I0597946

BY FORTHRIGHT

because I like to hold your interest

Table of Contents

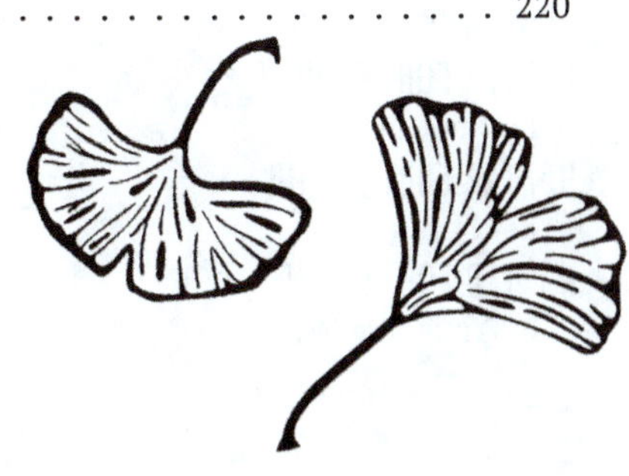

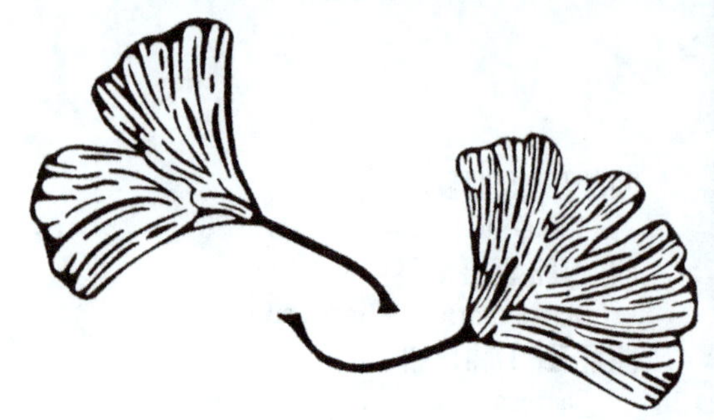

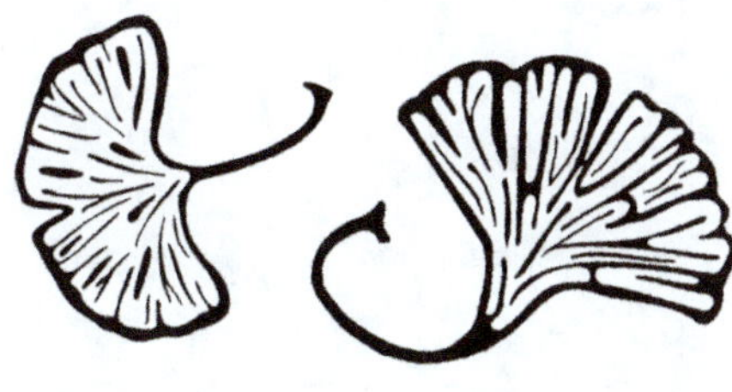

MIKOTO
AND THE
REAVER
VILLAGE

1
ONLY SON

Everyone seemed to think that Mikoto was ready to step into his father's place. Like it was only natural. An orderly progression. Seamless as the change of seasons. Gabriel's season had ended, leaving his son with a considerable legacy. And an overly considerate assistant.

The soft clap of clasping hands prefaced Yulin's light inquiry. "Are you avoiding me, young noble? Or is it the day's roster that troubles you?"

Mikoto bit his tongue and kept his face turned toward the early morning mists hanging thick among the trees on the neighboring mountain. He'd been quiet, even careful, when slipping out the gate in the back garden. Yet he'd been followed. Again.

All he wanted was a little normalcy. Simple things, like starting the day with a run. Maybe some sparring. Breakfast with the Guard. Or with their newcomers, if he'd been so lucky. But suddenly,

Mikoto had a schedule. And a minder.

It wasn't fair to blame Yulin. He was only doing his job.

This Amaranthine had been Father's administrative assistant. And *his* father's before him. And so on, all the way back, almost to the beginning. According to the family chronicle, Yulin had worked alongside every village headman since Gerard Reaver's grandson. Yulin did it all, and he did it flawlessly—secretary, accountant, correspondent, clerk, archivist, liaison, errand boy, and interpreter. As such, Yulin had a place in all of Mikoto's childhood memories. Father's shadow.

In the tradition of his clan, Yulin's designation was *scribe*. Scribe Yulin Dimityblest, son of Linlu Dimityblest, one of Wardenclave's less-famous founders. A moth.

"If you need escape, excuses can be made," offered Yulin. "You are grieving."

Which was true, but not the whole truth.

Mikoto's attention drifted woefully over the forested peaks and passes that made up the Denholm range. For nearly a week, an allotment of battlers had been entrenched on those slopes and on the plain beyond. Safe inside the oldest—and most formidable— barriers in the world, they were undergoing special training. All very secret. And like everything that went on in Wardenclave, all very exclusive. But Father had pulled some strings, begged a favor, gotten permission for Mikoto to tag along. Then undid all those plans by dying.

Disappointment was its own kind of grief, one that prickled with guilt and regret.

Mikoto had a battler's build and bloodline. When he was nine,

Father started letting him slip in among the other kids, attending camp like any other up-and-coming reaver, pretending he didn't live there year-round.

He'd taken every possible course their camp offered to young battlers—survival, tracking, climbing, close combat, ranged attack, stealth, and strategy games. Mikoto had gained proficiency in half a dozen traditional weapons. Had consistently ranked in the end-of-summer games. Had even been tapped for an Elderbough apprenticeship.

Father had been proud. Actually, the entire village was proud. But it had always been an indulgent, extracurricular sort of pride. Mikoto was a boy playing games. A kid with a hobby that would have to fall by the wayside. Because Mikoto was Gabriel Reaver's *only* son.

Heir to a piece of history.

Headman of Wardenclave.

"I wanted …." Mikoto trailed off with a shrug. His plans for the summer had been twofold—impress the instructor and impress the girl. The former was supposed to lead to the latter. So losing the first meant losing everything. Unless he could come up with another plan.

Yulin said, "You were looking forward to this summer."

He would know. He'd probably handled the arrangements.

Mikoto said, "I am selfish."

"No, brave noble. You are merely young." Yulin stepped closer. "Your progenitor was young once, too. He understood."

When it came to Father, *young* was impossible to visualize. He'd been sixty-five and already silver the year Mikoto was born. But *understanding?* Yes. Gabe Reaver had known what was important to his son because they talked. Not at great length. But always honest. Bedrock stuff.

"He knew what you needed." Yulin's fingers caught the hem of Mikoto's tunic. "You trusted him with your hopes, and he, in his turn, entrusted them to me."

Mikoto finally looked at the person who represented everything he'd lost and everything that would be required of him.

Like all Dimityblest moths, Yulin was short and slight, with hair mottled in a powdery range of creams and browns. The patterns were reminiscent of the clan's night-flying counterparts. A whole family in camouflage.

Yulin was a lot of things—quiet, efficient, pleasant, and darned near omnipresent. But what threw Mikoto straight out of his peevish mood was a pair of large, putty-colored eyes. Because Yulin was close to tears.

Was it his fault?

Or did Yulin have the same excuse he'd offered. *You are grieving.*

Mikoto blinked hard. He hadn't cried once since they'd found father. Couldn't. Wouldn't. He left that to his mother and his sisters, his half-sisters, and his nieces. Not because they were girls, but because Mikoto was himself.

Expressing wasn't his forte.

He tried to think what to do, but his emotional vocabulary—if you could call it that—was limited to vague hums, sympathetic grunts, and the occasional shoulder clap. His father had been so much better at connecting with people. Knowing what to say. Being in charge.

Resorting to a half-hearted pat, Mikoto mumbled, "You okay?"

"Time takes its toll, but it offers a way forward." Yulin whisked away a tear. "I daresay I will be *okay*. With your help, noble son."

Mikoto was used to Yulin finding new ways to tack *noble* onto his name. It was a moth-ish joke, playing off the kanji for Mikoto's given name, which was written with characters that implied nobility, lordship, and even divinity. Today, the endearment felt more like a taunt. Mikoto hadn't asked for status *or* its obligations.

Yet they were his. So he asked, "What can I do?"

"Work with me."

Mikoto cast one last, longing look at the slope where, even now, battlers might be learning new skills. "I know my duty."

Yulin's laugh was like rustling leaves, and his light touch was a plea. "The heads of the clans acknowledge your succession. Wardenclave is in your care." His words carried weight, as if this morning, this very moment, marked Mikoto's induction. "However, it has been suggested that your years are insufficient, compared to the full scope of the responsibilities that are your inheritance."

"I am not ready." It was an honest relief to hear someone else say it.

Yulin's gaze softened. "That is why you have been made an apprentice."

Mikoto longed for an outlet for all the tension that was building. "Whose?"

"Wardenclave's."

2

FIVE MENTORS

Across all classifications, reavers received training suited to their inherent strengths, usually in classrooms or in summer courses like those offered at Wardenclave. Group training. But an exceptional young reaver might be tapped for apprenticeship, either by a senior within the same specialty or by an Amaranthine mentor.

Selection was an unparalleled honor that opened many doors. One of those being the gates of Wardenclave. Glint Starmark's standards for attendees were the highest, so their village mostly welcomed in reavers with prestigious connections.

No one could help their parentage. Pedigree was a matter of record. But the only guarantee that came with good breeding was more breeding. Those with rank could expect excellent offers for maternity, paternity, and matrimony. And monetary incentives that encouraged large families.

Pedigree was about potential. But having promise assured nothing. That's where individual effort came into play. Those who worked hard were more likely to turn heads. And to gain the patronage of a powerful mentor.

"I do not understand," said Mikoto.

Mentors took one apprentice at a time. And apprentices only ever had one mentor. One-on-one. Personal attention. Mutual dedication. If the mentor was Amaranthine, the bond was so close that the apprentice could wear their mentor's crest and colors. It was the stuff of stories and dreams, for few could aspire to such intimacies.

It was different for Mikoto. Almost backward.

"How can I be apprenticed to a village?"

"You are the future of Wardenclave. You must build on its foundations." Yulin's fingers fluttered. "I am speaking of the Five."

Mikoto had grown up with the Five. Not the world-famous Five who'd brought about the Emergence. Theirs was the *original* Five— the five founders of Wardenclave. The Amaranthine who had allied themselves with Mikoto's ancestor.

Starmark.

Fullstash.

Duntuffet.

Alpenglow.

Dimityblest.

The clan leaders still considered Wardenclave home. Visitors were often impressed by them. Historians could get especially starry eyed. But to Mikoto, these guys seemed pretty normal. They were nice folks. Good neighbors. Family friends.

"I do not understand," Mikoto repeated.

"You are the first headman to take charge before his fortieth year. And you are the first to be inducted because of his predecessor's death." Yulin's voice softened with sadness. "Traditionally, you would have been mentored by your father."

But he was gone.

Yulin said, "Gabe left you to us."

Mikoto swallowed hard. "How could he have? It was sudden."

"Your progenitor lingered as long as he could. He lived to meet a great-great-granddaughter, but he knew he would never see your fortieth year." Yulin heaved a shaky sigh and repeated, "Gabe left you to us. Well, to *me*. But the others demanded their share, and you can only benefit from their council."

"I ... I *really* do not understand." Mikoto knew this should have been a great honor, but he hated the idea of being pulled in five directions. "Am I supposed to report to all of you? Will I be assigned courses? Apprentices usually live with their mentor. How can I ...?"

"No, my good noble." Yulin's hands sought his and supported them. "We will not add to your responsibilities. We will take them for a season, then share them for a season, then return them when the season is right, and you are ready."

"So I am *not* in charge?"

"You are." Yulin gave his hands a squeeze. "But you will delegate the majority of your duties to a staff of volunteers. Us."

Mikoto realized something that maybe should have been obvious. "Do you speak for the Dimityblest clan?"

"Yes. Until such time as my progenitor returns." Yulin got straight down to business. "I will be with you, and I will deal with all aspects of public relations. Your induction will undoubtedly garner the interest of the international press."

Reflexively, Mikoto grabbed Yulin's wrists. The moth smiled and matched the gesture in a silent pledge.

"Naturally, our first priority must be to our guests. The summer courses begin in a week, and this year's attendees include some special cases. We need to check with Merl, who will manage the instructors, their schedules, and any supplies they require. He is the Alpenglow designate."

Mikoto blinked and breathed easier. "Merl is one of my mentors?"

Yulin flashed a sweet smile. "At my request, since you and he have established a certain rapport."

"Thank you," he whispered.

"I am here to make things *easier* for you."

"Who else?"

"Salali, of course. And Bram stands by *any* Duntuffet, so you have your pick of the warren." Yulin gestured back in the direction of home. "Merl has promised an array of your favorites if you are willing to break your fast with him."

Mikoto nodded. Then hesitated. "What about the Starmark designate?"

"Ah." Yulin went up on tiptoe to deliver a fleeting kiss to Mikoto's cheek. An apology of sorts. One that made the answer quite plain. It would be Glint himself.

3

COLT ALPENGLOW

Wardenclave had been part of the Emergence, chosen for its historical significance. The New World village where an alliance between Amaranthine and reavers was first forged still flourished. A rustic locale where reavers sent their kids to summer camp. It made a good story. Both Hisoka Twineshaft and Harmonious Starmark made sure of that.

Mikoto had been five when the film crews first arrived. Journalists with their questions and angles and human interest. Politicians with their skepticism and their constituents and their upcoming elections. Tourists with their bravery and their bucket lists and their billfolds.

They were always so amazed when they passed through the outer wards, which hid an entire mountain range. Denholm's unveiling was used to prove the existence—by their very absence— of whole swaths of wilderness under Amaranthine protection. So while peacemakers and lawgivers were hammering out treaties, cartographers and cryptid hunters and conspiracy theorists hunted for more hideaways.

Like it was a children's game. Hide and seek.

Better than the alternative. Seek and destroy.

As headman of the reaver village, Mikoto's father had welcomed every group and escorted them around the campground. It was picturesque, with quaint cabins marked by bronze nameplates. All as original as possible, updated and renovated just enough to allow each generation their modern conveniences.

The circle with its amphitheater seating. The lodge draped in clan banners. The veritable zoo occupying their Kith shelter. Pastureland that now served as training grounds. Gabe Reaver had hosted countless tours, often with Mikoto at his side. And somehow, despite the abundant evidence, it never occurred to these wide-eyed humans that barriers could exist within barriers.

They saw a quaint village but missed the city.

They saw the forest but never noticed the tree.

They saw enough, but *only* enough. Never all.

Again, it was different for Mikoto. The close-kept secrets of Wardenclave were his inheritance. Part of a blood-bond passed down from father to son. But also in the tuning of the many illusions and barriers maintained by sigils, wardstones, and Salali Fullstash.

So when Mikoto rounded the bend that took him and Yulin out of the forest, he plainly saw the village, the city beyond, and the tree that dwarfed it all. Maybe after breakfast, he should go see Waaseyaa.

"He is waiting," murmured Yulin.

Mikoto needed a moment to realize that the moth was referring to Merl. Waving to his friend, Mikoto jogged across the Circle Green. Merl met him at his garden gate, forearm raised. Without a word, Mikoto crossed it with his own. Like the meeting of blades between sparring partners. Or the opening crack of quarterstaffs. Or ... well, it was their version of a fist-bump, really.

In truest form, Colt Merl Alpenglow was all muscle, a thickset draft horse who shared his sire Hannick's coloring—a coat of butterscotch gold, lightly dappled with the same rich ginger of his mane and tail. In speaking form, Merl was fair-skinned, and he pinned his pudding-hued hair in a bun that was more practical than fashionable, at least by horse standards.

"How are you?" Merl's wideset brown eyes were dark with sadness.

Mikoto shook his head, but said, "Better."

"May I beg a concession?"

"This once," he mumbled. Permission to touch.

The colt's arms enfolded him.

Merl had to be at least eight hundred years old, but when it came to Amaranthine, age had little to do with affection. Mikoto couldn't remember it clearly, but Father had told the tale often enough. Apparently, Mikoto had been a quiet kid. Always running off to play alone.

Probably to get away from a houseful of sisters.

But little Mikoto had taken a liking to Merl. Pretty soon, running off had turned into running here, to visit the camp's healer, whom he began referring to as his *big brother*. Everyone else treated it like a child's game, but Merl had taken the four-year-old seriously. Treated it as an honor.

Since Mikoto was welcomed, his family encouraged the fixation. He learned how to plant seeds and harvest flowers. About herbs and remedies and the best way to wrap bandages. But soon after he turned seven, Mikoto arrived earlier than usual and inadvertently buckled a barrier, badly startling the colt in the midst of a battle dance.

Everything changed.

After that, Mikoto also learned how to stand and how to fall. About wrestling holds and sticks and staffs and staves. Next came bladed weapons and drawing bows. And the knowledge that disrupting barriers was a useful skill in battler games.

Merl brought in more wardstones, worked with Mikoto's control, and guided him through the basics of tending. He recommended the best courses to take with each successive camp, then scheduled even better ones. Maybe Merl had been mentoring him, even then. But Mikoto never once felt like an underling. They'd simply been holding onto each other's secrets.

One a tribute.

One an heir.

The summer Mikoto turned fourteen, he joined a course taught by the head of the Thunderhoof clan. Mounted battle tactics, straight out of the history books. Riders with lances, with spears, with bows. Jumping to and from a moving horse. Standing barefoot on bareback. Keeping your seat on steep slopes. Knowing when to rein in and when to risk a leap.

While the registered campers all rode out on Alpenglow Kith, Mikoto competed as Merl's rider. As two halves of a greater whole. As equals.

And everything changed again.

The familial bond was there, for they'd begun as brothers. But Mikoto didn't need Merl the same way he had when he was four or seven. Now, they were sparring partners and comrades-in-arms. That summer, the colt had become something more—his best friend.

"How are your sisters?" asked Merl, already herding him up the walk.

"All home."

"*All*," Merl echoed. "Wren and Lily, too?"

"Yes."

"That must be a great help at a time like this."

Mikoto supposed it was. If only because they kept each other occupied.

Wren and Lily were his half-sisters, daughters of Lingering Light, who had been his father's first wife. That had been many years ago. In fact, those sisters were both in their sixties. Later in life, Gabriel had remarried. Probably at Glint's urging. Mikoto's mother, Sora, had come to Wardenclave from Japan. An arranged marriage.

Mikoto's full-blooded siblings were three older sisters.

Hikari had married and lived nearby with her husband and four daughters. Both Koharu and Hana still lived under the same roof, as did *their* daughters. Koharu served in the guard. Her three girls had been born under contract. Hana, who was closest in age to Mikoto, also had a little girl. With all the family pulling together, the females had more than tripled their numbers and noise level.

Which left Mikoto. And Yulin.

Mikoto stopped and looked back. "Coming?"

Yulin lingered at the gate.

Merl reinforced the invitation. "Come along. You can help make sure he gets enough to eat."

The moth clansman's gaze turned speculative. "How is your appetite, young noble?"

"I do not have one," he fibbed.

That decided Yulin, but it didn't get them through the door.

"*Here* you are!" boomed a voice everyone in Wardenclave knew. Glint Starmark walked toward them, three young Kith cavorting around him. The pups looked for all the world like over-sized golden retrievers, too clutzy and cute for anyone to believe they belonged to the pack known historically as the Demon Dogs of Denholm.

Yulin stepped forward, a polite smile on his face. "Glint, you are on Mikoto's schedule for tomorrow. If that is still ...."

Glint simply patted his head and walked on by.

"... convenient," Yulin finished bemusedly. Really, there was no getting in the way of Wardenclave's top dog.

Leaning down to look Mikoto in the eyes, Glint asked, "How are you, boy?"

Mikoto shrugged uncomfortably. As a kid, he'd adored the founder of the Starmark clan, with his big voice and his big hands and his big dogs. Glint was impressive—strong and manly. Well, *male*. When he was little, Mikoto had probably done his share of cavorting, just like these pups, eager to gain Glint's attention. To look into silver eyes, bright as the star that marked his brow.

Somehow, it was less fun to be in Glint's focus now.

Conversations always seemed to come around to the future. And who would share Mikoto's.

Glint was the village matchmaker. Pedigrees were his hobby. He had a reputation for bringing together strong bloodlines. In fact, most young reavers who came to Wardenclave hoped to consult with Glint with regards to their prospects. His stamp of approval—a very official-looking copper foil sticker—was highly coveted.

Mikoto didn't want to go through folios. Didn't need to.

He'd made his choice a long time ago. When he was nine.

And this summer, he was going to tell her. Somehow.

"... to make sure it was a good match." Glint touched Mikoto's arm, radiating concern. "Are you listening, my boy?"

"He wasn't," said Merl.

Glint's hand was warm. His gaze was soft. "In short, then. It is not good to be alone."

Mikoto wasn't. Far from it.

"It took me longer than I anticipated, but I think you will be pleased."

"With what?"

"With *whom*," corrected Glint, sounding unaccountably smug.

What had Mikoto missed? For a panicked moment, he thought he'd agreed to something binding. He darted nervous glances at Merl and Yulin. The former simply shook his head in a way that meant, *it's okay*. And the latter was covering a smile.

"Hold out your hands," ordered Glint.

Mikoto slowly obeyed, watching warily as Glint's big, brown hand dipped into a deep coat pocket. And brought out a puff of white fur.

Setting it carefully in Mikoto's waiting hands, Glint simply said, "Take care of each other."

And walked away.

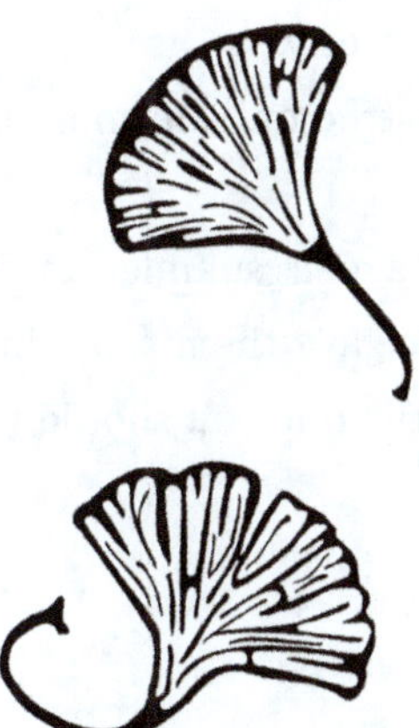

4

TO CATCH A DRAGON

Sinder's first instruction for Naroo-soh's rookie ranks was little more than child's play. "Find me."

The battlers weren't impressed. A hand went up. "That's all?"

At a glance, Sinder could tell that eighty percent felt insulted. Most of the rest seemed to be trying to figure out if he was joking.

"Where's Naroo-soh?"

"None of your business." Sinder smiled sweetly.

"We're meant to have an Elderbough instructor." Murmurs of assent rippled through the group.

"You think Naroo-soh was going to take a summer away from the hunt to hold your hands?" Sinder gave them a pitying look. "You'll get your Elderbough. But I'm the one you should be focusing on."

Another hand. "May we know your name, sir?"

"*Also* none of your business."

Glares. The insulted ones now radiated annoyance. If he could chivvy them into active dislike, they might actually *try*.

"You're Naroo-soh's picks, yes? His up-and-comers? Oodles of promise, just waiting to be tapped?" Sinder raised a hand. "How many of you believe that *you're* the one we've all been waiting for? With you on the rogue's trail, we may *finally* see results."

While no one raised a hand, they stood a little straighter in their ranks, pride and confidence in their posture.

Poor kids. This was going to be the worst summer of their lives. But if Sinder did his job well, they'd live to see another.

He wanted to sigh, but he plastered on a smirk. "I admire your courage. You'll need it."

When it came to capturing the rogue, all the skills and tactics in the world came to nothing if you couldn't find him in the first place. No easy task.

A dragon in truest form might seem showy, even garish, out of context. But drop them into nearly any landscape, and those markings allowed them to vanish. Even into a seemingly featureless plain. Sinder was on one such plain now, a wide stretch of tundra that wavered with green-gold grasses. Other than the occasional low bush, only the passing shadows of scudding clouds moved. They briefly washed the terrain in shadow, then cranked up the wattage with the squint-inducing glare of high summer sunlight.

Thirty rookies entered the practice field and waited. They scanned the area with hands over eyes, some with binoculars or spy glasses. A few began crafting sigils, which was the right idea, even though it wouldn't do them much good. They fanned out, moving with care, but obviously confused.

One of the Starmark guards had entered the zone with them. She stood with feet planted, gaze lowered, expression thoughtful. An observer.

A battler approached her. "Are you sure there's a dragon out here?"

"Yes. In striking distance."

Also the right idea. Trust *any* Amaranthine's senses over your own.

Another rookie quietly asked, "How can you tell?"

Which wasn't as stupid a question as it might sound. Knowing a predator is nearby is a good start, but *how* you know determines your next step.

But their observer wasn't on the team. She simply said, "There are boundaries, and he promised to stay within them."

This was too easy, but these battlers really were Naroo-soh's choices. They'd catch on. They'd learn, and then Sinder would have to try harder. But he'd impress them this once. Because the thing to remember when tracking a dragon, if there was any chance of anyone surviving the encounter, was that your eyes can deceive you.

When you're scanning your surroundings, and you're sure there's no place where any dragon could possibly hide, you're wrong. He's there, and he's still. He's listening, and he's laughing. And he's almost certainly behind you.

Sinder's jump-scare tactics didn't gain him any popularity. After three days, the rookies still couldn't find him in an open field. By the fourth, they were beginning to suspect they never would. Not without help. By the fifth, they were sure of it. Which was as ready as they'd ever be.

"Bring on the Elderbough," Sinder drawled, by way of introduction.

The ranks fell silent as their instructor stepped out of the woods.

Sinder eyed them critically. Yes, they were surprised. But by now, they should be desperate enough to take what they could get.

When this group was first selected, Boonmar-fen Elderbough was supposed to have handled their training. But things went south, and Boon was off the grid. It had taken a little convincing, but in the end, Naroo-soh had agreed to send another brother.

"My name is Torloo-dex Elderbough."

The battlers exchanged glances.

Sinder was pleased to see that the prevailing emotions were confusion and … awe. He was willing to bet that none of them had ever met an Amaranthine this young. Torloo looked twelve.

"Naroo-soh is my brother." With a soft smile, he said, "Here is his promise. If by midsummer your skills exceed mine, he will come here, and he will run with you."

Quite the incentive.

Sinder wondered how long it would take these rookies to realize that this kid had been running with Elderbough trackers since always. He was good. As in exceptional. Torloo could be ruthless, which might have been scary if he weren't so damned cordial about it. Adoona-soh's baby boy had already put Sinder on his back more than once. He was almost as good at it as Juuyu.

"New goal!" Sinder tossed his hair over his shoulder. "Now that you have an Elderbough to advise you, we'll make the game harder. Find me before I find you."

5

NIGHT MANEUVERS

As soon as Torloo took over, Sinder stopped talking. Well, he stopped contributing useful information. His little asides were bland or barbed. All part of the plan. These battlers needed a tangible enemy to curse, corner, and confine. Because the *real* rogue was the worst taunt, the biggest affront, and a true monster on two legs or four.

Twelve years gone, and he was still out there—rending lives and raping girls.

Human agencies didn't understand why it was taking so long to take this guy down. Every other year or so, they'd sling accusations and demand results. But a heart-to-heart with a few members of the Amaranthine Council, always with Lapis in attendance, sufficed to remind them what they were up against.

What these rookies were up against.

What Sinder could do with a few whispered words.

He tried not to look at them, to meet their gazes, to use their names. Otherwise, their hard eyes and muttered oaths might get to him. And this wasn't *about* him. This was a dress rehearsal, and they needed to fully embrace their parts.

Sinder wasn't thrilled to be the villain's understudy. Neither was he loving Wardenclave's rugged, rustic vibe. He was more of a climate-controlled penthouse kind of dragon. Communications and computer code. Social media and slipping onto servers. The team usually relied on him for information extraction, yet they'd shunted him to a place that time forgot. He was up a creek without wifi. Come to think of it, this might be the worst summer of *his* life.

Lost in a daydream in which Juuyu and Hallow were sent to extract him, Sinder nearly missed his cue.

Torloo crisply asked, "Do you understand?"

"We do," the reavers answered in unison. All eyes swung to Sinder.

He smiled and said, "Blink." And then he sprang away, knowing it would seem as if he'd vanished. Not because he wanted to impress them. That had been a warning. The only one they'd get.

Their orders were simple. Scatter. Search. They had one hour to find him.

In preparation, Torloo had given them each two bandanas—one green, one red. Every rookie went in with the green one knotted around their forehead and the red one in their pocket.

The next several minutes were more entertaining than most Sinder spent in the woods.

He wasn't often deployed in this manner. It really wasn't sporting. Wrapping up early, he returned to Torloo's side.

"How many did you get?" He slipped his hand into Sinder's.

"Not all," he admitted. A few of the rookies had Kith companions. "Most, though."

Torloo's big blue eyes never wavered from his face. "Most dislike you."

Sinder fluted disconsolately. "Can you blame them?"

"I might." The young wolf's hand tightened. "You are here to *help* them."

"I've just humiliated them." He gently extracted his hand, for the battlers were approaching, reporting back. "Let me goad them on. You be their ally."

As the battlers regrouped, Torloo split their ranks. Only five retained their green bandanas. Confusion and consternation radiated from the rest.

"Is this some kind of trick?" asked one.

"It was a massacre," said Torloo. "Everyone wearing red was either compromised or killed."

"I never saw him!" protested one, then another.

"You do not *remember* seeing him," said Torloo. "None of them ever do."

A hand lifted. "How did he switch them out?"

"He did not," said Torloo. "You did it yourself."

"No way."

Others shook their heads, muttered protests. But the proof was all around them.

"Tell us how it was done," urged one of the battlers whose green bandana was like a badge of honor. Sinder had noticed him a time or two. Best of the bunch, and not simply because of his feline companion. The patch at his shoulder read *Michaelson*.

Torloo smiled at him, and his tail lifted. Like he knew the guy. "Your prey is a dragon, and dragons have a way with words. When he told you to switch colors, you thought it was a good idea. When he told you to forget you had met him alone in the woods, you did as you were told."

"And it works on anyone?" asked Michaelson.

"Amaranthine and humans," said Torloo. "But not Kith, which is why partnership is an asset."

"Can we protect ourselves?"

"Yes." With that, Torloo spun off into an orderly explanation of the next phase of their training. Michaelson's questions encouraged others to speak up or interject. And if Sinder didn't miss his guess, that was the guy's intent. Because he got the impression that Reaver Michaelson already knew the answers.

He'd bear watching, that one.

Now that they had guidance, the rookies improved. Torloo introduced them to the survival tactics they'd need for the chase they'd be joining. Like working in twos and threes, so every reaver had eyes on their back. And learning tracker lingo, a verbal code that allowed them to communicate without tipping off eavesdroppers.

Those with Kith partners had the best survival rate, which hammered through the obvious. And put their futures into new perspective. To succeed, they needed to form alliances. Torloo brought in a group of Dimityblest scribes to guide the battlers through the application process for a Kith partner. Those who excelled over the summer could find themselves in a pairing program this autumn.

Talk about motivation.

Torloo decided they were ready for night maneuvers.

Sinder was finally forced to stay on his toes. His pursuers were getting better at limiting his options. Careful steps and the musical hum of crystals. Gruff commands in code and the eerie howl of wolves on the scent.

Torloo had brought two Kith with him. Torn and Yang were a matched set—light brown, blue eyed, and big enough to look a grown man in the eye. The wolves were packmates, companions, and bodyguards. Or possibly babysitters. Not that the kid needed babying.

No doubt Adoona-soh felt better knowing her youngest wasn't alone. Few wolves embraced a loner's status. But Sinder was in a position to know that Torloo's buddies probably weren't a gift from his mom. They'd been selected by his sire, for they had the Trebellair coloring.

Everyone was in fine form tonight. The encircling ranks were driving him toward a narrow place, likely in hopes of penning him in. It might have worked if they'd had the support of wards, but most battlers sucked at barriers.

Sinder streaked through the trees, circumventing the bulk of their ranks. Slowing to a stroll, he listened carefully, alert to movement in the treetops. One of the reavers had an owl Kith, and she was a regular stealth fighter. Hisoka should bring in more for support. It'd be in Sinder's next report.

Something hit him. Not hard, but not in a good way.

He'd been made.

Bolting away, Sinder strained his senses for the position of his pursuer. It should have been easy. Even if a reaver was warded, their stones and sigils whispered in ways that every dragon knew. For sigils were written upon the wind, resonating with the songs of stones. But Sinder was at a loss. And that meant he wasn't dealing with a warded battler.

There'd been a ward in the ranks after all.

Sinder leapt into a tree and quickly shed his tunic to check the back. A sigil shimmered against the cloth. Probably a tracer. He left it there and fled through the treetops. Which smacked of desperation, but it was also Sinder's best out.

Quick, but less quiet than he would have liked. And far from graceful.

Leaves smacked. Twigs scratched. Bark bit. Pausing to listen, he peered back over his shoulder and caught the telltale gleam of a sigil creeping over pale skin.

He hung his head and wished—not for the first time—for Juuyu.

His partner made short work of any form of sigilcraft.

This was *exactly* why Hisoka frowned on solo missions. And why Boon was in deep shit. And why Sinder needed to either shed his skin—*not* ideal—or go to ground. Camouflaged, there was a slim chance he could outlast the night.

Right then, a wave of dizziness washed over him. A moment later, he hit the ground, and pain lanced through his side. Sucking in a shallow breath, he forced his way onto his feet and focused on a silent retreat.

Was his pursuer aware that he was flightless? That little detail was *not* on the approved lesson plan. With wavering steps, he made for one of the grottoes he'd located during earlier reconnoiters. Not the best of bolt holes, but it was closest, and that's what counted.

Sinder crawled through a rocky narrow, tumbling into a den with an earthen floor. Perhaps it had once belonged to wildcats or wolves. It might have been a good hideaway if he wasn't so certain that the sigil that continued to spread was beckoning to its crafter.

Clutching at his side, he waited to see the source of his humiliation.

A scant minute passed. A few low words and a stealthy scuffle preceded Michaelson into the den.

"Go away," he muttered.

"Not until I remove that sigil."

Lovely. He was immune to Sinder's words, as well. "Sassing back to dragons? You are one annoyingly over-qualified rookie."

Michaelson lofted a couple of crystals, which took on a soft blue glow. He sighed and said, "You don't remember me, do you."

"Should I?" Sinder studied the young man. Caucasian. With dark eyes and hair, which hung in loose curls almost to his shoulders. In need of a shave. Built like a tank.

The battler shook his head. "Dragons don't rely so much on scents. Colors and sounds are what trigger your memories, and my voice has changed."

Sinder frowned. He didn't need lessons in being a dragon. He'd already been trying to pin down the man's voice, which was deep and lightly accented. As if English weren't the only language in his arsenal.

"I'll give you a hint." Beckoning with the fingers of both hands, Michaelson quietly ordered, "Touch my nose."

"We *have* met." Sinder's thoughts raced. "We met when you were a child?"

"Only once, so it's no wonder you don't remember." He showed his palms. "May I touch?"

Sinder tried to do the polite thing, only to reveal a bloodied hand.

"You're *injured*." Crowding close, the reaver ordered, "Show me."

"Is this the part where I'm meant to assure you that it's just a scratch?"

He snorted. "This is the part where I check for broken ribs."

Michaelson's hands were blessedly warm as he probed. Sinder bit his lip to keep from whimpering. "Kith partner, sigil crafter, *and* field medic? Where did Naroo-soh find you?"

"Hang on, Sinder. I need my kit, and Fend is carrying it."

He knew his name. Said it kindly.

They'd met once. But where? Sinder didn't know anyone else called Michaelson, but reavers chose their own surnames. Oh. What a dunce.

"You're Michael's son." And since the world was full of Michaels, he added, "First of Wards."

"Spot on." And there. He had his father's smile.

"Your mother's a battler." Sinder lifted his arms, giving the man access to his injury.

"And a healer, fortunately for you." Michaelson doused him with something that stung, then began wrapping. "I spent a couple of summers with the mares before being bundled off to Mum's people."

Sinder tried not to squirm. "Are you allowed to congratulate yourself for binding up wounds you've inflicted?"

"No." Those dark eyes sought his. "I'm truly sorry, Sinder. I wasn't even sure the sigil would work."

"It works."

"Can you describe its affects?"

"In excruciating detail." He shivered miserably. "So I'm an experiment?"

Michaelson removed his vest and peeled out of his tunic. "Hands up again."

Sinder lost the urge to be snide as warm cloth settled around him. It was just such a relief.

The man smoothed the shirt over his back, pulled free his thick braid, chafed his arms—all the fussing made Sinder miss Colt. "You have a lot of scars," he remarked.

"Old mishap with a skylight." Sinder shrugged, then wished he hadn't. "What's the diagnosis, Healer Michaelson?"

"Bruised, but not broken." He shrugged back into his vest, buckling it over a hairy chest, then checking his pockets. "I recommend a dose for the pain, and you're overdue for a long sleep. A proper tending wouldn't go amiss. Best thing for it, really."

Sinder was having a hard time keeping up. He shook his head, trying to clear it.

Michaelson looked away. "About the sigil."

Tugging up one sleeve, Sinder watched the progress of the pattern across his skin. It was sort of pretty, like molten body art. But it also made him uneasy. "Weren't you going to remove it?"

"About that." The reaver met his gaze pleadingly. "Would you mind if we let it run its course?"

Sinder made a grab for him, claws hooking into the fabric of his vest. "What's it doing to me?"

Michaelson took his hands and moved them to his face, pressing them to either side in a dragon's show of faith. "This one's not so bad. A trap nested within a tracer. It's singing you a lullaby."

This one. Which meant there were other ones. Worse ones. Sinder wasn't sure he liked the sound of that. "It's supposed to put me to sleep?"

"If it works right."

"Seems right." Slumping sideways, he asked, "What if it malfunctions?"

"I'll dismantle it." Michaelson's arm eased around him, pulling him close. "I'll be right here, making sure."

Sinder wondered if this is what it felt like, falling under the spell of a dragon's words. Helpless to protest. Stupidly trusting. Still, he managed to frame another protest. "What if it triggers a long sleep?"

"I'll take full responsibility." He smiled his father's smile and added, "I cannot offer you a harem or heights, but my home is yours for as long as you need it."

"Swear it."

"By all four winds," he said gravely.

Sinder thought that was a nice touch, but it wasn't what he'd wanted. "Upon your name. Swear it on your name."

A searching look. A small smile. "So be it. I swear to bring you safely home. Upon my honor and upon my name—Timur

Michaelson, partner to Fend, lately of Stately House, guest instructor at Wardenclave, and heir to the secrets of the Order of Spomenka."

Oh. Double dunce. First the legendary Junzi, now a throwback Spomenka?

He warbled a protest and knew how pitiful it sounded.

The man gathered him up like it was nothing. "Rest easy, Sinder Stonecairne. I've got you."

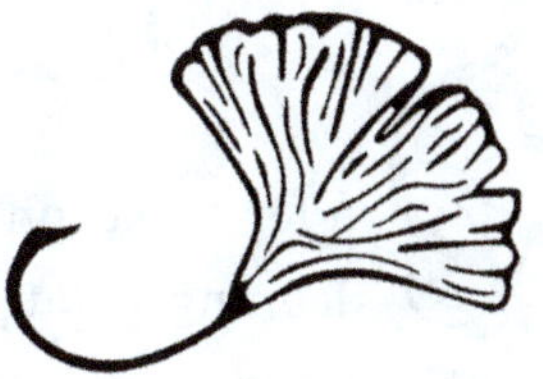

I SPY

inder woke on what could only be described as a sleeping platform. Which immediately brought wolves to mind, except for the distinct lack of shag. Boon's alcove always looked like it'd been paved in roadkill. This bed, while similarly spacious, was more sensibly fitted with smooth sheets, downy blankets, and a lavishly embroidered coverlet—greens, golds, and enough oranges to warm the heart of any Farroost.

But this wasn't a phoenix's nest. Sinder had enjoyed Harmonious' hospitality often enough. This added up to dog.

Turning his head, he noted a net of sigils, the basic sort intended to keep out noise and nuisances. Within that shimmering curtain, a big chair had been pulled up beside his bed. And upon that chair dozed Timur Michaelson, who had bathed and shaved in the indeterminate interim. His plain cotton T-shirt was battler teal, and when Sinder lifted his head, he glimpsed pajama pants.

His movement, though slight, woke his guardian.

"Hello," Michaelson murmured, sitting forward and extending a hand. "Any ill effects?"

Sinder allowed the brush of fingertips, even though he was pretty sure he hadn't dreamed up the late-breaking news flash with regards to the Order of Spomenka. "You're a dragon slayer?"

"Family tradition." Timur quietly added, "You had a right to know."

"A ringer among the rookies? Who knew about …?" He faltered, because he knew the answer. "Twineshaft arranged it?"

Timur glanced toward the door, then rubbed the back of his neck. "Sensei knows, sure. But that's *not* why I'm here."

"So it's pure coincidence that you're part of an intensive on tracking dragons?"

"I'm filling in for Boon."

Sinder snorted. "Torloo is filling in for him."

With a gesture that begged for patience, Timur said, "Boon was also scheduled as a camp instructor. I'll be working with the academy kids. But I'm mainly here because Argent arranged it."

"You?"

Timur seemed confused.

Sinder eased onto his side, testing muscles and gritting his teeth against several new aches and twinges. "No offense, Michaelson, but you can't expect me to believe you're Mettlebright's spy."

"Are we spies, then?"

"I never said that," he muttered, grateful the room was warded.

"Believe what you want. I can't deny that I'm here for … reasons." Timur's lips quirked. "But they're largely familial."

"But not *entirely* familial," he challenged. Sinder wasn't sure what kind of confession he expected to wrest out of the man. Why was he running at the mouth? And then it clicked. "What did you dose me with?"

"Huddlebud. You had a second dose two days ago. I can brew a tea that'll wash away any lingering effects." Timur came to perch on the bed's edge. "The room's been warded the whole time. Nobody heard."

Sinder's eyes widened. "What did I say?"

"This and that. Nothing worth repeating." Timur chuckled as he added, "Though I would like my phone back. Eventually."

He found it under his pillow.

Timur's eyes sparkled with laughter. "You were cuddling it like a teddy bear."

Sinder clutched it to his heart. "Wardenclave doesn't have wifi."

"Denholm does." As if on cue, the phone vibrated.

"We're in Denholm?" Sinder glanced at the screen. Someone with the handle BeastieBestie had texted, *I could walk faster than this bus is rolling.*

"No, we're at the heart of Wardenclave."

Something in the way he said it made Sinder take a closer look at his surroundings. That dose must have been fresh as flowers. Then again, Sinder was used to leaving setting details to Juuyu.

Daytime, roundabout mid-high. Bedroom, probably guest. And downright palatial, by Wardenclave standards. "They gave *me* a tent."

Timur laughed. "I have a little cabin, same as the other instructors. But this was both more secure and more convenient for ... reasons."

Sinder wasn't letting that go. "You *know* I know Inti, right?"

With a quick nod, Timur rejoined, "And you know where he is."

That hung in the air between them for several moments. "Right. Well," muttered Sinder. "The less said, the better."

"Now you sound like Boon," Timur accused.

Sinder hung his head, at a loss. Finally, he asked, "How much do you know?"

"More than I'm supposed to, but not enough to be dangerous. I'm trying to reassure you. We have people in common. You can trust me."

"Me, trust a Spomenka?" Sinder gave him the side eye. "That would be preposterous."

Timur nodded. "Almost as preposterous as having a phoenix for a partner."

Sinder flopped back and waved an accusing finger. "You're a harrowing, hulking security risk."

"Not a bit of it. But I *am* here for security reasons." He reached over and unlocked his phone with the touch of a finger. "How are they coming?"

More text messages from BeastieBestie.

I could walk faster than this bus is rolling
Unpaved roads = first line of defense
Lilya says to bring Fend
Smoother, faster ride

Next came a selfie that made Sinder sit up. Dark green seats and windows with a tundra view confirmed that the sender was on a camp bus. "The reavers are coming in already?"

"In a couple more days. Glint gave permission for an earlier arrival." Timur craned his neck to see the photo. "This room's for them."

The selfie showed a grinning male in a faded blue shirt that set off his eyes. His rumple of silver hair would have sent Juuyu into fits, but Sinder was more interested in his ears. Silver fox ears perched atop his head, marking him as a crosser. And a celebrity one, at that.

He was crammed into a seat with two children. A girl with long brown hair had her arms wrapped around the shoulders of a boy who clung to her waist. There was no mistaking his dark red eyes. Or the spotting and scales.

"Argent's kid?"

Timur leaned on an elbow to better share the screen. "They're both his—Ginkgo and Kyrie. And Lilya's one of my sisters. This is their first camp. My being here and needing Ginkgo made it easier to get all the assorted parental permissions."

"I can't believe Argent let Kyrie out of his sight."

"He trusts Ginkgo. And me."

"Kith partner, sigil crafter, field medic, and baby minder."

"Ginkgo's the baby minder. I get to play big brother." Indicating the phone, he said, "Go ahead and let him know you're keeping his bed warm while I brew that tea."

Sinder's fingers were itching to do just that. He missed technology. Liked to chat. "How will he react, knowing I've commandeered what's obviously meant to be a secure line?"

"He's a fox at heart. He *likes* intrigue." Timur laced his next words with more of his mother's accent. "You can be Hisoka's spy.

He will be Argent's. And I will play the Russian spy. Yes?"

"Unbelievable." Sinder couldn't keep a straight face. "Do you like intrigue?"

"Terrible at it, actually." Timur whispered, "Between you and me, Fend is the brains of the operation."

"You admit your Kith is smarter than you?" He was liking this reaver more by the minute.

"Part of why we're such a good team."

Sinder's curiosity piqued. "How do you communicate?"

Timur tapped his nose. "Whatever do you mean? Kith are intelligent, loyal, and make good pets. Everyone knows that."

"You're very good."

"Not at everything." His expression briefly closed, but his smile was soon back, if a bit sadder. "For instance, you're going to *hate* my tea."

7

AT THE HEART OF WARDENCLAVE

Sinder tapped and flicked his way through the contents of Timur's phone, assuring himself that all was secure before he toyed with Ginkgo.

I'm not Timur. Who am I?

Two beats. A third. Then Ginkgo responded.

Fend: the world's first typing Kith.

**You may rule out felines.
Try again.**

Friend or foe?

**Both/and
Depends on the game**

L – girl or boy?
K – half or whole?

All male, yet a damsel in distress
He's threatening me with tea
Should I be worried?

They sent him a selfie in which all three of them offered expressions of—what he hoped was—exaggerated distaste. Ginkgo might not know who he was, but he must have decided this was a family-friendly mystery.

K – you are doomed
L – are you sick?

To K – I will be brave
To L – injured in the line of duty
Will you rescue me?

Where are you?

Not sure
Guest room. Your room.

Two beats. A third. Then Ginkgo responded.

Warded?

Yes

Hosts?

No sign. I've been asleep
Should I be worried?

Yes and no
Do they teach little dragons about trees?

Clearly, this Mettlebright was privy to more information than Sinder had bothered to dig up. Had it been a mistake, taking this assignment at face value? Or had he been relying too much on Boon being here?

"O Captain, my Captain," he muttered. "Wherefor art thou?"

Even though his pause had to have been a giveaway, Sinder played it safe.

Every clan knows their songs

**Risky business,
sleeping under trees
Oh, and Sinder …?**

Damn.

Yes?

Let Timur know we're an hour out

Will do

Sinder rewarded the half-fox by sending a pouting selfie. And a parting shot for the kids.

Codename: Damsel

When Timur returned with a tray, Sinder scrolled back up to the picture of universal disgust. "This? *This* is what you're going to do to me?"

Timur smiled lopsidedly. "Too right. Mum's recipes are dastardly, but I brought afters. You must be hungry."

He sat up to receive the tray. There was a plate of roasted vegetables, crusty rolls, and cheese. And a fat turnover that smelled of honey, nuts, and cinnamon. Sinder realized that Timur's barrier must be blocking sounds *and* smells, which required unusually intricate wardsmanship. Skills like these bounded on the illusory. Rather foxish in nature, now that he thought about it.

"First this." Timur held out a brimming teacup. "It's cooled enough. Try to take it in one go."

Sinder made a face.

"You don't want any huddlebud left in your system when meeting our hosts."

Sinder chugged, coughed, and wheezed, "Vile."

Timur shrugged and borrowed from his mother again. "What is good is hard. But is good."

Breakfast could only be better. Sinder started in on the food. According to the date on Timur's phone, he hadn't eaten in four days, so this tray was going to be the first of many. Mumbling around a mouthful of pastry, Sinder said, "Ginkgo seems to think my virtue is at risk."

He passed along the phone. Timur scanned the whole conversation, smiling all the while. Finally, he said, "You *have* been sleeping under a tree. Practically inside it. One of the reasons we're so safe here is because most people have trouble remembering that *here* exists. We're in Waaseyaa's home."

Sinder had been briefed on this part. Twineshaft was very interested in the Amaranthine trees of Wardenclave. He chewed more slowly, then asked, "You know about tree-kin?"

"I do *now*. Glint introduced me when I first arrived." Timur admitted, "Three weeks later, and I'm still getting used to it. And them. Especially Zisa."

"Zisa." Sinder made the logical leap. "The tree half of their twinship?"

Timur nodded and leaned closer. "Fair warning. If you have personal boundaries, he'll be inside them before you can say, 'Kiss me again.'"

Sinder slowly shook his head.

Timur simply nodded.

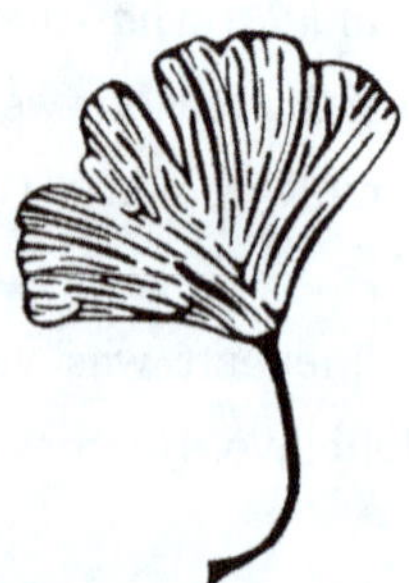

8

MAKING THE ROUNDS

The more Mikoto learned about his role as headman, the less he felt up to the task. Some things were honorary, like having a part in the annual Founders Day festival, playing host to important guests, and having his picture in glossy brochures and online articles. This was all part of being the son of the son of the son—through the centuries—of a historical figure.

But Gabe Reaver's day-to-day responsibilities had been much more prosaic. Head of Wardenclave's community association. And camp director.

The former was now under Duntuffet prevue, and the latter was being handled by Merl Alpenglow. They had it covered, so for the moment, Mikoto's primary responsibility was a scampering tuft of white fur.

The puppy was a big hit with Hana and with the nieces. Not so much with Yulin. Glint's gift had piddled one too many times in the moth's archive. So Mikoto's in-house mentor had prioritized long walks. He called it "making the rounds."

It was more freedom than Mikoto had expected. But the puppy was a bigger handful than he would have guessed. Not literally, of course. He was more of a scant handful, barely large enough to count as canine. Especially in a village where Kith-partnered battlers *rode* their dogs.

The girls had been quick to suggest names. All of them cutesy. But Mikoto firmly rejected them. He wasn't leaving something so important to them. Plus, he'd wanted a name with more dignity. Which had brought Yulin to mind. And then the name was suddenly there and perfectly right. A doggish name that was already an endearment. Noble.

Yulin had been amused. And pleased. Mikoto could tell.

Noble was quick and clingy, which put him constantly underfoot. While Mikoto made his rounds, the bouncing, twirling pup kept getting tangled in his own leash. Mikoto finally resorted to keeping Noble in the pocket of the long, sleeveless vest he was still getting used to wearing. Worn over Mikoto's usual summer tunic, the vest bore the crests of Wardenclave and its five founders. It marked him as headman.

So with a puppy in his pocket and time on his hands, Mikoto turned onto the narrow path that led into the pasture behind Glint's compound. And the enormous tree overshadowing it. The way in was a secret and well-warded, but not against family. Or against the headman. And Mikoto was both, for Waaseyaa's most recent wife had been Gabe Reaver's eldest sister.

"Uncle," Mikoto greeted.

Waaseyaa had ruddy brown skin and the straight black hair of many First Nations people. He was arrayed in a fawn-colored tunic trimmed with orange embroidery that was a sure sign of Glint's longstanding affection and protection. Waaseyaa always wore this same tunic. Or one similar. Maybe he had a trunk filled with nearly identical shirts. Or maybe his clothes endured because he did.

"Hello, Mikoto." Waaseyaa sat amidst his tree-twin's roots, his hands occupied with a child who couldn't have been two yet. The little boy was a determined climber. "I remember when you were much the same as this one."

"Not sure I do." Mikoto's glance flitted to the large feline sprawled nearby. "Except that you were patient with my hair-pulling."

Waaseyaa kept his hair in a braid that was remarkable for its length. If he wasn't in the habit of looping it around his shoulders, the trailing end would have dragged on the ground.

Mikoto awkwardly asked, "Is he one of yours?"

"Not of my line. His father is one of the instructors." Waaseyaa pulled the toddler into his arms. "Timur needed a hand, and both of mine were free. This is Gregor. And that one is Fend, Timur's partner."

Showing his palms to the Kith, Mikoto asked, "Where is Zisa?"

"Sulking." Waaseyaa looked up into the tree's canopy. "He cannot be as hospitable as he would like when the guest room is warded against him."

Mikoto addressed himself to the tree. "Would you like to meet my new puppy?"

Zisa's arms slipped around him from behind, hugging tightly as he hid his face against Mikoto's back. His question came out muffled. "You came to see me?"

"I did. You *and* Uncle." Mikoto patted one of the arms locked around him. "Glint gave me a puppy. He seemed to think I needed company."

Zisa lifted his head and Mikoto smiled into eyes the same shade of yellow-green as the tree's leaves. He'd never minded getting close to Zisa. Uncle had explained things a long while back, and Mikoto liked being trusted with the truth. Zisa loved to give, but he'd never take. And the more you accepted him, the less he flirted.

"Your house is farther than Brother lets me go." Zisa kissed his cheek. "Visit more, and I will be good company."

"I will." Turning in Zisa's embrace, he looped an arm around the tree's waist for a sideways hug. "But you are expecting more interesting company. I saw it on the schedule. *You* are someone's cabin assignment."

"Really?"

"Right there on Merl's spreadsheet. *Cabin: Zisa.*"

The tree looked to his twin, all dimples and delight. "Hear that, Brother? I am a cabin!"

"I can understand why Argent Mettlebright is so protective." Waaseyaa caressed little Gregor's mop of curls. "He asked nicely. How could we refuse?"

"Did you know we have company already?" Zisa asked coyly. "There is a *dragon* inside. He is beautiful."

Mikoto carefully lifted Noble from his pocket. "You think everyone is beautiful."

"Life *is*." Loosing his embrace so he could take the pup with both hands, Zisa exclaimed, "Why, he is no bigger than an Ephemera! What is his name?"

"Noble."

Zisa tittered. "How will Yulin tell you apart?"

Mikoto smiled and shrugged and … relaxed. He'd expected all the usual condolences, but Uncle and Zisa were simply glad he'd wanted to visit. Maybe that was how tree-kin had to be. Maybe that's why Mikoto liked coming here so much. They were always present in the moment, always glad to share it with him.

Uncle indicated the place at his side, and Mikoto joined him.

"I know this garment." Waaseyaa's fingers lightly caressed the vest's threadwork. "Is it heavy?"

He nodded, then changed his mind and shook his head. Uncle probably knew about his five-way apprenticeship, and he was tired of explaining it anyhow. So he asked, "You knew them all?"

"The headmen? Yes."

"They must have looked up to you."

"No," said Waaseyaa. "Not all. And not always."

Mikoto couldn't imagine it. This person was kind and wise and generous.

"Some of them were afraid of me. Some of them were disappointed in me."

"Why?"

His uncle looked away. "I think … they would have used my years differently. So instead of seeing me, they saw what I could have been. Or what they could have been, if there had been any way to trade places."

"They were jealous of you?"

"Not really. They were jealous of parts, but not the whole." Waaseyaa's smile was small. "And some of them met me during times when I was unhappy. I am sometimes sad. You understand."

Mikoto did.

"Some of them got along better with Glint than with me. Or … us." His gaze settled fondly on his twin, who was chattering softly to Noble. "Not everyone understands. Or accepts."

"I have always been more comfortable with you than Glint." As soon as it was out, it felt like a bold confession. Mikoto ducked his head.

"Yes." Waaseyaa patted his arm. "Glint loves you."

He grunted.

"It is true. He gave you Noble because he knew you were sad. Puppies are his answer to grief."

"Has he ever given you a puppy?"

"Many, many times." Tugging loose the end of his braid, he passed it to Mikoto.

His breath caught all funny, and his throat began to ache. This was how his uncle had always offered comfort, for everything from bossy sisters to bruised knuckles. And once or twice because he'd admitted to nursing a broken heart. Mikoto had never been one to go all weepy, but … that didn't mean he'd never sought comfort. Or known where to find it.

"Excuse me," came a voice Mikoto didn't know. "Sorry to interrupt."

A man stood in the door to Waaseyaa's home, practically filling it. Not quite dog clan stature, but close enough to rest an arm on the lintel as he leaned out. He wore battler colors and radiated competence.

"Can we get your healer back here? Colt Alpenglow?"

Mikoto saw the man notice him. Saw the man dismiss him. Knew what that meant among the ranks of battlers. Not a threat. Not a priority.

The man added, "He's awake."

For the barest fraction of a moment, Mikoto wanted to drop his uncle's braid and pretend he was strong or important or immune to the emotions he had no words for. And for a fraction of a moment, he was disappointed in himself. Mikoto tightened his grip and wound Uncle's braid around his fist, then his wrist. He would not let go. Not now. Not ever.

Waaseyaa accepted that much as he accepted anything. Without remark. Yet at this range, and tangled as he was, Mikoto briefly touched a vibrant bond that soared above them, even to the treetop, and deep into the earth, for Zisa was well-anchored upon this hill. And Waaseyaa was the beacon set upon it.

All of the sudden, Mikoto registered a deep rattle, and he tensed. The big cat was prowling toward him, all slink and sway. Like a black panther, but much larger. And far less threatening, since his alert was a purr.

Mikoto found himself staring into orange eyes.

"His name is Fend," reminded Uncle in an undertone. The toddler in his arms babbled and laughed, clearly happy to see the big cat.

Fend's broad nose touched Mikoto's forehead, the lightest of taps. And then the purring was loud in his ears, for the feline was rubbing his face against Mikoto's. Cheek to cheek. First one side, then the other. Over and over, like an affectionate housecat.

Was it a show of preference? That was really very flattering, especially in Wardenclave, where folks took pride in being dog people. Mikoto wondered what Glint would say if he saw this … and smiled.

Fend sat back. Making way for the man, who was definitely taking notice now.

Offering his hand, he cheerfully asked, "Who are you, then?"

9
CLAY PIT

Tenma had never considered himself impetuous, but there was no other word to describe his sudden urge to walk in the woods. He'd only meant to look around. Familiarize himself with the surroundings. Not strike off on his own.

But there was most assuredly *something* off in this direction. He'd learned to trust that certainty, even when it led him into strange situations.

Like this one.

He was in the woods below the village, that much he knew. So he couldn't be very lost. The creek hadn't been a surprise. In his mind, mountains and springs went together. At least, that's the way it worked back home. But when he'd reached a wide bend in its course, he found what looked like an exposed clay bed.

The grayish matter was just the sort of thing Goh-sensei liked to work with, and Tenma had thought to bring him a sample. However, in getting a closer look and trying to collect some, Tenma had somehow found himself stuck. And sinking.

Struggling only caused him to sink faster in the miry clay. He was up past his calves, helpless to free himself. Tenma rubbed at his nose, knocking his glasses askew, feeling like a child instead of a grown man.

He would be missed. If he didn't show up for the noon meal, Goh-sensei would notice and come looking. Unless he grew preoccupied with his work.

An hour might see Tenma sunk. Better to yell for help. There were plenty of Amaranthine in Wardenclave, and their senses were keen. They'd hear his voice, and they'd be strong enough to rescue him from his own foolishness.

A bird called then, sharp and close, and fluttered to the ground near the edge of the clay. Cocking its head to one side, it studied Tenma with a beady eye.

Despite his desperate situation, Tenma was taken by the beauty of the thing. Ever since graduating from New Saga High School, he'd traveled constantly. Usually with Goh-sensei. Until recently, also with Inti. And one of the things Tenma marveled over was the existence of so many birds. What was normal and boring to one region was strange and new to a traveler like him.

This bird had brilliant blue feathers, barred with black and white, and a distinctive crest atop its head. Striking and, Tenma hoped, overly large for its species.

"Hello," he called softly. "Good morning."

Tenma made a basic hand sign, identifying himself as a reaver.

Which wasn't entirely true, but he *was* part of the In-between now. And he'd always gotten on well with Kith.

"By some chance, are you a friend?"

The bird spread its wings and beat them once, adding a call.

Tenma was convinced. "I'm glad you found me. I seem to have become stuck. Could you send for help?" He waved toward the village. "I've only been here a few days. Well, not *here*. Not *stuck* for a few days." He was babbling, but he couldn't stop. "I only meant I've been here at Wardenclave for a few days. So I'm not sure who to ask for. But if this is your home, you'll know, won't you? Does Wardenclave have some kind of patrol or security team?"

"Both."

The voice came from above and behind, and Tenma twisted, trying to see who had arrived.

Someone had settled comfortably upon a nearby tree branch. Had he been watching Tenma struggle?

Lifting two fingers, he repeated himself, this time in Japanese.

Tenma bobbed his head and murmured thanks. He could get by in English, but in stressful situations, his many language lessons escaped him.

The Amaranthine slipped from his perch, landing lightly on bare feet and strolling around so Tenma didn't need to strain to see him. He wore loose pants of coarse cloth secured by a double row of buttons that marched up his midriff. The throwback style gave him a rustic appearance, like someone who didn't mingle enough with society to know when trends changed.

Not that Tenma was wearing the height of reaver fashion, which was a mercy. His good clothes wouldn't have survived this mudpack. It was no loss to further mangle the sturdy denim pants that he wore for work. They were already stained by clay from many seasons at the potter's wheel.

His rescuer's long coat looked like the sort of thing to keep off the weather, as did the hat with its drooping brim. He pushed it back on his head, revealing a remarkable thatch of gray hair and bright eyes. This Amaranthine was very much in need of a haircut. And quite possibly a bath.

"What have we here?"

The male's voice had a teasing lilt. A relief, since it meant Tenma probably wasn't in trouble. With formal phrasing, he said, "Thank you for your concern. I am sorry to trouble you; however, I seem to have become stuck."

"You certainly are. Quite trapped. In what, I wonder?"

The leading tone took Tenma aback. But he was used to the Amaranthine tendency to go all cryptic, especially when trying to explain him. So he stated the obvious. Again. "Clay."

"You have an interest in clay?"

He came close enough for Tenma to realize that his fair skin wasn't smudged with dirt or ash. He had freckles. Gray freckles. But he still gave an overall impression of someone who cared little for his appearance. Gauntlets covered the backs of his hands and forearms, but they left his palms bare and his claws on full display.

Tenma went with the simplest—if not the most accurate— explanation. "My mentor is a potter."

"That explains much." The Amaranthine stepped nearer, unmolested by the clay. "One man's lure is another man's mud puddle."

Offering his palms more in plea than in courtesy, Tenma asked, "Would you mind giving me a hand?"

"Pardon me!" He closed the distance between them, grasped him under both arms, and pulled.

Tenma had expected the sucking hold to steal his shoes along with his dignity, but instead of extracting him from the clay, the pit simply vanished. As if it had never been there. Held aloft by his rescuer, he could see the slight depression he'd been standing in. A stone etched with sigils lay at its center.

"A trap?" he asked.

"You walked right into it," said the Amaranthine. "Distracted, were you?"

He looked up into a pair of steely eyes. Now that they were touching, power tingled across Tenma's skin, and colors bloomed. None of this alarmed him in the least. He might be an oddity, but the novelty had worn away under the onslaught of training.

"Am I out of bounds?" Tenma asked. "I do apologize."

He hung limp in the Amaranthine's grasp, his feet dangling several centimeters from the ground. Proof of this person's capabilities. Though Tenma was pretty sure he'd be taller in stature, the Amaranthine was much stronger … and capable of flight.

Not a dragon, then.

The Amaranthine set him down, and Tenma sank further, ending on his knees.

"Did you injure yourself?" Pushing him to sit, the stranger ran his hands over joints and bones.

"I'm okay. Just a little disoriented." He waved aside any concern. "Was that your illusion?"

"The sigil is mine. The scene it painted was all yours." The Amaranthine tugged thoughtfully at the brim of his hat. "You're Goh's cosset."

Tenma sighed. As much as he disliked the label, it fit better than apprentice. Anyone who'd ever seen his attempts at pottery knew that Goh didn't keep him around for his artistic abilities. Hardly a night went by that Tenma wasn't cradled in the monkey clansman's arms, for Goh had picked up where Hanoo, Yoota, and Ploom left off. Nurturing and protecting the glimmer they'd discovered in his soul.

"He was my teacher at school." Tenma felt bad for stealing Goh away from New Saga. But he was immensely grateful for the monkey clansman's steady presence. He was a patient teacher, a capable protector, and a father figure for both him and Inti. Changing their friendship into brotherhood. Making them a tribe.

"And now you are his pet?"

"More or less."

While the term first struck him as insulting, Tenma had learned that it was neither demeaning nor derogatory. In Amaranthine culture, a close-kept human was referred to by a word that didn't translate exactly. *Pet* was close, since it implied choice and care and companionship. But also elevation and acknowledgement, in the sense that some people treated their pets like people. Which really did sound insulting unless you looked at it from the Amaranthine point of view.

Tenma only understood because Isla and Lapis had taken the time to explain.

Goh had no formal claim over him, yet he'd sworn a weighty

oath to the Five. To help Tenma get to the places he'd need to visit. Quietly. So he could do his thing without raising interest or attention. Except he always did.

The Amaranthine seemed to be waiting for more, so Tenma added, "We get along."

"Your classification?"

An inquisitive one. This never went well. Tenma shook his head. "No specialization."

"Aptitudes?"

"Not sigilcraft." It was a weak joke and a weaker deflection.

"An artisan like your mentor? No?" He edged closer and lowered his voice. "You must be sweet and nestle well."

Tenma doubted this was the appropriate time to point out that Amaranthine of the monkey clans *tangled*. "I really couldn't say."

"You don't have to say. I already know." Fingertips lifted his chin. "The mysterious Mister Subaru, honorary Starmark, apprentice to Lord Mossberne, and emissary to the clans. Word has it, your tending is more than sweet. It's salvific."

He couldn't deny any of it. Any more than he was allowed to confirm it. "Are you teasing me?"

"A little." The Amaranthine sat beside him, hands folded, gaze intent. "Ask me why."

"Why are you teasing me?"

He chuckled huskily. "Are you always this obedient?"

"Yes?"

"Sure about that?"

Tenma shook his head.

"I know you would have gotten around to asking eventually, but let's skip along, shall we? Salali Fullstash. We're lending a hand with security while the chief is out of commission." Beckoning to the blue avian, who flew to a perch atop Salali's hat, he added, "This one's Gent. He's Kith. A blue jay."

"And you …?"

"A bit of a stray, though I'll own to being a squirrel. Currently unencumbered by house or clan, mate or progeny. Much like yourself. Ask me how I know."

Tenma hunched his shoulders. "How did you know I'm still single?"

"Would you believe me if I said it's written in your scent?"

Although Amaranthine senses were unusually keen, Tenma knew their limits. He shook his head. "Did you talk to Goh-sensei?"

"No, but Glint did, and I *happened* to be nearby. So I heard about your upcoming nuptial tour."

He sighed and nodded. Really, there was nothing to say.

Theories abounded, but a consensus had yet to be reached as to why Tenma was able to mend the Broken. But everyone agreed that a gift like his should be preserved. Which was reaver-speak for producing a bunch of heirs. Although he'd overheard Hisoka lobbying hard for another means to their ends. Something about a golden seed.

"You are eager to secure a bride?"

Tenma said, "That's the plan. I'll travel to several enclaves. Participate in marriage meetings. They may place me in one of the outlying settlements."

"Are you always this obedient?" Salali repeated, a gentle taunt.

"Yes." He'd set the condition that had led to these arrangements, so he couldn't very well complain. "There are … reasons."

"So you'll go where you're told, do as you're told? Accept their plans for you?"

He looked away. "It's not as if I had any plans of my own."

"Very nice. So will you go along with mine?"

"Eh?"

"My plans for you." Salali had developed a mad twinkle. "Come with me. I'll show you a good place. We can do nice things there."

Tenma asked, "Are you teasing me again?"

"Even more than last time." The clansman smiled. "Have you worked out yet if you'll trust me? By all means, by *any* means, investigate the matter to your heart's content."

Permission.

This person really *did* know more than he should.

Forming a hand sign that begged for secrecy, he lowered his voice to ask, "Did you know there are all different kinds of blue? It's the moodiest color."

Salali rolled his eyes to indicate Gent. "Tell me about it."

With a sharp call, the blue jay beat his wings and might have stolen Salali's hat if the squirrel hadn't grabbed its brim with both hands.

"Is that what you see, Tenma Subaru?" he asked. "Am I a moody blue?"

Tenma was getting better at putting the things he saw into words. At helping people to understand the difference between what he saw and what it meant about them. So he dared to ask, "How long have you been friends?"

Salali sobered. "Long while. And then some."

"That's why." Tenma studied the bird for a few moments and

smiled. "Gent's blue is a part of you now, and he's taken on your hue. May I ask a personal question?"

"Go on, then."

"Is your blaze a reddish-purple?" The squirrel's expression was answer enough, and Tenma nodded. "When it's bondmates, the colors usually blend, creating a whole new one. But with longtime friends, they trade. As if they're each most on the other's mind."

"You are not the first to notice," Salali said softly. As if he'd already known.

Tenma pushed at his glasses, trying to think. All this time, had the answers been here in Wardenclave? None of the clans had a record of someone like him. Oh, but ... *oh*. Salali had said he had no clan. "You know about my secret?"

"First rule of keeping secrets is not letting anyone know you have one."

It was a little like a taunt, but a little like confirmation.

Salali casually asked, "Who sees the unseen world in colors?"

"Only me."

"Wrong."

Tenma couldn't believe it. Finally! "You know what I am? Are there others like me here?"

"Not here." He lifted a finger. "Not *yet*. But she's on her way."

10

SHARE AND SHARE ALIKE

People seemed to think Lilya didn't understand that she and her brother were different. Which was both silly and true.

She and Kyrie had always been together. They'd shared their first day and her mother's milk. They'd shared a crib, then a bedroom. Pets. Plans. Books. Biscuits. Siblings. Secrets. They even shared each other's parents.

And then there was Ginkgo. He belonged to both of them. Not in a parent way, because Ginkgo was terrible at rules and manners and bedtimes and boundaries. But in his own way, because Ginkgo was wonderful about holding hands and making faces and midnight raids and leading adventures. This being the biggest of all.

Ginkgo tapped the top of her head. "Something on your mind?"

Lilya said, "You."

"That explains the smile on your face."

Which put one there.

He cleared his throat and said, "I was worried you two would be homesick."

Kyrie tore his gaze from the passing scenery in order to check on Lilya. His eyes were more awake away from home. And not stuck to the pages of a book.

Slipping a hand into hers, Kyrie softly asked, "Mom wanted to know?"

"Nah. She's got too much faith to fret." Ginkgo's fox ears dipped, and he pocketed his phone. "But you know Dad."

"Send a picture," suggested Kyrie.

Ginkgo wrinkled his nose. "And end his suspense?"

"If he is not sure we are safe, he will come and *make* sure." Kyrie leaned into Lilya, composed and already posing. "You know Dad."

Out came the phone, and they took enough goofy pictures to reassure Uncle Argent.

Lilya tugged Ginkgo's sleeve. "Send them to Papka and Mum, too."

"You got it, little girl."

Not that her parents would be worrying, either. Maybe it was because they were used to the comings and goings of their children. There were six of them now—Darya, Timur, Isla, Annika, Lilya, and Vanya. And Ginkgo had told them a secret. That Papka and Mum would be adding *another* baby brother or sister to the family. By the time they returned home at the end of summer, they'd be able to tell that Mum was carrying.

Because of Lilya. That's what everyone said.

They were trying again because of her.

Ginkgo tapped again and tweaked her ear for good measure. "Where'd that smile run off to?"

"Not far. Right here." She leaned into him and shut her eyes against the future.

Kyrie whispered her name, and that gave her the courage to open them again.

"Right here," she repeated, because if she had a choice, she always would be.

He smiled for her, a small smile that mostly lurked in his eyes. Careful and quiet, as if he were always surrounded by timid creatures who would startle and flee the moment they noticed him. Kyrie was good at going unnoticed. A surprising quality in someone who didn't *look* subtle. All because of his heritage.

Kyrie's dad was slim and sly and sloppy and snooty, sometimes all at the same time. Uncle Argent was a fox with important friends. Sometimes he traveled, but he said he liked Stately House best. When home, he was never far from Kyrie's mom, who was small and dainty and wise and kind. And a beacon, too. Just like Lilya.

But Kyrie was a fosterling.

Aunt Tsumiko would only ever talk about the story behind his name. But Naroo-soh had once mentioned her being there for the birth. So she knew more than she was telling. And Lilya's sister Isla, who came back every time Hisoka-sensei visited Papka, had been arguing with Lord Mossberne about coloration and dragon clans when one of them let slip that Kyrie had a sire.

That meant Kyrie's mother had been the human, and his father had been the dragon.

Kyrie was a crosser. Like Ginkgo.

Only Kyrie didn't have fox ears and a tail like Ginkgo, who was a younger, scruffier version of Uncle Argent. Instead, Kyrie's heritage showed up in scales and spots and horns. And in full daylight—like right now—you could tell that his hair was the rich, dark purple of the aubergines from Mare Withershanks's garden, only glossier and swishier. Kyrie kept his hair long and left it loose. A curtain to hide behind.

Lilya's brother was stronger than Papka.

He was faster than Minx.

He was clever with sigils and stones.

He was levels above Lilya in school.

And still people found it necessary to remind her that they weren't true siblings. As if being the family's greatest disappointment had robbed her of sense. As if she didn't understand what was coming.

The knowing looks had begun this past winter.

All at once, almost overnight, the family noticed that Lilya was fifteen centimeters taller than Kyrie. Aunt Tsumiko had calmly reminded everyone that girls had their growth spurt earlier than boys. But she'd bit her lip and looked a little sad. Uncle Akira had pointed out that the Hajime family had always been shorter than average. And Mum proved the point by stealing up behind and looming over him.

Everyone had laughed and let the subject drop. Lilya wasn't taller because something had changed. Lilya was taller because she always would have been. Heritage came into play for humans, too.

For the most part, Lilya was like Mum—tall and sturdy, with dark eyes and straight hair. But Lilya had inherited the shape of her face and its features from Papka. She'd borrowed a little from each of them, like any crosser.

But crossers with Amaranthine blood always grew up in the Amaranthine way. Slowly. So even though Kyrie had been growing up alongside Lilya until now, that would change. Really, it already had.

Her eleven-year-old self would only be the same as his eleven-year-old self for a little while longer. Which meant *this* was their last summer together. She'd move on, getting older, and in another year or two, she wouldn't be half a head taller than him. She'd be head and shoulders taller. Then she'd gain Mum's height, and he would still be a skinny little boy.

Lilya's children and even her grandchildren would get to meet her brother and be eleven with him. Or maybe twelve. Or fifteen. Because she couldn't slow down time any more than he could hurry up growing.

They'd be like Aunt Tsumiko and Uncle Akira.

Because of the special bond Kyrie's mom shared with Uncle Argent, she was borrowing his years. Or something. Basically, she didn't get older. So even though she'd been born before Uncle Akira, he'd caught up to her. And passed her.

When Lilya asked, Papka had explained that sharing an Amaranthine's years was a mixed blessing. The very same thing that made Argent and Ginkgo and Kyrie so happy ... was making Aunt Tsumiko and Uncle Suuzu sad.

"Feel that?" whispered Kyrie.

"Flawless," marveled Ginkgo. "Talk about a blind approach."

They must be there. Lilya nodded, even though she had no idea which direction to look. "Where?"

Kyrie pointed out his window, at what looked to her like an endless sea of grass. Although her older siblings talked about their travels, she'd never left Stately House. This place seemed foreign and formless and void. But Lilya had spent much of her life in the care of foxes, so she knew that *seeming* meant little. Or nothing at all.

She couldn't manage sigils, commune with stones, or any of the other things that made Papka the best in the world. So the barrier that hid Wardenclave didn't interest her all that much. "Is Timur here?"

Ginkgo leaned down to look past them, utterly intent. "Wait for it," he murmured. "Any second now."

Something tingled against Lilya's skin, and she shivered. Ginkgo automatically slipped his hand around her wrist. Kyrie did the same on the other side. Making sure *her* walls were up. Making sure Papka's and Uncle Argent's seal held true.

The bus rolled to a stop before a high wall that looked positively medieval and entirely out of place. And doubly exciting because of it. There was no moat or drawbridge, but the gates were shut.

From a small log cabin beside the road came a white-haired Amaranthine wearing the Starmark colors. She boarded the bus.

Lilya wanted to ask Ginkgo to take a picture, but she didn't say it. It was exciting to think that this might be one of Ever's many aunts or cousins. She had the same eyes, all coppery.

Ever Starmark was the best friend who usually made them a trio. He was a crosser, but he lived in Keishi, a city too far from Stately House to make visits easy. But he came when he could, just like they visited him whenever Uncle Argent had meetings. Sometimes, the three of them would play at the Starmark Compound, and sometimes they'd explore Kikusawa, the neighborhood below the shrine where Ever lived with his big brother Eloquence.

They'd invited Ever to join them for the summer, since he was also eleven, going on twelve. The timing had been bad, but for a very good reason. He was about to become Uncle Ever. Kimiko was expecting a baby over the summer, and Ever absolutely needed to be there to greet his new packmate.

"Mind if we get a picture with that?" Ginkgo suddenly asked.

Lilya followed the sweep of his hand and saw a sign with bold lettering.

WELCOME TO WARDENCLAVE
FOUNDATION FOR PEACE

And in slightly smaller letters, a proud addendum.

HOMETOWN OF HARMONIOUS STARMARK

Kyrie's giggle was a melodious thrum that Lilya couldn't imitate. A dragonish sound that meant he was pleased.

Lilya knew how much he'd wanted this summer to include Ever. Before they left Japan, they made a solemn pact to send Ever a picture every day. Because even though they were often apart, they were part of each other. "For our first day. For his Da."

"You may. Please, do," invited the lady, who was staring at Ginkgo's ears, but trying not to be obvious about it. "Fans of his?"

"Friends," countered Ginkgo. He barely came up to her shoulder, but he was entirely at ease. You could tell by the gentle sway of his silvery tail. "I'm surprised you didn't get the memo. Or not. Dad equates secrecy with safety."

"You're Lord Mettlebright's son," she murmured.

Lilya backed into the aisle to allow Kyrie to slide out of their seat.

Immediately, the Amaranthine's expression changed—surprise, chagrin, and a promising smile. "By any chance, are you Ever's friends?"

Kyrie solemnly corrected her. "Best friends."

She beckoned them off the bus, then dropped to one knee before Lilya and Kyrie to offer her palms. "My name is Resplendence, and I'm one of the guards who helps keep Wardenclave safe. Harmonious is my big brother."

11

BIG BROTHER

Lilya was happy to clasp hands with Resplendence. She liked dogs. Maybe even liked them best of all the clans. Mostly because of Ever, but a little bit because of his Da, who was all rolling laughter and rumbling kindness. If Ever's Da was Resplendence's big brother, did that mean she loved him the way Lilya loved Timur? Did she miss him the way they missed Ever?

"Oh, lovely one," Resplendence said when their hands met.

That was strange. Lilya had been extensively warded, which meant no one should even realize she was a reaver. But the guard might simply be sorting her out by scent. Dogs did.

"Are you looking forward to your courses?"

Lilya bit her lip. Lying never worked with canines, so she gave a tiny shake of her head.

"Homesick?" guessed the guard.

She shook her head again.

Resplendence rolled her eyes toward Ginkgo and Kyrie. "Something you don't want the boys to hear?"

Lilya didn't want *anyone* to know. At least, not anyone from Stately House. But Resplendence was half right, so Lilya nodded.

"May we have a few minutes?" She signaled for permission and for patience. "Girl talk."

Ginkgo swooped in, searched Lilya's face, kissed her nose, and said, "Not even through the gate, and you're already making friends. Take whatever time you need."

Just like that.

Lilya doubted any parent would have let her go off with a stranger.

Then again, Resplendence was a Starmark. And they didn't *go* anywhere. Instead, the guard plucked a crystal from one of the pouches at her waist. Lilya knew about these—had one of her own—so she locked hands with Resplendence around it. Now, anything they said couldn't be overheard, even by the cleverest of fox ears.

Privacy. The first novelty of travel.

Ginkgo and Kyrie eased back, giving her room to speak for herself.

Resplendence carefully slid one hand into a supportive position under Lilya's. "May I know what you've been hiding."

"I'm a beacon."

Slim eyebrows arched. "That is well-hidden, but hardly the secret you wished to keep from these males. Therefore, it's not the truth I'm offering to protect."

Ever talked like this sometimes. Insisting he would protect them from anything that dampened their spirits, be it bad dreams, hurt feelings, or failing grades. Still threatened to *sniffen* them if she or Kyrie tried to keep something from him.

Lilya eased closer. "I'm a beacon," she repeated softly. "But being a beacon isn't a job."

"Your classification hasn't been assessed?"

She made a face. "Of course it has. Many times. I'm a beacon."

Resplendence frowned. "But that's not ... ah. Do they look no further?"

"They do. They've tried so many times." Uncle Argent was especially keen on helping her refine her superlative soul, to define her path. "It's no good. They can't pinpoint my aptitude because I don't *have* one."

"You are a tribute to your parents' strength, but you aren't sure how to stand in your own?"

She put it so simply, Lilya was all amazement.

"I understand a little." Resplendence rolled her eyes. "Try being Glint Starmark's daughter."

Was there a lot of pressure on her because her dad was First of Dogs? Maybe she did understand the weight of expectations placed on a daughter of the First of Wards.

"My case is a little different. You see, I have sufficient years to consider a suitor, and my sire wants my happiness. But his enthusiasm for the topic exceeds my own. If I didn't know my own mind, I might mistakenly conclude that my only value to the pack will be found in the number of pups I add to his lineage."

Lilya nodded.

"Then it's good that you've come to us. To Wardenclave. And you shouldn't fear your courses. They'll help you know your own mind." Resplendence smiled. "Then you'll stand proudly, sure of your place."

"Is that what you did?"

Resplendence brushed a kiss against Lilya's cheek. "It's what I did, and it's what I'm still doing. Making up your mind will be good, but changing your mind is also part of becoming."

That was a relief. It would be terrible to choose a course that didn't fit.

"You seem more at ease."

Lilya decided she was. "Thank you."

Taking back her crystal, Resplendence raised her voice to include Ginkgo and Kyrie. "If you need me, ask any of the guards." Standing tall, she proudly declared, "The sisters and daughters of Radiance Starmark are strong."

The bus carried them through the gate, up a steep series of switchbacks, and along the rim of a large green that looked to be a perfect circle. Buildings lined the road, and paths fanned away, leading to cabins. They pulled to a stop in front of a low building draped with banners representing the colors of every reaver classification, but Lilya was more interested in the man standing out front, holding a chubby toddler, accompanied by a large black feline.

Gregor had grown so much since last Dichotomy Day, when

Timur had arrived with their invitations to Wardenclave. He'd stayed long enough to convince their parents—and especially Uncle Argent—to accept Glint's invitation.

It had taken two whole months.

In the end, Lilya guessed that it was little Gregor who swayed the fox. For once they became attached, there was no way Argent was letting the little boy fall into anyone else's clutches. Ginkgo must go. No other minder would do for a son of Stately House.

Ginkgo was off the bus in a flash.

And it was nice to see Timur so glad.

"He is like us," said Kyrie, still in his seat. "Brother took care of him, too."

"All of us," agreed Lilya, who had spent as much time in Ginkgo's arms as Mum's. Maybe even more. "And all of our children."

Kyrie softly replied, "Yours, perhaps. If you stay at Stately House."

Lilya started to say that she'd never leave. She never *wanted* to, but she couldn't know that for certain. Darya had been contracted away, never to return. And Isla received offers from every corner of the world.

She tapped Kyrie's shoulder. "Your children, too."

He shrugged and shook his head.

"Crossers marry," she insisted. "Like Ash and Tami."

Kyrie's lips twitched into a little half-smile. "Ash's inheritance never frightened anyone."

"You might have wings one day," Lilya reasoned. "An attainment."

Her brother's eyes were soft with the gentle sadness that had always been a part of him. "Ash has the wings of an angel. With dragon wings, I would look even more like a devil."

Lilya's troubles seemed small and silly now. She dropped back into the seat and hauled him into a fierce hug. "No, *nyet*, *non*, and never."

Kyrie melted against her. "Sorry," he whispered. "I should not borrow trouble from my tomorrows."

"Today has enough worries," Lilya agreed, quoting Aunt Tsumiko. "Can we go to Timur, now?"

"May I hold Gregor first?"

Lilya giggled. "If you can get him away from Ginkgo."

With chorused thanks to the driver, they linked hands and hurried to join their brothers. What a sight they made. True to form, Ginkgo had secured the baby for himself, but that gave Timur the advantage. He scooped up Ginkgo *and* Gregor, proving he was strong enough to cradle both the half-fox who'd raised him and the son he was raising alone.

"Put me down, cuddle bud." Ginkgo's smile held nothing back. "I know I'm your favorite, but you really shouldn't neglect the rest of your denmates."

Timur landed a resounding kiss on Ginkgo's forehead, then turned him loose in order to capture Kyrie. He tossed him high, earning a warbling yelp, caught him close, and kissed his cheeks. "Have you grown?" Dangling Kyrie at arm's length, Timur let the boy squirm and smile under his scrutiny before nodding. "You have grown a little, I think. Yes?"

It always amazed Lilya that someone who looked so much like Mum could behave so much like Papka. Timur had been away for years. A training trip from which he'd returned with mixed baggage. A deeper laugh and a sadder smile. A richer accent and a baby son.

But no wife.

Lilya got the impression that Papka was somehow worried about Timur but delighted to welcome Gregor into the family. Mum was flat-out proud, but she tried not to let it show. And nobody was willing to pass along the particulars to a couple of kids.

While Timur quizzed Kyrie about their trip, Lilya offered a hand to Fend, one of the cubs from Minx's litters. He nosed her palm and tickled her with his whiskers, mostly to be polite. Fend was all business. Not one for indiscriminate cuddling or purring. But he sat beside her, watching Timur more closely than anyone. And Lilya waited her turn with the confidence of one who knows they are being saved for last … and will get the best because of it.

"Where is that sister of mine?" called Timur.

She raised her fist in a battler's hand sign. Or was it from wolf trackers? Lilya was always getting them mixed up.

Not that it mattered. Timur closed the distance in a handful of strides, dropped to one knee, and offered his hand like a burly prince charming.

Delighted, Lilya curtsied and placed her fingertips on his palm.

With a murmured endearment in their mother's first tongue, he tugged her into the circle of his arms. "Did you see many strange things along your way?"

For someone who lived with giant cats, flying foxes, and phoenix friends, the trip had been filled with fresh oddities. "A boat and a plane and a train and a bus."

"Wonders beyond compare?" teased Timur.

"New things," she replied seriously. "Kyrie and I have finally broadened our horizons."

Ginkgo swayed over, making silly faces for Gregor, and asked, "Do we need to check in with anyone?"

"As it happens, I just met the headman, and he wants to welcome you personally."

12

TREEBORNE BOY

Even knowing what to expect, Ginkgo had trouble making sense of reality. Once the promised Amaranthine tree towered into view, he understood the scope of the illusions that kept it safe. "Okay, that thing's beyond big."

"He is," agreed Timur.

Ginkgo peered around, senses alert. So much had been fine-tuned—the tree's presence, the shadow it cast, temperature differences, the view of the sky. There was probably a barrier similar to the one Dad used to keep his conservatory from being overrun. It made most people at Stately House forget the glassed-in garden even existed.

Straight out of a book of fairy tales and looking like someone's rendering of the World Tree, Zisa's trunk appeared to be smooth, and his leaves were an uncanny shade of chartreuse. But what really intrigued Ginkgo was the scent.

"You smell that?"

Timur slowed his steps. "I remember thinking there was a scent the first day I was here. Too used to it now to notice, I guess."

Kyrie asked, "Do you mean the flowers?"

Ginkgo nodded and peered at the village situated below. From here, their song circle was more obvious, as well as the bustle of activity around the cabins.

"That way," said Kyrie, pointing.

"Yeah?" Ginkgo indicated the next few mountaintops over. "What's that way?"

"No idea." Timur waved to the north. "Denholm, which is an undisclosed city, is just beyond the rise. It's the hub of all Dimityblest industry. In fact, it's where the scribes write the communiques that link reavers worldwide."

"Which other Dimityblest industries?" asked Lilya.

As the girl rattled off the diverse products for which the moth clans were famous, Ginkgo hung back to wait for Kyrie, who still gazed to the east.

"Eight different flowers." He spoke with a confidence that tended to sway the susceptible. But he also spoke from experience. Kyrie was Ginkgo's best helper in the gardens of Stately House—inside and out. When the kid's nose wasn't in a book, it was usually in a flower.

"Any you recognize?"

"All new." Kyrie eagerly begged, "Can we go find them?"

"Don't see why not." Ginkgo hated to admit it, but he wasn't picking up anything. "Eight, huh? How can you sort scents you've never encountered?"

"The wind helped." Looking up into the thick foliage overhead, he tentatively asked, "Do you hear that?"

Ginkgo swiveled his ears. "The birds?"

"Someone is singing."

Being only half Amaranthine, Ginkgo knew his senses weren't on par with someone of full blood. His little brother was also a crosser, but the mix was different. Dragon blood gave Kyrie a whole different set of aptitudes. Ginkgo dabbled in illusory sigilcraft. But there wasn't a trap or ward he'd ever created that Kyrie couldn't unmake with a touch.

The boy always blamed the wind. Probably thanks to all the dragon lore Tsumiko read to him. She'd been delving into Amaranthine history, scriptures, and songs ever since taking Kyrie to her heart as a son. She was as diligent as a Dimityblest scribe, especially when it came to the tales of dragons.

"What kind of someone?" asked Ginkgo.

Kyrie tipped his head to one side, then the other. "Someone new."

"Maybe it's the tree?"

His little brother brightened. "Maybe."

"We're due for an introduction." Ginkgo offered his hand. "Let's say *hi*."

They caught up to Timur in the kitchen of a modest house. He had his arm around the shoulders of someone who looked like a young samurai who'd mislaid his swords. Wavy black hair swept back from a broad face with strong cheekbones and a stronger jaw, but his quiet demeanor failed to intimidate. Largely due to the puppy in his pocket.

"This is my new sparring partner, Mikoto," said Timur.

By the look on the young man's face, this was news. And good news, at that.

"He's headman of Wardenclave, so mind your manners."

Not that Timur was showing even a smidge of respect. And Ginkgo judged that Mikoto appreciated the oversight.

Lilya greeted him in Japanese, which was understandable. Conversations at Stately House veered from Japanese to English to French without a moment's notice. Liberally sprinkled with Russian, usually for emphasis. But Japanese was default, and Mikoto looked the part.

To Ginkgo's surprise, Mikoto answered in kind, greeting them with polite formality. "It is my honor to welcome you on behalf of Wardenclave. May the coming season find you stronger for your efforts and richer for the bonds we will share."

Nice words, nice guy, if a bit serious for Ginkgo's tastes. But he was the sort Kyrie usually sidled up to. Quiet, conscientious types. Probably because they were slightly less susceptible. The kid clammed up fast around folks who couldn't help themselves.

Pleased, Ginkgo turned to urge his brother forward, only to realize his hand was empty.

Lilya, who had a sense for these things, blurted, "Where's Kyrie?"

Before he could break for the door, a hand hooked his arm. "Wait. He has not gone far."

"I'm responsible for him," protested Ginkgo.

The new guy, who was right about the same height as Ginkgo, smiled. "As your host, I have a share in your responsibility. He is safe."

"You're Waaseyaa." Ginkgo allowed the man to hold him back. "Where's my brother?"

"With mine. In a sense." Dark eyes dancing, Waaseyaa said, "Your brother is climbing the tree."

Kyrie knew better than to go off by himself without saying anything to anyone. It was a basic rule, especially when in strange territory. And he hadn't *exactly* broken it. Fend had seen him slip away.

Leaving his shoes among the roots, Kyrie touched the tree, which was so big, it was almost like facing a wall of wood. The surface wasn't rough bark, but smooth and rippling. Like the tree's trunk was made of many smaller ones that had twined together as they grew, folded together like the braids Aunt Sansa often wove into Lilya's hair.

If he used the grooves for footholds, he wouldn't need to dig his claws into the flawless surface of the wood. It would be a shame to leave marks. Probably rude, too, since this tree was special.

He searched for the best starting point, only to discover hoop of metal jutting out of the wood. It must have been there for a long time, because the wood seemed to have grown around it. Kyrie tested it. Definitely a rung!

Peering up, he spied another and smiled.

Someone else had been climbing this tree. Quite possibly in secret, or at least in private, since the hoop was set with a crystal.

Wards didn't work very well against Kyrie, especially when their anchor was purple. He touched the soft lavender crystal, which seemed to whisper its welcome. Reavers favored stones from the amethyst range as wardstones, but Kyrie had discovered that purple stones liked him best. They forgot what they were doing if he was nearby.

Barriers let him pass right through unless they were reinforced with sigilcraft to exclude him. But that only happened at home. And not so much anymore, since he was old enough to respect boundaries.

Balancing on the hoop, Kyrie reached for the next. Whoever had created this path was taller, so he had to stretch and scramble until he made it up among the limbs. Then his options multiplied with every branching path. And he began to search.

The song had ended, but a scent pulled at him. Stronger now, as if one of the barriers had been holding back the fragrance that teased him onward and upward.

Heedless of how high he'd come, Kyrie searched for the flowers, wanting to know their shape and their color. Then he could tell Ginkgo all about them. Maybe even add a tree like this to their garden at home. That way, he could enjoy this scent all the time. Or at least as often as the tree was in bloom.

He accidentally found the flowers by walking into them face-first.

They were unlike any blossoms he'd ever seen before—cupped petals like bells, cascading in clusters. Vividly orange and heavy with pollen, sticky gold dust that tickled until he sneezed. The noise sent several Ephemera zipping away like startled fish. But they came drifting back, as enamored of the flowers as Kyrie was.

He liked Ephemera. Dad's glass garden was filled with all kinds.

But these were new. And wild, of course. So when he offered his fingertips, they scooted away. With a whole summer ahead, maybe he could tame one. Bring it home to give to Dad. Ginkgo would probably help him.

Six-legged lizards nuzzled into the orange flowers, like they loved this tree.

Such a lovely tree.

Being here made Kyrie feel fuzzy and warm and glad … and a little bit sleepy. So he found a forked section right up among the flowers and lay back. Just for a little while.

Such a lovely tree.

Kyrie was so relaxed, he didn't notice that there was someone else nearby until he spoke.

"You are a long way up."

"It is a big tree," he pointed out.

The stranger balanced easily on their shared limb. "You like big trees?"

Kyrie nodded. "Especially this one."

"And why would that be?"

Inhaling deeply, he sighed his contentment. "Feels good."

The stranger glanced around, looking unconvinced. "So you say."

"You cannot feel it?" Kyrie asked.

"No." Peering around at the eager Ephemera, he quietly confessed, "I never could understand the appeal."

"Too bad. This tree is *lovely*."

That earned him a smile. "And you love it?"

Kyrie hardly needed to consider. He shyly admitted, "I think I do."

"Will you steal these flowers and bottle their pollen?"

"I would rather come visit every chance I get."

The stranger hummed approvingly. "Sensible boy."

Slouching a little further into his seat, Kyrie mumbled, "Feels good."

"It will not feel good if you topple."

Kyrie turned his head to check how high he was, but looking down tilted him sideways.

"Ope, ope, ope. None of that!" The stranger made a grab. "Messy business, cleaning up fallen boys."

All of the sudden, Kyrie realized that he was being cradled like a child, which wasn't such a great shock. He *was* a child. But not so little that he wanted to be babied. He would have said so, but he was distracted by his rescuer's hair, which was sprouting leaves of the greenest green, as vivid as the ones that surrounded them. His smile was nice, and his scent was lovely.

That's when Kyrie made a vast leap of logic. "Are you a tree?"

"I am *this* tree."

Struggling up, Kyrie brushed his lips against the underside of the tree-person's jaw, just the way Dad had taught him. It took quite an effort. Sagging back in limp delight, he said, "You are my *favorite* tree."

"Do you love me?"

Such a lovely tree. "I think I do."

The tree tapped his nose. "You are adorable."

A voice called out somewhere below.

"Come, and I will introduce you to my brother. Since you will be visiting me every chance you get, he will want to meet you." His eyebrows lifted slightly. "What name should I give when I introduce you?"

"I am Kyrie."

The tree caressed his hair. "What a beautiful name."

"My name is a prayer for mercy," he explained. Because an Amaranthine usually wanted to know.

With a delighted smile, he said, "And you are at mine, little dragon."

13

EACH ALLURING IN THEIR WAY

Kyrie came to himself in a tub of water.

Ginkgo cradled his head, but his attention was jumping all over the place, as if there were too many people in the room.

A man with gentle hands and kind eyes was washing Kyrie's face, so he noticed right away. "I have washed away the pollen," he said softly. "How are you feeling?"

Then Ginko filled his view, upside down. "Don't suppose you can sneeze on command?"

Kyrie had never considered trying.

"You got a snootful of fresh pollen, little bro." Ginkgo smirked. "Let's not tell Dad."

The man with the washcloth repeated, "How are you feeling?"

"Fuzzy."

Ginkgo quietly said, "He's Waaseyaa. Guess you met his twin.

Zisa brought you down."

Kyrie *had*, but all backwards. One didn't usually offer declarations of love before even knowing the other person's name. "Zisa."

"Here."

A finger trailed along his arm, then lifted his hand. The person from the tree smoothed his thumb over its back. Or rather, over one of the patches of the lavender-edged scales that showed up in different places on Kyrie's body.

He stirred uneasily and realized that they'd put him in the water with all his clothes still on. That was a relief. Kyrie didn't like for people to see all the ways he was different. Mom called modesty a virtue, but he wasn't sure he was behaving in a praiseworthy manner. He didn't want to be teased any more than he wanted to be feared. His mother thought him beautiful, but she was his mother. It almost didn't count.

Zisa was talking to Waaseyaa, eagerly recounting the rescue.

Without the haze of pollen, Kyrie noticed more details. Like the lack of fangs and claws. And the usual pointed ears and slit pupils. More interesting was the faint pattern of fine lines that decorated his skin like woodgrain. He wanted to touch it. Maybe for the same reason Zisa's thumb still stroked across the back of Kyrie's hand.

Suddenly, Lilya barged her way between the males and waved some sort of vial under his nose. The smell wasn't familiar, but it was potent. He sneezed. So did Ginkgo. Twice.

"His clothes," she groaned. "Where are our cases?"

Zisa asked, "Do you still love me without the pollen, merciful dragon?"

Kyrie felt heat creeping into the tips of his ears.

The man with the bar of soap repeated, "I am Waaseyaa, and this is my brother Zisa. You are in our home, which will be yours during your stay in Wardenclave. Your brother has been explaining how you found your way past the barriers. This time of year, we try to contain the pollen. Otherwise, it would make everyone ... fuzzy."

"This is nothing," interjected Zisa. "A token show of color. Hardly worth mentioning. You should see me on a fifth year in full bloom."

Waaseyaa murmured, "Yes, you are a sight worth seeing. But the barriers are in place for good reason. Too much of a good thing."

Yes, the scent of Zisa's flowers had been good. Such a lovely tree.

Kyrie took slow, deep breaths, willing the wind to bring him another whiff. In his mind's eye, he could see the cascading blooms, thick with granules of pure gold, fluttered on every side by Ephemera. Kyrie didn't want to forget the scent.

Was this what it was like for others? For the people who couldn't resist his words? Kyrie wasn't sure he liked being both helpless and happy about it.

"Are you all right, Kyrie?" asked Waaseyaa.

He stirred to fuller attention, tried to remember what he'd been about to say. There had been a question. Ah, yes. Kyrie sought the tree's gaze and solemnly answered, "Yes, Zisa. I still love you."

Sinder was working his way through second breakfast. Colt Alpenglow was a good sort, having the sense to bring food by the trayful rather than bowlful or plateful. So intent was he on tearing, scooping, and chewing that he didn't notice the subtle shift in Timur's sigilcraft until it did something very odd. With a whispery sigh, it swirled and resettled, as insurmountable as ever. But only after letting someone through.

Identity was no mystery, but his method was a surprise.

"Are you my knight, come to rescue me from Timur's kindly clutches?" Sinder indicated the door. "How'd you get past his barrier?"

The kid blinked and looked back. "I did not notice. I am sorry. Am I intruding?"

"Not at all." Sinder gestured to the tray on his lap. "Hungry?"

Kyrie surveyed the two emptied trays on the bed beside Sinder. "A little, but you need it more."

"Share with me," he urged. Mostly to see if it worked on a half-dragon.

The boy glanced over his shoulder, then eased closer to the bed. "May I ask you things?"

"I'll indulge your curiosity if you'll indulge mine." Sinder patted the mattress at his side. The boy obliged him, but for his own reasons. Which suited Sinder well enough. He wouldn't need to mind his words so closely.

Argent's foster son carried all the markers of his diabolical sire. In the course of their investigations, Sinder had encountered no less than eight children with some combination of draconic features. The hair, the scales, the speckling, the eyes. Kyrie's horns weren't always handed down, and one child's legacy had included a tail.

This boy had no way of knowing that he had siblings. Sinder

didn't doubt that they'd also kept that little detail from Argent. Perhaps for fear of what he might do. Then again, he was a clever old fox. Clever enough to stash his sons in safety for a season.

What mischief might Lord Mettlebright be up to, even now?

"Go ahead," prompted Sinder. "Your curiosity is both understandable and flattering. Though I know I'm not your first dragon."

Kyrie knelt beside him and offered his palms. "Lapis comes when his schedule allows."

"Not often enough?"

The boy shook his head. "And I have to share."

"How fortunate that Timur has provided us with so much privacy." He pressed half a pomegranate into the boy's hand. Plucking out his own half's ruby seeds with the tips of his claws, he added, "You don't have to be formal with me. Blurt away."

"Do you have horns?"

"In truest form, yes. Most dragons do, but there's a whole lot of variation by clan. Horns, antlers, tusks, ridges, even fins." He cleared his throat. "Horns of your sort usually come in sets. If I may?"

Kyrie dipped his head invitingly, and Sinder sifted through silky hair. Two pairs of horns curved gracefully from his hairline, up and inward, white as fangs. His questing fingers found a third set that had budded just behind and below. They were still small enough to be mostly hidden by his hair.

"I've seen something like this among the Winnowind and Galestrafe clans. There's a chance that the coming years will find you with a princely coronet."

The boy searched his face with eyes nearly the same color as the seeds he was toying with. Finally, he asked, "Do you have a tail?"

Sinder's curiosity was piqued. "Do you?"

Kyrie didn't answer, moving along to another question. "What about … your back?"

"Something there? May I see?"

With a small nod, the boy set aside his fruit and turned.

"May I touch?" checked Sinder.

"Please," said the boy, whose cheeks had gone rosy.

Sinder carefully lifted the boy's tunic, baring pale skin that looked human enough. But higher up, he discovered nascent ridges protecting his spine. And whorls of lavender that may have been his blaze. But were positioned in a way that suggested … wings.

"Do you have a blaze?"

Kyrie nodded.

"Is this it?" Sinder let the fabric fall back into place.

He shook his head, turned, and tugged at his collar. "Over my heart." With a tiny smile, he added, "Just like Ginkgo."

"Where has he got to?"

"Right there." Kyrie pointed to the barrier, and his whole expression warmed. "I think he is stalling."

"To give you time to interrogate the prisoner?"

"Just … time."

"That's very considerate of him." Sinder set aside his tray and folded his hands on his lap. "How about this. When our schedules allow, I know a spot. There's this secluded little lake, perfect for a grooming session. We can compare spots and ridges and horns and tails, and I can hand down wisecracks and wisdom. Rite of passage stuff."

Kyrie said, "I want to. Can Ginkgo come?"

"Okay, sure. Your brother needs to know what you need, right?" Sinder decided not to mention how desperate he was for company. He didn't really know Ginkgo, but they also had people in common. Maybe even common goals, if Timur's crack about spies proved true. "Fetch him in, and we can see what he thinks of our plan."

Scooting off the bed and hurrying to the door, Kyrie raised both hands, as if grabbing onto something. With a flourishing twist, the barrier vanished, allowing in a mélange of interesting scents and sounds.

Ginkgo gruffly called, "Watch yourself, Damsel!"

Belatedly, Sinder recalled *why* Timur had set such strong wards.

Some distant part of Sinder's brain was grateful that Juuyu wasn't here to see this. Because his partner had lived among Amaranthine trees and had coached Sinder on basic etiquette. Most of which went out the window long before Zisa drew back enough to smile coyly.

"Serves me right." Seeing Timur poised to intervene, Sinder shook his head and asked, "Is this where I'm supposed to say *kiss me again?*"

14

THE STUFF OF DYNASTIES

Mikoto guessed he was in the presence of greatness. Or at least great fame. This was Argent Mettlebright's family. Or more properly, his denmates, since Michael Ward also resided at Stately House. Mikoto knew the First of Wards by reputation, for Glint mentioned him often enough.

So much potential.

Glint had plied the man with proposals for paternity tours. Or a suite in his stable. Anything he wanted in exchange for greater multiplication.

All for naught.

Nothing frustrated Glint more than unions formed on the basis of mutual affection. At least, that's how it sounded when Wardenclave's matchmaker was grumping.

If the Eldermost Islands were in need of a new anchor, or when an enclave requested young diplomats willing to marry in, Glint wanted nothing more than to pull out his registries and ledgers and send them the individuals best suited to the task. But half the time, those best suited to some outlying enclave's need were already making plans of their own.

They'd formed an attachment at school or at camp. They'd agreed to a marriage arranged by a parent or mentor. They'd eloped with someone from the general populace that they'd met by chance. All disasters as far as Glint was concerned.

True love mucked up his charts in the worst way.

It happened all the time, but Michael Ward was a recurring theme. The exception that proved the rule. Because for once, a reaver's heart had guided him aright. Despite marrying for love, the First of Wards had achieved dynasty ranking by siring a beacon. A girl.

This girl.

Mikoto stepped back, dinging his hip against a bureau.

Glint must be delighted to have lured Michael Ward's daughter here. A brand new beacon, ripe for arrangement. No doubt he'd lovingly mapped out dozens of potential matches for her, complete with progeny projections.

A beacon wouldn't be sent out to prop up a flagging bloodline. No, Glint would want the dynasty to continue. A beacon could bear a beacon, given the right sire. And Mikoto had his suspicions about who topped Glint's list.

"Michaelson?" Mikoto murmured.

Timur, who'd returned to his side once it was obvious that Sinder didn't need help, angled his head to indicate he was listening.

"How old is your sister?"

The battler looked at him closely, as if Mikoto's fears were plain upon his face. "Eleven."

Young. But not too young.

Timur jostled him. "Planning to join the family?"

Mikoto couldn't think what to say, so he simply shook his head.

"She doesn't know. My parents never told her." Timur still watched him, amusement gaining strength in his expression. "You don't know either, do you?"

At an utter loss, Mikoto shook his head again.

Timur chuckled. "My father told me that Mum's been shredding your offers for years. By hand. With a ceremonial dagger. It's become one of her little Dichotomy Day traditions."

Mikoto paled.

"Not to worry. It's nothing too personal. My parents receive scads of offers. For all of us." He smiled easily. "Once she's done, we use the tatters to light a bonfire on the beach."

"I did not know." Mikoto wanted to defend himself somehow. "Glint must have sent them."

"Yeah. Same herald every time. Papka gets to chatting." Timur slung an arm around Mikoto's shoulders. "How old are you?"

"Seventeen." Older, but not too old. Not if putting off marriage meant securing a beacon for the Reaver bloodline.

"I've already told you more than I should, but Fend likes you. So do I. Here's the deal." He casually hooked him closer and lowered his voice. "Every Dichotomy Day, while the contracts burn, my parents remind us that our duty to the In-between need not cost us our happiness. We can choose any path, both for life and in love."

Mikoto wished he had that same luxury.

"Papka asked me to tell you that he's aware of the honor your offer represents, but Lilya's choices are her own." Timur hesitated. "Probably best I leave out Mum's message. She's mostly upset with Glint, anyhow."

Miserably, Mikoto repeated, "I did not know."

"Clearly." Timur's arm stayed where it was. "So … *are* you interested in my sister?"

He slowly shook his head. "There is someone else."

"You're contracted?"

"No." Mikoto put it into the simplest of terms. "I am not. But she is."

Sinder was in familiar territory. Most of his work involved listening in and extracting information. Observer. Eavesdropper. Informant. He loved to be in the middle of a muddle, taking in the drama as it unfolded, usually all unseen. Or at the very least, unnoticed. But not this week.

Captured by Spomenka.

Bandaged by a tribute.

Greeted by a headman.

Quizzed by a crosser.

Accosted by a tree.

Either he was a terrible spy or a brilliant one. In either case,

Sinder knew he was a terrible patient. Juuyu liked to point it out every time sickness or injury sent him creeping into his partner's personal space. Sinder got clingy. Juuyu got fussy. To be fair, the phoenix never turned him away. He was too restrained and too rigid, but he was totally reliable. And surprisingly missable.

Damn, he hated solo missions.

And roughing it in leaky tents.

He wasn't looking forward to his impending eviction from the guest room. Was it inevitable? If he remembered right, foxes knew how to nestle. But Ginkgo undoubtedly had his own agenda and might not be open to collaboration. Or cohabitation.

More out of habit than anything, Sinder took the room's measure. Not the picky little details that were Juuyu's specialty. He'd have cataloged everything from shoe sizes to shampoo brands, as well as the origins of every sigil in the room. Sinder was better with people. And especially with how much they let on without admitting to anything.

That balance of insight was the real reason Boon had paired him off with Juuyu. Although it didn't hurt that phoenixes were immune to dragon wiles.

Sinder assessed the room's occupants. In an homage to his absent partner, he even guessed at their shoe sizes. He'd include it in his next report. Let Twineshaft make what he would of that.

By far, the most interesting person in the room was Lilya. She didn't make sense.

Ginkgo bumped him over with a hip and sat beside him on the bed. "That's a speculative look if I ever saw one. Tell me, Damsel, why do you have your eye on Lilya?"

Sinder said, "She's warded."

"Thoroughly," agreed the half-fox.

Lowering his voice, he asked, "Why?"

"It would be funny if she weren't."

There wasn't any polite way to put it. "They're not working."

Ginkgo's eyes narrowed. "Those stones are of the highest quality."

"Befitting a daughter of the First of Wards." Sinder rolled his eyes. "But they're bored. They're not working because there's nothing for them to do. Is she an imposter?"

"She's the real deal."

Sinder slowly shook his head and voiced his first impression. "She doesn't make sense."

Ginkgo gruffly said, "She's just a kid. Let her be a kid."

"Uh-huh. Tell that to Glint."

"Don't think I won't." His lips quirked. "But you're the one staking out her room and sizing her up."

"Am I to be cast out?"

"Not my garden, not my tree, not my decision." Ginkgo adjusted his hold on the child currently using his shoulder for a pillow. One pudgy hand reached for Sinder, and he leaned warily out of reach.

Noting the string of beads at each wrist, Sinder asked, "Who's this?"

"Gregor is Timur's." Ginkgo corralled the kid's grabby hands and tucked him under his chin. "I'm his nanny for the summer. Officially."

Recognizing his cue, Sinder said, "There's an allotment of recruits training in the woods. I'm their prey for the summer. Officially."

"And ... *unofficially*?"

Knowing what they held in common, Sinder affected Boon's rumble. "The less said the better."

Ginkgo made a wolvish hand sign. "I won't tell if you won't."

They hadn't officially met—which left both with a tidy loophole of deniability—yet even without the exchange of names, Sinder liked the tenor of this relationship. Especially with how much Ginkgo let on without admitting to anything.

Pushing his luck, Sinder asked, "How likely are you to let me hang about?"

"Can't happen." Ginkgo's ears drooped. "Some of it's propriety. Some of it's proprietary. None of it's personal."

Sinder was offended. "I'm not here to woo your baby beacon."

Ginkgo snorted. "And that's gonna stop her from taking a liking? Face up to facts, Damsel. There's a *reason* they call hers an impressionable age."

That sobered him right up.

Beacons might be people, but they were also a commodity. Many Amaranthine equated potent souls with power, with acclaim, or with safety. Any ... no, *every* dragon lord would wish to add such a soul to their harem, in hopes of regaining the sky. Every enclave wanted one for its anchor. By the same token, every bloodline wanted a beacon as their boast.

Once Lilya reached her attainment, she would have her pick of husbands. But in the current climate and with public sentiment heartily in favor of inter-species mingling, this young lady might have her pick of the clans, as well.

Argent would definitely be protecting her interests. And limiting them.

"Get me out of here." Tossing up his hands, Sinder muttered, "On second thought, get *her* out of here. Or did you not notice that this tree has an amorous streak?"

With a wary glance at the room, Ginkgo leaned so close, his breath fanned Sinder's face. "It's *not* the end of the world if she likes it here. Waaseyaa's between wives."

Sinder swore. Twice. Then begged, "Get me gone."

He scanned the room, but Timur was absent. So was the headman. And Zisa seemed to be luring the kids away with the promise of food. Very tree-like. Leaving them with the only other person he hadn't met.

Waaseyaa smiled at Gregor, then Ginkgo, before studying Sinder's face. "I could not help but overhear."

Sinder glanced guiltily at Ginkgo and asked, "Which part?"

"You would like to stay." The man settled on the edge of the mattress. "Hardly surprising. You slept safely here. That is a kind of bond."

Entirely true.

"My brother was eager to meet you."

Sinder cracked a smile. "He's something else."

Waaseyaa nodded. "So are you. As it happens, you are our first dragon."

"Well, you don't get out much. And there are no clans native to this region." He gave a little roll of the wrist and flourish of fingers. "I am not the finest specimen, but I may be the most grateful. Thank you for your hospitality."

"Hospitality I willingly extend." Waaseyaa lifted a hand to forestall Ginkgo's protest. "This is my home, and my pledge to

Argent Mettlebright stands. However, Zisa has a little house of his own. It is empty."

"Why would a tree need a house?" Ginkgo asked.

Waaseyaa folded his hands together. "Some of my wives have been ... territorial."

He left it at that.

Sinder checked, "I'd be bunking with Zisa?"

"He would undoubtedly consider himself your host. The only other person who uses the cottage is Glint. I would inform him of your presence." With a small shrug, he said, "My brother is affectionate, and my oldest friend comes and goes as he pleases."

Sinder glanced at Ginkgo, trying to gauge the plan's acceptability.

"Any chance there's room for *two* in that cottage?" asked the half-fox.

Waaseyaa countered, "Who did you have in mind?"

Patting a sleeping Gregor's back, Ginkgo said, "I'd be happier with Timur closer."

Clearly, Sinder had a masochistic streak, because all he said was, "Fine by me."

15
FIRST DAY

Buses would begin arriving by mid-high, carrying hundreds of campers. First Day had always been a big deal for the Reaver household. Their responsibilities as hosts would soon have them scattered and scurrying for weeks on end, so before things got crazy, the family marked summer's arrival with a special breakfast.

Familiar smells wafted temptingly from the kitchen, but Mikoto didn't have much of an appetite. Facing the annual influx without Dad? It was hard. Gabe Reaver had loved First Day better than any festival day. This is what he'd lived for, and now he was ... well, he wasn't.

Mikoto couldn't hope to match his father's enthusiasm.

Wardenclave wasn't the same without him. Couldn't be.

Yulin murmured, "Brace yourself, brave noble."

He half-heartedly corrected his posture, though he was certain his soul was sagging.

A rap sounded at the door, and his eldest half-sister Wren went to see who it was. Yulin gestured for Mikoto to stand just as her voice carried from the front of the house. "Glint! And Uncle! Please, come in. Are you joining us? That's so kind. Be welcome."

Mikoto stood mute, unsure if this was good or bad. He hung back, leaving the greetings to Yulin. Not that Glint let the moth get very far.

Silencing Yulin with a fierce glance, Glint bore down on Mikoto, herded him into the corner, and folded him in strong arms. It took several startled moments for Mikoto to realize that Glint was crying.

Hot tears hit his shoulder, and Glint's soft whine filled Mikoto with distress. He wanted to look to Uncle for help, but he couldn't see past Glint's bulk. The head of the Starmark clan curled around him as if seeking comfort. As if Mikoto had any to give.

"I miss him," Glint muttered, arms tightening. "I miss my friend."

The broken confession broke Mikoto, who choked on a sob.

Waaseyaa and Yulin took charge then, hustling them in a clumsy jumble along the hall to Mikoto's own room. The moth swiftly warded walls and doors for privacy, barely in time to contain Glint's howl. Mikoto could *feel* his pain. After that came an uncomfortably messy torrent of grief.

It scared him.

It gutted him.

When Mikoto finally caught his breath, he was more wrung out than if he'd run a cross-country marathon with the Guard. He strongly suspected that Glint was the only thing keeping him standing. Which ceased to be true the moment Mikoto's feet left the floor.

"Brave boy. Good lad." Glint snuffled at his neck and mumbled childhood endearments and hoarse apologies.

Just this once, Mikoto decided he'd take it. Because today would go from hard to heartrending. For reasons that had his eyes watering anew. Gently wrapping his arms around the First of Dogs, Mikoto pretended he could keep anything simply by wanting it hard enough.

"Oh, my boy." Glint's whole body trembled. "I do not like letting go."

Mikoto just sort of grabbed, even though he might be pulling hair or spoiling embroidery. Because he understood what it was like, loving someone even though they would leave you. His summers were like lifetimes, and they always ended in grief. Over and over. Because he couldn't help staying loyal.

Every year, Mikoto lost Lupe.

Every lifetime, Glint lost a friend.

Waaseyaa coaxed and Yulin prodded Glint toward Mikoto's unmade bed.

"You need rest," said Uncle. "A long one."

"This room is best," added Yulin. "I will take responsibility."

Glint groaned and growled. Then gruffly muttered, "With your permission, boy?"

"Stay," Mikoto urged, his head aching, his nose plugged. Yet an offer of hospitality should never be stinting, so he asked, "Do you want tending?"

"I do." Glint set Mikoto on his own bed and sank to his knees beside it. "We do. Wardenclave does. It will strengthen our bond.

Renew my pact."

Touching the face of sorrow before him, Mikoto said, "Wardenclave does. We do. I do."

"Good lad."

He stood, making way.

Uncle straightened and folded aside the blankets. "Here is best, Glint. Take what you need."

Glint dragged himself onto the too-narrow mattress, looking wretched and weary and wistful.

For several moments, Mikoto grappled with the history behind this moment. How many times had Glint repeated it? Someday, would the First of Dogs howl for Mikoto and wrap himself in the scent of a future son? How many sons had helped Glint move forward into an uncertain future? Mikoto thought Glint must be very brave to face so many heartbreaks.

Mikoto helped Uncle tuck him in, then perched on the edge, taking one of Glint's large hands in both of his. Thanks to Merl, he knew what to do. But his experience with tending was limited to those lessons, during which they generally focused on refining Mikoto's control. Merl refrained from personal remarks, but Mikoto was sort of curious.

He watched Glint's face, wondering how his soul compared to generations of Reavers before him. What did an Amaranthine gain from this touching of souls?

Glint turned his head and one corner of his lips quirked. "There is nothing to fear from the likes of me. I may have been tasked with numbering the stars, but each has its own loveliness. You shine true, and I am grateful to know it."

Mikoto sort of … slipped. Like the warmth he felt couldn't be contained.

Somewhere behind him, Yulin gasped.

Glint's eyes fluttered shut, and he dragged in a long breath. "Maker bless," he whispered, though it sounded like an oath. Eyes widening, hand tightening, Glint said, "You should have told me you were in love."

Mikoto looked away. "Does it matter?"

"Always matters." Glint struggled against sleep, lids drooping, words slurring. "Changes everything."

Mikoto sat, dull and dazed, while Uncle pressed warm and cool clothes to his face. Yulin brought a tray, which contained a selection of his favorite First Day treats. Mother must have prepared it.

"Drink," urged Yulin, pressing a glass of water into his hand. "And listen."

Downing half the glass in one go, Mikoto took a moment to register its sweetness. It had been laced with something. A curative, no doubt. From the grove.

"Leave the formal attire for another time. *After* your induction," ordered Yulin. "Go and meet the buses as you usually would."

"Who will give the welcoming address?" Traditionally, that privilege belonged to the headman.

Uncle answered, "Radiance is both ready and willing."

Glint's bondmate was a force few knew they should be reckoning. Mikoto was more than a little in awe of her. And grateful. She was the reason he was allowed to mingle with the Guard, which was largely made up of her sisters and daughters, and *their* daughters in turn.

Mikoto drank the remainder of his dose before recalling something important. "How long will he sleep?"

"Days. Perhaps a week." Yulin quietly added, "He has not been getting proper rest."

Uncle murmured, "He still cries for Path."

Of all the Kith in Wardenclave, Glint had been closest to Path. They went way back. Perhaps all the way back. Mikoto had heard the red hound passingly referred to as the oldest Kith in Wardenclave. But for all their years, Kith had their limits. They aged. They ended.

Mikoto hadn't realized Glint was still grieving.

"Come by us," offered Uncle. "Zisa will make room for you in his little house, though you will have to share with Sinder and Timur."

His heart leapt, but he shook his head. "I should not impose on guests."

"You will honor them by your presence." Yulin clapped his hands, settling the matter with a soft smile. "And flatter them by the delight you take in theirs."

Mikoto gave in with a nod.

Yulin began packing his things.

Staring fixedly at the big hand Mikoto still held in both of his, he asked, "How did he know I am in love?"

Silence stretched for so long, he risked a peek at his companions.

Uncle's expression was soft, but he only shook his head. As if such mysteries had no answers.

Yulin's fingertips brushed Mikoto's arm as he offered the simplest answer. "Because you are."

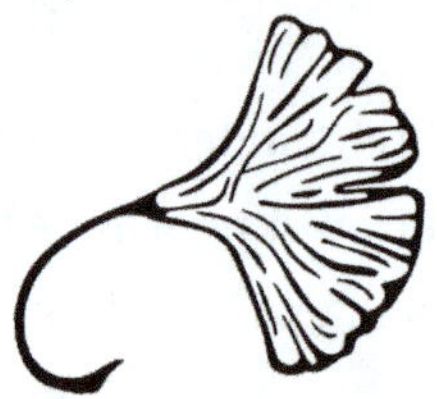

Mid-high had come and gone before Mikoto made his way toward the Circle Green. Buses were already arriving, and he wanted nothing more than to quicken his steps. But a little dog with short legs and a shorter attention span checked his stride at every turn.

Mikoto was sorely tempted to scoop up and pocket Noble. But no reaver set his own convenience ahead of proper training. It would go against everything the In-between was founded upon.

The Amaranthine were patient with humans, treating them as equals despite their differences. And each clan looked to the animals with which they were associated. Life was life, even brief lives. And young lives needed guiding.

So Mikoto slowed his steps and smiled over his puppy's antics.

Had he looked this silly and small to Merl when they first met?

Might Noble become a loyal friend if Mikoto was loyal first?

Loyalty. It defined him, yet his attachment was so hard to put into words. Maybe because it was a feeling. A sense and a sureness. A symptom of the season.

He breathed deeply and knew it was summer. Sunlight seemed to dance, and with it came the certainty that she was back. It was always like this when Lupe was near. Ever since the summer when a long jump to a slippery stone nearly ended in tragedy. But Lupe was a strong swimmer. She'd pulled him onto the riverbank, forced the breath back into his lungs, and hugged him tight until Merl arrived in a thunderclap and the day dissolved into confusion.

They downplayed the accident, since no harm was done. Yet Lupe's heroics brought about two monumental outcomes. One that stirred Mikoto's young heart to devotion. And one that would carry her far from Wardenclave. Because saving Mikoto brought Lupe to Priska's attention.

Priska of the Runefarer clan.

Priska of the Eldermost Islands.

She was a recruiter who traveled through the various camps, seeking young reavers whose aptitudes and inclinations fit the ever-shifting needs of her cooperative.

Nobody ever said what happened on those distant, undisclosed islands, except that it was important. As was secrecy. No reaver returned from a placement with the Runefarer clan.

Until now.

Lupe had sent word through her best friend, Mikoto's sister Hana, to expect her arrival and to arrange for accommodations. She was returning with Priska for one last summer.

One last chance.

Part of Mikoto knew it was too late. Lupe had made her choice, and his duty was to Wardenclave. It wouldn't do any good to confess his attachment to another man's wife. Even if the reaver way allowed for certain ... exceptions. But there was another part that refused to be ignored.

Against all odds, Lupe *was* returning. There had to be a reason. And Mikoto couldn't help hoping it was him.

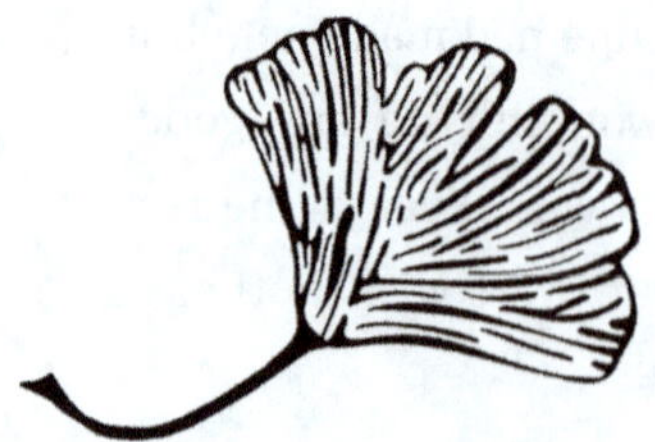

16
SOMEONE LIKE ME

Tenma gravitated toward Wardenclave's song circle, where buses unloaded streams of passengers and stacks of luggage.

Many of these campers would probably try their hand at pottery, and as Goh's assistant, Tenma would meet them, get familiar, maybe even learn a little about them. But he doubted he'd make friends. These kids were just … kids. To them, he was old. Hardly friendship material and worthless as a mentor.

Times like this, he missed Class 3-C at New Saga. And especially Inti.

Pulling his phone from the back pocket of his jeans, he kept a promise he'd made before leaving Japan … and texted a friend.

Lonesome today. Must be the crowds.

Isla's return text wasn't long in coming.

Where are you?

The Americas

Can you be more specific?

Northern Hemisphere

MORE specific, please

**A bench in front of ...
I think it's a gift shop**

**How long are you
going to draw this out?**

With a smile, Tenma relented.

**First day of camp
Surrounded by little geniuses
Reminds me of you**

**Summer courses!
Where is Goh-sensei teaching?**

Wardenclave

No

Yes

No!

His phone hummed in his hand, and he took the call.

Isla was already talking. *"Why didn't you* tell *me you were scheduled to be at Wardenclave?"* Her exasperation came through loud and clear.

"I didn't know myself." He reminded her, "Most of my travel plans are off the record."

"But you're at Wardenclave!"

"I am. For the whole summer." Tenma wistfully checked, "Any chance we're on your tour of duty?"

"No." Her tone gentled. *"Sorry, but listen. You have no reason to be lonesome. You see, my little sister is a camper this year. You remember Lilya?"*

"Kind of." Tenma couldn't imagine why this was such exciting news. "No offense, but it was enough of a stretch being friends back when you were twelve."

"Lilya's eleven," she reported, entirely missing the point.

He hung his head. "Isla, even if I were almost, sort of, secretly a distant friend of the family, hanging around with your baby sister would be just plain creepy."

"Yes, well. I do see your point. But listen! *I was getting around to telling you that my big brother is there."* Isla sounded entirely pleased with herself. *"If you're lonesome, all you need to do is find Timur!"*

Strong in the way Mum's strong, only with curlier hair and hairier arms.

With this scanty description, Tenma searched the crowds for a guy with sufficient heft, but it wasn't easy. All the biggest people divided neatly into two flourishing groups—dogs or horses.

Starmarks and Alpenglows, for the most part. Isla really should have given him more to go on. Despite being at Stately House several times, Tenma hadn't exactly been introduced to the family.

Back then, Isla had somehow talked Lapis out of his whole "eastern bride" notion, which had been an honest relief. Meanwhile, Argent had pushed for the protection offered by a formal apprenticeship. Much more palatable.

Both Tenma and Inti had been brought to Argent's estate, but secretly. Pretty much nobody knew they were there, not even Lady Mettlebright.

Those had been *his* summer courses, overseen by Argent, Lapis, and later on by Goh-sensei. But mostly by Isla's dad, who was the leading expert in sigilcraft and wardstones ... *and* a universal favorite when it came to tending.

Such a cheerful guy. Tenma missed his funny habit of calling him and Inti *young squires.*

For a while, his overseers tried to explain him. They'd certainly studied him. But for the most part, they simply let him do what he could. One by one, they brought in Amaranthine with heavy wards and haunted eyes, and he tended them. Mended them. And word began to spread that there was hope for the Broken.

The only other person Tenma *officially* met was Jacques, the butler. But there had also been a little boy, maybe six years old, who could walk through wards like they weren't important. He'd been quiet and polite and curious ... and in so much trouble from the fox crosser who'd tracked him down.

Kyrie and Ginkgo.

After that, Argent's sons would sometimes kidnap him and

Inti for crazy romps through the woods or walks on the beach at the base of Stately House's cliffs. Or for starwatching from the rooftops. Or to share some rare treat smuggled from the nearest convenience store. Which was a *long* way away.

Tenma missed those little breaks from the monotony of protection. The excitement of a secret friendship. But he was also glad those days were over.

Traveling with Goh-sensei was so much better. Tenma felt less like a prisoner, even if he did still have to stay a stranger to everyone he met. Safe distances and secrets kept him safe.

"What have we here?" A hand touched Tenma's shoulder. "Do you often stray so far from your protector's side?"

"Salali?"

The whole reason Tenma had come down to watch the arrival of campers was because of what Salali had said. That there was someone like him, and that she was coming. Didn't that mean she was on one of these buses?

Indicating the hundreds of milling people, Salali said, "This will take hours to sort out. Hours we could spend in pleasanter pastimes."

"What ...?"

Shushing him with a finger to his lips that triggered a burst of color before Tenma's eyes, Salali scooped him up and streaked away from the hubbub. Inti often resorted to this kind of thing. So did Goh, for that matter, so Tenma simply kept his eyes shut and held on tight.

If Salali Fullstash was part of Wardenclave's security, he had to be trustworthy.

But even more persuasive than role or reputation, Tenma was relying on the splash of blue that ornamented the squirrel clansman's soul. Gent was an avian, and from what Tenma knew about his former classmate Suuzu, the blue jay's high opinion of Salali could only mean good things.

Maybe Salali was only teasing again. But Tenma wasn't alone anymore. And he was grateful.

"Do you have trouble with heights?"

Tenma thought it a little late to be asking, since they had to be dozens of stories over Wardenclave. At least, that was the impression he'd gotten during Salali's final soaring leap into a tree that had appeared out of nowhere. Now, Tenma was surrounded on all sides by rustling leaves and gently swaying branches, for the squirrel had deposited him in what amounted to a rustic nest.

"Goh-sensei is from the monkey clans," said Tenma. "I learned to like heights a long time ago."

Salali tipped back his hat and smirked. "You really will go along with anyone's plans."

"Is that so bad?" Tenma reached into the leaves closest to his face, lifting them aside to reveal a delicate cluster of orange flowers. "I've seen more than I could have imagined because other people wanted to show me things."

"Not everything in this world is good."

Tenma's hand came away streaked in pollen. "I know. I've seen."

"What have you seen?"

Closing his eyes, Tenma took a slow breath. What a pleasant scent.

"What have you seen?" Salali held up a finger, silently commanding eye contact. "I want to know."

Why the sudden urgency? Tenma reached out, inadvertently smearing pollen across gray freckles. He shook his head. "I don't have any deep, dark secrets. *I'm* the secret."

Salali bit his lip, then gruffly said, "You've touched the Broken."

That was the label given to Amaranthine who'd become addicted to the hit of power they received by touching a reaver's soul. Some from constant indulgence. Usually tied to a quest for power. But Tenma had encountered several Amaranthine whose Broken status was a result of subjugation. Under certain circumstances, tending could be used as a means of control.

"Yes. They come to me, or I go to them." Tenma started tapping fingers, counting up the years. "It's all I've done since graduation."

"So you would know."

Tenma shook his head. "Know what?"

"If someone was nearly there." Salali seemed pale under his freckles. "Near to breaking."

"Is *that* what you're afraid of?"

Salali scowled. "I'm no coward."

"What do you want to know?" asked Tenma. "I'll help if I can."

"You? You are so very young."

Funny. That's what Tenma had been thinking, looking at all those little kids getting off the buses. "And here, I was feeling old."

"Mister Subaru, you cannot *comprehend* old."

"I can," he protested. "I love old souls like yours. Try me, and you'll trust me more."

Salali tweaked his nose. "Trust is meant to come first. And a proper reaver waits to be asked."

"I'm not really a proper reaver." Tenma quietly repeated, "Try me."

The squirrel clansman grumbled under his breath, then sketched sigils in the air over their heads. A puff of wind cleared Tenma's head even as a barrier shimmered into place, holding the scent of flowers at bay.

"Do you understand what it means if I tell you that my first taste was a beacon."

Tenma did. "For most, it's their *last* taste. There's no going back once someone's touched the rarest of souls."

Salali placed one finger over Tenma's heart. "I've never forgotten that long-ago sip. And I haven't dared take another."

Pondering that for a moment, Tenma asked, "How are you so strong?"

Salali snorted.

"I mean no insult, but someone of your strength gets that way with the help of many reavers over many centuries."

He snorted again, then sighed. "This is my nest."

Tenma considered the implications of that. Their perch was a comfortable mess of soft fur and overstuffed pillows, a haphazard tree fort for an afternoon's lounge on a sunny summer afternoon. But not any kind of house. "*This* is your home?"

"I have few requirements."

The nest's shallow bowl was comfortable, but there was barely room for the two of them. "Alone?" Tenma asked.

"Gent is good company."

Tenma had almost forgotten the Kith. "Where is he?"

Salali's smile regained its teasing twist. "Giving me some privacy."

"Because you want me to tend you?" he guessed.

Eyes averted, the squirrel said, "Just … check. I want a checkup."

"To see if you're Broken?" Tenma shook his head. "You're not."

All of the sudden, Salali was much closer, practically nose to nose. "Squirrels are greedy. I watched my clan shatter, so I abstain. But I've never stopped wanting another taste. I can be very … greedy."

This was a new one. Then again, every person's circumstance had been a little different from everyone else's. "You want me to tend you because you think I can't break you."

"The theory is sound."

"Understood. No problem. I'm pretty sure it's impossible for me to overwhelm you. You'll see." Tenma gently repeated, "Try me."

Salali sat across from Tenma, dragged the hat from his head, and rumpled his gray hair while studying him. The haunted, hungry gaze might have been frightening if Tenma hadn't spent the last few years coaxing people like Salali into a connection that would do them both good.

He began, and Salali's sharp intake began to worry Tenma. It took longer than usual for him to gasp for air. And mere moments for him to sway forward.

Different clans approached tending with a startling range of opinions. Some considered this a holy rite. Others took it medicinally. Tenma had met misers with jealously guarded cossets, and he'd spent time with reavers who spent all day, every day doling out little portions of their soul like a chain restaurant with a drive-thru window.

Tenma had begun to suspect that his only purpose as a reaver was this intimate give and take. "Do you think generosity is a job?"

Salali cleared his throat. "A time-honored one. Do you know why a cosset's tunic is yellow?"

For someone who saw a soul in terms of color, Tenma had never given much thought to the colors worn by the various reaver classifications. "Why yellow?"

Words softly slurring, he said, "Intoxicating as pollen, sweet as honey, gentle as sunbeams."

Tenma accepted that as a compliment. "You know, when they found out about me, I was barely anything but a spark. Some of my friends still call me *little glimmer*."

"You've gained."

"Yeah. There's a reason for that. Try tending me."

Salali favored him with a baffled look.

"I know, I know. It sounds backward." Tenma admitted, "It's sort of a secret, but you wanted mine. This one's especially nice."

Working out how to do what was needed took a few moments. Success tugged a soft whine from Salali, who toppled into Tenma's waiting arms.

"That's the way," he murmured encouragingly.

They hadn't really settled on official terms for this thing Tenma—and maybe one day, his line—could do. It had been described in terms of echoes and bouncing, of reverberation and even feedback. Those who were generous with him found themselves repaid tenfold. At least. And because Tenma was only returning what was given, his Amaranthine partner gained something compatible. Maybe even essential.

If tending was candy, Tenma was mother's milk.

"Don't stop," whispered Salali.

"I won't."

Taking a deep, shuddering breath, he again begged, "Don't stop."

"I haven't stopped."

"More?"

Tenma promised, "All you need."

Somewhere along the way, Salali began sniffling, and Tenma bundled him close. The squirrel softly demanded, "Not a word to anyone. Especially not Gent. Or Glint."

"This is between us."

And again, Salali demanded, "Don't stop."

Bumping his lips against his new friend's temple, Tenma confessed, "I'm glad I stumbled into your trap, Salali Fullstash."

"Is *that* what this is?" inquired a new voice, all intrigued innocence. "Entrapment. But which one of you is trapping the other? And may I join?"

17
MATHEMATICALLY IMPOSSIBLE

With the confusion of unloading happening all along the circle, Noble was safer back in Mikoto's pocket. He kept a hand on the pup, fondling one perked ear as he strolled along the edge of activity.

Wardenclave's citizens mingled with the crowd, greeting returnees and guiding newcomers. Mikoto's sisters barely acknowledged him, their fleeting glances holding little more than exasperation. Reprimanding him for arriving late. Reminding him that his pain was theirs, and then some. Hadn't they known Father better, loved him longer?

Shame seeped into the set of his shoulders.

A firm grip at Mikoto's elbow halted his progress, and he raised his gaze. Resplendence Starmark searched his face, firmed her grip slightly, and murmured, "Well met."

As she moved off, Mikoto was jostled on his other side by Reena

Duntuffet, who cuffed his shoulder and winked before hurrying forward to heft a young girl's travel cases.

His people. His friends.

Hannick Alpenglow patted his cheek in passing. "Someone's trying to get your attention."

Like the sudden pivot that can throw an opponent off balance, Mikoto's perspective shifted off himself. Familiar faces dominated the crowd. Many turned his way with grins, waves, and greetings. Chin bobs and hand signs from other battlers. Friendly remarks upon his increasing height. Teasing remarks about his tiny companion.

Mikoto found he was glad to see them back.

He began offering the same kinds of assurances he'd received. Touching an elbow. Clapping a shoulder. He spoke the names of those he knew and offered his name to new kids. As he patiently worked his way along, he felt fresh stirrings of certainty.

She was here.

Even though he couldn't explain it—not that he'd ever try—Mikoto always knew when Lupe was near. The pull that made his heart leap. The scent of summer that left him giddy. The way she always knew when to turn, where to look. Like she was as aware of him as he was of her.

But it was really quite hard to impress a girl who sees you as a little brother.

Mikoto worked hard, trained hard, tried hard. Wanting her to notice the man he was becoming. Catching up with something other than years.

Four years was an epoch for young reavers.

On her last year at camp, instead of flying home at summer's end, Lupe had journeyed to a port city with Priska, boarded a ship, and sailed to some far-off island where a new husband waited. She'd been eighteen, going on nineteen. He'd been fourteen and tongue-tied and inconsolable.

His only tiny sliver of hope was that they weren't a good match. Maybe Lupe would do her duty to the In-between and leave her island husband behind, making a second marriage possible.

Mikoto had done the math a thousand times over. Enough to understand the mathematical impossibility of grasping at that particular straw. To give Lupe time to fulfill her progeny quota, he'd have to figure out a way to stay single until he was twenty-seven. At least.

Glint might accept the plan. Well, maybe. If Mikoto could get Radiance to back him.

But deep down, Mikoto knew his plan was doomed. Lupe was so warm and accepting. She'd give her contract husband every chance to win her heart. And love him back with all of hers. That's just the kind of person she'd always been.

Mikoto still wanted to find a way of telling her how he felt, even though it would probably come to nothing. If she was safe and happy without him, he'd let Glint choose a bride with a good bloodline and secure Wardenclave's future.

It dawned on him then that in all his years of clinging to an impossible wish, he'd never once considered leaving Wardenclave. Not even for Lupe. Did that mean he didn't love her enough? Maybe. And maybe that didn't matter anymore. The decision was out of his hands. It always had been.

But if Lupe was even the littlest bit unhappy, he'd give her an alternative.

A whisper of wind flirted around his ankles and tugged at his hair, carrying a sense of summer's sweetness, drawing his attention to the second-to-last bus in the long line-up. It was always like this. The knowing part. He could always find her. As if they'd forged a connection eight years ago, and they shared it still.

He lengthened his strides.

She stood a little away from those mingling beside the bus, smiling skyward. A breeze caught her long, black hair and flipped the airy fabric of her skirt. Vastly different from standard reaver attire, but maybe they did things differently on whatever island Priska had chosen for her. It was pretty.

As he neared, she laughed lightly and turned his way, smiling as she tucked flyaway hair behind her ear. Lupe Navarro wasn't very tall; he'd surpassed her height when he was only eleven. She was all confident sweetness and crooked smiles. Bold with colors. Deft with crystals. Crazy about dancing.

Lupe was a reach. Reavers of their order acted almost like a tuned crystal, able to hone in on a location, so long as they had something or someone to reach for. They were prized as navigators, but it was said that reaches of the highest order could find their way into the thoughts of an Amaranthine with whom they shared close ties. Like telepathy. Or something.

"You're here," Lupe said.

Mikoto thought she sounded glad of it. "You are back."

She dimpled and accused, "You've changed."

Not fast enough. Wishing he could think of something clever to say, he mumbled, "You have not."

Lupe's brows arched over laughing eyes. "You're kidding."

"He is blind," cut in a sharper voice. Priska Runefarer casually balanced a trunk on one shoulder. Her pale blue hair was its usual mess of choppy waves, and her lip curled to reveal a dainty fang.

Mikoto gestured politely. "Wardenclave welcomes you."

Priska frowned, but her tone moderated. "You do your father proud."

"We're sorry for your loss." Lupe's eyes shimmered with sympathy. "Is there anything we can do?"

He didn't want this. Not even from her. Pasting on a smile, he slid into his role as headman. It was easier this way. "Hana will be so glad for your company. You should come by the house later. Once you are settled."

Empty words.

Expected courtesies.

"Do you remember the way?" he asked.

Priska snorted. "I've been trawling these waters for more centuries than you have years." With a scowl, she took Lupe's arm and guided her away toward the cabins set aside for instructors and recruiters.

Mikoto let them go with nothing more than an awkward wave.

He knew how to fall and how to fight, but there had been no fending off the blow Lupe delivered. Turning on his heel, he stumbled off the path and into the woods, desperate to be alone before coming to terms with three things he hadn't expected.

Despite Priska's snide remark, Mikoto *wasn't* blind.

He could see that Lupe was abundantly happy. He knew the significance of the ornamental sigil decorating her brow. And he understood the meaning of the curves Lupe's dress didn't quite hide. She was going to be a mother.

18

EASTERN BRIDE

Sinder limped along the path to his new quarters. Zisa's guest house was small by any standard, but it wasn't a comfortless, woods-damp tent. And it was safe. Right now, Sinder desperately needed that sense of security.

Even with Michaelson absent from their ranks, the recruits were getting on nicely, and Sinder was hiding fresh bruises. He'd barely managed to convince Torloo he could make it back on his own. It wasn't that far. It wasn't that bad. It wasn't going to get any easier.

All Sinder wanted was a soft bed. And he wouldn't refuse a dosing once Timur finished up his First Day duties with the campers. Sinder stumbled and swore, quickly straightening when he realized that Fend was sprawled across Zisa's doorstep. Very much alert.

"I'm fine," Sinder muttered.

Fend's lids lowered a fraction. So skeptical.

With a hushing motion, he eased around the big feline. "Between you and me, this is nothing compared to what's ahead. So leave it."

A foolish demand. Fend couldn't exactly spread Sinder's paltry secrets.

He laid back his ears and glared.

"You know, you're probably right." Indulging in a tired sigh, Sinder whispered, "I like that about cats."

Darned if the big feline didn't roll his eyes. Fend rose, stretched, and walked away, tail lashing.

Pushing through the door, Sinder drew up short. As grateful as he'd been for the company that Timur and Mikoto provided, he'd expected an empty house at this hour. Instead, he walked in on what could only be described as a drinking party.

Ginkgo lifted a beer bottle in greeting. "Grab a seat, Sinder. I'll pour you a glass."

Zisa frisked forward to kiss Sinder. "Welcome home."

"I didn't realize you were entertaining." Absentmindedly returning the greeting, he tallied up the tree's guest list.

Waaseyaa sat in the corner, cradling Timur's sleeping son.

Ginkgo's mood was as high as his color.

The man in their midst pushed up his glasses and offered a small nod.

"Salali captured him and brought him to me." Zisa fluttered over to the man, draping himself around the newcomer's shoulders. "He is mine now."

Rather than deny the tree's claim, the man smiled and touched

Zisa's arm.

Sinder's synapses belatedly fired, and he put a name to the face. "You've kidnapped Lord Mossberne's eastern bride?"

Tenma Subaru's hands formed a greeting. "Hello, Sinder."

Did *everyone* know his name?

Ginkgo grinned, "You've met Tenma?"

"No." With an apologetic posture to soften a blunt truth, Sinder admitted, "I've seen his file."

Tenma stood and offered his hand. "Nice to meet you. Sorry for imposing."

"Not a problem," he lied.

Something in the man's expression shifted, and he firmly said, "Sit by me."

"Yeah, join us." Ginkgo was already pouring a fresh glass, and he picked up the thread of the story he'd been telling. Something involving Isla, who was clearly a mutual friend.

Sinder eased to a seat at the crowded little table. Zisa plied him with snacks, but he only picked at them. A hand found Sinder's under the table. Tenma never looked away from Ginkgo as his fingers slid between Sinder's, pressing a crystal between their palms.

An offer?

Pretending fascination with the foam on his drink, Sinder triggered the ward that promised privacy. Almost at once, Tenma was there. A willing soul.

Sinder liked both the offer of comfort and the challenge it represented. Could he indulge without tipping off the others at the table? Probably not if Waaseyaa had been the one offering, but Tenma's reserves were modest. And unique.

If he were entirely honest, Sinder hadn't only seen Tenma's file, he'd helped compile it. He knew what this was. He even knew what to do—theoretically. Sinder tried a little squeeze that was supposed to mean, *Sure about this?*

Two heart thuds later, Tenma pulled Sinder's hand into his lap and covered it with his other.

So he composed himself outwardly and worked on a little inner investment. Because according to reports, Tenma Subaru turned pebbles into gemstones and dewdrops into deepening pools. Give a little; gain the sky.

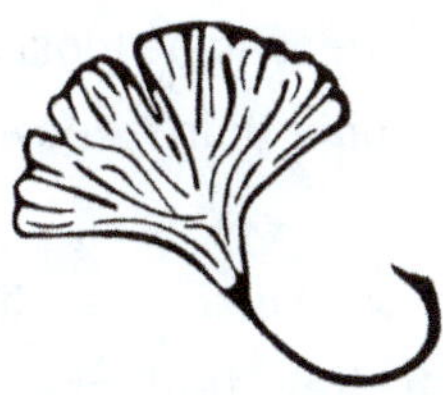

"Hey, there." A hand lightly pressed Sinder's forehead, and he twisted away from it. "Come on, Damsel. You're getting heavy. Tenma's only human, you know."

Sinder's eyes popped open, and he groaned.

Ginkgo chuckled. "Rough day?"

"Worst for me. Best for those recruits." Reluctantly pulling away from Tenma's warmth, he was grateful when the man didn't let go of his hand. "Can't really complain, since that's the goal."

"You should have said something," grumbled the fox crosser, who was *such* a nanny. "Are you hurt?"

"Me? I'm in heaven." Which wasn't really a lie. Tenma had a rep for good reason.

Tenma quietly contradicted. "He's in pain."

Ginkgo growled. "Want me to find Colt Alpenglow?"

"No." Easing more of his weight off Tenma, Sinder muttered, "Rather have Michaelson."

"No kidding?" Ginkgo looked ready to tease, but the door swung open.

Daylight was softening toward twilight, and Mikoto stood uncertainly on the threshold, eyes rimmed in red and ankles imperiled by his little nipper of a pup. The young man's confusion was no different than Sinder's upon finding the house cram-packed.

"Good evening?"

Mikoto didn't sound sure, and he looked emotionally mangled. Could be grieving, yet. Sinder didn't know the kid well enough to say for certain.

Waaseyaa stood and passed the napping little one to Ginkgo. Hurrying to Mikoto, he drew the young man further into the room and closed the door behind him. Zisa was there with soft words and tiptoe kisses, which Mikoto bowed his head to accept. He outstripped these ancients, yet he seemed young and lost and entirely overwhelmed.

Ginkgo gave them several moments, then repeated his earlier question. "Rough day?"

Mikoto nodded.

"Well, I'm glad you're here. You can shore up our gap. Once Timur arrives, Sinder will have a full harem."

Sinder couldn't help but snort. "A harem full of males?"

"Perfect for our Damsel." Ginkgo lowered his voice. "You're awfully ragged for someone who's just come off a long sleep."

Which was true. And sobering.

A chair scraped, and Sinder lost hold of Tenma, who moved around the table to offer his palms to Mikoto.

"Hello. My name is Tenma Subaru. May I know your name?"

With only a moment's hesitation, the young headman returned the greeting. "Mikoto."

"And your clan?"

Everyone in the room turned to stare at Tenma.

Pushing at his glasses, he asked, "I apologize. Are you ... unaffiliated? Some are, I know."

Mikoto finally found his voice. "I am Mikoto Reaver."

"But you're ...." Tenma glanced at Ginkgo before cautiously asking, "Are you a crosser, then?"

"No? I am a reaver."

"Glint can vouch for his bloodlines," said Waaseyaa. "Mikoto is a Reaver among reavers."

Tenma was staring hard and shaking his head. "But all the colors. I've never seen the like. You're positively ... prismatic."

19

SNOW

Although Kyrie's father gave every impression of *hating* the idea of sending his sons to Wardenclave for the summer, he'd also been the first and fiercest to banish all of Kyrie's qualms. "You are unique. They will be intrigued. Use that to your advantage."

Father was often blunter than Mother liked. But Kyrie liked being trusted with plain truths.

"Only indulge the bare minimum of curiosity. In most cases innocuous facts will suffice."

Kyrie had asked, "Am I forbidden to speak of home?"

"Not necessarily. However, choose what you say—and to whom—with care." Father smiled thinly. "Questions do not constitute obligations. And we have much to protect."

Since this was true, Kyrie agreed readily enough. But another point was harder to confess. "I doubt anyone will wish to befriend me."

Father had wreathed him in all his many tails and repeated, "Not necessarily. Use your judgment, which is sound. And bestow your trust, which is precious, when the time seems right."

"How will I know what is right?"

"If you were more like me, I would speak of scents." Tapping his nose, Father murmured, "Because it is you, I would say … listen closely to the whispers of your conscience and also to those of the winds who seek your favor. Neither has ever led you astray."

Kyrie liked the simplicity. It meant that no matter where he was, he would still be himself. And being sure of himself would make everything easier, even if that was the *only* thing he could be sure about.

First Day wasn't so bad. Even when the leaders divided the girls from the boys, Kyrie was more interested in what he'd learn than in worrying that he'd be parted from Lilya.

Now, he was conscience-stricken, for he could see from across the green that Lilya was tense and pale.

The moment their instructors released them for an afternoon of free time, Kyrie worked his way toward the sister of his heart. He knew her so well, he could tell she was trying not to run in order to get back to him. And he could tell tears were threatening.

Catching her hand, he redirected her off the path and into the shelter of trees. Ducking under the trailing limbs of an ancient conifer, he hugged her close and offered one of the warbling trills he'd learned from Lapis.

Lilya held him so tightly, it almost hurt. But Kyrie only crooned and waited her out. What had overwhelmed her? A second possibility caused him to blurt, "Was someone mean to you?"

"Everyone is nice. Very nice."

"Then ... why?"

With a wan smile, she confessed, "You were gone."

"Not far." He twirled a lock of her hair around his finger. "I am right here."

"But you won't always be."

Kyrie sighed. "That may be true. And we need to get used to the idea."

"A little at a time?" There was a smile in her voice. She always did bounce back quickly.

"Is that not why our parents let us come?" Because it was, at least in part.

Lilya took a deep breath and let go. Squaring her shoulders, she lifted her chin, "That sounds like something Uncle Argent would say."

Kyrie giggled. Because they both knew that what Father said and what Father meant were often two very different things.

"What should we do?" asked Lilya.

He tried to think what would please her most. "Explore the forest. Look for Resplendence. Take pictures for Ever."

She nodded in an indecisive way, then suggested, "Check to see if Ginkgo and Gregor missed us?"

"Yes. Good." Kyrie took her hand and asked, "May I choose the route?"

Lilya smiled. "Are the winds here friendly?"

He blushed and said, "Same as always."

"Where do they want you to go?"

It was almost a game, like pretend. Only Kyrie wasn't pretending. He really did catch impressions out of thin air. Lapis was the one who'd understood first. He'd begun singing ballads—some sad, some silly, some sweet—about dragons and their entanglement with wind imps. Kyrie hoped some of those stories were true. He'd love to meet a gentle breeze or a towering storm. Maybe even a monsoon.

Pointing in the general direction of Zisa, Kyrie said, "Back, but by a roundabout trail."

Lilya never questioned him, always trusted him. And it was nice to be believed, even when the truest of true things sounded impossible.

"What will we find?"

Kyrie cocked an ear and quietly said, "Someone is singing again."

Away from the cabins and halls of Wardenclave, it was possible for Lilya to pretend that these were the woods surrounding Stately House. She and Kyrie often wandered them, usually leading a small army of crossers. Or chasing after stragglers.

She could almost see Gilen's banded tail disappearing high above, with Tawny in close pursuit. And hear Mori's stern voice reminding everyone to stay with their buddy. Right now, she even missed Nonny, who was a terror and a tease with everyone except Uncle Jackie.

Kyrie stopped inspecting a cluster of mushrooms growing up the side of a tree like stairsteps to say, "Jarrah would call for a climbing contest."

So true. She said, "Finnick would have lost his shoes by now."

"Disa would beg to be carried."

"And Raife would give in first." Lilya tightened her grip. "I wish we could have brought everyone."

With a wistful smile, Kyrie said, "We miss them because we love them. They are a part of us. Our family."

"Maybe we can borrow Ginkgo's phone? Send messages."

"Yes. Good." With a finger before his lips, he quietly added, "Almost there, I think."

Although she listened hard, Lilya couldn't hear anything beyond the calls of birds and the rustle of leaves high above. "I miss the sea."

"I want to climb a mountain."

That was a good plan. "Can we?"

"Why not?"

Kyrie's winding way brought them around the hilltop, through a pasture, and over a fence with crystal-topped posts. They were well under Zisa's vast canopy. When Kyrie pulled Lilya through another barrier, they were there. But things looked different on this side of the tree. Waaseyaa had the bigger house, and Zisa had the tiny cottage. But there was a third building, partly buried in climbing vines. It didn't have many windows, and the door was big, so maybe it was a barn?

That's where Kyrie wanted to go, so that's where they went.

Now, it was possible for Lilya to hear the sound of singing—rich and mellow and belonging to a lady. Kyrie tried the door, a panel that slid easily to the side. The singing didn't stop. Closing the door behind them, they stole toward the voice.

Lilya could guess where they were now. They had buildings like this at the Starmark compound. A Kith shelter filled with cozy smells—dry straw and warm fur.

The song trailed off, and a voice cheerfully exclaimed, "Well, *this* is a surprise! If I'm not mistaken, we have guests."

Lilya only hesitated a moment longer than Kyrie before peeking around the final corner.

A beautiful lady reclined between the forepaws of an equally beautiful wolf. White hair. Copper eyes. They just *had* to be more of Ever's relatives.

With a laugh to add width to her smile, she beckoned to them. "Come and help me pamper this beast, for I love her like a sister."

"Hello." Kyrie immediately presented his palms. "Do you know who we are?"

"I could guess." She caught his hands and asked, "May I? I know it's not quite proper, but it's so much more fun!"

Lilya saw the way Kyrie relaxed. He liked this lady, and no wonder. She reminded Lilya so much of Ever, she half expected the lady to demand to *sniffen* them.

"You are two of the precious children belonging to Stately House." She gestured for them to join her. "You, young sir, are Zisa's merciful dragon. And you, dear heart, are the one Resplendence sang of during last night's moonrise."

"She remembered me?"

The lady laughed. "She *loved* you. Loves you still. And would love you ever onward, given the chance."

Lilya shyly took a seat at her side. "Are you one of Ever's aunts?"

"Alas, that is a privilege that belongs to my daughters."

Kyrie, who was quicker and cleverer by far, understood first. "You are his *grandmother*?"

She laughed again. "You may call me Radiance. And this sad beauty is … well, let's call her Snow. I always do."

Up on tiptoe, Kyrie lifted a hand to the Kith. "Why are you sitting in the dark, Snow? The day is fine, and the breezes are willing."

"Right you are! But will she listen to me?" complained Radiance. "Prop the shutters, will you? This time of year, the evenings are long and soft and sweet."

Lilya wanted to pet the Kith, but not until she'd nestled against Radiance's side a little longer. Because she felt as strong as Mum and as lively as Papka, and because Lilya knew how much Ever would have loved to be right here, hugging his grandmother. Probably for the very first time.

Kyrie fiddled with a set of wooden shutters, and more light flooded the shelter. Enough that Lilya could now see the small, silvery star that marked the center of Radiance Starmark's forehead. "Is that your blaze?"

"No." Her eyebrows arched. "It's a miracle."

"Truly?" asked Kyrie, coming closer and bending down to see.

Radiance hooked his elbow and pulled him onto her lap.

For a moment, Kyrie froze. Lilya understood his surprise. Most people were wary of a red-eyed boy with horns. Not her. When Lady Starmark proceeded to snuffle his neck, he collapsed into gasps and giggles.

"She's sniffening you!" Lilya exclaimed.

"Don't mind me," said Radiance. "Standard procedure for special guests. Especially wily, barrier-dropping dragons who may need tracking."

"Procedure?" Lilya remembered what Resplendence had said. "Is this for security?"

"Yes and no. I've always been nosy." With a knowing expression, she asked, "Who taught you about sniffening?"

"Ever." Kyrie relaxed with his head against Radiance's shoulder, all hazy and half-lidded while she petted his hair and traced his scales. "Ever is our best friend."

The lady's chuckle was soft and low. "When they were little, I used to sniffen Merit and Prospect and Valor. Although I think my brother started it. Moon always insisted on sniffening Harmonious whenever he'd visit."

"And Eloquence?" prompted Lilya.

"Not so much. He was still tiny when Harmonious decided to go away." More wistful now, she said, "But it sounds like his Da and big brothers kept up the tradition."

Lilya said, "We should take a picture."

"May we?" begged Kyrie. "We can send it to Ever. Oh, but we would need Brother's phone."

At this point, the wolf at their backs grumbled and wuffed.

"Worry wort." Radiance peered up at Snow. "There's such a thing as too much privacy."

The wolf laid back her ears and bared her teeth.

Radiance bowed her head. "Snow is camera shy. When it's picture time, she doesn't want to be included."

Kyrie's mother avoided cameras, as well. It was one of Uncle Argent's strictest rules. But why would a Kith have the same rule? Was Snow someone important or hiding ... or maybe both? Lilya was curious but asking felt like the wrong place to begin. Papka would start with trust.

Getting to her feet, Lilya showed her hands to Snow. "May I pet you?"

Vividly copper eyes narrowed.

"May she?" asked Radiance.

Everyone held still for several moments, waiting for some sign. Even the tiniest wag of Snow's tail would be good. But she was utterly still.

Radiance laughed. "Really? Well, then. Snow *might* allow it if you'll let her have her way with the young sir."

"What does that mean?" asked Kyrie.

"She wants to sniffen you, merciful dragon."

"I do not mind." He stood and spread his arms wide. "Please, do."

Radiance rose and urged Lilya to get out of the way. Snow soon had Kyrie sprawled in the straw while she snuffled and growled to herself. Kyrie's expression remained peaceful, and he began petting Snow's muzzle whenever it was in reach.

"You're very patient," remarked Radiance.

"I have many, many younger brothers and sisters, and they are always curious." Almost as an afterthought, he added, "Once they are not afraid anymore."

Snow jerked back and looked to Radiance, who asked, "Why would they be afraid?"

Kyrie pressed his lips together.

Lilya tried to distract them. "Once they get to know him, Kyrie's their favorite."

Radiance touched Lilya's cheek and promised, "And you shall

be mine, my angel. But Snow and I would still like to know why."

To Lilya's surprise, Kyrie told the truth. "The little ones do not know, and the bigger ones will not say."

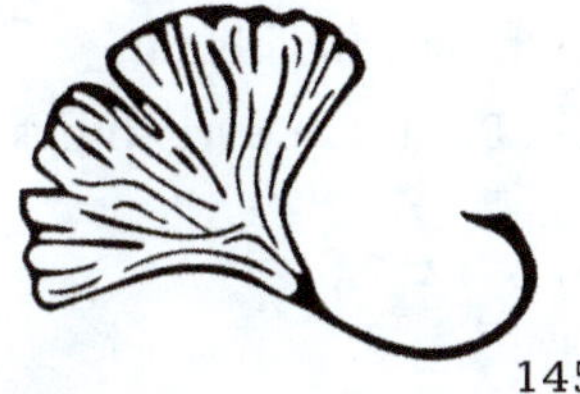

20

BONDS OF BLOOD

Timur needn't have worried about whether or not he could cut it as an instructor. Managing a bunch of reaver kids was hardly any different than playing with a houseful of crossers back home. They'd test his endurance more than his patience.

Every one of them was eager to improve, to distinguish themselves, to impress him. It was almost too easy. Suggest a game. Explain the rules. Play to win. Timur honestly felt like he'd spent the day goofing off.

Very different from the tension-inducing challenge presented by working with Naroo-soh's recruits. He was glad he'd have both. They'd give his summer some balance. But right now, all Timur wanted was a shower, some soft clothes, and his son.

Well, maybe not *all* he wanted. But these were things he could have.

Running his hand through the tangled mess of his hair, Timur stumbled into memories that weren't quite regrets, even though they made him sadder than anything.

Fend butted his broad forehead against Timur's hip.

"I know." He found one of his Kith's ears and scratched. "I know, but I can't help wondering. In a few years, they could be in classes just like these. Would I know them?"

With a growl, Fend pushed him off the path. Backing him up to a tree, the big cat reared up, planting velveted paws on Timur's shoulders and looming over him. Then he nosed his forehead and began to purr.

Fend only ever did this sort of thing when they were alone. Timur grabbed hold with both hands, grateful for this reminder that Fend knew. And even if he didn't fully understand, he cared.

Timur guessed his family was as close-knit as any reaver family could be. His folks were unusual in that regard, and they'd set a high standard for their own children. To choose for love. To nurture the next generation. To cherish the bonds of blood.

But Papka and Mum hadn't seen the progeny projections and heard Uncle Sergei's grudging admission that the Order of Spomenka was a dying breed. Timur had seen the villages, entered the enclaves, tended to dragon lords and their harems. Nobody had pressured him, but the facts were compelling.

Maybe they'd guessed he would offer.

He knew they'd been hoping.

Timur fulfilled his first short contract when he was nineteen. Quietly, but not off the record. Because pedigree was everything.

The following winter, he accompanied Uncle Sergei and a

healer from the Canterbelle herd to a remote village belonging to members of the Order of Spomenka. Long days of training. Brief sessions as a one-man stable. By spring, he had more than fulfilled his contract, but he'd had enough. Because in the end, he wanted something more like what Papka and Mum had chosen.

So he'd told Uncle Sergei to refuse any other offers.

Instead, he watched for likeminded women. And he'd begun to dream about the children who were growing up without him.

Finally, he'd written an inquiry to the registry at Wardenclave, wanting to know how many sons and daughters he could claim. And if possible, to learn their names.

What he received in return was a mixed blessing. Ten sons. Fourteen daughters. And a plea from Glint Starmark himself. To meet a woman named Manya. To help her fulfill her obligation to the In-between.

She was exceptional—single digit ranking and an intellectual, a crystal adept specializing in cutting and tuning. But she would be reporting under protest. And with conditions. Because like most of the elite, she was choosy.

Manya required a top-class ward, but there were none of sufficient rank in Glint's stable.

However, Timur's record had tempted her out of seclusion. Battler though he might be, he was the son of the First of Wards. She would have him and no other, in the fervent hope that Timur would pass along his father's genes.

Timur had done it before. He could do it again. And the bonus he'd receive would set him up nicely for the future. The only problem was, he wanted a better future than this. So he'd drafted a response with his own set of conditions.

He wanted to live with Manya for as long as it took to impregnate her. He wanted them to remain together for the duration of her pregnancy. He wanted to be in attendance at the birth of their child, along with Mare Rilka Withershanks. And he would take full responsibility for the child. Their baby would be his to keep.

Naively, Timur thought that with all that time and closeness, he'd be able to win Manya's affection. On paper, they seemed suited. She could become the one true love he'd share his life with.

She accepted all his terms, provided she'd have a workshop on the premises.

Quarters were arranged at an enclave famous for both its healers and its crystal mines, and from the start, she was cool toward him.

Manya had little patience for closeness or conversation. He tried a range of thoughtful gestures and cautious flirtation, but she rebuffed everything. Most of her days were spent closed up in her workshop. She employed tests to determine when she was ovulating. What intimacy they shared was both scheduled and monitored for success. It had only taken three attempts before a pregnancy test showed positive.

All that remained was the contracted waiting period.

Little by little, Timur's hopes grew stale and crumbled. He'd never been lonelier in his life. That's when he finally confessed to Papka—where he was and what he'd done. That very night, he'd been visited by the silver fox who'd loomed large in his childhood. Argent Mettlebright whisked into his room, pulled him into an embrace, and let him cry.

The next night, Deece had arrived with Fend, who'd been born to Minx's first litter. Timur remembered when that set was born, had played with the cubs. Fend had been his favorite. Apparently Timur had been Fend's favorite, as well, and was demanding a pact.

From that day forward, Timur was never alone.

Argent or Ginkgo would come. Sometimes Deece. Even Suuzu and Akira had shown up once, when the rest of the family were caught up with their many obligations. And Fend was a constant.

His exile ended the day Manya went into labor.

Mare Withershanks kept him close, talked him through the stages, plied him with the same teas she brewed for Manya. Before he was fully prepared, the healer placed a squirming baby in his hands. And there was a tiny person squalling angrily at him.

"Your son," Mare Withershanks said. And with a doting smile and a familiar inflection, she asked, "He is beautiful, yes?"

Timur laughed and cried and babbled nonsense to his son in every language he knew. He was awestruck and happy, and when he looked up to find Manya watching, he said, "Thank you."

She only nodded. But it had been a nice sort of nod. Like maybe she agreed with Rilka about their son.

The very next day, she left. He stood awkwardly by the door, babe in arms, heart in his throat. "I'll miss you," he managed.

Manya gave him the oddest look, one of those rare moments when she looked him in the eye. As if seeing him for the first time. Or perhaps startled that he would have formed any sort of attachment. Because she obviously hadn't.

"I'll let you know how he's doing," Timur offered.

She nodded again and murmured, "You do that."

Timur filed Gregor's registration and received a letter from

Glint in return. He'd been tempted to let Fend shred it unread, for he was determined never to take another paternity contract. Instead, he'd found the job offer. Filling in for Boon. And a small postscript. *Your line is established. Look to your house.*

"Fend?" Timur leaned into his partner's bulk. "Let's go home."

Whiskers tickled. Paws kneaded. A tongue rasped across stubble.

"I'm all right now. Let's reclaim our boy."

Fend dropped to all fours, and they returned to the path. Waaseyaa was waiting on his front step, singing a song in what Timur suspected was Old Amaranthine. He admired the man, who'd probably raised more sons and daughters than any human alive. Maybe it was his confidence. Maybe it was the singularity of his attention. When Gregor was in Waaseyaa's arms, the boy was all he saw.

"We're a little late."

Waaseyaa only smiled and said, "Welcome home, Timur."

Gregor bounced and reached, and Waaseyaa turned the toddler loose. Timur swooped him up and grinned. "There's Papka's little battler! Miss me much?"

"Pah-kah!"

Timur grinned and glanced around. "Where is everyone?"

"Most of us were at Zisa's. I brought Gregor out because things were becoming … noisy." Waaseyaa's smile tilted, and he chuckled. "I believe Ginkgo is intoxicated. Or pretending to be. He is trying to cheer up Mikoto."

"Is something the matter?"

Waaseyaa nodded. "Although I am more concerned about Sinder."

Timur was already backing toward Zisa's house. "What happened?"

"I think he needs a healer. Ginkgo thinks he needs a harem." Waaseyaa waved him onward. "Either way, he asked for you."

Timur spun on his heel and whispered to Gregor, "We shall catch us a dragon, yes? I can teach you how. It's a family tradition."

One that all his other sons and daughters were probably already learning.

One that might bring them back together someday. In a place like this.

21
PERSONS OF INTEREST

Sinder was in familiar territory—fading into the background, overhearing more than people realized. Without really meaning to, he was filing away details about Tenma and Mikoto. They certainly counted as persons of interest.

The Savior.

The Successor.

But to Sinder's wearily jaded eye, they seemed like a couple of close-kept and cosseted kids. Maybe he envied them their safety. Maybe he should be proud that he was one of the guys who kept them safe.

"Prismatic?" Mikoto looked too confused to be hiding something. "Are you talking about colors?"

Ginkgo's attention fixed on the young headman. "Sure you're seeing straight, Tenma? He's definitely human."

"Do me!" exclaimed Zisa, who eased between the two men.

"Look at me."

Sinder couldn't shake the idea that the tree knew exactly what was going on. Easing away so he could watch everyone's reactions, he focused his senses, trying to catch the import of Tenma's mistake.

"Oooh," breathed Tenma. He looked between Waaseyaa and Zisa, then beamed at Mikoto. "You're tree-kin?"

Zisa tittered.

"No?" Mikoto scooped up his puppy like he wanted to hide behind it. "Just a reaver."

Ginkgo held up a hand. "Maybe we should start over."

As they began a rehearsal of bland and useless facts, Sinder slipped into the only other room in Zisa's house. While some snide part of his personality was amused because trees shouldn't need toilets, Sinder appreciated the spacious shower stall, which had surely been built on a scale to accommodate the First of Dogs.

Sinder let the drumming of hot water on tiles drown out most of the inanity in the other room and eased carefully out of his clothes. Stepping under the steady flow, he wondered if he had enough range of motion to get properly clean.

He belatedly began unraveling his braid, but he could only lift one arm high enough.

Swearing under his breath, he turned and nearly leapt to the ceiling. Zisa was perched on the sink, watching him.

"You have *no* concept of privacy!" he grumbled.

"I do. Brother has explained it to me many times."

"So, what? You don't believe in privacy?"

"I do not see the necessity." Zisa smiled sweetly. "You did not ward this room against me."

It hadn't even occurred to Sinder.

"May I help with your hair? Brother lets me. His is even longer than yours."

Relief washed over Sinder, and he mumbled, "That's very generous of you."

Zisa hopped down and stood just beyond the streaming water. Sinder turned and tilted his head so the tree could untangle his increasingly sodden hair. "Your clothes are getting wet."

"Should I disrobe?" Zisa asked hopefully.

"Maybe not."

Like a well-trained bath attendant in a dragon lord's harem, the tree handled him courteously. Blunt nails scraped circles against his scalp. Then a hand took Sinder's chin, guiding the angle of his head, the other lifting sections of hair to rinse away the suds.

Sinder basked in the heat and in the attention. So much, he was sorry when Zisa turned off the tap.

Still in silence, which was its own kind of privacy, Zisa brought out an enormous stack of towels and proved he was adept at toweling without tangling. Sinder bowed his head and let the tree do as he pleased.

Zisa had begun braiding before he spoke again. "You have more injuries today."

"You keep track?"

"Are you being bullied? Children are sometimes bullied."

What a thing to ask. "I'm hardly a child."

"No?" Zisa sounded amused.

Sinder lifted his head. "Do I look like a child to you?"

"How many centuries do you have?"

Fudging a little, Sinder held up three fingers.

Zisa shook his head and pushed down one of the fingers. "You are *barely* old enough to tempt a tree."

"I know I'm young. Prodigies usually are."

"Finished." Zisa dropped a kiss on the blaze decorating Sinder's shoulder. "Thank you for your trust, beautiful dragon."

Sinder turned, only to find himself in a careful embrace. It was so easy to give in, sagging against Zisa, who held him up, stalwart as beams.

"Timur is coming," Zisa murmured. "He will know what to do."

Sinder sighed. "Oh, sure. I suppose he could just put me out of my misery."

"You will show him your injuries and drink his tea and trust him as you have trusted me." Zisa sternly added, "Or I will tell on you."

"I suppose."

"Promise it."

Sinder smiled, for Zisa wasn't very convincing as a commander. He missed Juuyu's crisp orders and Boon's growling. But since either of them would have backed up Zisa at this moment, Sinder lifted his face and whispered, "I promise."

Zisa kissed his nose, stepped back, and vanished.

While he pulled himself together, Sinder tried to decide if he should make a note in his report about Zisa. While it was plain as pebbles that Amaranthine trees could manifest, it had never occurred to Sinder that they could de-manifest. Or would it be un-manifest? And presumably re-manifest at a different location. How quickly? And what was the limit of their range?

Surely there was some strategic significance here. Offensive and defensive potential? A possible means of protection, both for them and for their sibling? Hallow would figure it out if anyone could. Sinder would simply leave out the circumstances surrounding his little discovery.

Exiting the bathroom, he fielded a nod from Ginkgo, who was in the middle of trying to explain what it was like, having characteristics of both Amaranthine and reaver bloodlines.

Zisa stood poised by the door, hand on the knob. If his expression was anything to go by, Ginkgo, Tenma, and Mikoto were off the mark, but getting warmer. If no one else thought to ask the tree what was going on, he'd do it himself.

But then Zisa was ushering in Timur, whose gaze locked on Sinder with unnerving intensity.

He knew. But how ...?

Then it registered that Michaelson had carried Gregor in, which meant Waaseyaa must have brought the boy to his father. Between a likely tip-off and the threat of tattling, Sinder wasn't getting out of this. Damn. He hated explaining things that weren't the business of anyone outside the heights.

Timur's arrival set off a chain reaction. Ginkgo jumped up, all pretense of drunkenness gone, to introduce Tenma. Mikoto rallied considerably. He was clearly taken by Timur in a very "notice me, sempai" way.

Waaseyaa came to the door long enough to ask if Mikoto and Tenma would help him prepare the evening meal. And invited them all to share it. Ginkgo stole Gregor and announced they needed to track down Kyrie and Lilya.

Zisa smilingly closed the door on the entire lot, offered Sinder a wink, and vanished. Leaving him alone with Timur and Fend.

The former crossed the room in two long strides and loomed over him. "Tell me what you need."

"Who says I need anything?" Sinder rolled his eyes at Fend and grumbled, "*You* told, didn't you?"

Timur looked between them, then slowly asked, "Sinder, are you afraid of me?"

The idea. "No. I wanted you more than anyone."

"Good." His expression softened, and he repeated, "Good. Who prettied you up?"

Sinder drew a blank.

"Your hair."

Slowly reaching out, Timur pulled the heavy weight of Sinder's braid forward. In addition to helping and holding him, Zisa had woven his own flowers through the entire length of his braid.

"Sneaky, flirty imp of a tree." Sinder closed his eyes. "I couldn't manage alone."

"Show me."

Sinder eased up the hem of his tunic. Timur quickly knelt and took over, hands tracing welts and abraded skin.

"No bones broken," Sinder assured. Always a bright side.

"Who kicked you?" Timur's voice was low, dangerous.

"Doesn't matter." Anger radiated from the battler, and Sinder sighed. "Trust me when I say I was asking for it. And dragons usually get what they ask for."

Timur's expression abruptly closed off. "Sinder, are you afraid of me?" he repeated.

"Not ... specifically."

The battler rose to his full height. "The idea of me," he quietly amended. "You called me a dragon slayer."

"Aren't you?"

"I am a member of the Order of Spomenka." His voice deepened, and his accent thickened. "My heritage. My training. We are legendary, yes? Do little dragons grow up fearing the storms we can bring?"

Sinder muttered, "I'm not a child."

"What are your comfort colors?"

"Wh-what?"

Timur gripped him by the back of his neck, but before the move could register as threatening, he was pinching one of Sinder's vertebrae. Then the one below it. As he added more pressure, Sinder fluted an oath, his eyes crossing.

"Can you raise your ridges in speaking form?" Timur asked.

Sinder leaned into the man, head lowered. He trilled a weak protest. Humans weren't supposed to know this stuff.

"Which of the winds do you favor?" Timur continued. "When was the last time you were properly oiled?"

"Why?"

"Why do I want to know? For your comfort."

Sinder shook his head. "Why do you know *at all*?"

Timur's other hand began working in tandem. "I am a member of the Order of Spomenka. We only know what's been entrusted to us. Who do you think teaches us your ways?"

Swearing miserably, he filled in the blank. "Dragons."

"I started living among dragons when I was fourteen. Most of my early training revolved around pampering and pleasing dragons. I was a harem attendant. I was a healer in the heights. I made friends and helped three of your brethren gain the sky."

Sinder looked up then, stunned. "They let you into the heights?"

"Not many humans learn what I know."

"Tracking and trapping and marking."

Timur hummed an affirmative. "Don't forget pedicures."

Sinder snorted. "Only if Fend goes first."

In silence, Timur convinced him. Even Juuyu didn't know things like this. Sinder probably wouldn't have told him if he'd asked. But this Spomenka had him in his proverbial coils. Long-ignored instincts stirred, and Sinder crumbled under the weight of his need.

"Please?" he whimpered.

"Glad to," Timur promised.

And because this man knew what it meant and how much, Sinder whispered, "Yellow."

"Right. And?"

"East."

"Ah, a contrary wind. Not at all surprised." Timur's smile was easy to trust. "And which of the oils should I have shipped?"

Sinder had never been asked before. In his line of work, you made do or did without. How strange to be offered such consideration during the worst summer of his life. With a low trill and a long sigh, Sinder asked, "Ever heard of spikenard?"

"I know it." Timur promised, "You'll have it."

22

ASKING THE RIGHT QUESTIONS

ikoto was grateful for the distractions, even the confusing one offered by Tenma. The man kept stealing glances all through dinner, which was a little unnerving. Mikoto couldn't help but wonder what he was seeing.

Reavers weren't supposed to touch one another's souls. But Tenma had admitted that he wasn't exactly a reaver, although he had to be something similar. Otherwise, how else could he tend at all? Which was apparently his method for healing the Broken.

A mystery and a miracle worker.

His *prismatic* remark made no sense. And colors? That wasn't how Mikoto saw his connection to the Amaranthine.

But Tenma seemed harmless. He meant well, and he presented himself as a modest and unassuming man. Though hard to fathom. All through dinner, Tenma sat quietly, ate sparingly, and mostly listened to everyone else's conversations.

With traces of chagrin, Mikoto realized he was probably being equally inscrutable. Though he ate with better appetite. Uncle was a good cook, and Zisa fluttered around the table, nudging extra onto everyone's plates. Even Noble, who'd curled up between Fend's front paws, received the odd morsel.

Had there ever been such a dinner party? Mikoto doubted the years had brought such a group to Uncle's table.

They lingered over the meal, but Ginkgo finally announced it was time for the young ones to prepare for bed. Their cue to disband.

Making his way to Uncle's side, Mikoto mumbled his thanks and surrendered his hand, which Waaseyaa held until Zisa wafted over and cozied up. Nothing was said, exactly. Not even *goodbye*, since Glint was still monopolizing Mikoto's room and Yulin's attention.

Tenma migrated over to offer parting courtesies.

"Mikoto will walk you home," said Zisa. "Unless you would like to sleep here? I have a house."

"That's not necessary," Tenma murmured. "You've been too generous."

"I insist!"

Mikoto gently squeezed Zisa's shoulders. "You are a good host. I am certain he will want to return."

The tree pouted. "That is not why. And I still insist. I will even go along, to make sure."

Waaseyaa quietly reminded, "You cannot pass our boundaries, Brother."

"I know." Zisa lay his head against Mikoto's chest and murmured, "I only want to help them."

To appease the tree, Mikoto said, "We can walk Tenma to the boundary. That way, he will know the way back to you."

"Yes!" All brightness, Zisa gave his brother a soft-eyed look. "This is important."

"I will be waiting," Waaseyaa promised.

Tenma followed the conversation with an expression of polite confusion. Mikoto wasn't sure what else to do, so he reinforced Zisa's invitation. "Let us walk you to the boundary. It would be our pleasure."

The man accepted with a nod. "I would appreciate knowing how to return."

Zisa seized their hands and nearly skipped to the door.

Tenma didn't seem to mind the handling at all. In fact, he laced his fingers with Zisa's and held on tight. Mikoto found himself hoping the man would stay in Wardenclave. Not many were so accepting of Zisa's little ways.

Barely halfway to the boundary, Zisa stopped short. "Now," he said, as serious as Mikoto had ever seen him. "Tell Tenma what happened."

"Something happened?" Mikoto's brows furrowed. "When?"

"When you were smaller than you are now, but not as small as Gregor." Zisa wasn't very good with timeframes, but when he let go and stepped back, he put out a hand, describing the correct height. It was a good hint.

"Zisa, are you talking about when I was nine?"

"No. You talk." The tree made little flutters with his hands. "Tell him about the day when everything changed."

Which could only mean ... Lupe. Lowering his voice, Mikoto asked, "Do you mean the day I almost drowned? Why do you want me to share that story?"

"It matters," said Zisa. And again to Tenma. "It *matters*."

"I believe you." Tenma took a receptive posture. "If Mikoto-kun is willing."

Mikoto didn't mind telling, but he didn't understand why. Touching Zisa's shoulder, he asked, "Why does it matter?"

"Because that is the day everything changed," he patiently replied.

"I do not understand."

"Maybe *I* will," Tenma suggested.

"It was an accident," Mikoto awkwardly began. "We were down by the river. I slipped and fell in."

Not much of a story, really. A dozen words covered the basics.

Zisa frowned. "You left out the important part."

"L-lupe ... she ...." Mikoto stopped and restarted. "A friend of the family dived in after me and pulled me out. She saved my life."

Tenma was listening closely, watching closely. He asked, "Were drastic measures required?"

"I ... I guess you could say that. The other kids teased me some, saying she kissed me." Mikoto offered an awkward shrug. "I needed CPR."

"Breath," said Zisa, who bounced on his heels. "*Wind.*"

To Mikoto's way of thinking, the kiss was the important part, even if he couldn't really remember it. Only the elation and how the air had tasted. And the warmth of being hugged and how Lupe smelled like sunshine. And the whole falling in love thing.

"This friend of the family," Tenma said, watching Zisa now. "She's Amaranthine?"

"No. She is a reaver." Mikoto lowered his gaze. "She is here. For the summer."

Tenma shuffled closer, maybe to try to read his expression in the dark. "Are you sure?"

"That she is here? Yes." He swallowed hard. "I met her bus."

Reaching out to touch his arm, Tenma quietly asked, "No. I meant … are you sure she's *human*?"

Zisa tittered.

Mikoto whispered, "Of course she is human. The same as me."

"Yes," Tenma said slowly. "But you and I aren't the same kind of human. Maybe she's another kind entirely."

"Closer." Zisa clapped his hands the same way Yulin often did. "Close, but not quite."

Tenma turned his attention to the tree. "Do you need us to figure this out, or can you tell us more?"

Zisa looped his arms around Tenma's waist and said, "Look at me."

Mikoto edged around to the other side so more moonlight fell on Zisa's face. But he knew he wasn't seeing the same kinds of things Tenma was.

The man stood quietly for several moments, then breathed, "Oooh."

As much as Mikoto wanted to hurry them along, he bit his lip and waited. Because Zisa said this mattered. And it was about Lupe.

"What am I?" prompted Zisa.

Tenma said, "You're a tree."

Mikoto thought he understood, then. "You are an Impression."

Zisa's smile was beautiful. "I am."

"Is Mikoto's friend an Impression?" asked Tenma.

Zisa hummed happily. "Close, but not quite."

A thought occurred "Is she the one Salali said was coming?"

"Salali noticed," confirmed the tree. "Salali knows."

Tenma's gaze bounced between Mikoto and Zisa, as if comparing what he'd found. "Would you mind if I made a call?"

"To?" asked Mikoto.

Pulling out his phone and pushing at his glasses, Tenma said, "My friend is an expert on … well, just about everything. May I ask her about Impressions?"

"No pictures." Zisa gave a little shimmy of excitement. "Could you use the speaker?"

Tenma smiled and nodded, but he also waited for Mikoto's verdict.

Funny that his first big decision as headman was to allow Zisa the rare treat of a phone call. "May I know who you plan to call?"

"Someone trusted." With an abashed expression, he said, "Actually, you may know her already. She's Timur's sister, well *one* of them. I want to confer with Isla Ward."

23
CONFERENCE CALL

Isla do you have several minutes to spare?" Tenma spoke over his phone. "You're on speaker, by the way. My friends and I have need of your expertise."

"Which one?"

Tenma hesitated. "Which friend?"

With exaggerated patience, Isla asked, *"Which expertise? I have several, you know."*

Isla wasn't twelve anymore, but she still seemed awfully young to have so much confidence. She was as bossy as ever, still eager to share her encyclopedic knowledge on any and every topic, and patient with the gaps in Tenma's understanding. A force of nature. A friend he could count on.

"We're interested in anything you might know about Impressions."

"Oh!" Isla sounded delighted. *"I like your friends already. How*

secure are your surroundings?"

"Unrivaled, I should think." Tenma searched Mikoto's face. "Am I allowed to say where we are?"

"Do," urged Zisa. "How else can you introduce me?"

Still, Tenma waited for Mikoto to give some sign. Young though he seemed, even younger than Tenma had been when he started at New Saga, Mikoto was the headman of Wardenclave. He would know how much was too much.

Mikoto asked, "How secure are *your* surroundings?"

"If this is a competition, I might win. Sensei and I are at Lord Mossberne's home in the heights." She was smug now. *"He gave me your room, Tenma. The east-facing one."*

Tenma groaned. His friends might forever tease him for Lapis Mossberne's grateful impulse, especially Isla.

Isla glibly went on, *"A secure line. A secure room. I've also begun adding wards, since you sounded concerned."*

Mikoto nodded and said, "You may explain our circumstances to Reaver Ward."

Tenma began, "Isla, I'm at Wardenclave. And that was Mikoto Reaver."

"Oh!" Isla's voice radiated warmth. *"It's a pleasure, Headman. But Tenma, this is* wonderful. *Have you met my brother?"*

"Just this evening. A nice man." More softly, he added, "A good father."

"Isn't Gregor a dear?"

"He is never at a loss for admirers."

"And my sister!" Isla exclaimed. *"You met Lilya."*

"I ... suppose I did." Tenma had been rather more interested in

Mikoto. He couldn't recall much about the girl. "Quiet. Very quiet. Not much like you, I think."

Sisterly concern overflowed. *"This is her first time away from home. I hope she's not withdrawing. Did she seem unhappy?"*

To his embarrassment, Tenma couldn't answer. He looked to Mikoto and Zisa, hoping they had something to contribute.

Zisa leaned closer to the phone. "Your sister has courage and ended the evening with a smile."

"Ah, that is good to hear. Who is this, please?

"I am Zisa."

Silence reined for three full beats. *"Oh? Oh, dear."* Isla was clearly flustered. *"Oh, this is a pleasure! Tenma, you're not teasing, are you?"*

"You know who he is?"

"Of course! While the name of Waaseyaa's tree twin is not listed in any contemporary literature, any student of history can uncover the occasional mention. And, well, I've had several opportunities to chat with Dickon Denholm on the subject of trees."

"He is one of ours," said Zisa.

Mikoto quietly explained, "Waaseyaa's youngest son."

"Baby of the dynasty," boasted Zisa. "We have a dynasty, you know. That is what Glint calls our family tree."

"Yes, I am aware." Isla's tone softened. *"Papka was recently awarded dynasty status. We're all very pleased for him, of course, but ... well, it's also a lot of pressure."*

"Oh? Oooh!" Zisa leaned so close to the phone, his nose nearly touched the screen. "Glint likes linking dynasties. Are you part of ours?"

"No, no." Isla veered off into a brief overview of her lineage, which carried down almost exclusively through Northern Europe. Never crossing with the fabled bloodlines that flourished an ocean away.

"He might consider you, then."

Isla's fell silent. Finally, she ventured, *"Pardon?"*

"If you are not descended from Waaseyaa, then you could come and belong to Brother and me."

Tenma knew that this was a sensitive subject for Isla and led in with a chuckle. "Are you matchmaking, Zisa?"

The tree pointed to the screen. "She likes me. I like her. Brother might choose her if he knew she would be nice to me."

His expression was so hopeful, so wistful. Tenma had no idea what to say, but Mikoto wrapped his arms around Zisa and said, "Isla *is* nice, and we need her help. Is it all right if we talk about Impressions now?"

Zisa leaned into Mikoto's larger frame. "I *like* her."

"Yes. We all do. And you can tell Uncle all about her later." Mikoto calmly added, "He will be glad to know you made a new friend."

Until now, it hadn't occurred to Tenma that a tree whose legacy had been all but erased and who lived in hiding might be a little lonesome. Reading between the lines, this would be especially true if his twin's wife *wasn't* nice to him.

"Complementary genealogies aside," Tenma interjected. "Isla, what can you tell us about Impressions?"

"Yes. Right. Quite." He could hear the relief in Isla's acceptance of the change in subject. *"As it happens, I've had access to most of the old sagas. The collection at Kikusawa Shrine remains the most*

extensive, and thanks to the Miyabe family's efforts, completely uncensored."

"Sorry, sorry," interrupted Tenma. "By sagas, do you mean stories like the one Kimiko borrowed for her courtship?"

"The Wolf and the Moon Maiden," Isla supplied. *"And yes. The sagas refer to the oldest heroic tales. Some belong to individual clans. Some are shared freely, usually by storytellers during a Song Circle. Oral tradition is more common, but many clans—like the Dimityblest—are compulsive about written records."*

"True," Mikoto offered. "There is a Dimityblest chronicler attached to our family. He has preserved our whole history."

"Really!" Isla's fascination carried easily over the phone. *"I'd love to read a record of Wardenclave's founding."*

Before she could be further sidetracked, Tenma asked, "So the sagas are historically accurate?"

Isla hesitated. *"Some think the stories are figurative, but there are just as many who call for a literal interpretation. Scholars like to point out that many of the essentials don't change, and not only through the compendium of sagas. There are also the songs, which are sometimes called psalms, countless short fables, a handful of lullabies, and the Amaranthine equivalent of nursery rhymes."*

"I know some of the fables and rhymes," Tenma said. "When I … do what I do, I'm often repaid in stories. For many it's all they have to offer."

"Oh, I want to hear more about that!"

"Another time?"

"Right. Yes. Where was I?" Isla seemed to be drumming her fingers. *"Taking corresponding histories into account, the*

Impressions predate Amaranthine culture. Many of the classic tales involve encounters between the Amaranthine and the Impressions. And in all, the imps inspire awe. They're beautiful, desirable, and often depicted as existing just out of reach."

Zisa shook his head and said, "I am here."

"So you are!" Isla agreed. *"We cannot deny the existence of the clans of earth, sky, and sea when people like you confirm the truth."*

Tenma's attention skipped ahead. Isla knew how his abilities worked, so he simply asked, "Why would I look at a human and see the same kinds of colors only found in Amaranthine?"

She hummed. *"Logically, it means that they aren't human. Or that they're not entirely human. Or it could mean that you are changing."*

That last one hadn't occurred to Tenma.

It was so simple, he wondered why not.

Isla lowered her voice and asked, *"Can you see Zisa's colors?"*

"Yes." Smiling at the tree, Tenma added, "He's glorious."

"Can we assume that means you will now recognize another tree if you were to meet them? In much the same way you're able to differentiate members of different clans?"

"Maybe." Tenma asked, "Aren't there supposed to be many kinds of trees?"

She hummed again. *"Who is the human involved?"*

"Me," said Mikoto.

Isla immediately countered, *"Well, that makes* no *sense. Your bloodline can easily be traced."*

"An original Reaver," agreed Tenma. "Yet I see colors."

"Wait." The drumming quickened, then a sharp sound carried through. A snap. *"Do you still see swapped colors? Or a shared*

color when two souls accept a bond?"

"Yes, of course. That hasn't changed." Tenma rather enjoyed picking out colors in a crowd. In a way, he was matchmaking, only after the fact.

"Could you be catching an echo of Mikoto's attachment to someone?"

"Closer," crooned Zisa. "So very close!"

Mikoto shook his head. "Lupe is human."

Zisa reached up to touch the young man's cheek. "She is," he assured.

A new idea rushed at him. "Isla, are imps and the Amaranthine … compatible?"

"Oh, yes. Many of the old stories are romantic, even erotic."

Tenma shook his head. "I meant … are there crossers?"

She took a moment to react. *"What in interesting question! I'm not sure. I'm not even sure how to find out!"* The sound of scribbling accompanied her muttering. *"If Impressions are compatible with Amaranthine, and Amaranthine are compatible with humans …! Well, reavers are compatible. And Mikoto is undeniably a reaver. Hmm."*

Tenma's attention jumped from face to face, trying to read the others' expressions.

Mikoto looked more and more like a frightened boy. For his part, Zisa hung on their every word, eager for them to understand.

Isla rambled on. *"How would something so ethereal … ah, but the wolves! And in the tales of stars … of course! Tenma, this is brilliant."*

"Which part?"

"All of it, really. This single shift in premise could have monumental repercussions. In a good way, I think."

Tenma sighed. "You've always been a big picture kind of girl."

"I'm sorry. Well, not sorry, exactly. This is all so exciting. But I understand that this isn't why you called." He could almost see her straighten up and clasp her hands. *"Did you have a more specific question?"*

"Yes. And I'd like Zisa to share his answer with you." Tenma eased the phone closer to the tree. "What changed the day everything changed?"

The tree looked up and away. Night breezes toyed with leaves festooning his head, and he smiled at the stars. *"Mikoto would have died if she hadn't shared her breath."* He placed his hand on the young man's chest. *"She blew wind into your lungs, and she saved you."*

"Wind?" Mikoto rubbed at the back of his neck and glanced around.

Little gusts were puffing around them. Tenma's skin prickled into gooseflesh.

On the other end of the connection, Isla echoed, *"Wind? Zisa, are you saying you know of a wind imp?"*

The breeze grew more agitated, and Tenma tried to catch a glimpse of it. But he had no idea where to look. But this hint was better than the others, and Zisa hadn't told them they were close or closer. *This* was their answer. "Isla, do you know any helpful stories about wind?"

"Entire libraries are dedicated to wind lore, and I'd wager Lapis knows every ode and epic." With a little laugh, Isla said, *"If you want to woo the wind to your side, all you really need is a dragon."*

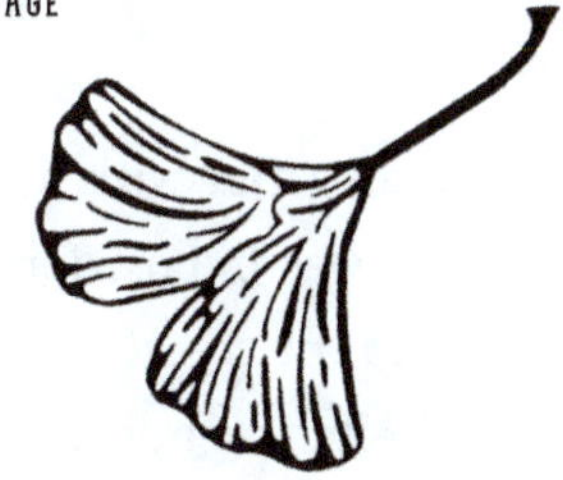

24

NEW MOON NIGHT

Sinder saw no reason not to report for training exercises at his appointed position. Torloo was taking advantage of the new moon to push the rookies through more night maneuvers. From what little he could hear, they were definitely up to something. New code words. Different team comps. For some reason, they'd gone to groups of five instead of three.

Fine by him. All he had to do was evade.

Thanks to Tenma and Timur, Sinder was feeling much more like himself. Refreshed. Elated. Maybe a little keyed up, but he'd have every opportunity run off the excess energy. Torloo was getting more serious, too. Limiting how much Sinder knew in advance. Forcing more realistic outcomes.

The training wheels were off.

Sinder dodged a swooping owl, only to find his way barred by a lone battler with a crossbow. He dove for cover, but a second archer was in position. The first dart grazed his shoulder, and he took to the trees.

Sheltering in the boughs of an evergreen, he did a swift self-check and cursed. A sigil fizzed against the fabric. Improperly anchored, Sinder was able to dispel the thing. For a few moments, Sinder wrestled with the sting of betrayal. This was Michaelson's handiwork.

But ... not really, or it would have worked.

Which meant they were applying his tactics. Or adapting them. Which was the whole point of these exercises.

A wolf howled, and another answered. They were flanking him, and he hadn't even noticed.

Dropping to the ground, Sinder flashed through the woods at speed. Not quite worried, but no longer comfortable with his chances. He kind of wished Michaelson was here, but the man had been sound asleep when Sinder stole away.

And what good would it do to have him here? Timur wouldn't be on his side.

Another dart whizzed past Sinder's nose, stopping him in his tracks. That's when two more hit his upper arm. They pattered to the ground, having delivered their shimmering sigils.

Sinder caught one up and inspected it as he ran.

Blunt tips. They weren't meant to break skin, though there would be more bruises.

Embedded crystals. And that was going to be a problem.

"Are they insane?" he muttered. Hallow was obsessed with tuned crystals, so Sinder had been exposed to every variation known to carry Cadmiel's song. That's why he *knew* that this rookie scheme might actually work. But not necessarily in the way they hoped.

Another dart found its mark, smack dab in the center of a spreading sigil. Targeted. Good for them. Bad for dragons. This one bit deep. Scenting the air with Sinder's blood. Bowing him over with a pain that wasn't entirely physical.

A red remnant. He *really* hated the red ones.

Sinder was frightened beyond clear thinking. Sweating and swearing, he stumbled onward. He needed to get away from his pursuers before any of them died.

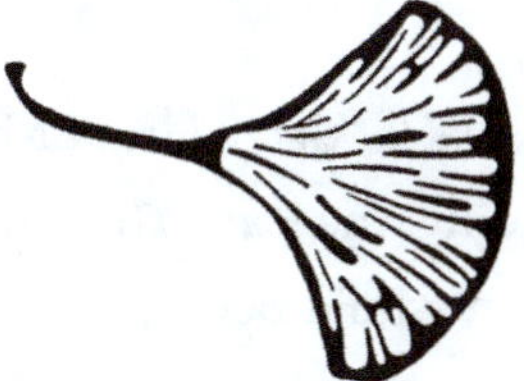

Ginkgo's phone chirruped impatiently, startling him from a light doze. He snatched it up and squinted at the time, already thumbing to accept the call. "I'm here."

"Where is Sinder?"

"This second? Not sure." Ginkgo eased from the bed and padded to the window. There wasn't much to see in the dark.

Another voice carried along the line. Someone else. Sounding worried. Ginkgo's ears twitched. "That Hallow?"

"Yes. We have cause for concern. I will need you to check. Now."

Ginkgo lifted the sash on the window and slipped outside. "On my way next door."

"What about Timur?"

"They're rooming together. See? I made good on my promise."

An impatient grunt. An ominous silence.

Ginkgo eased open Zisa's door and half-stumbled into the tree's waiting arms.

"Sinder here?" Ginkgo whispered.

Zisa eyed the phone in his hand and shook his head.

From the bed in the corner, Timur quietly called, "Ginkgo?"

Hallow must have grabbed the phone because his voice came sharp and clear. *"Get to him. Immediately. His crystal's vibrating nearly to pieces, and its song tells of pain."*

"On it," he promised, signaling urgently. Timur's feet hit the floor. "Juuyu?"

Sinder's partner was back. *"Get to him,"* he begged. *"For I cannot."*

"On our way." Ending the call, Ginkgo hurried to the bed and scooped up Gregor, who'd been tucked between Timur and Mikoto. "I'll sneak him in with Kyrie and Lilya. Don't wait on me. I can catch up."

Mikoto stirred. "Trouble?" he asked.

"Sinder's probably hurt."

"Need help?"

Ginkgo didn't stay to answer. Whisking across to Waaseyaa's house, he hurried the sleeping toddler to the guest room. Kyrie was not only awake, he stood at the window, fingertips touching the screen. "Hey, little bro. Watch Gregor for me?"

Kyrie shook his head and asked, "Sinder?"

"Not sure. Probably injured. We're going." He scooted Gregor under the sheet at the center of the bed, right next to Lilya.

"I will come."

Only then did Ginkgo realize that the boy had already dressed.

He'd probably interrupted him in the process of going out the window. "Dad wouldn't like it."

"Dad will not scold." Kyrie turned wide eyes to him and solemnly said, "Sinder is screaming."

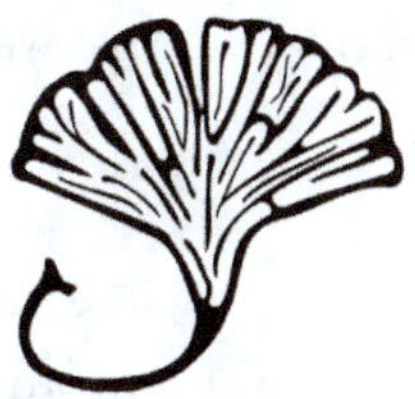

Mikoto had been training for emergencies for more than half his life, so he was in his basics and boots even faster than Timur. But he was a long way from Colt and his arsenal. "Do I need a weapon?" he asked.

Timur spared him a glance. And a second glance. "No. Ever ride?"

"Yes."

"You're with us, then." Timur led the way outside. "Fend is going to be cranky, having to carry two of us."

"I will run," offered Mikoto, lengthening his stride to keep up with the battler.

Timur laughed. "No need. He'll run twice as fast, just to be rid of us. Right, friend?"

Fend slunk out of the darkness and yowled testily.

Mikoto mounted first, but he wasn't sure what to do with his hands. Dogs had ruffs, and Merl's mane was fair game. "Where …?"

Timur crowded him from behind, one arm locked around Mikoto's chest. "He's just a big kitten. Scruff him. I'll be your brace."

Following his example, Mikoto buried his hands in thick fur and muttered a low, "Apologies, Fend."

The big feline grumbled and leapt, and Mikoto lowered his body and adjusted his hips.

Bowing over him, Timur said, "Quick learner."

Mikoto hoped he'd have the chance to show Timur that he could do a whole lot more than ride. But that wasn't the most important thing here. "Orders?"

"You want some?"

"I am a battler. I run with the guard. I know these mountains."

Timur hooked his chin over Mikoto's shoulder, putting his mouth right next to his ear. "Ever face a dragon?"

"No."

"Then you're at a disadvantage. Listen well. Dragons in truest form are formidable. Claws and jaws and horns and ridges. Don't *ever* lose track of their tail." Timur's tone was grave. "Most believe that dragons become even more dangerous in speaking form. Speed becomes a factor. And with a few words, they can ensorcell a whole rank of battlers."

"Which will we be facing?"

"We'll be facing *Sinder*." Timur's hold tightened. "Our friend needs us, and we'll do whatever's needed. Got it?"

"Yessir." But Mikoto needed more information. "What happened to him?"

"Something bad if we received a call." As lights began showing between the trees ahead, Timur's grip nearly robbed Mikoto of breath. "Faster, Fend. He's suffering."

25

SCREAM

Kyrie had no trouble keeping up with Ginkgo, who lofted a handful of illuminated crystals to zip ahead and light their run through unfamiliar woods. Long before they reached any kind of destination, Kyrie knew something bad was happening.

The wind carried frightening scents. They made him want to run faster, but also to stop.

"Okay, little bro?" Ginkgo asked.

Before Kyrie could answer, he heard his first dragon scream. It made him want to scream back.

Ginkgo scooped him up and ran on. "That bad?"

"He is trying to say, 'Stay back. Go away. Leave me.'" The words hurt because they offered a terrible kindness. "Sinder does not mean it, though."

Ears askance, eyes worry-wide, Ginkgo asked, "How can you tell?"

Tapping his fingers over his heart, Kyrie admitted, "I might only half understand. But that is the truth of his call. He wants a rescuer."

"That'd be us, yeah?" Ginkgo kissed the top of his head. "Timur's just ahead, and I'm catching Torloo's scent. They'll need our support."

Kyrie simply nodded.

" ... the next trial," Torloo was saying. "An experimental technique combining sigilcraft and crystal-tipped bolts. Crossbow delivery."

"But why *red* crystals?" Timur was pulling at his hair.

"We must test all hues, and the samples provided were arranged in a spectrum." Although his tail was puffed double, Torloo's voice was steady, his answers succinct. "Red was first."

Ginkgo let Kyrie down and shouldered his way between Timur and Mikoto.

Torloo continued. "He reacted poorly. He is contained, largely thanks to Salali, but he has not calmed. There is some concern with regards to the damage a rampaging dragon can cause."

"To the village, or to himself?" growled Timur. Kyrie thought Lilya's big brother looked dangerous right then. Like he was daring the assemblage of battlers to say the wrong thing.

"He knows us. Trusts us," said Ginkgo. "What I want to know is who cut him?"

"No! Well, *yes*, a dart pierced him. But after that, Sinder hurt himself." Torloo pointed to the sigils that danced in midair, forming a roughly hexagonal barrier. "Once we had him penned, he began thrashing. Trees shattered, and he threw himself against the resulting splinters."

Kyrie felt bad for Torloo, whose misery was palpable.

Timur growled something, but Kyrie slipped away. He saw no reason to worry about the village. Sinder should be everyone's first concern. Saving him would keep everyone safe.

Bent branches and bare roots made it obvious that the area was freshly cleared. Little breezes stank of bare earth, bruised leaves, tree sap, and blood. And in the center of the wreckage huddled Sinder, head low, sides heaving. Glittering green eyes roved along the line of battlers, who ranged around the boundaries.

Sinder could not escape.

Not because Salali's barrier was strong. Only because Sinder was holding himself back. Keeping to a form that posed less of a threat, should he falter. Kyrie was impressed by Sinder's resolve— to accept pain rather than deal it.

Behind him, Timur was saying, "I'm glad you learned something of value from this, because you aren't going to have another chance. This cannot continue."

Ginkgo said, "Dad'll bust chops if anyone gets stubborn."

Mikoto spoke up. "I will file a formal protest. Allow us to find other means of training while Sinder recovers."

"This can't continue!" Timur repeated.

Kyrie glanced back, still intrigued. Lilya's brother always laughed and smiled at home. But that was far away and full of children. This was a face Timur didn't usually show. But Kyrie approved of his fury. If he was entirely honest, he shared it.

Sinder's claws raked the ground. Blood matted his mane, and there were splinters the size of pikes in uncomfortable places.

Kyrie's patience for the adult's conversation faded entirely. Talking things through *could* be important. Mother liked to say that patience was a virtue. But so was mercy.

He trotted along the line, paying more heed to the barrier than the battlers. It was good and strong, but one of the anchors had a lovely lavender hue. Just what he needed.

Kyrie could have dismantled the whole assemblage with a touch, but that wouldn't be safe for the humans. Instead, he found a little ripple and pressed his fingers through. Nudging and leaning, he whispered encouragement. Potent words. He didn't often need them, but this was a *very* good barrier. Its clashing layers scraped, but he whispered and teased and wiggled past the first layer … only to find no further impediments.

Disappointing, really. If Dad had been in charge, there would have been a series of failsafes and fallbacks. That's the way foxes were, always making certain they accounted for the unexpected. Then again, this was a rush job, and it worked to keep Sinder in. But whoever made this barrier hadn't known about Kyrie.

They'd know better next time.

Fiddling with a sigil, Kyrie worked his way across battered ground. Unseen. Ginkgo had taught him this one for sneaking into the pantry, which wasn't exactly against the rules since Aunt Sansa was generous with everything, even snacks. Sharing cookies at midnight was one of the best ways to help skittish new orphans feel like part of the family. And sometimes … well, sometimes little kids were afraid of Kyrie.

Mother asked him to be gentle and kind and patient. Give newcomers a chance to see past the red eyes and horns and scales, to see how much his other denmates liked and trusted him. And mother was wise, because that's how it always worked out. Even the worst crybaby—which was Be'el-garva, a little half-cobra— would trail after Kyrie, wanting to hold hands.

The youngsters were cute. Kyrie liked being a big brother.

For now, at least, he was the only half-dragon at Stately House, but Kyrie often wondered if Dad might someday bring home a little cousin. Maybe they would be like Sinder, who looked like new shoots in springtime. Or they might be like Lapis, whose blues shimmered like deep water. And he could be their big brother. But right now, he needed to be a good *little* brother. Or a good cousin, at least.

With a series of trills, he let Sinder know he was coming. That was only polite.

When the injured dragon's near eye rolled his way, Kyrie offered a small wave, but he wasn't sure Sinder recognized him.

Foam dripped from his jaws, flecked with blood, and there was an unhealthy slick upon his scales. With each blink of his eyes, they rolled a little, and their pupils wavered between thin slits and black pits. Could he even see?

Kyrie said, "Hold on, Sinder. I am here."

Scales shifted, and the dragon dragged his chin, trying to see.

"I am not alone. You are not alone."

Sinder's wail made Kyrie's stomach plunge, but he didn't stop.

"Let me see." He used a bossy tone that would have suited Lilya just fine. Words that could compel. "Show me where."

The answering whine ended in a sob.

Kyrie wrapped his arms around Sinder's muzzle as far as they would go. He warbled a lullaby that Lapis had taught him, a silly rhyme about the winds in each season. All lovely. All loving.

With a creaky warble, Sinder tried to sing along. But he was still suffering.

"Let me take it from you." And when Sinder widened his eyes and squeaked alarm, Kyrie said, "I know, but I am only half. And sometimes, that is a very useful thing to be."

Sinder gave him a direction with a small jerk of his head.

Kyrie had to paw through fur, but it was there, buried. "Take the shield of faith, with which you will be able to quench all the fiery darts of the wicked one." And wrapping his hand around the offending bolt, he jerked it free.

Sinder yelped and shuddered.

All of the sudden, the barrier was gone, and voices were shouting. Ginkgo reached them first. "Hold still, Damsel. Let us pull a few of these slivers before you try to move."

Timur crashed to the ground beside Sinder and spoke right into his ear. "Do *not* transform. Hear me? Not until I say it's safe." And to Kyrie, "Keep him calm. This will hurt."

So Kyrie stroked the angles of Sinder's face and made sounds low in his throat. Ones he knew meant peace and home and brotherhood. Because they were the very things Lapis knew he craved.

Timur was talking, too. A growly harangue that sounded more like vows. "No more battle games. No more night maneuvers. No more experimental weapons. No. More."

Kyrie babbled on, telling Sinder about the garden at home and about nearly falling from Zisa's branches. About Lilya making him sneeze and the mysterious scent of flowers that the winds brought to tease him.

Then Ginkgo was back. "Their healer's here with supplies, and Timur's ready. Nice and easy, Damsel. We've got you."

In a whirlwind that only partially hid a groan, Sinder shifted. On his knees before Kyrie, he reached for him, pulling him against skin that must have hurt—battered and bloodied and bruised.

Kyrie crooned and kissed his cheek, then used his sleeve to blot tears.

"Let me through," grumbled Timur. "We need to stop the bleeding."

Once he was sure Lilya's big brother was close enough to catch him, Kyrie let go of Sinder. Next to Timur, caught in the light of Ginkgo's crystals, the dragon looked pale and frail.

Sinder tugged at Timur's vest, his voice was cracked and hoarse from screaming. "Tell them I'm sorry."

"Zolottse," Timur murmured, gathering Sinder close. "That's exactly what they asked me to tell you."

26

FREE DAY

Lilya woke to find Gregor in Kyrie's usual spot, which was nice in its way. She enjoyed having her nephew all to herself. At first. But breakfast was a spare affair, with only Waaseyaa—who gently suggested she call him Uncle—for company. And his attention was mostly taken up with Gregor, who was content to be spoon-fed his portion of porridge with berries.

"Are you missing your brother?" Waaseyaa asked.

Prodding at her breakfast, Lilya only shrugged.

He wasn't offended. "My brother has always been as near as he can be. I would be lonesome without him."

Lilya stole an envious peek. "So you're never lonely?"

He smiled a little. "Do you understand the difference between us? It is similar to the difference between you and Kyrie."

She shrugged again. "Lifespan."

"A tree's years are many. And so are mine." Waaseyaa focused on Gregor, as if not wanting to meet her gaze. "I am sometimes lonesome for those who have gone away. And for those who have ... gone before."

Lilya pushed her bowl away and let her chin drop onto folded arms. "Like who?"

"My children. Their mothers. My grandchildren. And their children in turn." His dark eyes were soft and sad. "And friends. Like you and your brother. I am glad you came to us, Lilya."

"Do we make you less lonely? Or *more* lonely because we'll go away later?"

Waaseyaa's smile was nice. "Both."

Lilya indicated Gregor. "You like children."

"I have raised many." With an impish smile he confessed, "I pretend to lose count, but it is a little joke between me and Zisa. He likes to remind me of their names."

"Are you all out of children?"

"Not entirely." Waaseyaa offered a cup of milk to Gregor. "But my youngest grew up and left Wardenclave several years ago."

"Ask Uncle Argent."

He searched her face. "Pardon?"

"For a crosser. Or a bunch of them, if you want a big family. This is a safe place, and you're nice. They'd like you for their papka."

Waaseyaa stared at her for so long, Lilya thought he didn't understand. But then his chin trembled. And he looked like he wanted to say yes, except he'd lost his voice. And Lilya knew she was right. Some of their crossers were going to be *so* happy here.

She asked, "Do you know where Kyrie went?"

"Yes." When she stared pointedly, he bowed his head. "Your

friend Sinder was injured last night, and your brother is the only other dragon in Wardenclave. Timur seemed to think having Kyrie close would be a comfort."

Lilya couldn't believe it. This was their first free day, and she and Kyrie had planned to chase the scent of strange flowers into the mountains. She opened her mouth to offer her help, but closed it. Mum and Timur were both healers, but Lilya's usefulness in that arena ended in the herb garden. She could weed and water. Stuff anyone could do.

"So they'll be busy all day." Lilya had no idea what to do instead.

Waaseyaa scooped up Gregor and beckoned for Lilya to follow. At the front door, she stepped into her boots and followed him outside. He circled to the back of his house, which was tucked close against a steep hill, and paused at the foot of a stairway. Every step was a slab, touched by lichen and moss, weathered by enough seasons to give the stairs a magical feel.

"Go to the top," he directed. "There is a door, and it is unlocked. Pay a visit."

"Whose house is up there?"

"Glint and Radiance are my closest neighbors." Waaseyaa propped Gregor on his hip. "She told me you found the Kith shelter and asked me to teach you the way to her door."

Lilya hesitated. Was it really all right to do something fun without Kyrie?

"Am I correct in assuming that Kyrie is capable of tracking you, should he return earlier than anticipated?"

She nodded sheepishly.

"Go on, then. And enjoy your visit." He lowered himself to the bottom step and turned loose a squirming Gregor. "We cannot anticipate your return until you find the courage to go."

Lilya bent to kiss Waaseyaa's cheek. "Thank you, Uncle," she whispered.

He laughed a little and waved her off.

With a spring in her step, Lilya hurried toward the unknown ... and felt quite daring on her own. Not at all like her usual self.

When Lilya arrived in a wide, sunny room at the back of the large house atop the hill, she was immediately surrounded by three floppy-eared Kith pups with curling golden fur. They were hardly more than babies and innocent in their curiosity. Lilya knelt and accepted their interest and adoration, giggling when their little tails whipped the way Ever's did when he was at his happiest.

"What a lovely surprise! I've been wanting to see you again!" Radiance sauntered over and joined the muddle on the floor. Hauling one of the big pups into her lap, she remarked, "You're used to Kith, I take it?"

"Mum is partnered. We've had two litters. Cubs. The feline kind." Lilya tugged silky ears and addressed the little ones, "But I like dogs just as much. Even better. What are your names, you rascally pups? What should I call you?"

Radiance laughed and handled the introductions. "These three are from Myth's latest litter, and they're here because Glint dotes. I'm holding Lyre, who is the only female. Her brothers are easy to tell apart. Lute is the blue-eyed one, and Lore's eyes are silver."

Lilya greeted them with her best manners.

With a widening smile, Radiance said, "Join me in a game, Lilya of Stately House?"

"I have all day." Lilya was glad to have found such a warm welcome.

"I want to play a little trick on my bondmate, and you must cooperate." Radiance leaned forward. "Let's see how long it takes Glint to realize who you are."

"I won't lie to a dog. I couldn't. And I wouldn't want to." Lilya softly added, "Then he wouldn't trust me."

"Not a lie," Radiance quickly assured. "Misdirection. He's easily distracted, especially when there are pups underfoot and pedigrees to puzzle together."

Having grown up with foxes, Lilya understood the appeal of such games. Ginkgo delighted in riddles and secret meanings and hiding things in plain sight. She found herself nodding, "What should I do?"

"We'll fudge the introduction, and you mustn't mention how you know Ever." Radiance waggled her eyebrows. "You *wanted* to meet Ever's grandsire, didn't you?"

That was true. She was curious if Glint Starmark was as nice as Ever's Da.

"You will not lie, and I will not lie. And I think in the end, when all is known, it'll make for a pleasant surprise." She flicked her fingers toward the ceiling. "Or so the stars do sing and say."

Lilya looked up. The entire ceiling had been decorated with a pattern of stars, both in silver and copper. She wanted to ask what Radiance meant about talking stars, but the lady eagerly went on.

"First, we'll lay a false trail!"

Which amounted to Radiance taking her into Denholm, the hidden city that most of the world didn't know anything about. They spent the entire morning exploring its spires and bridges and gardens and shops. Radiance bought a parcel of pastries for Glint. "His favorite, and he's ravenous for days after a long sleep."

She also insisted that Lilya choose new clothes.

"Scents," Radiance explained. "We'll give up the game before it's begun if you go in smelling like the nice boys who keep you close."

So their last stop was a bathhouse. The attendants were from various songbird clans, and they couldn't have been kinder or more flattering. By the time they were through with Lilya, her hair was wound into dozens of tight braids. It was just the sort of thing favored by wolves and battlers, and Lilya couldn't wait to send a picture to Mum.

"Thank you," she said, for what seemed like the hundredth time.

Radiance caught her hand and laced their fingers together. "If you want to repay me, spare the odd hour for Snow. She may have grumbled, but she's too often alone."

Which led to a quick side jaunt into another shop, where the lady purchased a bag filled with savory pastries. "Snow's favorite," she confided. "I'll smuggle them in later. While you and Glint are away."

"Me and him?" Lilya hadn't heard that part of the plan.

Radiance winked. "Just follow my lead."

They returned to the Starmark home, which was very nearly a mansion, and Lilya could see that this was the trail Glint was meant to pick up. If he knew she'd entered through the front door, he might not notice that she'd first arrived through the back.

"Wander as you wish, then return to Myth's pups," said Radiance. "Glint is awake and will return soon. I need to work quickly to get the rest ready."

Lilya poked her nose into a few of the rooms.

They were large and mostly empty, just like the many halls and pavilions of the Starmark compound in Keishi.

Lyre, Lute, and Lore were ecstatic to find her returned. Lilya may not have been a very good tracker, but she knew enough to lead the pups into a game of follow-the-leader that crisscrossed her old trail. And hopefully disguised the fact that she'd begun her visit here.

"Shh!" she warned the cubs. "Do as Radiance says."

Mere minutes later, an Amaranthine strode into the room. His step checked at the sight of her, and his confusion was obvious. But then he showed his palms. "Peace, girl-child. You have an interest in Kith?"

"I like them, yes." She felt as tongue-tied as he looked. "Yours are very nice, sir."

Hands still framing his peaceful intentions, Glint walked closer. He was tall and broad in the same way as Ever's Da, and his hair was the same kind of auburn—thick and wavy. But Glint's skin was a rich brown, his eyes were silver, and his manner was overly serious.

All three pups tumbled over each other in their eagerness to reach Glint, who lowered himself to the floor and gave them the attention they craved.

Lilya didn't know what to do, let alone what to say.

Then Radiance whisked into the room and beckoned to her. "Fear not, my angel. He is not so gruff or so growly once you know him. And know him, you shall!"

Glint turned to his bondmate. "Growly?" He sounded hurt. "Are you afraid of me, little angel?"

Lilya had often wondered if she'd ever earn a pack nickname. Was this hers?

"Come, angel. You may trust my mate. He knows this territory better than any." Lifting a cloth-wrapped bundle, she added, "I even prepared a picnic."

"Radiance?" Glint spared Lilya a glance, then demanded, "What new scheme is this?"

27

WOODLAND WANDER

At first, Lilya thought Radiance's plans were spoiled, but Lady Starmark must have liked to play these pranks a lot. She seemed the sort. A little like Uncle Argent's mother—mischief and teasing and tricks and fun. Glint knew she was up to something, but his stance indicated his willingness to go along with it.

Radiance wasn't at all flustered by her bondmate's remark. "I've taken a liking to this girl, and you will, too," she announced. "Be a dear and take Angel for a walk. Show her around. Give her reasons to feel at home with us. Myth's cubs are due for a romp. Bring them along."

Glint dipped his head and looked to Lilya. "Would you like that?"

"Is it really all right?"

He didn't quite smile, but his gaze was kind. "If you can match my pace, we can share a path."

That was worrisome. Lilya knew just how fast Amaranthine could move. "Will I need to run?"

"You will need to walk," he rejoined, taking the bundled lunch from Radiance.

Lyre, Lute, and Lore frisked around Glint as he aimed for the front door. With a quick wave to Radiance, who blew her a kiss, Lilya hurried after him.

They only followed the road for a little while before Glint veered off onto a much narrower trail that wended its way into the woods. There was just enough room for her to walk beside him, but Lilya let her steps lag. He was paying more attention to the pups than her, and she didn't want to interrupt. Plus, well ... she couldn't think of anything to say.

Glint paused. "Am I walking too quickly?"

"No, sir."

He held out his hand. "Not *sir*. Just Glint. Come, little angel. We can make this journey together."

Lilya slipped her hand into his and felt safe. Dogs were nice that way.

"Are you new to Denholm?" asked Glint.

"Today was my first day."

Only after she answered did it occur to her that he might think she meant she'd moved into the city. Wouldn't it be more natural to assume she was a camper? Oh. Not necessarily. Papka and Uncle Argent had done something new that was supposed to hide the truth of her ranking from all Amaranthine. Ever hadn't liked it.

Now, his grandsire didn't know anything and couldn't sense

Lilya's soul. Did he think she was an ordinary human girl? That idea was … nice.

She relaxed enough to look around.

Right away, she began to notice things that would interest the others. Flowers for Kyrie. Animal tracks for Ginkgo. Wardstones for Papka. Trail blazes for Timur. Berries for Mum. Lilya stopped to study the shrub, wanting to memorize the shape of its leaves. It was different than anything in Ginkgo's garden

What have you found?

"I don't know." Lilya touched the leaf's serrated edge. "Mum is a healer. She taught me about plants, but I don't know this one."

He snapped a twig and offered it to her. "Bring it to her. These woods will not miss a few sprigs or berries, and she will be glad to know you were thinking of her."

Which was true. And Ginkgo would certainly let her take pictures to send to Mum. "Thank you."

Glint hummed and ambled along. Slow enough to give her time to explore some more.

It was strange. Lilya knew exactly what interested every other member of her family, yet she had no idea about herself. Except that she *wasn't* really interested in flowers, tracking, wards, trailblazes, or healing herbs. She worried about it a lot. Was it all right to be eleven-and-a-half and not want anything?

Aunt Tsumiko said that not wanting for anything meant she already had everything she needed. A great blessing.

Mum was similarly unworried. Her big, strong hands had been as gentle as her tone when she cupped Lilya's face and promised, "Wanting will come, and when it does, you will know. And once you know what you want, you will seize it for yourself. This is good, yes?"

Lilya had dared to ask Mum what she'd wanted most.

Chin lifting proudly, she'd answered, "Your papka."

She'd thought Aunt Tsumiko would say Uncle Argent was the thing she'd wanted most, but her answer was different. In a nice-ish way. "I wanted Kyrie. More than anything. And he became the beginning of everything."

Lilya picked up a chunk of fallen bark and turned it over in her hands, admiring the pattern of lichen and the wiggling trails on its underside left by burrowing insects. And because she didn't think he'd mind, she asked, "What did you want to be when you grew up?"

Glint stopped walking. He gazed for a while at the pups, who were nosing around nearby, probably chasing rabbit trails. Finally, he said, "I wanted to be a good brother."

"I didn't know you were a brother."

"I rarely see the brother I loved before all else. But in the long-ago time of my boyhood, I could not imagine ever leaving his side." He smiled crookedly. "Surprising things happen in this life."

Lilya found herself nodding. "I like surprises."

"Then you are braver than I ever was. May you be twice as happy for it."

"You're happy, even without your brother?"

"Happiness is one of the best surprises life holds in store." With a confidential air, he said, "I find it in the strangest places."

Since he seemed to want her to ask, she did. "Like where?"

"Here," he said, tugging Lore's silken ear. "And here," he said, tapping her nose.

The compliment made Lilya happy. Maybe this was what Aunt Tsumiko meant when she talked about a double blessing.

"You are good company, little angel."

"You, too." And recalling the parcel Radiance packed along, Lilya asked, "Where is the best spot for a picnic?"

Glint hummed. "The *best*, you say?"

"Yes. Someplace you love to go."

He smiled, then pressed a finger to his lips. "Can you keep a secret?"

"I can."

Beckoning for her to follow, he strolled on. But every time he looked back, it was with that lurking, quirking smile. Like a promise of good things. Like a surprise in the making.

Lilya had expected Glint Starmark to be more ... important-ish. Which was silly, really. Because Papka was ordinary and Lapis was silly and Hisoka-sensei was nice. Even though most people expected them to be *extra* important-ish.

"What do you like best to do?" she asked.

Glint frowned in a thoughtful way. "I like ... possibilities, I suppose. I like helping things along. I want the things I love to continue."

Lilya didn't understand and said as much.

With a soft huff, Glint gruffly said, "I suppose you could say I like children."

"That's a *good* best." Lilya was thinking of all the crossers back home. "I like children, too."

She picked more leaves and a few of the tiny flowers. Enough that it was getting hard to hold everything. Glint noticed and took a book from his pocket.

"Press the leaves in here, between the pages," he offered. "That will keep them safe."

So before moving on, he helped her insert leaves and flower petals between the pages of a journal. She couldn't help but notice the penciled lines that filled every page. Along with the names of people and places.

He said, "These are some of those possibilities. People sometimes ask me to help them decide on a path for their future."

"I know about family trees."

"These are the pedigrees of some of the most promising young reavers who are visiting this summer." Glint traced one line and then another. "I introduced this girl's parents. And I knew her maternal grandparents, as well. A bright and beautiful line. May it continue to shine."

It sound like a prayer. Or possibly a blessing.

She knew about these kinds of contracts. She even knew that Glint was famous for them. And that Mum hated them. Did that mean Mum wouldn't like Glint? That would be a shame. Ever's grandsire was kind, even to someone he'd mistaken for an ordinary girl.

Glint carefully closed his book and slipped it into his pocket. "Almost there." Whistling for Lyre, Lute, and Lore, he took a turning and climbed a slope.

Using saplings as handholds, she scrambled after him.

All of the sudden, the ground leveled, leaving Lilya on a wide grassy ledge that backed up to a tall stone wall that glittered in the sunlight. Dozens—no, surely it was hundreds—of crystals were set into its surface. Their sweet harmonies pulled at her heart, making it beat a little faster, and the air smelled like flowers.

Kyrie would have loved it.

Glint sat with his back to the wall and stretched out his legs. "Will this do for a picnic, little angel?" he asked.

"Where are we?" She wanted to show this place to Kyrie if she could.

"A favorite spot. I like to come here."

"Is it a secret?"

"Rather a big one." Glint didn't seem worried though. "Are you hungry?"

They shared out the food, which included the pastries Radiance claimed were her bondmate's favorite. She'd even included an entire tray of special meatballs, which Glint allowed her to feed to the pups.

After every last crumb was gone, Lilya began to explore. First the wall, then the plants edging their little haven.

"Do not go far, and do not approach the gate." Glint offered a solemn wink. "Otherwise, I will be in trouble with my daughters."

So while he lazed in the sun with the pups, she tried to guess where she was. And how to get back. Kyrie had been smelling strange flowers, and this was probably the source. Knowing there were crystals involved as well, Kyrie would be able to track down this place even faster. Potent stones liked him nearly as much as the winds.

Just then, she caught the flash of something moving—quick and light—amidst the shady greenery. Ephemera? They were certainly Uncle Argent's favorite thing. Wouldn't it be wonderful to be able to report to him about a new variety that was native to this far-off place?

Lilya moved carefully and listened close. She was actually pretty good at stalking these little creatures, though Papka had gently pointed out that she also attracted them. Ephemera were part of the Amaranthine world, rarely seen by unendowed humans. Mum considered them pests, since they flitted about, fitting through every crack and crevice, nosing their way into food bins. Papka warded Stately House's grounds against wild ones, but Lilya liked them. They were small, harmless, and cute.

She softly clicked her tongue as she pushed aside leaves. Adding a coaxing song she and Kyrie had invented. Baby nonsense. And it attracted something, all right.

"Is that Japanese?" Glint was crouched right behind her.

Hushing him with a finger, she whispered, "Something's here."

His nostrils flared, and he nodded. "We do get some interesting creatures in these woods, but they mostly avoid humans."

"I *know* about Ephemera," she grumbled, lifting aside another clump of foliage.

Glint asked, "Is one of your parents a reaver, then?"

"Both." She felt a little foxy, not telling the whole truth. "I know it's hard to tell. Sorry about that."

With a perplexed expression, he looked between her and the bushes. "Not sure what to make of either of you."

Before another word could be spoken, something streaked into the open and wrapped itself around Lilya's neck. She started, but held very still, trusting Glint to deal with the threat if there was one. As she waited and watched him, Glint's eyes slowly widened, then went all misty.

"Child," he said softly. "Where do you find your courage?"

She reached up to tap his nose. "Here." And because she couldn't see what was tucked snugly around her neck, she asked, "What did we find?"

"Something ... new?" Glint's nostrils flared. "An unfamiliar scent. But I suppose it must be an Ephemera."

Lilya's fingers found silken scales. But also fur. "Who are you, please?" she murmured.

"Yes. We need a better look at you."

So saying, Glint gently worked a finger under the critter. When it tightened its hold, he lapsed into crooning, but Lilya didn't know much Old Amaranthine. Mostly just the lullaby that Uncle Argent used to sing. And a couple of endearments.

She tried one, letting it roll of her tongue, and wished her soul wasn't quite so locked away. Calming little ones was so much easier when they found her lovely.

"How many languages do you know?"

"Fluently?" she countered, not really wanting to admit to more than she already had. "Four, I guess. Bits and pieces of more."

Glint gave her a sidelong look. "You remind me of my best friend."

She knew he must mean Waaseyaa, but she doubted a newcomer to Denholm was meant to know about him. So she simply asked, "I do?"

"The first thing we ever did was learn each other's languages. He knows dozens." Finally disentangling their mystery creature, he murmured, "You were right. He does look a bit like a dragon."

Lilya's confusion must have shown.

"That is what you called him in my language." Glint repeated the endearment, then translated. "Little dragon."

The creature wasn't anything Lilya had seen before, which was amazing, considering how extensive Uncle Argent's collection was supposed to be. It wasn't very big—probably as long as Lilya's forearm, with most of its length only as thick as her thumb. Fine scales shimmered slightly, the soft gold of sunlight, but with a faint bloom of pink low on its chest, right above his first set of legs.

"Showy little thing." The critter twined around Glint's fingers, not exactly trying to escape, but not exactly happy to have been dislodged.

Lilya amended her original impression. The creature's first set of legs was its *only* set of legs. The rest of its body was more serpentine, with a mane of creamy yellow fur tapering towards the tip of its tail, which ended in a thorny spike.

"Poisonous?" she asked.

Glint shook his head. "Nothing toxic in his scent."

The little one lifted a narrow muzzle to sniff at the air. There was a prominent tuft of fur on top of his head, which flexed and fanned, almost like the crest on a cockatoo. Then he butted Glint's big knuckle and reached for Lilya with dainty claws.

Chuckling, Glint said, "You are the one he wants, and I see no harm in letting him have you."

Lilya reached back, and the little dragon grabbed her thumb, coiled around her wrist. His eyes were dark gold, without whites, and exhibiting the narrow pupils that were characteristic of both the Kith and the clans. But not Ephemera. "You really don't know what he is?"

"He is not native. Probably a stowaway." Jerking a thumb at the wall behind them, Glint said, "We receive guests and shipments from all over."

Tiny claws, soft as a kitten's, caught in Lilya's clothes and hair as the little one clambered swiftly up her arm. Once again, he settled around her neck. She couldn't see him, but she stroked his silken sides and tickled his fur. "He's heavier than he looks."

Glint smiled crookedly. "He is holding his own tail to stay in place."

"Would it be okay if I named him?"

"Are you asking to claim him?"

Lilya supposed she was. "Is that allowed?"

The little one rubbed his wedge-shaped head under her chin and offered a musical trill. Glint chuckled and pointed out, "He has his own opinion on the matter."

With another burble of high notes, the little dragon coiled just a bit tighter. And into the middle of Lilya's warm thoughts, she heard a single word. High and sweet, like a child's.

Mine.

Clearly unaware of this development, Glint said, "We are supposed to have a dragon somewhere hereabouts. I think we should try asking him."

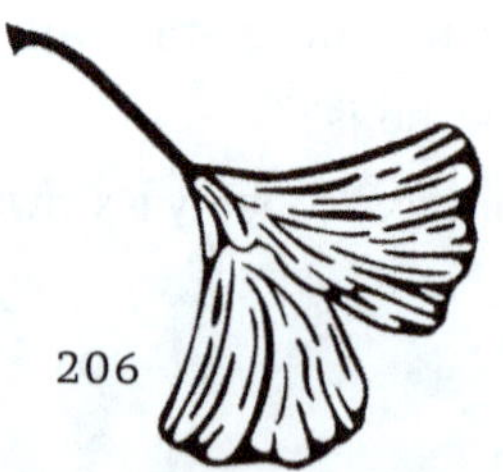

28
WINDOW DRESSING

Shortly after sunrise, Yulin sent Mikoto a message, letting him know that Glint was finally up and about. He could return home. But Mikoto couldn't bring himself to leave his post, seated on the floor at the foot of the bed where Timur had tucked Sinder in with Kyrie.

Maybe it was stubborn. Maybe he was selfish. But Mikoto wasn't leaving without something he could hang onto. "If you want to woo the wind to your side, all you really need is a dragon," he murmured. That's what Isla Ward had said. And that meant Sinder. They'd never hosted a single dragon in Wardenclave before this season, and it felt as if they were about to lose him. Mikoto had overheard enough to know that powerful people were upset.

There might be repercussions.

His to deal with as headman.

But right now, Mikoto couldn't have cared less about the wider world. He wasn't here in any official capacity. This was personal.

He picked a bit of meat from his handroll and fed it to Noble. Tending to the pup's needs. Teaching Noble to look to him.

Looking to. Looking after. Mikoto could see how they were linked. Had Glint meant to comfort him or to teach him how to lead?

With a muffled bump, Timur bustled through the door, barely able to see past the ungainly bundle in his arms. Ginkgo jumped up to help, so Mikoto stayed put. In such a small room, he'd only be in the way. Worse, Noble would get underfoot.

"What's all *this* for?" asked Ginkgo, who pulled free a couple of embroidered cushions.

"Just some things," Timur said shortly.

More textiles came to light—blankets, bed linens, towels, and a loomed rug. Even a few bolts of cloth that had the distinctive shimmer of Dimityblest workmanship. Expensive stuff. And all of it in shades of yellow.

"I'm sensing a theme here," remarked Ginkgo.

Timur's jaw worked. "I know what I'm doing."

"Well, I don't." Frowning slightly, the half-fox added, "But that doesn't mean I can't be useful. Boss me around, cuddle bud. I care about Damsel, too."

Right then, Fend sauntered through the open door, tail high enough for the tip to biff Timur across the face. The man's whole posture changed—chastened, apologetic. After a husky affirmative and a few lines in what sounded like Russian, Timur switched to Japanese and began to issue orders.

When Timur finally registered his presence, Mikoto silently offered his hands. Well, his hand. Noble was occupying the other.

Timur's expression softened, and he sighed. "Right. Sorry." He adjusted his posture to include them, and in a slower, deeper voice, he started over. "Ginkgo, help me with the windows. Mikoto, do you know how to tune your soul to another's? The way you would for tending?"

Mikoto's lips quirked. Then again, how would he know? "My mother is a cosset."

With visible relief, Timur urged, "Be inviting. He needs more than he's taken." He glanced at the door. "Also, I asked Colt Alpenglow to replenish my supplies. He'll be here soon. If I'm not back, will you explain things?"

"Where are you going?" Ginkgo asked.

"Lady Starmark is getting more of the things I need. I have to meet her. And make a call." In a weary voice, Timur added, "Sinder's partner wants regular updates."

"And by regular, he means hourly?"

Timur messed up his hair. "Can you blame him?"

"Sure, I can. I can also *call* him. Let me handle the updates." Ginkgo nodded at Mikoto. "We've got this. Fetch what you need from Radiance, then get your butt back here before he wakes up."

After some hasty instructions, Timur rushed out, Fend close on his heels.

Mikoto asked, "Can I help?"

"With this?" Ginkgo shook his head. "I'll work on the trimmings and trappings, you coax him into a better tending than my little brother can offer."

Mikoto turned Noble loose and stood to survey the larger of the room's two beds. Sinder lay on his back, clad in little more than bandages, with a sheet modestly folded at his waist. Kyrie had been tucked in with him. The boy had warbled himself to sleep, nestled against Sinder. Easing to a seat on the opposite side, Mikoto slipped his hand under Sinder's limp one. This was something Merl had worked on with him, providing an atmosphere that would promote healing. It wasn't exactly tending, and it worked better if there were crystals adding their resonance.

Sinder sighed, and he turned his face toward Mikoto.

A good start. On some level, the dragon was aware of him.

Mikoto's focus turned inward as he loosened the restraints enough to affect the ambiance inside the little house. Almost at once, there was a rustle of leaves as arms came around him from behind.

"Me, too?" coaxed Zisa. "You are usually so stingy."

"You are hardly wanting, brother of beacons." But Mikoto bussed the tree's cheek. "You can stay if you help keep Noble out of trouble."

"I will stay." Zisa retreated to the corner to coo and sing nonsense over Noble.

"He's right. You're good." Ginkgo flashed a smile over his shoulder. "I'd be more surprised if I didn't live with a battler who's also a healer. Timur's mother. Timur, too, for that matter. But I've never been this close to a cosset before. It's … nice."

Mikoto mumbled something grateful and kept his gaze fixed on the fine-boned hand in his. Sinder was cool to the touch. Was he cold?

Ginkgo worked quickly and confidently, removing panes and screens from every window. He carted them outside, muttering about dust and bugs. Returning with a bucket and rags, he wiped the frames and sills, then conferred briefly with Zisa. Ginkgo trotted off again, returning with a toolbox. Drawing a sigil in the air, he somehow managed to banish the sound of his hammer as he tacked layers of sheer fabric across the windows.

Soft yellow, it changed the quality of light in the room, drenching them in honeyed gold. Breezes slipped through the cloth, though, stirring his hair and tickling up his arms.

A shadow fell, and Mikoto wondered how he'd missed Merl's usual call. Zisa twirled to his side, leaning into the horse clansman and babbling something as he showed off Noble. Which clued in Mikoto. Ginkgo must have warded the bed, not himself.

Only when Merl joined him at the bedside did Mikoto register his footfalls, the subtle ripple of sleeves, the low hum of concern. And not for Sinder.

"May I?"

Mikoto grunted an affirmative.

His best friend touched his face, running the pad of his thumb under one eye. "Sleepless night?"

"Stuff happened."

"Nothing you cannot handle?"

"You know me," Mikoto gruffly countered. "He is the one who needs a healer."

Merl let his hand drop to Mikoto's shoulder as he considered the dragon. "This time, I am merely a courier. Sinder will benefit more from Timur's knowledge and your presence."

"About ... Lupe." Mikoto risked a glance into his best friend's face. "Did you know she is pregnant?"

"Priska brought her around for assessment after their long journey."

"Nothing was strange?"

"No. Such things are part of the natural course." Merl gently added, "She and her child are healthy, and Priska will make sure she takes care."

"You would know if Lupe wasn't human."

Merl blinked several times, inadvertently fluttering long lashes. "She is human," he cautiously confirmed. "Completely human. Ah. He is waking."

Mikoto looked down just as Sinder opened eyes made strange by whatever Timur had dosed him with. A slim ring of eerie green encircled pupils blown wide.

"Oh, dear. He has been thoroughly pollinated." Merl asked, "Do you need anything, Sinder?"

The dragon shook his head, then nodded. "You, with the soul. Come closer."

Mikoto saw no reason not to oblige, even though Merl's grip tightened. He shrugged out from under his hand and mumbled, "I am here."

"Closer," whined Sinder. "It's cold."

"I could bring a blanket."

But Sinder wouldn't let go. "Stay here. With me. In bed. That's the way. Won't bite. Don't tell Juuyu. He's so pissy about protocol. Please, stay."

"I will stay." Mikoto didn't mind. Why would he? He'd wanted to help.

"More, more, more," Sinder chanted, wriggling a hand under Mikoto's tunic and sighing against his shoulder. "Warm."

There were other voices around him, but Mikoto was having

trouble focusing on them. He was too busy listening for Sinder's next words.

Somebody swore, and Mikoto pulled the dragon closer, pretty sure he should be protecting Sinder. That's what Timur had said to do. Wasn't it?

Then a blanket settled over them, and a voice growled something about needing sleep anyhow. And Sinder crooned softly and whispered, "Sleep."

So Mikoto did.

29
TRADE WITH ME

A voice entered Mikoto's oblivion.

"Seriously, *wake up* now. Otherwise, I'll be in the deepest of deep sh– ... oh, there you are. Stars and storms, you weren't too deep to hear me. You might have gone on sleeping forever, you susceptible softie." Sinder patted his cheek. "Don't scare me like that."

Mikoto's only real thought was that he was more comfortable with Zisa's eyes than with Sinder's. Because Zisa's green was dappled with gold and alight with smiles, but Sinder's green was faceted like stones and flecked by fear.

"Nothing bad happened," Mikoto soothed, pulling him closer. "Are you still cold?"

"Are you listening?"

He grunted. "Timur will know what to do. Wait for Timur."

Sinder pointed.

Mikoto was startled to find Timur looming over them. "Which one of us is he angry with?" he whispered.

"Me. Very much me. You missed all the shouting. Bellows like a thunderclap, that one." And with a tweak to his nose, Sinder muttered, "Seriously, wake up."

Someone flicked Sinder's ear. The half-dragon boy. Kyrie.

"I only did it to make sure he's coming out of it," grumped Sinder.

Kyrie tapped his own nose, then touched Mikoto's. "He did not mean to use swaying words. Timur drugged him, which is only another kind of sway, but Sinder resisted. And he did not ask for anything bad. You did need sleep."

"Yes." Mikoto's attention strayed back to Timur, who was so tense. "I am fine. Nothing bad happened."

"It might have."

"All is well," insisted Kyrie, who seemed too young to be any kind of authority. To Mikoto, he said, "I will teach you when to listen and when to resist the words of dragons. And half-dragons."

"I would appreciate that," Mikoto murmured, more to be polite than anything. He was still a little hazy on what had happened.

"I owe you an apology," Sinder said meekly.

"I am fine. Truly." And because Mikoto thought the words were needed, "All is forgiven."

Ginkgo bustled past, loudly declaring, "You're making too big a fuss over a little mistake. Are we done here, Timur? I need to pack enough food for everyone."

"May I help?" asked Kyrie, scrambling off the bed to follow his brother.

Sinder bowed his head, hiding his face against Mikoto's chest. "You're *completely* vulnerable to dragons. No surprise. Most are. Working with Kyrie will help. I'll do what I can, too. Should be easy enough if you're here."

Unsure what else to say, Mikoto repeated, "I would appreciate that."

"You're very okay with this. The closeness, I mean." Sinder cleared his throat. "Can't say I've ever been cuddled by prey before."

"Most of my friends are Amaranthine." Easing away with a mumbled apology, he nearly fell off the bed.

Timur steadied him to his feet, still stern and serious. "I'm dosing you. Just to make sure there aren't any lingering effects."

Mikoto simply nodded.

Only after they strode out did Mikoto recall that he'd been waiting for Sinder. He turned back to the bed, then hurried to assist the dragon, who was gingerly making his way to his feet.

"May I ask you something?" checked Mikoto.

"Go for it."

"Do you know anything about wind?"

Sinder rolled his eyes. "I'm a dragon."

"So ... yes?"

"Yes. Lots and lots of *yes*. It's part of my heritage." He smiled faintly. "Not every tale of dragons is a warning, you know."

"I did not know." Mikoto balled his fists. "But I think I *need* to know. Maybe about dragons, but mostly about winds."

Sinder coaxed the story out of him. It didn't take long. There wasn't much to tell.

Tenma's mistake.

Zisa's hints.

Isla's speculations.

"You're wind-touched?" Sinder eyed him speculatively. "Can I have a look?"

"Yes." Mikoto ventured, "Wind-touched?"

"There are stories about people who win the wind's favor. Honestly, there are just as many stories about people who earn the wind's wrath. Those are pretty funny, but only because they're so farfetched. Imagine being chased by ominous clouds or a dust devil. Things like that." Sinder placed a hand on Mikoto's chest and muttered, "You, uhh … you might have to hold me up."

Mikoto quickly grasped him by the shoulders. "Do you want to lie back down?"

Sinder groaned. "Thanks, but no thanks. I'd rather not let Timur see how hard it is for me to move."

"He is your healer."

With a poke to Mikoto's chest, Sinder said, "We'll see if you feel the same way *after* you taste his tea."

Sliding his hands under the dragon's elbows for additional support, Mikoto waited for Sinder's assessment.

"While I'm getting personal, do you mind if I get *more* personal?" Sinder's eyes were closed, his brows furrowed.

"Go ahead."

"This woman. Lupe. Do you know where she is right now?"

"Yes. My house." Mikoto explained, "She is staying with one of my sisters."

"But do you know where she is *right now*," pressed Sinder.

"My house," Mikoto repeated.

"It's a big village. She could be anywhere."

Mikoto simply shook his head.

Sinder opened one eye. "You're sure that's where she is? How do you know?"

"I just … always have."

"Try to define the feeling for me. What senses are involved? Where is your certainty coming from?"

He'd never tried to explain it before.

"Can you hear her? Can you taste her?" Sinder asked patiently. "Oh, don't give me that look. The wind can carry more than scents."

Mikoto's grip tightened. "Wind."

"Hmm?" Sinder invited more without actually saying anything.

"There are always little swirls of wind, just puffs and breezes, that only happen when Lupe is close."

Sinder hummed again. "So you weren't setting off windchimes last summer, while she was elsewhere?"

It had been a lonely summer. Mikoto shook his head. "It was quiet."

"And these things—the noticing, the knowing, the scent and sense of elation. They feel like love to you?"

Mikoto's face heated. "Yes."

Sinder sighed and said, "Could I tell you a story? I think it'd help."

"All right."

Ginkgo returned right then. "Ready, Damsel?"

The dragon frowned. "Will Kyrie mind if Mikoto joined us?"

"Today is for you more than him."

Sinder looked to Mikoto. "Timur insisted we spend the rest of the day at one of your more secluded lakes. It's partly to keep a promise I made Kyrie, but I also need water and sunlight and Timur."

"His cosseting wouldn't hurt," said Ginkgo. "Sure. Let's kidnap the headman. And his little dog, too. Where'd that bit of fluff get to?"

Mikoto hesitated. "I do not want to intrude."

"Trade with me, in the way of friends." Sinder smiled wearily. "Share your strength, and I will share what I know. And if there's any truth to the tales, I should be able to help."

"Friends," Mikoto agreed, then scooped up Sinder to carry him out the door.

"I can walk!"

"Can you?" he challenged. He knew better. Knew how tired and lonely and scared this dragon was.

Sinder swore. And went limp. And whispered, "I promise, Mikoto. It's a good story."

"I believe you." He wryly asked, "Is that because you are a dragon?"

"That reminds me!" Sinder's eyes glinted, and he slyly urged, "Touch my nose."

30

THE FIRST RULE OF DRAGONS

Kyrie had been looking forward to the trip to the lake, but not quite like this.

He was used to sharing. His home. His room. His mother. His father. But when he'd spoken with Sinder about this trek and its purpose—rite of passage stuff—he'd sort of thought it would be less crowded.

Yet as he followed Ginkgo, who braced a crate on one shoulder, Kyrie couldn't honestly imagine asking anyone to leave.

Timur, who had taken charge.

Ginkgo, who was taking orders.

Mikoto, who was finally taking notice of the way the wind danced for him. In Kyrie's opinion, it was sort of like the way Fend made all sorts of little bids for Timur's attention. Such a friendly wind, but more focused than the ones Kyrie usually met in passing.

He'd never seen a wind *stay* before.

Kyrie was a part of this party, too. Kyrie, who had been taken along, even though the day would be less about the dragon half of his heritage and more about helping Sinder recover.

Making four. At least, four in speaking form. Kyrie cuddled Noble under his chin, since minding the puppy was his current contribution, freeing Mikoto's hands. The headman had a backpack and two big duffles, their straps crisscrossing his broad chest.

Four.

Kyrie knew as many stories of dragons as Mother could find, and in every story, fours were important. Did Sinder need things in fours? Was he more at ease now that he'd asked Mikoto along? Kyrie would need to watch for other examples.

Could numbers be inherent? Surely, they were only tradition. Kyrie didn't think he had an instinctual need for fours. Except ... he'd been raised by four parents. With enough siblings to make a dragon lord proud. Was some part of Kyrie more at ease because he longed for a harem?

Maybe he should ask Lapis the next time he visited. Or maybe Sinder would know.

"Hey, little bro." Ginkgo was looking back, his free hand extended.

Quickening his pace, Kyrie laced his fingers with his brother's.

"Something on your mind?"

Kyrie sifted through the many ideas niggling at him and selected something safe. "Can crossers tend?"

"Not sure. Never really tried. Not on purpose, anyhow."

His brother's face had gone suspiciously pink. Kyrie pressed, "Accidentally?"

"Me and Kel, I guess. We got a little tangled up once. His brothers kept a closer eye on us after that." Ginkgo admitted, "I was probably his first taste. Though the Elderboughs decided it didn't count."

"Because crossers do not count?"

"Nah. They counted me as a packmate, so I mattered as much as anyone. But we were too young to be messing around with stuff we didn't understand. Kind of like underage drinking."

"You did not try again?"

"Not ... exactly. Well, maybe. With Dad."

Kyrie wasn't sure why his brother wasn't sure.

"Mostly, I like to be on the receiving end of tending. Michael usually sets me up, but Mom's the absolute best." Ginkgo gave his hand a squeeze. "You getting curious about this stuff?"

He was curious about most stuff. But Kyrie understood the underlying question. "Not enough to get tangled."

"When you are, go to Michael."

"I will." And because Ginkgo would be honest, he asked, "Will I be in the way today?"

"Hardly. Or did you forget you're the whole reason for today."

Kyrie ventured, "Sinder is hurt. This is for his healing?"

"The outing will do him good. Being in truest form will do him good," Ginkgo allowed. "But Timur didn't redecorate Zisa's house just so we could get out of there. He probably would have kept his patient there if he could've. But Damsel insisted."

"For me?"

"For sure. And maybe for himself. You might be the only other dragon on the continent." Ginkgo's gaze tracked to Timur, who'd insisted that Sinder ride Fend. And further insisted on riding with him, to prevent him from sliding off the sleek cat. "Dragons are really social. Loners are rare, and Sinder *isn't* a loner. He's had it rough."

"We are here. He has us."

"We'll remind him of that." Ginkgo's smirk promised mischief. "Juuyu insisted."

On the mossy bank of a pretty little lake, Sinder sank to his knees before Kyrie and said, "Little cousin. I'm like you, and you're like me. Not the same, but alike. And I like that."

"Me, too," admitted Kyrie.

"Let's start simple. I'll revert, and you may make a full inspection." Sinder hesitated. "Will you be able to hear my voice in truest form?"

"I do not know." Kyrie looked to Ginkgo.

The half-fox shrugged. "I can sometimes hear Dad, but only if we're touching and he's trying. Not sure if blood ties are part of that or if clan ties are enough."

Kyrie really wished Ginkgo was more interested in the duality of his existence, but introspection had never been his strong point. Kyrie's most probing questions had never occurred to his big brother, who didn't even *have* a philosophy of life. Just a motto. *You're alive, so live.*

Some of their crossers really needed to hear that.

Like Ginkgo was giving them permission to exist.

"Guess we're here to find out." Sinder shrugged. "If not, no big deal. Save up your questions for after."

"I will," promised Kyrie.

"Two steps back," urged Sinder.

He sprang away and waited breathlessly.

With a solemn wink, Sinder transformed.

Even though he knew what to expect, Kyrie's heart squeezed as Sinder seemed to shatter like light through a prism, scattering before gathering into a new shape. Scales rippled outward, and curving claws flexed against soft soil.

Sinder's scales were like opal—translucent, even luminous, and sparked by colors that shifted in the gaining sun. Two white horns spiraled above a pale mane threaded with green. Familiar eyes glinted, clear and calculating, as sharp as any fox's.

Kyrie suddenly understood something about himself. He was drawn to Sinder's intelligence even more than his beauty. Here was another person—like Dad—who would speak the truth, even if it wasn't easy.

Needing to touch, knowing it was all right, Kyrie let his fingertips glide over silken scales. While the overall impression was certainly green, the vivid colors that marked Sinder's speaking form were only apparent on close inspection. Hidden facets. Ribbons under ice. Flowers in the snow.

Beautiful.

Achingly, flawlessly beautiful.

Until Kyrie's questing fingers snagged upon a rough patch.

Something had rubbed Sinder raw, marring his opalescent perfection. Kyrie hastened to Sinder's other side, standing ankle-deep in the lake in order to inspect his opposite flank.

Long scratches. Deep punctures. Trembling muscles.

"Please," Kyrie quavered, reached urgently for Timur. "Please, hurry. Please, help."

"I will," Timur answered absently. He was rummaging through the contents of the crate. "I will, and you'll help me. We'll help him together, yes?"

Ginkgo flicked Kyrie's ear then. A sharp reprimand. "Mind your words, little bro."

Kyrie clamped both hands over his mouth. Mortification set in. He hadn't meant to try to sway Timur.

"Hey, now," Ginkgo gruffly chided. "I'm glad you care so much about Damsel. Enough to forget yourself. It's not like you, but in a good way. You know?"

No, no. There was no excuse. Kyrie knew better.

"Are you even listening?" Ginkgo gently eased Kyrie's hands away from his mouth. "Be more careful with your words, but don't take them back. All I'll ask is that you take responsibility."

Kyrie followed his brother's gaze to Mikoto Reaver, who hovered uncertainly at the water's edge.

"What can I do to help?" asked Wardenclave's headman.

He'd influenced someone. Shame burned in Kyrie's eyes as he offered his hands. "I apologize," he whispered. "Please, forgive me?"

"For what?"

Mikoto's confusion only made it worse.

Ginkgo jumped in. "Seems you're susceptible to half-dragons, as well."

Sloshing back onto shore, Kyrie confessed, "I was careless with my words."

"You did no harm," Mikoto quickly assured. "I am here to help."

Kyrie adjusted his posture into something the headman was sure to understand, living as he did among dogs. "There is no excuse. I will own my mistake and learn from it."

Mikoto dropped to one knee and searched Kyrie's face from a closer quarter. "I believe I understand." Meeting his palms, the headman gravely said, "All is forgiven."

He offered a grateful smile.

"Truly, Kyrie." Mikoto slipped his hands into a supportive position. "Tell me how I can help. Sinder is my friend."

"And me?"

Mikoto pressed his thumbs gently into Kyrie's palms and asked, "Are you asking if we can be friends?"

"Let there be peace between us," he replied formally.

The headman bowed his head, firmed his grip, and smiled shyly. "You have made me glad our paths crossed."

Kyrie felt somehow … richer.

Mikoto looked at him with something akin to awe. Which seemed silly when there was a flawlessly beautiful dragon beside them. Mikoto said, "You are very colorful. Is that rude of me to say?"

"Crossers are born with clear indicators of their clan. My colors surely echo those of my Amaranthine parent." Kyrie quietly added, "Since my foster father is a fox, Sinder offered to teach me about my heritage."

"Then we are *both* curious about dragons."

Suddenly, Sinder's claws slipped between them, closing around Kyrie, lifting him away from Mikoto. Kyrie already knew that a dragon's digits were as dexterous as human fingers. Lapis had proven he could write while in truest form. And pull delicate sigils out of thin air.

Sinder gave Kyrie a light toss over his shoulder, then reached for Mikoto, ferrying him onto his back. He gave the young man more time to find his feet before letting go.

Mikoto's eyes were wide, and he seemed at a loss where to put his hands.

"The first rule of dragons," intoned Timur. "Once you spy the beast, do not look away. They deserve one's full attention. And they *know* themselves to be deserving. However, they like to be reminded. Compliments are encouraged."

Ginkgo propped his hands on his hips. "In other words, keep the center of attention where it belongs. Am I right, Damsel?"

Sinder arched his neck and warbled a series of notes that Kyrie could feel through his feet.

Timur directed, "You two check for any lingering splinters. They can get lost in the shift between forms. Meanwhile, I'll warm the ointments and balms. Dragons are fussy about temperatures."

A gusty huff.

Timur grinned. "I'm not criticizing. You should thank the four winds I'm not the kind of well-meaning fool who'd slather you in chilly glop."

Kyrie could feel Sinder's shudder.

"You're a fortunate dragon, indeed, to have gathered a

fellowship of four." Timur promised, "We'll take our time. We'll do this properly. We'll stir up your embers. We'll bank your fires."

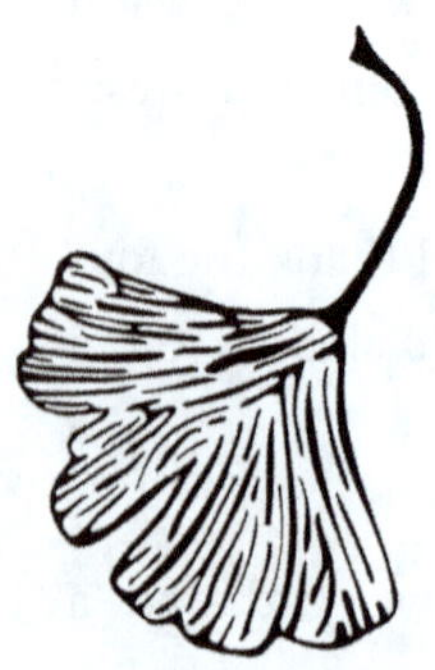

31

ULTERIOR MOTIVES

ow do you know so much about dragons?" asked Mikoto.

Timur fussed with the contents of the crate—mesh bags, labeled pouches, glass vials, and clay pots. "I worked with them and lived with them throughout my teen years. You *could* say dragons are my specialty."

"I have never heard of battlers who partner with dragons."

"You wouldn't have." Timur spared him a glance. "We're quite the secretive bunch. My own siblings don't know where I've been or what I did there."

An expert. "We are fortunate you happened to be here."

"Not really." Timur's next glance was amused. "I'm here by design. Or designs. Every time I turn around, I trip over an ulterior motive."

Mikoto plucked up a bundle of fringed fettle. "Should I be

worried? As headman, I mean?"

Timur glanced at Fend, whose lip curled. "Not as headman. But you struck your own bargain with Sinder, yes?"

"I did. You heard?"

"Not much, no details. But a dragon's pledge has a certain ring to it. Hard to miss."

Mikoto sighed. "You have confided in me. I would gladly offer a return of trust, but my secret is more of a mystery. In truth, I already confided in your sister."

"Lilya?"

He backed up. "The first time we met, Tenma somehow mistook me for an Amaranthine, Zisa began dropping little hints about Impressions. After that, Tenma placed a call to your sister Isla. She is very knowledgeable."

"Oh, she is at that. And did she sort your problem?"

Mikoto studied his hands, then glanced toward Sinder. "She said I needed a dragon."

"And did Sinder sort your problem?"

"Not yet." With a sigh, he admitted, "Nobody has said so outright, but I am beginning to think I fell in love with the wrong girl."

Timur went still, his gaze sad. "Tell me about it."

"May I help with these?" Indicating the warming pots and crushed herbs, Mikoto asked, "Do the standard proportions change for dragons?"

With a bemused look, Timur said, "For dragons, I double the mallow pulp, and I've added some lemongrass for Sinder, since he favors bright scents. You know the healing arts?"

Mikoto supposed it was his turn. "I have been working alongside a healer since I was old enough to sneak off. Merl Alpenglow is my best friend, my brother."

"Fandriel's foresight, you're a welcome surprise." Timur shoved several implements into Mikoto's hands. "Prep four full measures. Once he's had a wallow in the lake, daub it on thick and hot."

"Four measures," he confirmed, calmly lining up ingredients in the order he'd need them.

"Steady hands and a sweet soul. Looks like *I'm* the fortunate one, having you here." Timur scratched at the stubble on his chin. "If you can also handle Sinder's tending, I can focus on closing the smaller wounds with sigils. It's the dragon way."

Mikoto was eager to see that sort of treatment but only asked, "Is there an ideal temperature?"

Timur rattled off an acceptable range while poking through a small pouch on a cord around his neck. Withdrawing a pale green marble—undoubtedly a remnant—he addressed Sinder. "Ever had a wound warded? Medical barriers? Sigil-soothing?"

Sinder's claws gracefully formed a *no*. It hadn't even occurred to Mikoto that hand signs were an option. In hindsight, he felt silly.

"Advanced sigilcraft wrought upon the body." Timur held up the green marble. "This will anchor my sigils. You can keep it under your tongue, or you could swallow it. Either way, I'll need it back. Eventually."

There was a teasing light in Timur's eyes.

Sinder extended a clawed hand to accept the crystal. He held it up to catch the light, studying it for several long moments, then took it into his mouth.

"Did you swallow it?" asked Kyrie, sloshing around to peer

curiously into Sinder's face.

The dragon's brow ridges arched, but he kept his own counsel on the matter.

"Oh." Kyrie's giggle had a fluting quality.

"Did he say something?" asked Mikoto. He'd lived among the clans long enough to know that not all communication was verbal.

"No." The boy's smile was wide enough to reveal fangs. "But the stone did."

"Dragons have an especial affinity for both wind and stone, which are rudimentary for all forms of sigilcraft." Timur grappled out of his boots and sat on the lakeshore in order to roll up his pantlegs. Finding them already damp, he shucked off his breeches and dropped them over a nearby bush. "Amaranthine scholars believe sigilcraft originated with the dragon clans, but some of the lore suggests that they learned it from the stars."

Kyrie said, "Mother thinks that sometimes when the stories say *star*, they mean *angel*."

"Who can say for sure?" Timur pointed out, "The stars are listed among the lost clans of sky, so they could have been Impressions. But nobody seems to know for certain."

"Hisoka-sensei might," said Kyrie.

Timur grinned. "Cats do love their secrets. Which puts us right back at … who can say for sure? Because everybody—especially the illustrious Spokesperson—rarely says all they could."

Mikoto wasn't sure what to make of the teasing tone. His hesitation must have shown on his face, because Timur wagged a finger at him.

"Hisoka Twineshaft is an old friend of the family. My respect for him is second only to my fondness." Turning to Sinder, he made a shooing motion. "Into the water. You need a long soak before I work my magic."

Sinder slowly eased back on his haunches. Clearly, he was still in pain. Mikoto checked for—and found—the numbing agent to add to the ointment.

"Signal if the little fishes start to nibble," Timur drawled. "Kyrie can chase them away."

The dragon's response was to pick Timur up and toss him into the center of the lake, then slip sinuously after him, Kyrie clinging to his mane.

With a backdrop of calls and splashing, Mikoto turned his focus to the level of flames and the viscosity of the warming ointment. Familiar tasks. Soothing motions.

His thoughts returned to the Amaranthine Council.

In due course, probably for his induction ceremony, Wardenclave would likely play host to some of their members. Yulin probably already knew the schedule. And the guest list.

The council had expanded its membership to fifteen with the induction of Krail Basqwend during this past spring's celebration of the Emergence's anniversary. Krail spoke for a people remembered by humanity as the Naga, making him the first representative from one of the so-called fabled clans. Small and secluded, yet equal to every other voice.

Would someone someday speak for the trees? Or for any of the other lost clans?

Maybe if Hisoka Twineshaft really did show up in Wardenclave, Mikoto could ask. If anyone knew the answer, surely it was him.

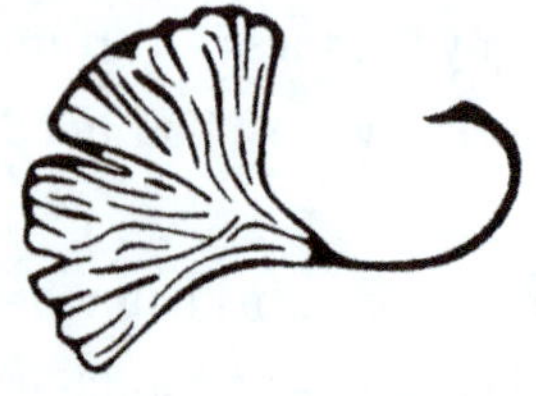

Mikoto studied the glowing lines that decorated Sinder's scales. They were a practical necessity, but Mikoto suspected that Timur had taken the time to be pretty about it. Even Kyrie had contributed a couple of sigils. They were small and simple, but they burned even brighter than Timur's. Was it because he was part dragon? Maybe his soul resonated more closely to Sinder's, and that made their bonds stronger.

Kinship.

"Will the sigils hold when he takes speaking form?" Mikoto asked.

"Should do." Timur stepped back to admire his handiwork. "You awake enough to try, Sinder?"

The dragon lifted the lid of one eye.

Mikoto studied his pupil and murmured, "Was my dose too strong?"

"Not even close." Timur came to stand beside Mikoto. "He's content."

They'd eased his pain, bound his wounds, and lavished his scales with fragrant oils, massaging it in until they were all redolent of spikenard. And throughout the whole process, Mikoto had encouraged the rapport that would allow Sinder to take from Mikoto's strength.

He'd also been keenly aware of Kyrie's presence—neatly contained, closely warded—and of Ginkgo's enjoyment. The half-fox sprawled on the grassy bank, hands behind his head, ankles crossed, and a half-smile on his face.

"I wouldn't budge either, if it weren't for all those fish we caught." Ginkgo sat up and rumpled his wild hair, then slapped his own cheeks. "You're easy to take, Mikoto. Thanks for the pick-me-up."

"My pleasure."

Ginkgo moved toward the jumble of kindling he'd collected in a shallow pit near the shore. "I'll get this going. Make with the shifting, Damsel. There's no way we're feeding you in truest form."

A moment later, Sinder was kneeling in the protective circle of Timur's arms.

"Steady on," said Timur.

"I'm feeling *much* better, thank you. Stop fussing. It's insulting."

But the burly battler didn't leave off until he'd checked every sigil still gleaming faintly against Sinder's pale skin. Once satisfied, he unceremoniously thrust a too-large hoodie over the dragon's head and went to help Ginkgo. "Food will do you good. You're hungry, yes?"

Sinder struggled to pull the length of his hair free of the hoodie and came to sit beside Mikoto. Kyrie hurried forward and quietly set to work braiding. Sinder sat still, head bowed, and let him.

Curiosity brought Noble sniffing, and Mikoto scooped up his puppy.

Timur returned, this time with a squat thermos. "Get this down. It's a restorative. It'll clear your head."

Sinder made no move to take it.

So Timur unscrewed the lid himself, releasing a burst of fragrant steam. Citrus and spice. Mikoto caught another, richer scent and knew that Timur had added a generous splash of liquor.

By the look of things, enough eggs had been added to make it more custard than liquid.

"Do you have a spoon?" asked Mikoto.

Kyrie immediately volunteered, "I can feed him."

Sinder grumbled, "Give a guy a chance. He pollinated me, you know."

"This will clear your head," Timur patiently repeated. And to Mikoto, "Make sure he takes every drop."

With a longsuffering sigh, Sinder took the thermos and took a long swallow. Then another. "Bauble my halls, Timur. You're better at this stuff than my own mother."

Timur simply tugged at Sinder's eyelids, checking his pupils, and ordered, "Every drop."

"Heard you the first time." But Sinder was smiling now. The restorative must have been especially potent. Mikoto had to wonder if Merl would want the recipe.

Not until the dose was more than half-downed did Sinder speak again, this time to Kyrie. "Did you save up any questions for me?"

"Yes." The boy came to sit before Sinder and Mikoto, creating a triangle that didn't exclude anyone. "Will I have a tail when I get older?"

Sinder took another mouthful while pondering his answer. "Horns and antlers and every kind of spike and ridge can come in as a dragon ages. But tails are different. If you were meant to have a tail, I think you would have been born with one."

Kyrie bounced right to his next question. Although it was more of a remark. "Lapis has wings."

"And ...?"

"You do not."

"Yet." Sinder kept his gaze fixed on the steam rising from his dose. "I aspire to wings."

"How old do you have to be?" asked Kyrie.

"While horns and the like come with age, wings are a matter of power. Given your markings, I think you can hold out some hope. Especially since you live in close proximity to so many potent souls." Sinder asked, "Haven't you ever undergone some kind of assessment?"

"There is no need. I am in good health." Kyrie glanced at Ginkgo before adding, "Dad does not approve of the kinds of tests people propose. Reavers are curious about crossers, but not for the right reasons."

Sinder made a derisive sound. "There's a big difference between learning more about your inheritances and being turned into a test subject."

"Yes. Exactly." Kyrie explained, "Many crossers are fostered at Stately House."

"I know. I've been there." Sinder smiled around another slow sip.

"But ...!" The boy plucked at his sleeve. "When?"

"You were still a baby. I only held you once." With a small shrug, he admitted, "I was all awkward, and your father was *so* looming. You liked my partner better."

Kyrie turned to ask Ginkgo, "You knew Sinder?"

"Nope. Not to speak to." The half-fox said, "Dad has his share of secrets. Usually, he's protecting somebody, so I try not to meddle. Much."

Mikoto would have liked to ask a few questions of his own, but this was Kyrie's moment. So he held his peace and held his puppy. Noble was happy enough to have so much of his attention.

"Are we related?" asked Kyrie. "Even a little?"

"Not closely, but that doesn't really matter. By the custom of our clans, we are dragons of the heights, and that makes us brothers."

"Lapis has a home on a mountain." Kyrie softly added, "I thought it was because he liked stars."

Sinder's brows arched. "Perhaps he does."

"I … do not think that is the reason."

"Males like Lapis and me are not granted mates. Or more accurately, we are not permitted to attract a dragoness, since the generations before ours have gathered harems for themselves." Sinder drank deeply and sighed. "One in five become fathers. They are the strongest and best, so their sons and daughters are also strong."

"You cannot have a family?"

Sinder shook his head. "My family is made up of a small brotherhood of celibate dragons." His voice took on a lilting quality. "The Fathers are strong, but the brothers are not weak. We are learners or healers or crafters or questers. We keep all our clans' stories and sing all our clans' songs."

"Lapis says he is a scholar."

"He is."

"Which are you?" Kyrie asked.

"Well, I'm not exactly a dragon of the heights anymore. That's where I'm *from*, but I have things to do." Sinder's claws tapped lightly against the side of the thermos. "This summer, I'm playing dangerous games with battlers."

"You *were*. You're done." Timur traded Sinder's empty thermos for a portion of fish.

"No. I have a job to do, and I'll finish my job."

Timur's tone held menace. "I won't let them turn you into a test subject."

"You can't stop me. You shouldn't try. This is way over your head." Sinder's gaze was unwavering. "If you want to help me, keep me on my feet. I don't want to delay the battalion's training."

Mikoto's interest levels spiked. "You are training battlers?"

Ginkgo snorted. "Timur, take pity and recruit the boy. He doesn't like being left out."

Timur's fury bled away. "Not my decision to make. None of them are, yes?"

"Yes." Sinder firmly redirected the conversation. "Kyrie, did you have another question for me? I see one shining in your eyes. It must be the last. For now. Because while I promised you answers, I promised Mikoto a story, and such things take time to tell."

"Is it a story of dragons?" asked Kyrie.

"A story straight out of the heights," Sinder promised.

The boy admitted, "I do have a question."

Sinder simply beckoned for it.

"Do we have any Kith?"

"Have you ever asked Lapis?" Sinder's expression turned inscrutable.

"I have," admitted the boy.

"What did he say?"

Kyrie mumbled, "That it is a great secret."

"I can say with considerable authority that he understated the matter." Leaning toward the boy, Sinder gravely said, "It is a *very* great secret."

32

BECKONTHRALL AND BETHIEL

In long ago days, when dragons were enemies of all the world, including one another, one brave soul departed from the valleys of war, climbing into the austere heights of a lonesome mountain. The place he settled wasn't good for hatching eggs or succoring young, but Persiflage Beckonthrall—for that was the brave soul's name—felt as if he'd become part of the sky. The nights were clear, and the stars were close. The winds came and went in a rush, and the stone at his feet sang with remnant songs."

Sinder had barely begun his story when Kyrie realized he knew it. Or at least a version of the tale. The one he'd learned from Mother was sprinkled with questions along the way, so that the listener could interact with the teller. A kind of catechism intended for young dragons. With every retelling, woven as it was with rote questions and answers, its lessons were reinforced.

A lonesome dragon.

A merciful angel.

A careless wish.

A miraculous outcome.

Kyrie could even guess why Sinder had chosen this particular story for Mikoto, and that made the telling even more interesting. Settling back, Kyrie watched Mikoto face. The story had drawn the headman in. That was only natural. Few could resist the words of a dragon.

"He labored alone, coaxing brilliant crystals from the mountain and gaining wisdom from their songs. Unwilling to waste stone, he fashioned a home for himself—columns and arches and chambers and halls. Over time, he embellished every room, lavishing them with all his attention and affection, for there was no one else with whom he could share them."

There was a lesson there. Mother always paused upon this point. Beauty upon beauty. Yet the loveliness echoed. A soul longed for more.

Sinder went on. "To fill the halls, Persiflage took to singing. He harmonized with the stones he'd collected, and he sang the ballads of beginnings. When he ran out of old lyrics, he began to compose new ones. Rich in detail. Threaded with longing. Captivating in unforeseen ways, for the very stars bent low to hear him.

"Only Persiflage did not realize it.

"Not until a summer's eve when a star drew near and spoke. He gave the name Bethiel and asked, 'Why do you sigh?'"

"Wait a sec," interrupted Ginkgo. "I thought Bethiel was one of the seven angels. Or was it ten?"

"Who can say how many angels there might be?" Kyrie was quoting his mother, who knew a lot about such things. "But yes, he is commonly numbered among the angels who visited the Amaranthine clans in times past."

"Like Soriel of the Dawning," interjected Mikoto. "And Cadmiel of the Echoing Song."

Timur said, "Bethiel is a frequent figure in the lore of avian clans and dragon clans. Those who fly and those who live in high places."

"Yes, this is *that* Bethiel," acknowledge Sinder. "And if you want tales of Cadmiel or Auriel or Fandriel, we can trade tales on other nights. But Beckonthrall met Bethiel. And that's when his story gets … interesting."

"Please, continue," urged Kyrie. Sinder's storytelling was even better than Mother's, for his voice changed with each part, giving personality to the players. Solemn and sonorous for the lonesome dragon. Warm and winsome for his angelic visitor.

Sinder composed himself and took up the narrative.

"'Why do you sigh?' asked Bethiel 'Why are there tears upon your face?'

"'I am unloved,' complained Persiflage.

"'Not so. You are greatly loved.'

"The dragon supposed that Bethiel was referring to the Maker's unwavering ways. But that was little comfort. He clarified. 'I am alone.'

"'Not so,' repeated the angel. 'Your companions are as constant as they are inconstant.'

"But Persiflage knew every handsbreadth of his home. He began to suspect that this was no star and no angel, but a trickster come to mock his pain. 'Am I blind, then?'

"'Not so,' Bethiel said yet again. 'If anything, you are deaf.'

"'What am I meant to hear?'

"The angel held a finger to his lips, and Persiflage fell silent. For long moments, he listened. But the only sound was the wind sighing through empty halls. Nothing had changed.

"Not wanting to seem ungrateful, Persiflage opened his arms and said, 'You are here, and for that I am grateful. Come inside and enjoy what hospitality I can offer.'

"'Answer me this,' countered Bethiel. 'Why do you—a dragon— take humanity's guise?'

"Persiflage thought the question odd, but he craved conversation. 'I like this form, this size, this voice. Is it not the same for you, starry one?'

"Bethiel asked, 'Who taught you this form?'

"'My father.'

"'And did you wish to learn?'

"'Very much.' Persiflage smiled. 'I wanted to be like him. To become his companion.'

"'Was it easy?'

"'Not at first, but his words helped me. He guided me into his arms, which is where I wanted to be.'

"'Well said, dragon.' And Bethiel turned to speak to empty air. 'He can teach you the way.'

"'Who is there?' Persiflage asked softly.

"Touching a finger to his lips, the angel urged, 'Listen.'

"Again, the dragon tried to hear. Again, he shook his head. 'My voice, your voice, and the whistle of a lonesome wind among the stones.'

"Bethiel said, 'Your songs are pleasing, and your prayers have been heard. An answer is all around you. Woo the wind to your side.'"

Mikoto blurted, "What?"

Sinder arched his brows. "What?"

The headman's voice was barely a mumble. "That is what Timur's sister said, too."

"Naturally. It's in *all* the stories." Sinder waved his hands. "Beckonthrall's story is the first and most famous example. He's become a byword. Along the lines of 'be careful what you wish for.' Because in his enthusiasm, he wooed all four winds at once, which resulted in quite the tempest."

"Four brides," said Kyrie. "East, west, north, and south."

Ginkgo whistled softly and eyed Mikoto speculatively.

Sinder shrugged and skipped ahead. "It's said that the Waning never touched Beckonthrall's household. His children arrived in every color known to creation. His sons became our fathers, and his daughters the jewels of the harems they graced."

Mikoto looked lost. "Are you trying to say that I was never in love with Lupe?"

"I'm not sure. I can't exactly relate." Sinder frowned. "I'm suggesting that your love—while earnest and true and good—may have been a teensy bit off target."

"Because I am actually in love with the wind."

"Not the wind, in the broadest, general sense. A wind. Singular. A south wind, I think."

Kyrie helpfully added, "She is a summer breeze."

Mikoto brushed absently at his hair.

"I'd need to chat with Miss Lupe to be certain, but it sounds as if she and that breeze became entangled somewhere along the way." Sinder fanned his fingers wide. "And by your tale, I'm willing to bet that on the day you nearly drowned, that wind is the one who saved you."

"Breath is life," murmured Kyrie. "She cleared your lungs."

"Leaving a bit of shine behind." Ginkgo slyly asked, "Does that count as a claim?"

"There's a word for it in our stories." Sinder waited until Mikoto met his gaze. "Mikoto, I think you're wind-kissed."

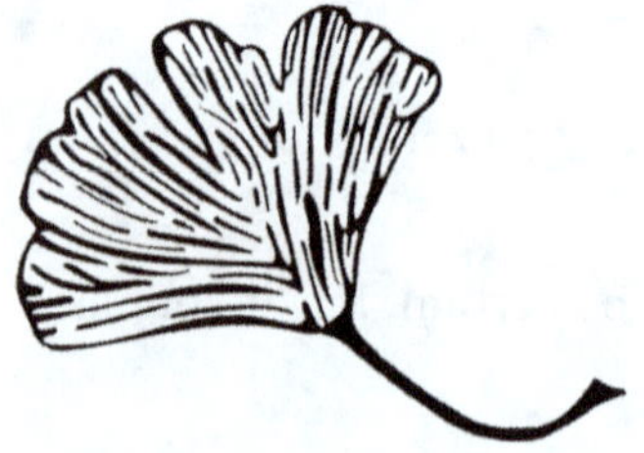

33

STRATEGIC ALLIANCES

lint held Lilya's hand all the way back to his home, chatting about ordinary things the whole time. The strawberry harvest. A new bakery in Denholm. The morrow's gathering of clover blossoms by the Alpenglow healers. A visiting delegation from the turtle clans. But their conversation always cycled back to the fuzzy creature that rode upon Lilya's shoulders, head tucked up under her chin.

"Have you given thought to a name?"

Lilya hummed. "Are you sure he's a boy?"

"Quite sure."

She asked, "Is it all right for *me* to name him? Names are important."

"Very important," Glint agreed. "He will carry it all his days, and its story will be yours to tell."

"I've never named anyone before."

Glint gave her hand a small squeeze. "There is no hurry."

But Lilya thought maybe there was. Once people started making suggestions, it would only become harder to decide. And if Kyrie proposed something, she knew she'd give in. So she asked, "How do you say *friend* in Old Amaranthine?"

With a faint smile, Glint pronounced something with too many syllables and sharp edges.

"That doesn't sound very friendly."

He chuckled. "The old words aren't in a hurry to make their point."

"Is there a word that means ... *yellow flower*?"

Glint hummed and offered a few, but none of the words he suggested sounded right.

"How about *sigil*?"

Patiently, he translated all of her suggestions.

Lilya reached out to tug at the hem of his tunic. "Is there a word for this?"

"Embroidery?" Glint almost laughed and offered another complicated phrase.

"This embroidery is prettier than anything I've seen, but it doesn't make a very pretty name."

"Thank you." He searched her face and gently asked, "May I give you a word that is close to your suggestion?"

Lilya supposed they were in this together. "Yes, please."

"Ribbon is *rifflet*."

"Oooh," she breathed. "I like that."

"I do, too." Chuffing Lilya's passenger under his chin, Glint asked, "Do you approve, little dragon?"

He answered with a light trill.

Lilya couldn't help wondering how much he understood. "May I call you Rifflet?" she asked.

Once again, the sweet voice touched her mind. To her amazement, he spoke her name. Or her borrowed one. *Angel.*

She almost corrected him, but she remembered just in time that Radiance wanted her to hide her identity for as long as possible.

At the Starmark residence, Glint urged her to follow the three pups inside. Lyre, Lute, and Lore tumbled through the door, vanishing toward the back of the house. Radiance didn't appear to be home, and Glint peered thoughtfully out the window.

Eventually, he asked, "Will you stay? Radiance will want to meet Rifflet, and I have had a message sent. You see, I have been out of pocket for several days, so I cannot say for certain where our dragon might be. But I know who to ask."

"I'll stay," she agreed.

Glint poured two glasses of chilled tea and even offered a bit in a saucer to Rifflet. Then he led Lilya to a sort of side room. It was a little like an alcove in that it was curtained off instead of walled off. But *alcove* sounded small, and Glint's office—for that's what it must be—was spacious.

Ducking past heavily embroidered drapes that sang with sigilcraft, Lilya peered around an area that was both orderly and cluttered at the same time.

"Yulin will be here shortly," said Glint. He'd gone to a table that was easily as large as the one in Stately House's dining room. Only instead of using it to feed crossers, Glint had turned it into his desk. Ledgers lay in rows along one side, and Lilya had never seen books so big. Their pages were taller than the communiques that Papka collected. Wider, too, since she could see that many of them folded out.

By their thickness and shimmer, she guessed the paper was Dimityblest-made. And well warded. Lilya might not be able to create sigils, but she could feel them just fine.

Glint gently unfolded one of the pages and traced his finger along a line.

These must be the thrice-dratted pedigrees. Mum might not like them, but Lilya suspected she might be impressed by them. It was like standing in a war room, surrounded by dozens of strategies. Oversized family trees were tacked to the walls, some with bits of colored thread linking them to the branches of other trees.

Was Glint matchmaking between dynasties? Did that mean Lilya's name was here somewhere? She began searching the walls for familiar names.

While she explored, a light call came from the front of the house. A moment later, an Amaranthine whisked in, his arms filled with packets.

"These are the last of them, Glint." The Amaranthine wearing the Dimityblest crest smiled at the sight of her. "Hello, dear child."

"So many?" Glint grumbled, taking the stack. "Thanks, Yulin. And this is Angel."

The moth clansmen offered his hands to Lilya. "Scribe Yulin Dimityblest. Radiance mentioned a new friend."

His mild expression was hard to read, but his slow wink was reassuring. This person knew exactly who she was. And that Radiance was playing games.

Lilya placed her hands on his and skipped her half of the

introduction. Instead, she admitted, "You're my first moth."

This was the sort of thing Amaranthine enjoyed learning. Indeed, Yulin's whole countenance brightened. "I would be honored to indulge your curiosity in any detail."

Just then, Rifflet uncurled enough to *peep*.

Yulin's soft eyes widened. "Well, hello to you, as well."

"Ever seen the like?" Glint's eyebrows lifted. "Say, Yulin, do you have your progenitor's knack?"

Cool, dry hands gently enfolded Lilya's as Yulin explained, "I am the son of Linlu Dimityblest, one of Wardenclave's founders. The *knack* Glint is referring to is his sensitivity. Linlu has always been attuned to Impressions. He hears voices where others do not."

Lilya tried to fit that into a context she was familiar with. "Like a crystal adept?"

Yulin's lips curved upward. "Those who work with crystals are often able to hear their remnant song. They hear the echoes of impressions long gone. My progenitor hears the voices of impressions who have remained near."

Glint cleared his throat. "Even among Amaranthine, hearing voices is considered … odd."

"Yes," Yulin agreed easily. "Those without ears to hear remain skeptical."

Lilya wondered if he meant that people thought his dad was crazy. Didn't Amaranthine understand about faith? Aunt Tsumiko would have called it hope in unseen things. And it was silly not to believe in imps. She'd chatted with Zisa every day since their arrival, and *he* was technically an Impression. But saying as much would give away who she was. Something else worried her, though. "You think Rifflet might be an imp?"

"Ah." Yulin presented a fingertip for Rifflet's inspection. "I cannot think of a more plausible explanation as to why I have never heard of this creature."

Lilya said, "He may have come from somewhere far away."

"I may not be well-traveled, but I am exceptionally well-read." Yulin's eyes danced with interest. "Which means your Rifflet is either an imp, a clan secret, or … both."

"Could he be Kith?" she asked.

"Unlikely," said Glint. "Our Kith always look the same as we do in truest form, but this little one only bears a passing resemblance to members of the dragon clans."

"And Kith are sentient," added Yulin. "They have a voice."

Lilya decided to speak up. "Rifflet *has* a voice."

"You heard something?" Glint came over, bending down to study their mystery critter. "I hear nothing."

"Would we?" posed Yulin. "Rifflet is neither a dog nor a moth."

"But why would Angel hear a voice."

"She could belong to one of the attuned classifications—candor, fellow, reach. Rare, but not without precedence. The trait does crop up from time to time in most bloodlines." Yulin shrugged. "Or it could be an impish or ephemeral quirk, making Rifflet himself the cause."

"Which brings us back around to our original plan. Where is that young dragon who has been … err … here?"

Glint's abrupt self-censoring made Lilya feel a little better about keeping her own secrets.

"Out of contact, for the moment. I can arrange for them to

meet tomorrow."

"Could we do that here?" Glint bargained. "I want to hear what he has to say."

Yulin clasped his hands together, giving a significant look to the piles of paperwork. "Are you certain you have the time? Dichotomy Day is near and nearer."

"We do not often see new things," protested Glint.

Inclining his head, Yulin conceded. "Perhaps if you made significant headway tonight …?"

Sensing an end to her visit, Lilya raised her hand. "May I have the flowers and leaves I collected for Mum?"

Glint straightened and patted his pocket, bringing out the small journal. "Nearly forgot," he muttered. "What would make these safe to travel?"

Yulin jumped in. "Allow me."

He located a box with delicate slips of paper, thin and veined with copper threads. He showed Lilya how to fold them into a protective sleeve. Each of her specimens was carefully preserved, then bundled into an envelope he created from a fold of heavy paper.

"If you plan to collect more over the summer, I can show you how to make a press," Yulin offered. "Perhaps tomorrow."

"You'll be here tomorrow?" she asked.

His laugh rustled pleasantly. "How could I resist? We do not often see new things."

Lilya riffled through Glint's journal, making certain she hadn't left any of her botanicals behind. Again, the names and charts caught her attention, and she slowed to read.

"Hoping to find a good match?" Yulin asked mildly.

"Not today." She closed the book and offered it to him. "Are all these charts part of your job, too?"

"No, no." With a wave to the walls and piles, Yulin said, "This is Glint's labor of love. My own affections bind me to the headman."

He must mean Mikoto.

Glint snorted. "You cannot deny an interest, Yulin. You have been hovering like the proverbial moth to a flame these past weeks, all because the current headman is at that age, and more than half of these piles are offers for him."

"We are *all* interested in his future. And who will share it."

Lilya was curious. "You're going to arrange his marriage?"

"Not ... precisely." Glint rubbed at the back of his neck. "I do try to bring strong bloodlines together. Usually indirectly. Our summer courses have exceptionally high standards. For those wanting a match, there are no poor choices."

She walked over to one of the trees on the wall. "Did you make this match?" she asked, tracing a green thread to another chart farther along. "Did you decide they should meet?"

"Yes." Glint patiently explained, "This young man wished to leave home and see new things. His academic mentors agreed that his aptitudes and interests would make him an excellent addition to the isolated enclave that this young lady calls home. When I sent them a progeny projection, they agreed to meet, even though neither can speak the others' language."

"Brave souls," murmured Yulin.

"What if they don't get along?" asked Lilya.

Glint rubbed his chin. "What if they do?"

She couldn't help smiling. He reminded her of Ever, who always believed the best of everyone and everything.

"Is everyone willing to do whatever you say if it means their children will be strong?"

"Hardly," Glint retorted. But then he scanned his desk and gruffly corrected himself. "Usually."

Yulin opened one of the huge ledgers on the table and began paging through. "Most young reavers these days are seeking an *advantageous* match."

"In recent years, there has been a trend toward career over family, but in another generation or two, love matches may be in vogue again." Glint tried to turn the tables. "Do you want me to look to your future, Angel?"

"Probably not." Lilya knew from her older sisters' experience that his offhand offer was beyond generous. "I'm only eleven."

Glint waved that off. "Traditionally, the offers begin when a child turns twelve. And many parents and patrons begin discussing options earlier. Especially those hoping to improve their ranking, because those with exceptional pedigrees are usually swamped with offers."

Lilya surveyed the table and felt a little sick. "Can I avoid this?"

"Easily," said Glint, who was kind enough not to doubt her ability to bring in mountains of offers. "It happens all the time. Make lots of friends. Watch for someone with similar plans or interests. See if they want to contract with you."

That did sound easy. Except Lilya knew it wasn't. Darya had turned down hundreds of men. *Hundreds.* And Isla had it twice as bad because she was as fussy as she was famous.

Glint was still talking, and one phrase jumped out to Lilya. "An early contract is the answer."

"Why?"

Yulin beckoned to her, saying, "Properly filed contracts with matrimonial exclusivity clauses make it clear to everyone that no further proposals will be entertained." At her puzzled expression, he simplified. "The bidding stops."

That sounded good to Lilya. Pick and be done.

Shuffling through one of his piles, Glint continued. "On Dichotomy Day, many of our oldest campers—those ranging from sixteen to eighteen—will formalize their intentions by filing contracts with Dimityblest scribes."

Oh, she knew all about contracts and Dichotomy Day. Lilya wasn't about to mention that they toasted marshmallows over them.

Yulin's finger traced lightly along a neat diagram. She was used to reading genealogical charts, partly because Kyrie found them fascinating. Perhaps because his was sort of … lost. Nobody talked about his bloodline, but every person born had one. This particular pedigree was easier to read than most because it was hers.

Beside her name, someone had added a neat notation in copper ink—**BEACON**. And in pencil, someone else had scrawled a list of names. She was confused at first, until she realized that these people were probably meant as possible husbands for her. More than half of the names were Amaranthine.

Yulin quietly said, "Glint does not always choose. He arranges the groups and the housing to ensure that compatible people will have the chance to meet."

Lilya read the list again. Mikoto was on it. So was Uncle Waaseyaa. Lord Mossberne. Suuzu Farroost. And even Hisoka

Twineshaft. Worst of all was the last name. She really, *really* wanted to talk to Ginkgo.

A hand on her shoulder brought her attention up to Yulin's gentle expression. "What kind of future will you choose for yourself?"

Now, that was interesting. Because the wife of a member of the Amaranthine Council would have a very different life than the wife of a tree-kin. And her choice could affect her lifespan. If she took an Amaranthine husband, could she stay with Kyrie?

Yulin quietly closed the book.

Lilya carefully shifted into a grateful posture. "I don't know yet."

"Plenty of time," Glint murmured distractedly. "Might try a preservationist or an ephemerologist, should wee Rifflet refuse to be parted with you. Or there's a bloodline with close ties to dragons. One of our instructors carries on the tradition. He's the settling sort. Good father."

Did he mean Timur? Lilya glanced at Yulin. The scribe's lurking smile and slow wink confirmed it. Her own brother.

"You remind me of … him." Glint's head snapped up, and he goggled at her. "Of all things! It is *you*, and here I have been …! Lilya?"

The jig was up. "Yes."

"Did you know, Yulin? And where is my Radiance?"

Glint grumbled and sniffed and apologized and asked to start over. But it was too late. She didn't want to go back to being a name and rank in Glint's files.

No, she'd made up her mind. On the matter of husbands, she *would* choose for herself. And the sooner the better. If she could secure an early contract—this summer—bids for the world's newest beacon would end before they started.

34
THE MOST IMPORTANT THING

Iisa took one look at Rifflet and dropped to his knees before Lilya. "I love you already!"

While he tried to discover what kinds of things the little creature would eat, Lilya watched the moonrise from Waaseyaa's front step. And waited.

Glint and Radiance had escorted her back together, fussing at each other in fond ways the whole while. After extracting a promise that she'd keep tomorrow's appointment, Glint gruffly vowed to not to meddle ... much. But he might know of a boy in France who was an up-and-coming ward. And how did she feel about tree-kin in a hypothetical sense?

Lilya leaned into Waaseyaa, whose arms must be strong to have been cradling Gregor for so long. He was a nice man. She liked him and Zisa both. But marrying Waaseyaa would mean staying here. It might be different if she happened to fall in love, but there wasn't time for that.

"What's the most important thing?" she asked.

Waaseyaa hummed.

Maybe there was no answer. Kyrie would have known a better way to ask.

But Waaseyaa said, "Listening, I think."

That sounded very wise. Almost like something Aunt Tsumiko would say.

"Here they come," announced Zisa.

Waaseyaa murmured, "He always knows."

"Because he's a good listener?"

His twin nodded. "Zisa pays better attention than people realize."

That made her want to pay closer attention. As Zisa hurried to greet his guests, it occurred to Lilya that she usually only paid close attention to Kyrie. Could watching someone else be considered part of growing up?

And then Ginkgo was crouched in front of her. "New scarf?" he asked lightly.

"His name's Rifflet."

Lilya held up her arms for a hug, and Ginkgo immediately gathered her close. "What's wrong, little girl?"

"My turn," she whispered.

They were magic words. Like a pact, they were so important. She saved them up for emergencies, for those times when she needed to have Ginkgo all to herself.

Without letting go, Ginkgo turned his body. "Kyrie, watch over Gregor until we get back."

"Gladly."

Lilya looked up into Kyrie's face. He spared Rifflet a quizzical glance, but simply asked, "Later?"

"Yes, please."

Ginkgo scooped her up and sprang away—strong and sure and straight into mischief. "I know where the camp's kitchen hides their ice cream. How about a midnight snack?"

"It's not midnight."

"Might be if we hang around long enough." Ginkgo sprang playfully from one rock to the next along the edge of the song circle.

Lilya tightened her hold around Ginkgo's neck. Her family was everything she cared about and the only thing she'd ever wanted. Even if she grew up, she couldn't imagine that part ever changing. But maybe that just meant that she wasn't grown up yet. Being eleven was a bigger problem than she'd ever suspected.

Ginkgo carried her to the kitchen behind the dining hall and worked a little foxish magic. He never used a door if there was a window available. Scooping two bowls of butter brickle, he sprinkled their dishes liberally with pecans. They found seats at one of the long tables in the empty dining hall.

"Ready when you are," Ginkgo said.

"Remember when Darya needed to get married?"

"Sure. Won't soon forget it, either." He eyed her. "I'm surprised *you* remember. You were pretty little. Six, going on seven."

"It was bad."

"No question it was a hassle. Everyone got so worked up, myself included. But I wouldn't say it was *bad*."

"Darya cried for a week before she left."

"So did I." Ginkgo offered a sheepish smile. "It was hard letting her go like that. But your sister wasn't crying because she didn't want to go. She couldn't help it. She knew how much she was going to miss us."

"Not just that. All the heralds. All the applicants."

"Oh, that. Yeah, that was no fun." He poked at his ice cream. "Between you and me, Darya's always been too smart for her own good. So she saw through all those hopeful offers. None of those young men did anything wrong, but they weren't doing right by Darya. She needed more than they knew how to give."

"How did she find somebody?"

"Didn't you hear that part?" Ginkgo chuckled. "It was Hisoka, of course. He came one day with a packet. Only it wasn't the usual kind. Just a letter and a snapshot. But it was enough."

"She didn't know him?" That surprised Lilya. She didn't remember that detail.

"No. Which was why your Uncle Argent escorted her personally. If the guy was any kind of unworthy, my dad would have brought Darya straight back."

Lilya asked, "Why can't we talk to her?"

"Sometimes, enclaves have strict rules. They need to stay a secret." With a wave in the direction of Waaseyaa's house, he blandly added, "Darya's husband has a twin. Y'know?"

Tricky foxes had their way of saying just enough without saying anything.

She whispered, "I saw a list."

"Yeah? What kind of list?"

"People that Glint Starmark thinks I might marry."

Rather than being shocked, Ginkgo said, "Best not tell Dad.

He's edgy enough about Isla. For that matter, don't tell your mum. She might turn it into a hit list."

Lilya knew he was mostly joking, but she couldn't quite smile. "Ginkgo?"

"Hmm?"

"Your name was on the list."

"No kidding?" He eyed her thoughtfully. "That gonna make things awkward for us?"

"I don't want to marry you."

Ginkgo chuckled. "Thank you for letting me down gently."

"But I love you almost more than anybody."

"I know, little girl." His smile was the same as always. "Family's nice that way."

She sighed.

"Don't worry too much about that stuff. If nobody's good enough, Hisoka will probably come through again."

"He was on the list, too."

Ginkgo snorted. "Just goes to show how much Glint *doesn't* know. Sensei isn't looking for a bride."

"Why aren't you married?"

"Mmm ... lots of little reasons. Most of them are just excuses, though." He nodded to himself, then shrugged. "I guess nowadays, I'm a little like how Darya was. Too smart to believe anyone might want me for more than my connections."

"Do you get contracts?"

"Yep. All kinds of offers from all over the place. Strangers who like the idea of me, even though they've never met me and haven't a clue about what's important to me."

"If you chose somebody, the offers would stop."

Ginkgo grinned. "Interesting strategy. Maybe I'll propose to Damsel."

"Do you think he gets offers, too?"

"Doubt it. I don't think many people know he exists. Hard to build a fanbase when you're intentionally obscure."

Another voice interjected, "That's worked for me for years."

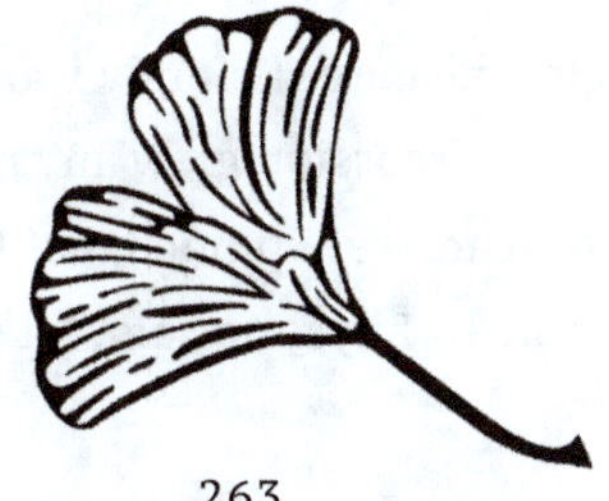

35

WONDERS NEVER CEASE

Gingko had been fighting hard to ignore the little dragon casting shy looks at him from his clinch around Lilya's neck. Even though all things draconic would be considered notable. Didn't matter. His girl needed him to be focused on *her* right now. To the exclusion of all else.

A decent excuse, but it was still mortifying that he'd missed the presence of a potential threat. Not that Wardenclave's trickiest protector had any designs on Lilya. But if word got back to Stately House, Dad wouldn't see it that way.

Rubbing wearily at his face, Ginkgo asked, "How much trouble are we in?"

"None, my young reynard. I simply wanted to alert you to my presence before your discussion grew any more personal."

Ginkgo knew his ears were pinned, but the wily squirrel didn't rub it in any further. To Lilya, he said, "It's okay. Salali's head of security around here."

"*Acting* head."

"He's also the whiz who disappeared an entire mountain range."

With a faint smirk, Salali murmured, "You're too kind."

Lilya scooted off her chair and went to offer her hands. "I'm Lilya. He's Ginkgo. And this is Rifflet."

He stood and bowed with a sweep of his floppy hat. "Salali Fullstash."

"One of the founders?"

Tossing aside his hat, he rested his hands atop hers and quirked a brow. "That's what the history books say."

"*Are* we in trouble?" asked Lilya.

Salali waved toward the front door and explained, "I arranged to meet a friend here. We have similar designs on the contents of the freezer, so I can hardly fault your choices."

Ginkgo was proud of his girl's manners. And the unflappable streak that was part nature, part nurture. Rather than being off-put by Salali's sudden appearance, she embraced the opportunity. Edging closer to the squirrel clansman, she asked, "Could you please tell me if you've seen someone like Rifflet before?"

"A *someone*, are they?" Bending close, Salali murmured, "Wonders never cease."

Rifflet tootle-peeped.

"Yes," Lilya said firmly. "He's someone."

Even though she sounded a little like a child defending her favorite stuffed animal, Salali didn't brush that aside. Ginkgo nearly slapped his forehead. He was way too slow on the uptake tonight.

"What did Yulin say?" checked Salali.

"To ask a dragon," said Lilya.

Okay, that was some more name-dropping. Salali clearly had more of the facts, and Ginkgo needed to get up to speed. Giving up on his ice cream, Ginkgo asked, "Can I have a look?"

Lilya turned to him with a smile.

He mumbled reassurances as he worked his fingers under Rifflet's lithe body, but he needn't have worried. The little one came easily, winding around Ginkgo's fingers, then forearm. With more soft vocalizations, Rifflet rubbed his jaw against Ginkgo's knuckle. It was tough to say who was taming whom.

"Darn cute. Dad'll want a dozen." With extreme care, he pressed the smooth side of a claw into Rifflet's mouth. "Give us a look, little mister. What are you packing?"

"He's not poisonous," offered Lilya. "Glint said so."

"Ephemera aren't aggressive. No stingers, no fangs, no poison. They don't bite, they don't hunt." Pulling free, Ginkgo tickled Rifflet under the chin. "Which is why I seriously doubt your new friend qualifies. He has a proper set of teeth, and that usually spells carnivore."

"Interesting," remarked Salali. "May I?"

"What do you say?" Ginkgo asked the little dragon. "Do you have room in your affections for this scruffy squirrel?"

Lilya giggled.

Rifflet's answering twitter sounded like laughter.

"I do apologize, Miss Ward. I know nearly everything that can be known about Wardenclave and its environs, but he isn't from these parts." Salali stroked Rifflet's crest with one finger. "By all means, ask Sinder. Though if you tarry a little longer, my friend may offer some insight."

Ginkgo glanced at the door. "Who *is* this friend of yours?"

Salali angled his head toward the front door, which swung open.

Tenma dragged through, looking—and smelling—like he'd lost a long siege against a mud puddle. "I'm late. I'm sorry. Goh-sensei needed me to prep tomorrow's clay since he's filling in for Sinder tonight. Good evening, Ginkgo. Hello, Lilya-chan."

"Already friends?" Salali's eyes were bright with interest.

Without hesitation, Tenma provided some oblique context. "I've been a guest at Stately House."

Ginkgo wondered how often. Dad definitely depended on him to help Tsumiko with the running of the household. But when it came to grand schemes, Lord Mettlebright kept his own counsel. Or confided in Jacques. And despite appearances, Tenma was a top tier, grand scheme kind of guy.

It was becoming increasingly difficult to follow the strategies that kept his dad busy, but Ginkgo was okay with his need-to-know basis. His focus was on the den, not the world outside.

Which made this summer exceptional.

At first blush, Dad had sent him to watch out for the kids—Kyrie, Lilya, Timur, and Gregor. With understated instructions to keep his ears and eyes open. Information about trees. Information about foxes. Information about dragons. All the sorts of things you'd expect.

Except Ginkgo couldn't shake the idea that Dad was doing Dad things. Which meant he might be in the middle of a very foxish endeavor.

No place was safer than Stately House. But people knew about it. So Dad had stashed them someplace that *wasn't* on any maps. Borrowing Salali's longstanding barriers and Denholm's pack of over-protective dogs, he'd limited—if not outright eliminated—the chances of discovery.

Argent Mettlebright's eggs were no longer in one basket.

Was he acting on Hisoka Twineshaft's advice? Or had he arranged things because he was acting on his own … and unable to personally ensure his sons' safety while away from Stately House? Where was Dad now? Ginkgo had no way of knowing.

"Your ice cream is melting," Salali called as he escorted Tenma to the freezer.

While he was out of earshot, Ginkgo nudged Lilya. "We okay?"

"Better than," she assured. "But … do you think we can talk to Sinder tonight?"

"Not sure. We can try, though. But let's see what Tenma has to say about Rifflet."

Lilya shook her head. "He didn't even notice."

"I dunno, little girl." Ginkgo had heard plenty of gossip about Tenma's capabilities. "I don't think he misses much."

Lilya fished a pecan out of her ice cream and offered it to Rifflet, who was now tangled between Tenma's long fingers. The little dragon clasped the morsel with dainty forepaws and nibbled contentedly.

"No," Tenma admitted, his gaze soft. "I haven't seen anyone like him before."

"You're sure?" Lilya pressed.

He nodded. "I wouldn't be able to forget. He's all rainbows."

Salali leaned forward. "As in … *prismatic*?"

"Hey, now," grumbled Ginkgo. "Where'd you hear that?"

"I'm a squirrel," he replied innocently. "I spend a lot of time in trees."

"Eavesdropping."

Salali smiled and changed the subject. "How do you like your courses, Miss Lilya? Have you learned anything useful?"

"I like it here," she offered, since that was a safe answer. She didn't really see the point to most of the courses available to her age group. She and Kyrie had matching schedules, but she'd let him do the picking. So it mostly felt like she was tagging along. Same as always.

"And it's *your* first summer camp, as well?"

It took a moment for them to realize Salali was addressing Ginkgo.

"Never been to a camp," he answered blandly.

"Are you making the most of the opportunity?"

Ginkgo's ears dipped. "I'm here for the kids."

Salali's voice softened. "Are you implying that they're unsafe behind my wards?"

"No."

"Which must leave you with time on your hands," continued the squirrel clansman.

Lilya passed another pecan to Rifflet. She knew about squirrels. One of their crossers was a gray like Salali. They were one of the

269

trickster clans, just like foxes. Was Salali messing with Ginkgo in the same way Uncle Argent sometimes did?

"Gregor's a toddler. He needs full-time attention."

"Something Waaseyaa and Zisa can lavish in abundance." Salali pushed aside his empty bowl. "Would you be interested in my guiding your summer courses?"

Ginkgo's expression was something Lilya had never seen before.

Salali casually added, "I don't usually bother, but I'm interested in exploring your potential. Part fox. Part reaver. That's a heady mix."

When Ginkgo's gaze leapt to hers, she knew how much he wanted to say yes. And how guilty that made him feel.

"You should," she said.

Ginkgo muttered, "That's not why I came."

"Are you sure?" Lilya asked. "It's a good reason."

His gaze jumped warily to Salali. "Did my father arrange for this?"

"No."

Lilya pointed out, "You might learn a bunch of things Uncle Argent doesn't know."

Ginkgo chuckled and squirmed and finally said, "Yeah. That'd be great."

"Come along, then." Salali rose and moved toward the front door.

"Now?" Ginkgo scrambled to his feet, but hesitated.

Tenma cleared his throat. "I can escort Lilya-chan back."

Ginkgo hurriedly kissed Lilya's forehead, then Tenma's. Seeing that Salali was already gone, Ginkgo swore, muttered hurried thanks, and sprinted away.

Lilya giggled.

Tenma smiled.

And for a little while, silence hung awkwardly between them. Lilya broke it by admitting, "I don't remember you. Not really."

"Did Isla never mention me?"

"Are you one of her friends?"

"Yes. We were classmates."

Lilya saw Isla irregularly, and her older sister was usually doing important things for Hisoka-sensei or practicing her French with Uncle Jackie. "You're Isla's age?" she asked doubtfully.

He chuckled. "No. She skipped several grades. I'm six years older than her."

Which might as well have been a riddle. "I'm not great with math."

Tenma shrugged. "I'm twenty-six."

Even older than Timur. It seemed only natural to ask, "How many children do you have?"

"Oh, I'm not married." Tenma kept his gaze fixed on Rifflet. "With one thing and another, well ... let's just say I'm behind schedule. Shall we?"

Since his hands were full, Lilya gathered up their bowls and carried them to the kitchen. Then they left—by the door this time—and strolled up the path toward Waaseyaa's. He spoke first this time.

"I can see the resemblance."

"To Isla? She looks like Papka, and he's the pretty one." Lilya was used to being compared. Everyone did it. "Unless you meant to Timur?"

"Oh, no. Well, I suppose." Timur searched her face. "I actually meant that you're extremely warded."

She lifted her wrists so that moonlight gleamed across the

heavy bracelets at her wrists. Rifflet seemed to think this an invitation. Wriggling free of Tenma, he glided through the air and landed in her hands.

"Wow," Tenma whispered. "He flew."

"I didn't know you could do that." Lilya caressed the little dragon's back. "You don't need wings to fly?"

Rifflet peeped in a pleased way.

They continued along, and Lilya decided it was her turn to ask something. "What's your classification?"

"I haven't formally declared one."

At his age? "I didn't think you could graduate without one."

"It's easiest if you think of me as an unregistered reaver." Tenma ambled along, hands in the back pockets of his grubby jeans. "Ever since I graduated from New Saga, I've been traveling. Going different places, meeting all kinds of people, and making a lot of really ugly pots."

Lilya laughed. "Is there something you're good at?"

"Tending." He offered a small shrug. "I like tending."

She nodded. "My papka does, too."

"I know." Tenma favored her with a lopsided smile. "Michael-sensei was my teacher for a while. So ... what's *your* classification."

Lilya kind of wished he hadn't asked. "Beacon," she sighed.

His hand strayed to her shoulder, just a light touch. "Strange. I thought the beacon must be a different sister. You give nothing away."

"Precautions." She tapped his hand. "Reavers aren't supposed to be able to sense other reavers."

"I do a lot of things I'm not supposed to do." Tenma lifted both hands. "Sorry for being strange."

Lilya decided to answer more than he'd asked. "They sealed me. That's why you can't find me. That's why *no one* can find me."

Then she told him about Radiance's silly plan and her day with Glint. Tenma's steps lagged to a stop, as if walking might keep him from listening well. He was all smiles and nods, with questions that had her spilling out more of the story. All the way up to her discovery of Rifflet.

"Should we stop by Zisa's and see if Sinder's awake?" he offered.

"It's late."

"He's Amaranthine," Tenma pointed out. "And don't you think he'll want a look at your new friend?"

So she let him lead her to the little house beyond Waaseyaa's.

Tapping on the door, he opened it partway and quietly called, "Is everyone decent?"

"By whose standards?" sang out a familiar voice. Zisa appeared, wreathed in smiles.

Kyrie skidded in his haste to reach her side. "Lilya?"

Inside, Timur was lofting crystals. In their soft light, she could tell that Kyrie had been in bed with Sinder and Timur. Hurrying forward, her big brother quietly demanded, "Trouble?"

"Peace." Tenma's posture matched his words, which helped to calm everyone. "Lilya-chan has a question for Sinder."

The dragon grumbled something, and Mikoto left the other bed to offer his arm. Sinder shook his head and stayed on the edge of the mattress. "I'll hold audience from here, if you don't mind."

Kyrie caught Lilya's hand, pulling her around Zisa and drawing her inside. "Damsel was hurt, but Timur is a good healer."

Timur reached for her but pulled his hands back when Rifflet lifted his head. "Sinder?" he called. "Are you seeing this?"

"Can't be." Sinder looked from Lilya to Rifflet with an expression of utter bewilderment. "That's a wind dragon."

"Is that what he's called?" It was nice to have a proper term.

"They're extinct."

Lilya knew better, and she could tell Sinder did, too. His wonderment only multiplied when Rifflet's voice chimed sweetly in both their minds. *Damsel.*

36

SECRET APPRENTICE

Ginkgo had been so sure that Dad was joking when he referred to this summer as his eldest son's proving journey. A bad joke, at that, given the monumental disaster that had been Argent Mettlebright's first foray into the wider world.

Betrayal. Capture. Enslavement.

Looking back on all those dreadful memories, Ginkgo often wondered how Dad had managed to survive. Except ... now that things were better, he thought he knew the answer. Argent had toughed it out because he'd had a kid to protect. All those centuries. More than a millennium. He'd dug deep and kept going because his son needed him to.

Maybe it was easier to see now because Ginkgo felt the same way about Michael's and Sansa's kids. His first brush with a real family. His first time really belonging. They'd quietly encouraged the attachment, and he'd taken every last one of them to his heart.

Darya, Timur, Isla, Annika, Lilya, and Vanya may have been born into Rilka's hands, but she'd promptly handed them off to him. Like an honorary uncle. Or a big brother. Not until later did he learn that it was an actual thing. Fostering.

Their kids were *his* in every way that mattered.

So he understood, now, just how far a parent would go for their child. And that scared him more than anything. Because Kyrie was Dad's in every way that mattered.

The worldwide threat that the rogue represented was intensely personal to Argent. Sure, that murderous dragon kept eluding the trackers, but what were years compared to millennia? Argent Mettlebright knew how to dig deep and keep going. He wouldn't stop until he stopped Kyrie's sire.

All without Ginkgo. Or maybe it was fairer to say, without endangering Ginkgo.

Unless this really *was* a proving journey. Maybe he'd go home better equipped and able to help. Somehow.

Chasing Salali through the treetops, Ginkgo drummed up the courage to ask, "Are you my mentor?"

"Up to you." The squirrel crouched on a limb and waited until Ginkgo settled beside him. "Not everyone wants this sort of thing getting out."

"Because I'm a crosser?"

Salali snorted.

"Is it a clan thing? Am I not supposed to learn the squirrel clan's secrets?"

"Closer." He tipped his hat back and grinned. "People like you and I don't usually advertise the tools in our kit."

"So I'd lose the element of surprise if folks found out I'd picked up some seriously squirrely tricks."

Salali offered his hand. "Traditional secrecy aside, this *is* an apprenticeship. I'm willing to teach you everything I can. I'm interested in the possibilities represented by your unique heritage."

Ginkgo grimaced. "Guinea pig time, huh?"

"Sensitive on that score?"

"Can you blame me?"

Salali sighed. "Untuck your tail, Ginkgo Mettlebright. To me, you represent untapped potential. I'd like to see if there are any new tricks up your sleeve. Do you want an advocate to make sure I don't take unfair advantage of our arrangement?"

"Is that usual?"

"Common enough, and quite useful in our case." With a faint smirk, he said, "I recommend Hannick Alpenglow."

Ginkgo recognized the name. "One of the other founders? Why him?"

"I really couldn't say." Salali casually scanned their surroundings. "But as my apprentice, you'll gain access to the kinds of places I go. Which will undoubtedly please Lord Mettlebright, should you *discretely* pass along certain details."

He wasn't going to turn down that kind of help. "Want me to call you *sensei*?"

Salali tweaked his nose, then pulled something from behind one of Ginkgo's ears, presenting it with a wink. "Wear this at all times."

"Is this so you can keep tabs on me?"

Salali snorted again.

A necklace. Holding it up toward the moon's light, Ginkgo recognized it for the treasure it was. The crystal was nearly colorless, with a faint seam of green at its heart. Slipping the heavy chain over his head, he studied the sigils etched deeply into the stone's surface. "This is to keep me safe?"

"You're my responsibility, now." Salali solemnly asked, "May I place a sigil on you?"

What to say? Trust for trust was a good way to begin. But he knew better than most that it could lead to betrayal, capture, and enslavement. Voice catching, Ginkgo asked, "What for?"

"You can't learn from my sigilcraft if you can't *see* my sigils." Salali showed his palms. "I intend to open your eyes. We can wait for Hannick if you have reservations."

Ginkgo gave a small shake of his head. "Where do you want it?"

With an approving little chirr, Salali playfully asked, "Are your feet ticklish?"

It took a few minutes for the squirrel clansman to complete the intricate pattern on Ginkgo's heel, but the moment it took, Ginkgo's view of the world changed.

Sigils wheeled at regular intervals overhead.

Networks of hidden crystals sparked with inner light.

Nocturnal varieties of Ephemera swirled into view.

Barriers fizzed at trailheads, limiting choices.

And as he slowly adjusted to the dizzying array of new information, Ginkgo noticed a pattern. The surrounding trees bore a softly gleaming mark. Finding the silvery sigil on the tree in which they'd stopped, he looked to Salali in disbelief. "You named them? *All* of them?"

A modest shrug. A faint smirk. "I'm a squirrel. I spend a lot of time in trees."

Ginkgo found Waaseyaa dozing in a rocker, Gregor sprawled on his chest. "Was he fussing?"

Zisa laughed quietly. "Brother has always kept his children close. He knows no other way."

Lifting the contented toddler to his own shoulder, Ginkgo nudged Waaseyaa. "Get along to bed, old man."

Waaseyaa smiled sleepily. "Welcome back."

"Good to be. Thanks for this."

"Anytime."

As the man eased from the chair and stretched, Zisa swooped in, getting a shoulder under Waaseyaa's arm. "Bed, bed, bed," crooned the tree. "I will tuck you in."

Waaseyaa chuckled and allowed himself to be led away. "You do not need to fuss."

"I know no other way," retorted his twin.

Ginkgo slowly swayed his way toward the guest room, but an unexpected sound set his ears quivering.

A moan? Almost a howl.

Without stopping to put Gregor to bed, Ginkgo hurried back outside and paused to orient himself. He squinted against the dazzle of sigilcraft that kept Zisa's existence under wraps. It was going to take a while to get used to all the extra stuff revealed by Salali's mark on his sole.

"*That* wasn't there before," he muttered, making his way to a shed on the far side of the tree. It must have been, of course. Probably for a century or more, judging by the vines. But Salali must have hidden it from view for some reason.

Another halfhearted moan set his hairs on end.

He tried the door. Not locked.

Ginkgo's ears flattened against a whimper that turned to soft keening. Had this been going on every night? Or worse, day and night? Why would anyone sequester an animal here?

Opening his mouth, he tasted the air, which was close from being closed up. Wolf. Well, probably a dog, given the locale. Not injured, but not happy. The scents finally matched a memory, and he adjusted his hold on Gregor as he hustled to help.

Planting a hand on the rail of a pen, he launched over, landing lightly in the straw beside a large white Kith who was crying in her sleep.

"Hey, lady, what's the matter?" He crouched to rest his free hand atop her head. "Wake up, now. It's only a dream."

He rattled on until she finally roused, her whimpers cutting off with a snarl.

When she lifted her head to bare her teeth, he ducked low to nuzzle her jaw. "Sorry to wake you, lady, but you were having a bad dream. You need anything? I can get your friends or a healer. Or a drink of water. Or we could keep you company until you fall asleep."

The *we* must have caught her attention. She angled her head to get a better look.

"This is Gregor. He's not mine exactly, though I helped raise his daddy." Scooting back to make it easier for her to see, Ginkgo lofted one of the pocket crystals he carried for nightlights.

Copper eyes blinked in their glow.

"Well, now," he said. "Aren't you a beauty?"

Straightening so he could reach, he fondled her ears in the way he knew felt awesome. Her nose bumped his belly, a good reminder of how vulnerable he was, but Ginkgo smiled. It was best to let a wolf—or dog—know that they had the upper hand. She could easily push him back. Or with a single snap, he'd be a goner.

Instead, she lowered her head to butt his hip, allowing his rough caresses. He explained about his years running with the Elderbough pack and sang his pack nickname. His wolvish wasn't great, but it earned him an amused huff.

She nipped his ear.

"Curious, are you? That's fine. Everyone is." Ginkgo wiggled his ears at her. "I'm half fox, which explains the ears. And the tail, for that matter. How about you? If you don't mind my asking, you look like a wolf, but that doesn't mean you aren't part of the dog clan."

She snuffled him, then Gregor.

"Guess it's not fair to ask questions you can't answer. Wolf?" he tried.

Her ears flattened.

"Dog?"

Her tail flashed an affirmative.

"Guess that means you're related to Glint?" At her soft growl, Ginkgo revised his assumptions. "Right. Sorry. With your coloring, you'd be related to Radiance Starmark."

The Kith's posture remained neutral, which could indicate a snub.

Ginkgo decided to go all in. Sitting between her forepaws, he leaned back into the thick ruff of fur covering her chest. "Y'know what? How about we hang out with you until morning? It'd do Gregor good to get a feel for a canine. We would have bundled him off for Harmonious to cuddle, but this trip came up, and that dog's schedule is always ridiculous."

More ear nipping. But a quick lick reassured him.

"If I hang around long enough, will someone come by who can cover your half of the introductions?" He resettled Gregor and reached up to touch her muzzle. "Bet you have a beautiful name."

She crooned a few notes.

"Did you say … *frost*? Wait. I take it back. If I guess wrong, you'll be insulted, and my shaky grasp of wolvish nuance will ruin our friendship right from the start."

A tongue bathed his cheek.

"I wonder why you're here, of all places. I know she-wolves who withdrew into their dens for the last few weeks before whelping." Ginkgo asked, "Is it getting close to your time?"

She whined.

"Hey, it'll be fine. Better than fine. Pups are almost as cute as kits." He chuckled. "That's what my dad used to call me when I was just a squirt. It might have been the only joke he ever made. Or just his version of an endearment. Kit was short for *kitsune*, which is a kind of fox spirit from folklore."

Ginkgo rambled on with no real purpose except to distract her from her troubles.

"Any chance you were brought in to strengthen bloodlines?"

That earned him another nipped ear.

"No offense. It's just a guess since that happened to a friend of mine. Only he never mentioned it to anyone, and then all the sudden our Kith was having kittens under the kitchen table." He smiled at the memory. It'd been a fiasco at the time. "Quite the feat, since Minx is considerably larger than the table. At least she spared my couch."

A thought occurred.

"Anyone figured out how many pups you're carrying?"

She made a low sound that was decidedly inconclusive.

"Want me to check?" He stroked her jaw. "I got pretty good at it. Guessed right for both of Minx's litters."

A small lick felt like permission.

"Okay. Mind the baby for me." Ginkgo bundled Gregor in his shirt and nestled him between the Kith's paws. "I need to push and prod a little, but it shouldn't hurt. I'll watch your ears. Flick them back sharp-like, and I'll stop."

She rolled an eye.

He knelt at her side, petting before adding any pressure. "I'm sure if you're here, you're under all kinds of watchful care, so let's face it. I'm just being nosy."

The scents were good. Much of the sadness had faded, leaving the deep, warm, waiting flavors he associated with pregnancy. With half an eye on the disposition of her ears, he kneaded into her side, searching for clues.

He found one.

A big one.

"Hey, you in there," he called softly. "Are you making your pretty mama wait? Seems to me you're about ready. Between you and me, she's ready, too. So no dawdling."

Under his hand, the lone pup wriggled, almost like they were trying to get closer.

"Clever pup. Are you a beauty like your mama? Or as handsome as your da?" Which really should have occurred to him earlier. "Say, lady. Is your mate going to take exception to my being here?"

She closed her eyes, threw back her head, and opened her mouth in a silent howl.

37

EARS TO HEAR

Mikoto woke to the skitter of tiny feet, only to realize that Kyrie had taken Noble out for him. His apology came out low and hoarse as he rolled from bed. "Thank you for sparing Zisa's floors, but Noble is my responsibility."

The boy glided over and boosted the puppy onto the bed. "I was already awake. I do not need as much sleep as you."

"Because you are a crosser?"

"Because I am a crosser," Kyrie solemnly confirmed.

Sitting on the edge of the mattress, Mikoto was nearly the same height as the boy, who was compelling at close range. His fingers twitched, but he recalled himself and lowered his gaze.

"Curiosity can be a compliment." Kyrie carefully picked up Mikoto's hand and brought it to his face. "Some people need to touch me to be sure I am real."

"They do?"

The boy smiled. "Touch is part of familiarization. And I find it reassuring."

Mikoto's fingertips grazed freckled scales. "You do?"

"I do. Because you are neither afraid of nor disgusted by me."

What a thing to suggest.

"Not everyone finds the marks of my heritage beautiful."

That remark was even more telling than the last.

The boy could see right through him. Had weighed Mikoto in a balance and somehow found him worthy. But Kyrie was also baring something vulnerable. People feared this gentle child? Flinched away or thought him ugly? Mikoto felt a surge of indignation, of protectiveness.

Kyrie shuffled closer. "We are becoming friends …?"

"We *are* friends." Mikoto pulled him into an embrace. "And not simply because you are beautiful."

The boy practically melted into him, which was such an Amaranthine thing to do. It put Mikoto back on familiar footing. How many colts and bucks and pups had he carried and cuddled? And the whisperlings of the Dimityblest clans, who flocked to his side as if he were their flame. Children needed this.

He gradually became aware that they were alone in Zisa's little house, even though sunlight still angled sharply through the eastern window. A breeze puffed past sheer fabric, stirring the tiny chime Timur had added. Mikoto had the sudden impression that the puff of wind had been looking for him, which was probably his imagination. Even though it riffled through his hair.

Kyrie was watching his face. "I am curious about you, too. You are the only other person I know who is loved by wind."

"You are? Because you are a dragon?"

"I used to think so, but … no. I have come to believe that I am loved because I listen. I was born with ears to hear." Kyrie tipped his head to one side, as if catching faint sounds. "In stories, only a few rare souls ever win the trust of the lost clans. Moonbeams are only ever caught by those who can cherish them, and stars only set their feet upon the earth when love compels them."

Mikoto dared to ask, "What about wind?"

"The most elusive of all impressions." Kyrie pulled himself up onto Mikoto's lap. "Did you know that sigilcraft would not be possible without the wind's cooperation?"

He shook his head. He'd only really paid attention to the stories of fabled weapons and epic partnerships between reavers and their Kith. Battler stuff.

Kyrie's fingers traced through the air, pulling luminous strands into a pattern. He gave it wings and blew it a kiss, and it twirled into action, dancing around Noble's ears like a butterfly.

"We write upon tame winds, or so the stories say."

"I did not know."

"Not all winds are tame, of course. Most are fickle, but I have always been able to make friends."

"Because you listen."

Kyrie nodded. "The ones that like me best will bring me things. Scents or sounds or secrets. Sometimes, I know how they feel."

Mikoto couldn't bring himself to ask. He didn't need to.

"You make yours happy."

"I did not know," he mumbled again. "How could I know?"

The boy nodded. "That is why you need a dragon. Because a willing wind can be captured by their words. If that is your wish."

Mikoto had been wishing along an entirely different line. But he wanted to know more. "Are there stories besides the one Sinder told?"

"Yes. Quite a few." Kyrie said, "Woo an ethereal one to your side, and feel their kisses. Teach them your form, and you shall find pleasure in theirs. Twain lives, thus entwining, bring new light and life. For such are the ways of love."

It was suggestive enough to make Mikoto blush. "Are you not a little young for this kind of thing?"

"Yes. But you are not." Kyrie folded his hands together. "Your wind has been trying to catch your attention. Have you begun to notice, now that you know she is near?"

Mikoto glanced toward the windchime, which stirred enough to offer one dainty *ping*. "What am I supposed to do?"

Kyrie calmly studied his face. "You could release her."

"How?"

"Reject her. Winds hardly ever settle or stay. Most scholars believe it is not in their nature." He hesitated, then added, "Something that makes her attachment noteworthy."

"Alternatively ...?"

"Invite her to stay." Those deep red eyes were soft. "That would make a nice story."

For Mikoto, there had only ever been Lupe. But what if the things he'd always loved most about her were actually the workings of an imp? "But to take a wife, sight unseen?"

"It is my understanding that such contracts are commonplace in the reaver community." Kyrie breezed on. "It is not easy for those of the sky clans to stand upon the earth, but neither is it impossible."

"And you know the way?"

"I know the stories." Kyrie quietly asked, "Are you sure you want to know?"

Mikoto hugged the boy close and confessed, "I am confused and embarrassed and uncertain of everything. But I *do* want to know."

"You are very brave." Kyrie nodded approvingly. "According to the old tales, you would give her a name. 'Call to her, and she will hear you. Reach for her, and she will reach back.' But I think she already has a name. Perhaps Lupe gave it to her."

"Lupe knows?"

"Yes, I think so. It may be what binds them."

Mikoto had desperately wanted to believe that Lupe had returned for his sake. And maybe she had, in a roundabout way. But why hadn't she told him? He cringed inwardly. "Lupe is staying with my sister, but I have not been back to the house since First Day."

"Go to her," urged Kyrie. "Ask her for the name. Only ...."

"Yes?"

The boy shyly asked, "Can I be there when you call for her?"

Not *if.*

When.

Mikoto liked this boy. "I want you there, my friend. I will *need* you there. You and Sinder both."

38

INVISIBLE FRIEND

Mikoto clasped Waaseyaa's hand and mumbled, "I need to go home."

"They will be missing you, I am sure."

He couldn't bring himself to let go. "I have been neglectful."

"You have been where you needed to be." Waaseyaa slipped the end of his braid into Mikoto's hand. "Now, Zisa and I will have a turn at missing you."

"I may come hurrying back," he joked, winding and unwinding the black braid around his fist.

Uncle smiled. "You will always be welcome."

Because he knew it was safe to ask, Mikoto did. "Have I been running away?"

Again, Waaseyaa said, "You have been where you needed to be."

Mikoto accepted that with a nod, released his uncle, and pocketed Noble. He turned to leave, nearly bowling over

Zisa. The tree twin threw his arms around Mikoto's neck and whispered in his ear. "Are you running away now?"

"No," he promised. Even though there was a sizeable part of him that didn't want to face Lupe. "Can anyone outrun the wind?"

Zisa giggled.

Mikoto sighed. "I need to go home. Lupe is there, and she might know the name I need."

"Your Lupe?" Zisa's smile faltered.

"She is not mine," he mumbled, avoiding the tree's gaze. "Sinder thinks she is the one who has been bringing the wind."

"Her … twin?"

"Maybe a little like that." Mikoto gently extricated himself from Zisa's embrace. "I will not know until I ask. Or until the wind has words."

Zisa made a little shooing motion, although he said, "Come back soon."

Mikoto nodded and set his face toward home, though his steps lagged. Feeling overly conspicuous, he left the path, sneaking through the trees until he reached the back gate. He hesitated there, suddenly feeling like an outsider.

How long had he been at Zisa's? Ten days, more or less. Yulin would know for sure. Was that all the time it took for him to become a stranger to everything?

Even grief?

Even heartbreak?

Maybe he had allowed himself to become wrapped up with the newcomers in order to distract himself. Had he been putting off coming home because pain would ambush him here?

Mikoto let Noble down, putting off the inevitable long enough for the pup to piddle on a fencepost. Trudging to the door, he slipped inside and stood listening.

After so many days of male companionship, he worried about returning to a house filled with females, but time had been passing here, as well. He peeked through enough doorways to confirm that his older half-sisters had gone back to their own houses. Were they done with mourning and getting on with Wardenclave business? Picking up Mikoto's slack. Seeing to the needs of their annual guests.

He supposed he was feeling less blighted by his father's absence. Although he really would have liked his opinion on wind lore.

The achingly familiar rustle of paper came from the next room, and Mikoto turned toward it. Yulin was here. He would hear Mikoto out. He might even know something helpful. Mikoto hurried forward, totally unprepared to find Lupe lounging on a sofa, nibbling on toast while paging through a communique.

Stumbling to a stop, his mind stalled.

Lupe. He'd barely given her a thought in all the days he'd been at Zisa's. And for the first time in his life, the sight of her brought mixed feelings.

The air in the room seemed to swell and settle, and Lupe looked up. "Hello, Mikoto. I was beginning to think you were avoiding me."

He shook his head. "Not really."

"Glint emerged from your room days ago." Her lips tipped teasingly. "Where have you been?"

"My uncle's."

She searched his face. "Are you doing okay?"

Mikoto was tempted to make an excuse and shy away from

the things that made him want to run. But he felt as if he'd made promises—to Zisa, to Sinder, to Kyrie. And that in a way, they were at his back, lending their support.

"I am better. I will be fine. The founders are watching over me."

Noble scampered into the room. Lupe exclaimed over him, and Mikoto explained about Glint's gift. She listened and laughed and put him at ease. And still, he had a hard time broaching the topic they needed to discuss.

Thinking to work his way up to it, he blurted, "May I ask you something?"

Lupe settled back, her hands folded over her belly. "What's on your mind?"

"Is it possible that you brought a stowaway when you came here?" Backpedaling, he clarified, "Not you *personally*. I meant your traveling party."

"I'll need you to be more specific," she said carefully.

"A little creature." He measured Rifflet's length with both hands. "Looks like some variety of Ephemera, probably because of its size. We think it belongs to some branch of dragonkind. My friend believes it to be a wind dragon."

"Oh," Lupe said, sounding disappointed. She turned toward the back of the house and called, "Priska!"

Her Amaranthine mentor stepped into view, making it very clear that they'd not been alone.

"See? I didn't miscount." Lupe's chin tipped to a stubborn angle. "I knew one went missing."

Priska inclined her head, then addressed Mikoto. "Where is the hatchling?"

"He is in good hands."

Her slit-pupiled eyes narrowed. Mikoto had no idea which animal was attached to Priska's clan. That, along with most everything else about the Eldermost Islands, was veiled in secrets. But he guessed it must be something fierce.

"A male, then? That is less tragic. Unless he is a rare color."

Mikoto hadn't expected to find the source of their mystery so quickly. "Light yellow. Sort of creamy."

"A shame," Priska said flatly. "Many favor that hue. It is auspicious."

"I did not know."

She curled her lip. "You know more than you were ever meant to."

He shuffled his feet. "I am headman, now."

"This is *grove* business," Priska countered snappishly.

Mikoto conceded that with a nod. Waaseyaa was the most noteworthy tree-kin in Wardenclave, but he wasn't the only one. However, Denholm's ancient grove was under the founders' protection, *not* the Reaver family's. Mikoto wasn't sure where the trees were hidden, but he knew they were nearby. And secure.

Guessing wind dragons were a safer topic, Mikoto asked, "So there are more of them?"

Priska sniffed. "Enough that one will not be missed."

"My friend knew of them, but he thought them extinct."

"It was a close thing." Priska's tone mellowed slightly. "Their return bodes well for the finding of other lost things."

Mikoto came to sit on one of the chairs across from Lupe. Again, he couldn't quite bring up the most essential subject. "Can you tell me anything about your new home?"

Lupe's smile was an apology. "You know I can't."

"Not secret things." He carried plenty of those himself. "I only want to know that ... that you do not regret your choice."

She looked to Priska, who grumbled and shrugged. Which seemed to mean that she'd allow her apprentice to speak. But the Amaranthine stalked to the bookcase and pretended to peruse the titles. A chaperone? Or simply ready to jump in if Lupe seemed close to giving too much away.

"I live on an uncharted island," Lupe began. "A safe place, untouched by storms. No one can find us, even by accident. Life is simple, but also more magical."

Mikoto nodded to let her know he was listening.

Her tone warmed. "There are sea turtles, and we ride them through turquoise lagoons. And on calm nights, the sea is a mirror, so that the stars seem to be both above and below."

"Are the people nice?" He resisted the temptation to add, *or are they all as prickly as Priska?*

"My husband is gentle and generous." Lupe smoothed a hand over her abdomen. "He's awaiting our return. Probably quite anxiously."

"Is he ...?" Mikoto fumbled for a nice way to ask. "Are you ...?"

Lupe cut a glance in Priska's direction. "He's gentle and generous and ... quite a bit older than me."

Priska snorted.

"And I get along well with his sister, who is his twin."

Mikoto guessed that the hint was big enough. Her husband was someone like Uncle Waaseyaa, someone bound to a tree in some far-off grove. Lupe's children would be strong, for their father's life was inextricably bound to a rare tree.

When he finally found his voice, Mikoto dared to ask, "Is it a good match?"

"Tzefira thinks so."

He stopped.

Stopped hearing, stopped thinking, stopped breathing. But a breeze caressed his cheek and tickled his nose and threatened to fill his lungs lest he collapse from lack of air. And then he was hyperventilating, and Priska was pounding his back, and Lupe was laughing and crying and babbling in Spanish.

"You finally noticed?" Priska asked. "By all that is sacred, it took you long enough."

Lupe raised a slim hand. "Let's not get ahead of ourselves. Mikoto, is there anything you'd like to ask me?"

He did. Ever since he was nine, he'd wanted to ask her to be his. It was embarrassing to realize that it had always been the wrong question. Or that he'd always been the wrong one to ask it. That someone far, far away had been longing for a bride like Lupe. And that someone closer than his next breath had been hoping he would notice her.

"Lupe," he croaked. "I am sorry."

She wagged a finger at him. "Ask *properly*, now. This is important."

Mikoto agreed, but that only made him more tongue-tied. "W-was there another stowaway?"

"Yes."

He cleared his throat and fought to steady his voice. "As it happens, there are two dragons here. Well, one and a half. And they have been telling me stories about the wind."

Lupe sank back on the sofa. "She has the most amazing luck."

Priska's snort seemed to be agreement.

"Mikoto, please," said Lupe. "Will you listen to my story? The short version, anyhow."

"I will listen." He offered his fingertips to Noble, who'd wriggled free of Lupe in the excitement. "Help me understand."

"I've always had a second voice in my head. When I was very little, my parents assumed I'd invented her. But once I was a little older and better at expressing myself, I was able to convince them that I had more than my imagination for company. I was assessed, and that sparked off a bunch of excitement." Lupe smiled. "I am the first reach in the family since my paternal great-grandfather."

Mikoto had known, had always been impressed. "A rare classification."

"No one knows for sure if my invisible friend was drawn to me because I would be able to hear her ... or if she nurtured and amplified my nascent talent so we'd be able to communicate." Lupe flicked that aside as inconsequential. "Either way, I was promoted to First of Reaches during my last summer here."

He hadn't known *that*. Then again, she wasn't one to brag.

"My family searched for answers, but all we really know is that Tzefira came to me after a long journey. She was in a weakened state, and I was the refuge she needed. We've never been apart, and we might have continued as one. But then *you* happened."

"The day I fell into the river?"

Lupe laughed. "Long before that. It's her fault that I became friends with Hana. She liked your mother and your sisters, but *you* were always her favorite. The beautiful boy with the sweet soul and the sturdy build and the steadfast heart."

Mikoto knew he was blushing. Wouldn't anyone? Priska watched him closely, arms folded, and when their eyes met, she smirked. But not unkindly.

"She wanted me to wait for you."

His attention jumped back to Lupe.

"But that wouldn't have been fair. To either of you." Lupe didn't shy away from the hopes she must have known he harbored. "And you would have come between us."

Mikoto wasn't sure what she meant. "Is that not what I am about to do?"

Lupe quirked a brow. "Are you?"

"If I woo the wind to my side, she would be leaving yours." Mikoto glanced self-consciously at Priska. "If that is what she wants, of course."

Another derisive snort from Priska's direction. "Are you addled, boy? Why do you think we risked the voyage?"

"Heir to Wardenclave, now headman, with a line to secure. Glint will have you contracted by this solstice and wed by the next. But we had to *try*." Lupe gestured broadly between him and the seemingly empty air. "This summer was her last chance to win her first love."

39

BREEDING PAIRS

Lilya and Kyrie tried not to rush through their breakfast. That would be rude to Uncle. But Waaseyaa noticed their efforts and smiled. "You are not half so excited as Zisa was when Sinder suggested he go along."

As planned, Sinder would go to Glint's home in order to give his official opinion about Rifflet. Lilya had special permission to skip her morning courses in order to bring the little wind dragon, with Timur for an escort. But Zisa's inclusion had sparked off a chain reaction of joy.

He didn't often go from home. Indeed, he couldn't range far or be seen. So the trip to the Starmark home atop the hill was a rare treat. One that had his treetops swaying in anticipation.

"Keep an eye on my brother for me." Hoisting Gregor onto his hip, Waaseyaa added, "We will be here when you return from your adventures."

Lilya agreed and hurried out the door, only to stop on the front step. She looked uncertainly at Kyrie. Here they were again, going separate ways.

"Should we ask again?" she mumbled.

He took her hands into his and trilled soothingly. "I *do* want to meet Ever's grandsire, but I also want to learn more about brushwork sigils from Scribe Yevlu. I will *also* be here when you return from your adventures."

She pulled him into a fierce hug, and Rifflet gabbled a protest.

Kyrie replied with a fair imitation of the little one's tootle-peep.

Rifflet still grumbled, which was cute enough to make Lilya laugh.

Relaxing into her embrace, Kyrie promised, "All will be well."

Since he was so smart about everything, Lilya chose to believe him.

"Ready?" called Timur, who hadn't strayed far from Sinder's side since his injury.

Lilya was used to thinking of her brother as a big, strong battler. In all her childhood memories, he was running, climbing, sparring, and winning. This past winter, she'd had to rethink him a little. It had been strange at first, seeing him as a father.

This summer, she was learning even more about Timur. When other campers found out she was his sister, they were jealous. Because Timur was a favorite teacher. And now, he was acting like Mum in healer mode. All while managing to keep on being himself.

She couldn't help wondering if she'd ever have as many sides. Or be half as good at any of them.

Zisa was waiting on the bottom step. Timur offered his hands to help the Amaranthine to his feet. Zisa accepted the help, only to spring too high, wrapping his arms around Timur's neck. But it was pretty clear that Timur had expected it.

They all had. Because Zisa was uncomplicated. He *always* wanted a hug, from all of them.

For her part, Lilya didn't mind a bit. Zisa was always so happy, and he smelled nice.

Timur gathered Zisa up, cradling him to his chest as if he weighed no more than Gregor. "Are you asking to be carried?"

"Would you?" Zisa asked, clearly taken with the idea.

"Would it please you?" countered Timur.

"Immensely!"

So Timur strutted ahead, trailing flower petals.

Lilya fell in step beside Sinder and asked, "How are you feeling today?"

"Much better. Don't worry on my account." He stared straight ahead. "In fact, don't spare me a second thought."

She wasn't sure what to make of that. "It doesn't work on me, you know."

Sinder's eyebrows shot up. At least he was looking at her now.

"Kyrie and I shared a cradle. I'm completely immune. I can also tell when someone's trying." She raised her own eyebrows. "*Why* don't you want me to spare you a second thought?"

He slowed to a stop and glanced guiltily after Timur. "Tell me something about yourself."

"Like what?"

"If I tell you not to do something, would you turn around and do it just to spite me?"

Lilya smiled. He was so serious, so she answered with as much formality as she could muster. "No. I was raised to respect the wishes of family and friends alike."

Sinder raised a warning finger and leaned close to mutter, "It would be enormously inconvenient if you developed a crush on me."

He meant it. With a shrug, she said, "Likewise."

Relaxing his posture, he averted his gaze. "Right. Good. As long as that's understood."

Lilya moved to the step above Sinder's and faced him squarely. "I need a *human* husband. Because I'm going to help build Papka's dynasty."

"I suppose that *is* the reaver way."

"No," she argued. "Well, yes. I suppose it is, but I'll do my own choosing."

Sinder hummed skeptically. "Will they let you?"

"They'll have to." Lilya raised her own warning finger. "I've seen Glint's list, and his ideas are *terrible*."

Interest lit his features. "Can I get a look at this list?"

"What for?"

"I'm an unabashed snoop."

She didn't fancy Mum finding out about the list. "The fewer who find out, the better. It's a dead awful list."

"One name," he wheedled. But in the ordinary way, not with dragon wiles in force.

Lilya spread her hands in a show of disbelief and whispered, "Hisoka-sensei."

Sinder shared her shock. "Never happening."

"I know! Right?"

"You're correct to question the pedigree committee's grasp on reality."

Lilya started climbing again. "It's safe to be friends with me, Damsel."

He sprang to her side and walked with her. "Sorry for the sway. It creeps in sometimes."

"Are you sloppy?" And because that might be insulting, she hastily added, "I am."

"I've often been accused of saying more than I should. But since I can *usually* tell people to forget what they've heard, it hardly matters." He sighed. "Maybe I'll outgrow it? I'm young. Well, young*ish*. My partner is fond of pointing it out whenever I blunder."

"You have a partner?"

Sinder blinked, then grinned sheepishly. "Whoops."

Lilya gave his elbow a squeeze. "I'll pretend I didn't hear that part."

Lilya hung back while Yulin mediated the introductions, and not only between Glint and Sinder. An Amaranthine female named Priska was there, and—somewhat to her surprise—so was Tenma. Even keeping the usual formalities to a bare minimum, Lilya knew it'd take forever for all the necessary connections to be made.

Yulin was going on about the Eldermost Islands when Tenma edged over to the couch where Lilya waited and sat next to her.

"May I skip to petting Rifflet?" he murmured.

She hardly blamed him. "Be my guest."

Tenma made little coaxing sounds, and Rifflet unscrolled from Lilya in order to twine through his fingers again. They paid more attention to the wind dragon than the longwinded greetings, but Lilya picked up a few words here and there.

Beacon wasn't a big surprise. People were always talking about her as if she wasn't there. But *spomenka* caught her attention, since it was Slavic. She knew the word because of Mum, but what did forget-me-nots have to do with anything? And Zisa seemed especially pleased about something called a *scattering*.

"But where is Linlu?" demanded Priska. "Is he still missing?"

Glint gruffly said, "We are looking into the matter. We take care of our own."

Timur's posture shifted. "Linlu Dimityblest is missing?"

"For quite some time." Yulin smiled thinly. "His absence, while troubling, is unlikely to have any connection to *other* matters at hand."

"Have you involved the trackers?" Timur persisted.

"Sure they did," said Sinder. "My boss is on the job."

Timur frowned. "Who's your boss?"

Sinder looked incredibly uncomfortable, then gestured for secrecy. "The less said about that, the better."

Her brother's expression cleared, and he nodded once.

Yulin clapped his hands and suggested, "Shall we move on? Lilya has been very patient."

She and Tenma hurried into the circle of Amaranthine, and Rifflet was passed around. He preened under their compliments, clearly happy to be the center of everyone's attention.

Sinder began, "Although I was under the impression that wind dragons were extinct, there's little doubt he's a fine specimen. I assume we have preservationists to thank?"

"You are welcome," said Priska blandly.

"Do you have breeding pairs?" he asked curiously.

She only stared at him, stone-faced and silent.

"Surely you're better equipped for this," Sinder complained. "All I know are the old stories."

Priska remained implacable.

With a whistling sigh, Sinder continued. "Wind dragons were … pets, I suppose. Gathered and kept by dragons. They're not true dragons, by which I mean they're not dragon Kith. They fly in the same manner as Ephemera, skimming effortlessly along air currents, but they're sentient."

"They *do* have voices?" interjected Glint.

"Yes. I've heard Rifflet." Sinder tapped his forehead. "It's baby talk, but he's just a little guy. For now. I've seen paintings of dragon clansmen riding through the clouds astride wind dragons. They were treasured by the ancients as mounts."

"And you brought them here?" Glint looked to Yulin for confirmation.

The moth clansman inclined his head. "They require the pollen of certain trees for nourishment, and we are one of the few secure areas capable of accommodating them. The Alpenglow herd welcomed a clutch of eggs. As best we can tell, one hatched before all the necessary wards were in place. Salali is quite put out."

Glint chuckled. "No harm done."

"Yet! They are an undisclosed species," snapped Priska. "We

cannot let the girl walk about camp with a wind dragon."

"True." Glint pointed. "Zisa can look after her pet while she attends to her courses."

"And when summer ends?" The blue-haired female wasn't backing down.

Yulin calmly said, "Stately House's application for a Scattering is on file, and a rudimentary support system is already in place. Their enclave's approval is inevitable. Rifflet is a foretaste of things to come."

Timur chuckled. "Trust me, Argent will want as many breeding pairs as you can spare."

"That's probably not going to happen." Sinder looked to Priska. "You don't have any, do you?"

"No." Priska folded her arms over her chest and said no more.

"Where do little Rifflets come from, then?" Timur asked.

"It's true then?" Sinder asked.

Priska's mouth thinned.

"Oh, fine. Be that way. As improbable as this may sound, wind dragons are crossers. It's one of the reasons their population fell off. Or so the stories say." Sinder cleared his throat. "If it's true, it's good news. And an enormous secret."

One by one, everyone in the room made the hand sign for secrecy.

Sinder said, "The mothers are true dragons. Either wild ones or dragon Kith. That's why they look like they belong to our clan."

"And the sires?" prompted Glint.

"Imps." Sinder shook his head in wonderment. "Take your pick of any of the sky clans, but most especially the wind."

40

NO MORE

Where is Radiance?" asked Lilya. She'd been hoping to secure a future invitation for Kyrie, but Glint's bondmate didn't seem to be home.

"Lady Starmark is seeing to a family matter," said Yulin. "Would you like me to pass along a message?"

Lilya hesitated. "It can wait until next time. Unless I would be intruding."

Yulin turned to stare at Glint, who started guiltily. "You are always welcome, Angel," he said, reinforcing his invitation with his whole posture.

"Her name is Lilya," said Yulin.

"I am aware. Now," grumbled Glint. "Does my nickname offend, Miss Lilya?"

She took a receptive stance. "How could I be anything but complimented?"

He crossed to kneel before her. "Can we remain friends, Angel?"

"That depends."

Silver eyes creased at the corners, hinting at a smile. "Upon?"

"How many of the packets over there are meant for me?"

Glint's gaze slid sideways.

Lilya had seen the very same hangdog expression on Ever's face at least a thousand times. Throwing her arms around his shoulders, she hugged him tight. "No more," she whispered.

His growl was the weakest of protests. "You will need one by and by."

"What if I promise that you'll be the one to draw up my contract when the time comes?"

He leaned back to search her face. "I would consider it an honor."

"And until then?" she prompted.

Glint ruefully inclined his head. "No more."

Lilya kissed his cheek.

Timur talked over their heads. "Tenma, where will you be next?"

"I'll be assisting Goh-sensei with his afternoon pottery class."

"Will you walk her there?"

Lilya realized he meant her. She pulled away from Glint and would have protested, but Tenma looked so apologetic, she didn't have the heart. Instead, she helped Priska disentangle Rifflet from a flustered Yulin. Bringing the wind dragon to Zisa, Lilya said, "We're counting on you."

The tree kissed her forehead, then Rifflet's, then Sinder's for good measure. And in Lilya's mind the wind dragon's voice chimed. *Sweet.*

"No, you," crooned Zisa, who twirled toward the door.

Sinder smirked and sighed. "Back to work."

"Back to bed," growled Timur.

"Wrong, Michaelson. I have a job to do, and I'll do it."

"You're injured."

Striding toward the door, Sinder called over his shoulder, "On the mend. Thanks to you. Let's see how long you can continue that trend."

Timur was still arguing when they disappeared toward the back door.

Lilya shook her head and asked, "May we go out the front? It'll be quicker. And quieter."

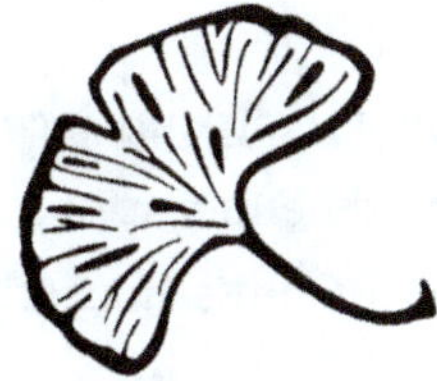

Once they were away from Glint's place, Tenma said, "I'll understand if you want to run ahead."

"Ever since he became a daddy, Timur's been extra protective. Which isn't fair. Mum says he was all risks and dares and disasters when he was younger."

Tenma laughed. "You're safe as can be here, and we both know it."

"He does, too. Deep down." Lilya smiled up at Tenma. "It's fine. We're going the same way. Do you mind if I ask some things?"

"Feel free." His lips quirked. "It's actually nice to be able to converse in Japanese again."

Lilya hadn't realized she'd switched. "We mostly use Japanese at home. Except with Uncle Jackie, who pretends not to be fluent."

"I'm grateful. Words come easier this way." He gestured with both hands. "Please. Ask anything."

She started with the obvious one. "Why were you there this morning?"

"I wondered that myself." Tenma slipped his hands into his back pockets and followed the flightpath of a group of doves. "I suppose it could be that I've traveled. But none of the places I've visited so far have had wind dragons. Or … Glint wanted to give Priska a look at me."

"Why?"

"Mm … well. They're hoping to place me somewhere. And it's pretty obvious that wherever she's from, it's safe."

"You need a job?"

"I have one. Sort of. I'm not really sure it counts." Tenma seemed to realize he hadn't answered her question. "I need progeny."

She glanced back toward Glint's house. "You're going to the Eldermost Islands?"

"Maybe. Maybe not." He shook his head. "I'm hardly the strongest candidate. Sure, the Amaranthine think I'm wonderful, but reavers are looking at ranks and pedigrees. I have neither."

"Because you're an unregistered reaver."

"And uncategorized. And unquantified. But interesting enough to try to replicate. Hence the general consensus that I need progeny."

"You don't want children?"

"It isn't that." He hummed again. "I want to make a good choice. One that satisfies both my duty to the In-between and the secret wish of my heart."

Lilya couldn't tell if he was being teasing or truthful. He was speaking so casually. "*You* have a secret wish?"

"Doesn't everyone?"

"*Nobody* knows?"

"My closest friends do," he admitted.

She considered that and asked, "Does Isla know?"

"Naturally. She's been my go-between in the past, and she's fully prepared to weigh in again if I need help."

"You want Isla to pick a wife for you?"

"Mm ... I *do* trust her. Maybe even that much."

Lilya realized something then, because Isla was careful about everything, especially trust. And this man had hers. That was rare.

"What about you, Lilya-chan? I couldn't help but overhear you setting Glint back. Are you as opposed to practical match-making as Isla?"

"I *do* want to choose for myself."

"When the time comes, you'll get your way." He smiled toward the sky. "You have many people who will make sure of it."

She knew he was right. Papka and Mum would back her choice. Uncle Argent had pull, and Hisoka-sensei could make anything happen. She'd have all the help she needed. "How are *you* going to pick?"

"I have no idea," he admitted. "Favorable circumstances. Willingness on both sides."

"So you'll tell her your secret and see if hers matches?"

"That might work." He quietly added, "Assuming there's no language barrier."

Lilya's steps lagged and she studied her feet. She'd thought it would be easy, picking a husband before the flood of contracts began. But she hadn't considered that her someday husband might have a secret wish. Her cheeks heated with shame.

"You okay, Lilya-chan?"

"I forgot to consider my future husband's feelings."

Tenma nodded. "That's important. Did you already have someone in mind?"

"No." She sheepishly admitted, "I think anybody would say *yes* because I'm a beacon, but I don't want that to be the reason someone says *yes*."

"Isn't that why you're here?" Tenma waved toward the camp. "It's a good place to meet peers. You have time to figure out who you can get along with."

She didn't have that kind of time. "I might not be back."

Tenma stopped, glanced about, and indicated a bench. Once they were seated, he said, "Keep it simple. What do you want most?"

"You first." Maybe it would help if she had an example.

He pushed absently at his glasses, then nodded. "When I was your age, I was lonely, but I didn't understand why until Harmonious Starmark added me to his pack. Suddenly, I was learning Amaranthine ways. All the little tender touches. And the wordless ways they find to show the depths of their trust and affection. I don't want to give that up."

She wasn't sure if it was boasting, so she held her tongue. But she'd grown up with all those things, surrounded by Stately House's crossers.

"I used to think that I wanted to be happy. But it turns out, that isn't a very good wish."

"Why not?"

"Because I'm *already* happy." Tenma's eyes were sparkling. "When I realized that, I had to edit my wish."

"You changed your mind about what you wanted?"

"Mm … no. I think it's more that I understand myself better." He tapped his heart. "I want to share my happiness. I want more than progeny. I want a family. A wife who's glad she chose me. Children who know what its like to tangle or nestle or coil. I want to teach them clan ways so I can say I love them with the set of my shoulders or the flick of a finger. I want to give them reasons to be happy."

He rambled to a stop and looked away. It was funny how secrets—even good ones—could be embarrassing. Lilya touched his elbow, and some of the tension eased from his shoulders.

"I like it," she said.

Tenma sighed. "I think I have a chance. Maybe in an enclave."

Lilya jumped to her feet and stood before him. "I like it," she repeated. "I'll make that my wish, too. I want my children to grow up at Stately House."

"That's an important decision," said Tenma. "It will help Glint refine his search."

"I've made another decision." The words weren't hard to say. They blurted right out. "I know what I want most."

Tenma tipped his head to one side, looking more closely. "You're much better at big decisions than I am. What is it you want, Lilya-chan?"

"*You*, of course."

41
BYGONES

Ginkgo slipped inside the Kith shelter and dropped onto the straw at the white dog's side. "He's trying to kill me. Or at least humble me." Flinging his arms wide, he let himself go limp. "Behold, I have been humbled to the very dust."

She snuffled his neck and nuzzled his ear.

"That Salali." Ginkgo blindly reached for the dog and petted. "Does anybody realize how amazing he is? Because the things he does aren't just next level. They're on par with miracles."

She shuffled closer, trapping him between her forelegs.

He felt safe and relaxed further. "Heaven help me, I need a nap."

It felt so good to rest his eyes after spending half the night studying interlocking sigilcraft and the other half trailing Goh Impleer. The monkey clansman had apparently taken Sinder's place tormenting that allotment of young battlers. Salali made certain he and Ginkgo remained undetected.

Observation, he called it.

Stealing tricks, more like.

"Monkey clans are all risks and rigamarole. Goh pulled tricks I've never seen, let alone imagined." Ginkgo curled onto his side. "His nonsense works, but I don't know why. And it's going to drive me crazy until I figure it out."

The dog licked him.

Even as he burrowed closer, Ginkgo reminded himself that he shouldn't be zoning out. "Need to tell Waaseyaa. Supposed to be the one … bring Gregor next time."

"You should ask him."

Ginkgo's head snapped up.

"Goh Impleer is a teacher at heart. If you want to know something, ask for a lesson."

He sat up and slumped into the white dog's chest. "Well, hey. I was hoping someone would show up to make introductions. Figures it'd be you, Lady Starmark."

Radiance's posture was all dominance, but her smile offered nothing but welcome. "It's nice to put a face to the scent, young Master Mettlebright."

"Ginkgo," he corrected.

"And you shall call me Radiance." Brows rising, she asked, "Is Kyrie to blame for your arrival in Snow's domain?"

Snow, was it? He reached up to give the dog a friendly scratch. "Salali changed my security clearance, and that brought this place to my attention. Not surprised to hear that little bro found it first, though. Barriers are no match for him."

With a sharp look at Snow, Radiance asked, "Is this a common trait of all dragons?"

"Nope, not at all." Recalling Salali's hopes for him, Ginkgo suggested, "Could be an upshot of having both Amaranthine and reaver blood."

"So crossers make excellent cat burglars?"

"The heists we could pull," Ginkgo joked. "But seriously, let's not give Kyrie any ideas."

"He's a good boy. A tribute to Argent's care. And yours." Radiance arched a quizzical brow. "Although I really must ask why you've decided to ignore boundaries."

Ginkgo looked up, trying to catch Snow's eye. "Is she complaining?"

"Usually. But not about you in particular." Radiance remained where she was, studying the two of them as if trying to unravel a mystery. Finally, she said, "I wouldn't have expected her to tolerate a fox."

"You've got fox issues?" Ginkgo was wide awake, now. This was one of the topics on Dad's information-gathering wish list.

"Historically." Radiance seemed to be listening. Probably to Snow. "*Feud* would be too strong a term, but Wardenclave had some trouble with foxes at the very beginning. Linlu's ink was barely dry on the charter when a trio of hungry foxes attempted a raid."

Ginkgo had heard similar stories from Dad. "With an appetite for reaver souls."

"Yes." Radiance's lip curled. "Glint helped Gerard Reaver and his people drive them off, which gave Salali time to reinforce the barriers. But not before a life was lost."

"You lost someone?"

"Not personally. This was before my time. Nor anyone from Wardenclave." Radiance's expression grew troubled. "One of the foxes caught the full brunt of a battler's fury. When his sisters retreated, they dragged his body away with them."

"Wardenclave's people defended themselves."

Radiance inclined her head. "Times have changed, and bygones are bygones."

"Except?"

"Salali warded against foxes for more than a millennium." She quietly admitted, "Up until a scant century ago, when Hisoka Twineshaft came with his hopes for greater cooperation between the clans."

Ginkgo said, "Seems a long time to hold a grudge against foxes."

"Turn that statement around in your thoughts, young Master Mettlebright." Radiance's chin lifted. "Those foxes have long held a grudge against Wardenclave."

"You got proof of this?"

"Against foxes?" She laughed mirthlessly. "They smile and say all the right things. But they delight in dropping hints that all is not forgiven nor forgotten."

"And you can't keep them out?"

Radiance smirked Snow's way. "Our security team knows its business, and upon my eldest son's recommendation, Salali refined his wards. That was eleven years ago."

Ginkgo ran through all the things that'd happened eleven years ago. Tsumiko's arrival. Kyrie's birth, close on the heels of Lilya's. Dad's freedom, at long last. And his appointment to the Five. Replacing ... oh, boy.

"Two sisters," he said warily. "Which clan?"

With a grim smile, Radiance answered, "Hightip."

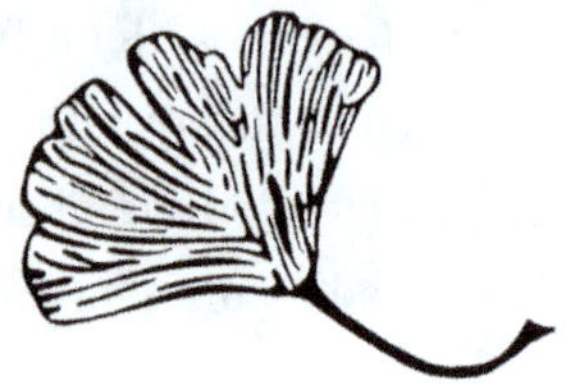

Ginkgo was still composing a report to Dad when Tenma stumbled through Waaseyaa's kitchen door and sagged to his knees beside Ginkgo's chair.

"Classes done for the day?" Ginkgo asked with a glance out the window. It was too early. Pushing back his chair, he crouched beside Tenma and grabbed his shoulders. "What happened? Is it one of the kids?"

"Safe," he gasped. "They're fine."

Tenma's heart was pounding, and his scent was a far cry from his usual calm. Ginkgo chaffed his arms and grumbled, "Get ahold of yourself and tell me what's going on."

His confusion only mounted when tears sprang to the man's eyes and he begged, "Kill me quick. You'll be kind about it, at least."

Ginkgo couldn't help laughing. "Who in their right mind would dare raise their hand against a packmate of Harmonious Starmark, let alone the almost-bride of Lapis Mossberne."

"Sansa-san, for one. Isla, I think." With a cringing posture, he whispered, "Maybe even you."

"Back up. Start over. Shouldn't you be up to your elbows in clay right about now?"

"I begged off. Goh-sensei realized I wouldn't be any help today."

Ginkgo tried to pull Tenma to his feet, but the man lowered himself further, kowtowing dragon-style. With the beginnings of genuine concern, Ginkgo demanded, "Who did this to you?"

"Lilya-chan."

Impossible. "She's just a kid."

Tenma curled into an even tighter knot of distress and whimpered, "I'm sorry."

"For what?"

"I'm sorry, I'm sorry, I'm sorry," he chanted.

Ginkgo couldn't understand what had gotten into Tenma. Neither could he ignore what was obviously a plea for help. He hauled Tenma into his arms and carried him to the guest room, a clumsy task since the man was easily head-and-shoulders taller than Ginkgo.

Depositing Tenma on the bed, Ginkgo jumped up beside him, hauling the man into his arms. "Hey, hey, hey, now. Want me to get Eloquence on the phone? Hanoo? Lapis? Dad?"

Tenma groaned.

Ginkgo wasn't getting anywhere. "Show me your hand."

He surrendered both, palms pleading.

Tracing a sigil that made secrets safe, he said, "Nobody but us. You and me, okay? Now, what happened with Lilya?"

"She asked me why I'm not married yet. She wanted to know my wish for the future." Tenma hid his face against Ginkgo's shirt, so his words were all muffled. "I'm a teacher here. I thought it was one of those ... those teaching moments."

"You've always been patient with folks. A good listener."

Tenma raised his head. "She's *eleven*."

"Yeah, I know."

"She's even younger than Isla was, and Isla was practically a baby!"

Ginkgo snorted. "Be glad Isla didn't hear you say that."

Tenma laughed a little, relaxed a little.

"Out with it, Tenma."

"She proposed."

Ginkgo was stumped. "Lilya has a crush on you?"

Tenma slowly shook his head. "This wasn't *that*. Not a blushing girl making her first confession. This was a calm, calculated bid. She's going to have Glint work up a contract."

"And you came to me … why?"

"Talk some sense into her!"

"Oh, I'll talk to her," promised Ginkgo. His mind was racing, and he kept coming around to the same conclusion. "So … you're turning her down?"

"Of course!"

"What's your reason?"

"She's *eleven*."

"Age difference. That's all you've got?"

Tenma gaped at him, glasses askew.

"For an uncertain entity like you, it's not a bad deal, landing a beacon bride. Your future home would be in a secure location. Most of the household is conversant in Japanese. And the amenities are top notch—beachfront property, onsen baths, and a live-in nanny. That'd be me."

"The age gap. It's nearly *fifteen* years."

"That works in your favor. A young wife will boost your progeny projections."

Tenma shook his head. "Why are you even considering this?"

"Because I think Dad would approve. Put bluntly, you'd be a strategic acquisition for Stately House. And Glint'll probably be giddy, matching the Amaranthine Messiah with a girl whose birth established a dynasty."

Tenma rested his head on Ginkgo's shoulder. "You really think they'd allow it?"

"You really expected bloodshed?"

"Yes."

"I'm not going to kill you for putting your signature on a contract. And I'm not going to criticize Lilya's choice until I hear her reasoning. Realistically, you'd stick to your itinerary and come back when she's sixteen or seventeen. Do the whole courtship thing, then."

"W-we'd be family?"

"You and me? Sure. Along with a few dozen crossers, a partial herd of horses, a sedge of cranes, a nest of mice, one honeybee, two grumpy bear brothers, our French butler, and several members of the Amaranthine Council. Yay, verily, our Kith shelter runneth over, and we're always expanding." Ginkgo gently reminded, "Once he's back safe, Inti will also be calling Stately House home."

After a long silence, Tenma admitted, "Sounds too good to be true."

"What was that future wish you shared with Lilya? What do you truly, actually, honestly want?"

He whispered, "This. All of it."

"Even the eleven-year-old girl who proposes to give it to you?"

Tenma's words were like a vow. "If she is resolved, I will devote myself to her happiness."

Borrowing from the wisdom of cranes, Ginkgo asked, "Can such generosity lead to anything but joy?"

42

SMART CAT

Sinder was accustomed to getting his way. Every dragon was. But it was pointless trying to sway Timur and Torloo. Only when Sinder lost his temper did they bend, but his triumph left him feeling like a petulant child. They were obviously humoring him, because Torloo had lowered the stakes so far, Sinder and the rookies weren't doing anything more menacing than playing tag in the forest.

Well, to be fair, it was tag with traps.

Trapping an intelligent person wasn't the same as outwitting a dumb beast, especially one on their guard. To keep things interesting, he'd worked in several traps of his own. If the four winds favored him, Michaelson would fall for one.

It made an amusing daydream, but Sinder wasn't holding his breath.

Timur of the illustrious Order of Spomenka was undoubtedly

wise to a dragon's ways. They preserved knowledge and techniques that were supposed to be lost to time. Sinder knew for a fact that dragons from the heights had been tasked with the monumental chore of snuffing out any songs or fables that mentioned the tricks of the dragon slayer's trade. In the tales that remained, knights were praised for their bravery upon setting off and showered with glories upon their return. *How* they'd succeeded wasn't a matter of record.

Humans should have been no match for dragons, who were larger, fiercer, and stronger than any other predator. Yet every dragon was driven by three instincts—to fill a harem, to reach the sky, and to move with the seasons.

All dragonkind embraced a migratory existence, and it was the predictability of those courses that had led to their near demise. Learn the patterns. Lay the traps.

Of course, urges could be curtailed. Or more often, channeled.

Ancient dragon dwellings were sprawling affairs, invariably cross-shaped. Lords moved their entire household from one wing to the next with the turning of the seasons. And in more modest, modern harems, lords maintained four bedchambers, one for each bride—east, south, west, and north.

Sinder understood the pull. He kept his sanity by rearranging the furniture. Juuyu never minded. It gave him an excuse to clean. Maybe it was team building. Maybe it was group therapy.

Dragons were isolationists, obsessively secretive about their idiosyncrasies, now more than ever. Sinder understood that, too. Their traditions were already remarked upon, even criticized. The lords were reluctant to expose their culture, opening the way for mockery, speculation, psychoanalysis, or future attacks.

Which were a real possibility, thanks to the rogue.

Because that dragon wasn't immune to the pull of instinct.

The women he stole were stashed in makeshift harems. Many profilers believed he was after progeny, a frustrated male who'd refined his techniques once he realized he could only impregnate females of reaver descent.

A noteworthy discovery, to be sure. Lapis Mossberne was especially interested in that particular point, but Sinder was skeptical. If the rogue wanted his children, wouldn't he show more interest in gathering them up? Yes, some infants had gone missing, but those disappearances didn't correlate with the reports of fresh kidnappings and killings.

Sinder thought it more likely that an even greedier instinct drove the rogue. He wanted to gain the sky.

The rogue was after wings, something that traditionally took a thousand years. But the truth was far less poetic. It went without saying that dragon lords had long been forming alliances with reavers and benefiting from their tending. What most left unsaid was that those who consumed the souls of reavers—even the undisciplined, unrefined souls of unregistered reavers—could gain those selfsame wings.

And damn the rest of them.

The lords had looked on in horror when mounting evidence pointed to a dragon as the perpetrator of heinous crimes against humanity. Immediately, they'd put the scholars of the heights to work. Registries were opened. Lineages traced. Eggs tallied. Identities confirmed. And to the mystification of all, every male was both found and found innocent.

Meaning the rogue dragon was an impossibility.

No male had sired him. No female had carried him.

And nobody would believe them.

Despite every protestation of peace, dragons would be vilified. So when Hisoka Twineshaft approached the lords, asking for any detail, no matter how small, that would give trackers an edge in the chase, the dragons pledged their cooperation.

And when the cat smiled and singled out the Graennturn enclave's IT specialist, nobody questioned his choice in emissaries. Sinder was plucked from the heights of an urban high rise, thrown to the wolves, partnered to a phoenix, and trusted with more secrets than anyone should have to keep.

His musing were interrupted by the arrival of three reavers in the small clearing at the base of his hideaway. Had they managed to track him? That was promising.

No Kith in evidence. Should he trip a new trap? Just to see if they'd learned their lesson.

Earlier, the rookies had taken two hours to realize he'd compromised four of their members. If not for the Kith in their midst, they might never have realized that they'd begun trapping each other instead of him.

A low growl. A soft hiss.

Sinder glanced over his shoulder and winced as the twist pulled at his injuries. "He warded you? Smart."

Timur's feline partner crouched in the shadow of a bush, orange eyes burning with predatory zeal.

"Then again, he said you were the smart one." Sinder did *not* like the twitch in Fend's tail. "You going to let me off easy?"

The panther's lips peeled back, baring fangs, and his growl escalated into a snarl.

Sinder swore and sprang away, barely evading Fend's pounce. The animal's scream alerted the battlers and spurred Sinder through the treetops. He'd have to add a line in his report about warding the Kith, which was terrifyingly effective. Hisoka would be pleased. Michaelson and Fend were exactly what Naroo-soh needed—invulnerable and innovative.

Teetering to a halt on the sagging limb of an old pine, he worked his way closer to the trunk and climbed to one of the hideaways he'd created back when the rookies were more gullible. The scent of tree sap wasn't the best cover, but if he was lucky, he could catch his breath.

"Let me have a look."

Sinder started violently enough to lose his balance, but strong hands grabbed his wrists. Which was a little too much like being held captive. But his captor turned him loose and raised both hands.

"Peace, Sinder. Or should I call you Damsel?" Salali Fullstash grinned at him from under the brim of a battered hat. "I'm a neutral party in these games, so you're not caught."

"Salali," he mumbled. "Right. Thank you for your concern, but I'm fine."

"Let me have a look," he repeated with calm authority. "Or the scent of blood will give away your position quicker than a sneeze."

Was he bleeding? Sinder pressed a hand to the stitch in his side.

"Hold this." Salali pressed a blue pebble into his hand. "Gent, pass him Merl's bundle."

An overlarge blue jay dropped through the pine boughs and hopped sideways along the branch. From his beak dangled a cloth bag. Sinder accepted it with a puzzled nod.

"Eat," ordered Salali, who was busily unwinding lengths of gauze.

The bundle contained bite-sized squares of dense cake, thick with dried fruit and nuts. Popping one into his mouth, Sinder slowly chewed. And immediately felt better. He hadn't realized he was hungry. Rookie mistake. "Thanks," he mumbled.

"Thank Ginkgo." Salali slowly daubed a greenish paste onto the worst gash. Something antiseptic but laced with spikenard. "He owes me a favor. The goo and goodies are from Merl."

Sinder mumbled around a mouthful. "As much as I needed a friend in my corner, this feels like cheating."

"For all we know, the rogue has allies, too." Salali shifted in midair to doctor a different abrasion. "It could explain why there are glimmers of brilliance in a pattern dominated by baser instincts."

A second individual, somehow party to the crimes? Did the rogue—like Timur—have a smart partner? Someone with intelligence and influence. That was a chilling thought.

"Can I add that bit of speculation to my next report?" Sinder asked.

"Depends who you're reporting to."

"Twineshaft."

"Tell him," said Salali. "Tell him everything. Even if it doesn't seem important. Even if it doesn't seem related."

Sinder muttered, "I'll know."

"What'll you know?" countered the squirrel clansman lightly.

"I'll know if it's important. I'll know if it's related."

Salali pushed a second crystal into Sinder's hand like he was bartering for secrets. "Why?"

"Because Twineshaft tells me things." And it was important for this person to know it.

"Things? Or *everything*?" With a low chuckle, the squirrel clansman made an impressive leap. "You're his stash. Smart."

43

LIGHTS OUT

Lilya held Kyrie's hand all the way back from movie night. They'd been treated to back-to-back episodes of *Dare Together*, with hints that special guests would be arriving the following weekend. Rampant speculation pointed toward a visit from Caleb and Josheb Dare ... or any number of the cryptids they were so famous for tracking down.

It was long past curfew, but the event wasn't quite over. All the lights had been switched off, making everyone's trek back to their cabin a final hurdle. Growls and yelps and nervous laughter came from all sides. Older teens in ward colors lofted crystals, while battlers formed ranks around the younger kids in their cabins.

After all that spooky cryptid footage, every thin howl and slinking shadow took on an aura of menace.

"They are only teasing," murmured Kyrie.

Lilya tightened her grip on his hand. "Can you see?"

"Quite well. Do you want more light?"

Tempting as that might be, she shook her head. "That would only expose our location."

Kyrie pulled her into the shelter of the shrubs alongside the path. Up on tiptoe, he whispered in her ear. "We should go the long way around."

"Danger?" she breathed, placing her hand over his heart. Partly to show she trusted him, partly to see how fast it was beating.

"They are only teasing," he repeated. "Trust me."

Even though she was taller now, Kyrie was still many times stronger, so he didn't so much as stagger when Lilya climbed onto his back and tucked up her long legs. Once her arms folded around his shoulders, he carried her away. And with every giddying leap and swerve through the trees, she tried to stifle her giggles.

"Are we winning?" she whispered.

"I am good at these games."

"Who's chasing us?"

"Four dogs, two rabbits, and a monkey," he reported smugly. Kyrie reached back and touched her hair. "You are especially bright tonight."

"Am I?"

"Did something happen? Something pleasing?"

"I hope so." She prodded his side. "I'll tell you once we're under covers."

And just like that Kyrie was done playing games. With more speed than he usually displayed, his turned his darting course toward Zisa, neatly setting Lilya on Waaseyaa's doorstep before his dark hair had time to settle about his shoulders.

They changed for bed and nestled under the embroidered coverlet in the guest room, Gregor and Rifflet between them.

"I like this blanket," whispered Kyrie. "It hums."

She thought he might be right. But the tapestry in Glint's office had been more distinct.

He found her hand, then found her soul, which took longer than it used to. Papka's and Argent's new seal gave him trouble, but Kyrie was Kyrie. Eventually, a low melody thrummed against her senses, and she smiled.

"It's like a lullaby," she whispered.

"Yes. The sigils are for protection, and the song is a promise. All who sleep here are safe."

"Can you tell who made it?"

Kyrie hesitated. "I will not know for certain unless I touch him, but ... Glint Starmark. Probably."

"Not Radiance?" Lilya hadn't expected something so thoroughly beribboned to be the handiwork of an entirely masculine male. No wonder he'd been pleased when she complimented his embroidered tunic.

"Well?" Her brother squeezed her hand. "Why are you sparkling like star wine?"

"I want you to be the first person I tell."

Kyrie's voice lilted warmly. "I usually am."

"And you are again, but maybe not always." Lilya needed to acknowledge this out loud. "I'm not sure yet. Things will change."

"Change is natural. Not something to fear."

Taking a deep breath, Lilya announced, "I chose a husband today."

Kyrie took more time than usual to answer, but he was as calm as ever. "A person or a packet?"

"I wanted a person."

He hummed. "I would, too."

"I'm going to have Glint make the contract. It can be settled before our birthdays. Twelve is when it begins." She was feeling rather smug about it. "I've outwitted them all."

"All ...?"

"Matchmakers, applicants, bidders, prospectives." She scowled defiantly. "None of them can waste the heralds' time."

Kyrie caught on. "No one can propose to you because you proposed first. That is a fine strategy."

"I thought so, too."

"The process has always seemed arduous. How did you find someone so quickly?"

"Luck?"

Her brother trilled a pleased note. "Are you going to make me guess your choice, or will you tell me for yourself?"

"It's my news," she grumbled. "Don't listen to tattling winds."

"I am listening to you. Tell me who gained your favor."

She didn't think that was the right word. Not in the sense of having a favorite. Or maybe he meant favorable, which was a little like luck. "I chose Tenma-san."

"Oh, him." Kyrie didn't hesitate to say, "I like him very much."

Lilya was relieved to hear it. "Do you think it will work out?"

"Is that what you want?"

"Yes."

Kyrie said, "If that is also what he wants, it will work out."

"I'm not sure." Lilya remembered the stunned expression on Tenma's face and the haste with which he'd excused himself. "He looked like he might say *no*."

Kyrie held Lilya's hand until he was certain she was deeply asleep. Only then did he slip from the bed in search of his brother. Zisa appeared the moment Kyrie stepped outside and pointed the way. Ginkgo was inside the Kith shelter, lolling between Snow's front paws as he told her stories about Stately House's swimming club.

Ginkgo's ears pricked. "What's up, little bro?"

"I have been thinking." Kyrie offered his hand to Snow before sitting in the straw. "I would like to be assessed as a reaver."

Slinging an arm around his shoulders, Ginkgo said, "This is where I have to point out the obvious. We're not reavers."

"We are half."

"Granted." He pulled his tail around so it lay across both their laps. "So ... you want someone outside our family—a neutral party—to assess your reaver half?"

"Yes."

"To what end?"

Kyrie was used to having to delineate his points clearly and without any trace of a dragon's sway. "I would like to be ranked. How else will I know if I am improving?"

"Sure, I'll buy that." Ginkgo nudged him. "What else?"

"I would like an opinion as to my classification."

Ginkgo snorted. "It doesn't take a specialist to figure out you're a ward."

"What if my affinity for sigilcraft is part of my Amaranthine heritage?" Kyrie quietly pointed out, "Lapis is also a crystal adept."

"Lapis might speak for the dragon clans, but he's hardly typical. Take Damsel, for instance. He's useless with all but the most basic sigils. Remember how Timur took him out?" Ginkgo sketched a sigil in the air and sent it spinning toward the ceiling. "There's as much diversity within each clan as there is within humanity."

"I understand that an assessment would be largely speculative," Kyrie said slowly. "But that does not mean it would have no value. Assessment could uncover hidden aptitudes, which in turn could direct my studies."

Ginkgo searched his face, and his gaze softened. "Glint Starmark has the necessary experience to give an honest reckoning, but I cannot recommend you try him."

"Why not?" Kyrie winced at his own sharpness and softly added, "I would like to know why, please."

"You probably already know." Ginkgo's ears flattened sideways. "Every assessment begins with parentage and pedigree. He would ask all kinds of questions you can't answer. Questions Dad would consider intrusive. Even forbidden."

"Dad will not allow it?"

With a huff, his brother gruffly said, "He's protecting more than you and me with his silence."

This had occurred to Kyrie as well. "Is he protecting the woman who carried me?"

Ginkgo's ears flattened further, then bounced forward in false cheerfulness. "He would if he could, I'm sure"

A foxy answer. The kind that meant they were dancing close to secrets.

"I think," Ginkgo began cautiously. "I think it would be wiser to ask Sinder for an assessment."

"Is that one of his jobs?"

"Not likely, but he could offer an opinion. And he wouldn't ask all kinds of awkward questions." Ginkgo's gaze begged him to understand. To catch what was left unspoken. To hear what he wasn't allowed to say.

Kyrie sat up a little straighter. Was it possible? He was almost afraid to ask. "He will not ask the questions because he already knows the answers …?"

"Probably."

"Do you know who my birth parents are?"

"Of course I do, little bro. I've always known."

"Will you tell me?"

Ginkgo smiled and hugged him. "That's Dad's right and responsibility."

"Will he tell me?"

"Yeah. He was just saving it up until you were older."

Kyrie asked, "Like now?"

"I'm thinking … yeah. Seems to me this is our proving journey, and when the sons of Argent Mettlebright return home, he'll have things to say to each of us."

He took a slow breath and released it fully. "May I talk to Sinder?"

Ginkgo looked up. "Mind if I clutter up the place with a dragon?

Or should we take our conversation elsewhere?"

Snow lowered her head to nip Ginkgo's ear.

"Right. Sit tight, little bro. I'll go see if our fair Damsel's awake."

"What if he is sleeping?"

With a playful tweak to Kyrie's ear, Ginkgo answered, "I'll wake him with a kiss, of course!"

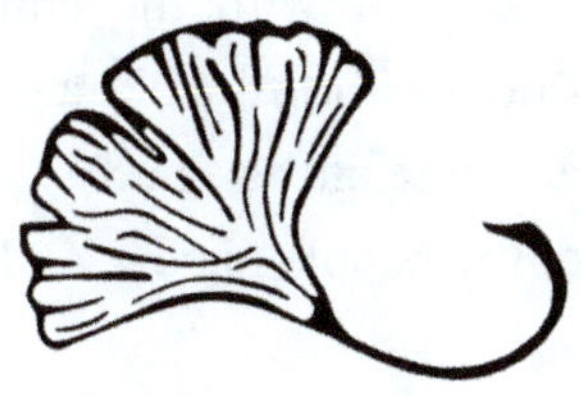

44

SET STRAIGHT

Ginkgo closed the shelter door and lifted his nose to the night wind, hoping to catch a whiff of spikenard. There were a lot of places Sinder might be. Including away.

With no warning whatsoever, arms slid around Ginkgo from behind, and Zisa nuzzled his shoulder.

"You're a regular ninja," Ginkgo accused.

The tree petted his ear. "Did you forget I am here?"

"Would I do something that silly?"

"You are sometimes silly. Usually with the children." Zisa quietly added, "Thank you for not treating me like a child."

That took him aback. "Zisa, you're old as ages."

"I am younger than most of the people I know. And people call me ... simple."

"That's hardly a bad thing." Ginkgo turned in the tree's embrace to study his expression.

"They are *not* complimenting me."

"Do you want to be complimented?"

Zisa brightened. "Yes, please."

Ginkgo rubbed their noses together. "Your kindnesses are uncomplicated, and if your flowers are sweet, it is because your nature is doubly so. Your strength resonates through both halves of my soul, which makes me want to linger in your shadow. And your generosity is steadily turning me into a glutton. I can't help wanting more."

Wonderment widened Zisa's eyes. "Are you teasing?"

"Every word is true."

"You are good at compliments."

Ginkgo grinned. "I've learned a thing or two from wolvish ballads."

Zisa looked heartbreakingly hopeful. "Do you love me?"

"Are you surprised?"

The tree stole a kiss.

Ginkgo let him.

"People usually work harder to resist me," said Zisa. "You do not even try."

"You and I have something in common. I love the attention." Ginkgo rubbed their cheeks together. "Zisa, you have become my home away from home."

With a happy little croon, Zisa said, "You are lovely."

"And *you* are distracting. I'm supposed to be finding Sinder. Any chance you know where I should look?"

Nodding toward his little house, Zisa said, "He is resting."

"Really? He shouldn't have needed more sleep."

"Timur captured him and will not let him roam."

Ginkgo pricked his ears and smiled. "My kind of challenge. I'm going to steal Damsel back."

"Should I let you?"

That was an interesting idea. "Could you stop me?"

Zisa's smile turned sly. "Anyone under my branches is at my mercy."

"He'll thank me," promised Ginkgo. "Trust me."

"I will allow it. For your brother's sake."

"Do you know *everything* that happens under your branches?"

With a finger to his lips, Zisa whispered, "Usually."

Easing out of the tree's embrace, Ginkgo jogged to the house and let himself in. From within the circle of Timur's arms, Sinder reached pleadingly. With a jaunty salute and a sound-dampening sigil, Ginkgo crouched beside Fend, whose tail lashed the floor in silent annoyance.

"Work with me, Fend," Ginkgo bargained. "I get Damsel. You get your usual spot."

The big feline rose and stretched lazily.

Ginkgo used a bit of foxish finesse to deepen Timur's sleep, then lifted his arm. Sinder slipped free and minced toward the door, giving Fend a wide berth. The panther hissed softly, then sprang onto the bed, inserting himself into the vacancy at Timur's side.

Even before Ginkgo had them tucked in, Timur had burrowed into his partner's fur. Ginkgo's grateful bow was lost on Fend, who turned his back on the rest of the world in a feline snub.

Back outside, Ginkgo drew up short at the sight of Sinder in Zisa's arms.

"I'm *fine*," Sinder sighed. "And I know why I'm fine. Thank you for sheltering us."

"Good dragon," crooned Zisa "Brave boy."

"Up for a bit of a puzzle?" asked Ginkgo. "Kyrie's waiting on us."

Sinder took a gratefully receptive posture. "I'm yours until the dawn patrol."

"Wait." Zisa's head turned. "Mikoto is coming."

Ginkgo angled his ears toward the trail. Sure enough, the slow, soft tread of boots approached. Moments later, Mikoto lifted an arm, left the path, and cut their way. Zisa abandoned Sinder in order to welcome the headman with characteristic affection. Which was clearly mutual.

With a gurgle of laughter, Zisa stole Noble from Mikoto's pocket and skipped to Waaseyaa's door.

"Hello," Mikoto greeted in a low voice.

"Couldn't sleep?" asked Ginkgo.

"Not really." He shrugged awkwardly. "Am I intruding?"

Ginkgo hooked his arm. "Kyrie's waiting on us, and you're welcome. Did you know there's a Kith shelter just over there?"

"Yes." With a faint smile, Mikoto remarked, "I did not realize you were acquainted with Transcendence."

"Who now?" His ears went cockeyed.

Sinder interrupted to grumble, "Well, *I* didn't know this was here. Why are there so many barriers around a barn?"

"I know, right?" said Ginkgo, pulling open the door.

"It is a wolvish custom," said Mikoto. "Glint and Radiance supported her decision to go into seclusion."

"You mean Snow?" Ginkgo turned to Sinder. "The Kith in here knows you're coming. Best I can tell, she doesn't mind."

"About Snow." Mikoto touched his shoulder. "Did Radiance tell you she is Kith?"

The question confused him. "She introduced her. How else would I know her name?"

"Nickname," gently corrected the headman. "Radiance has a playful manner. She finds misunderstandings like this amusing."

"I'm sorry?" Ginkgo didn't like the direction Mikoto seemed to be going. His ears drooped.

Mikoto took the lead and offered his palms to the white dog. "May I enlighten our guests?"

Snow's gaze locked with Ginkgo's, and she dipped her head.

"I am pleased to introduce Transcendence Starmark, who is chief of Wardenclave's security team. They are often referred to as the Demon Dogs of Denholm. Transcendence has been in seclusion since the death of her bondmate last winter."

"You're a traditionalist?" asked Sinder, who'd lowered himself into a passive crouch just inside the entrance.

Mikoto hesitated, but Snow—who Ginkgo really needed to think of as Transcendence—made a sharp gesture with her muzzle.

"This was her choice, but also a necessity." Mikoto's whole posture radiated respect. "The chief's bondmate Path was a Kith of the Starmark clan."

45

BY YOUR DEEDS

Now that he had a name, Mikoto had sort of hoped that Sinder could call out to the whisper of wind that was suddenly, achingly missing. The stillness was unnerving. An absence he'd always associated with the end of summer. It had always meant that Lupe was gone from Wardenclave. Except now he knew that he'd lost touch with his imp.

The lonesomeness left him empty, breathless, but Kyrie needed Sinder. Something about an assessment.

"Why me?" asked Sinder, looking between the Mettlebright brothers.

Ginkgo's tail puffed and settled. "Because you won't ask unnecessary questions."

Sinder made one of those pretty little fluting sounds that reminded Mikoto of the avian clans. Finally, the dragon said, "I'm willing, so long as you don't ask how I came to my conclusions."

The boy, who was usually really reserved, all but abased himself.

Lowering himself carefully to one knee, Sinder touched Kyrie's hair. "Hey, kid. I get that this is important to you, and I'll give it my best shot. But I doubt I can tell you anything your family hasn't already figured out."

"But you are a dragon," said Kyrie.

"So's your friend Lapis."

Kyrie caught the hem of Sinder's sleeve. "He is like Mother. He loves me too well to see anything but the best."

Sinder's lips quirked. "For all his scholarly pursuits, he's certainly a romantic. Fine, then. I won't ask a bunch of questions. More than words, I need deeds."

As the boy eagerly presented his palms, Mikoto began to wonder if he was intruding on something private. He edged away, trying to fade into the background. And out the door.

"Mikoto, stay," said Sinder.

Of course he'd stay. Why would he leave? Not when Sinder wanted him.

Ginkgo thwapped the dragon's shoulder. "Don't *do* that!"

Sinder swore and hurried to pat Mikoto's face. "My bad. I get careless with friends because they're mostly immune. Sorry."

"I did not notice," admitted Mikoto.

"Even worse." Sinder turned to Kyrie. "Help me work with him? I know there aren't any dragons in Wardenclave, but leaving a world leader vulnerable is just asking for trouble."

"I am willing." Kyrie jumped to his feet. "It is one of my responsibilities at home."

Mikoto inclined his head and answered in Japanese. "I am in your hands."

Kyrie slipped to his side, went up on tiptoe, and asked, "Why are you alone?"

"Noble is with Zisa."

He shook his head and whispered, "Did you send her away?"

"She is missing," Mikoto admitted, surprised by the tremor in his tone.

The boy cocked an ear toward the window, then the door. Patting Mikoto's hand, he solemnly said, "Trust me."

And he wanted to. So much. But not because the half-dragon was trying to sway him. Perhaps it was a case of having no other choice. Mikoto took a receptive stance and cleared his throat.

Mercifully, Kyrie interpreted this in a positive light.

"I'll need to see him in action," Sinder was saying. "How much leeway will you give me?"

"Whatever you need," said Ginkgo.

Sinder frowned at the sky. "Could he join the rookies for maneuvers?"

Ginkgo gestured for his younger brother to speak for himself. Kyrie asked, "Why, please?"

"Because you're eager, and it's next. And it doesn't really matter where we start. I'll need to see you in different settings. All I know so far is that you have a way with barriers." He pointed in the vicinity of the boy's shoulder. "And that you have a way with crystals."

Kyrie loosened the ties on the yukata that must have been his sleep clothes. Pulling free one arm, he displayed an armband set with pale crystals—lavender, blue, and green.

"Personal wards?" asked Sinder.

"Not precisely." Kyrie shyly admitted, "I passed every test. I do not require safeguards, but ... if I did not keep these crystals close, they would miss me."

Sinder's incredulity came out in a soft whistle. "Crystal adept?"

"Quite the charmer," confirmed Ginkgo.

"Well, then. I propose a practical test. The battlers in these mountains are trying to work out how to track a dragon. And catch one. See if you can outdo them. Chase after me. I want to see how you fare with tracking. Bonus points if you can show off a bit of sigilcraft on the fly."

Ginkgo raised a hand. "Aren't you worried all those rookies will get between you?"

"I could stay with him," offered Mikoto.

Kyrie turned his wrist gratefully, but he said, "You would not be able to keep up."

"Not a bad idea to have friends to fall back on," countered Sinder. "How about we pair Mikoto with Timur. They'll do well enough. And Kyrie can run with Torloo."

Mikoto didn't recognize the name, but Kyrie flushed with pleasure. "He is my friend."

Ginkgo hesitated and turned to Transcendence, who'd been listening closely to every word. "What do you think? I'd feel better with one of your people on hand. Just in case."

The white dog nosed his shirt, nipped his ear, and huffed.

A sharp rap sounded on the door. With a murmured apology, one of the guards let himself inside. Mikoto was a little surprised to see Glint and Radiance's youngest son.

"Da?" Kyrie blurted, only to dissemble. "You look like Ever's da."

"Well met! My name is Reveille Starmark. You must be Ever's good friend Kyrie."

The boy quickly presented his palms.

Ginkgo waved a casual greeting. "The resemblance is uncanny."

"You're not the first to mention it." Reveille met Kyrie's palms and smiled faintly. "May I consider your mistake a compliment?"

Kyrie blushed to the tips of ears. "Please, do! I love Ever's da almost as much as my own."

"Then trust should come easy and linger long." He took a conspiratorial tone. "I was whelped after my eldest brother left Wardenclave, so I don't really know him. I'm a little jealous."

"Come and visit?" the boy suggested.

"Maybe someday. But let us concern ourselves with *this* day." With a jaunty flick of fingers toward Transcendence, he said, "Since my aunt cannot run with you herself, I will share your path."

46
PRACTICALLY FAMILY

Lilya woke to Gregor's finger in her nose. His delight when she opened her eyes was contagious, and she was still smiling when she lugged her freshly dressed nephew into the kitchen.

"Good morning," murmured Waaseyaa, who was setting breakfast on the table. He had Rifflet tangled in his hair and Noble bouncing around his ankles, trying to reach the little dragon. Yet the man seemed pleased to have their company.

Ginkgo strolled through the door and laughed. "Which one of you wants my help most?"

"'Ko!" called Gregor, reaching eagerly.

So Ginkgo swooped in to pluck up Gregor, freeing Lilya to rescue Waaseyaa from Rifflet's antics.

Not until they sat to eat did Lilya ask, "Where's Kyrie?"

"With Sinder. I've already made his excuses to the morning

instructors." Ginkgo casually added, "You can stay back, too. If you want."

Lilya smiled. It was good timing. "May I visit Glint?"

"Something important come up?" Ginkgo asked, inviting her to say more.

"Yes."

He waggled his ears at her and said, "Best take care of it, then."

Lilya wondered how much Ginkgo already knew. For once, she hoped it was everything, because that meant he had no complaints. Stuffing the last of her breakfast into her mouth, she stepped into her boots and hurried away.

The morning was overcast, with more wind than usual. The ordinary weather-making kind, not Kyrie's secret-telling kind. Maybe it was going to rain? With half an eye on the sky, she jogged up the long stairway to the Starmark's back door and let herself in. Only to stare in astonishment at the sight before her.

Lyre, Lute, and Lore weren't alone. From under the tumble of pillows and puppies, white fur showed. A furred foot that was more like a paw. A clawed hand covered in fur. Shaggy white hair falling across a face that was almost familiar.

He had to be a crosser. Yes, there was his tail. She barely ever saw adult crossers besides Ginkgo. One or two on television. This one was completely relaxed, despite her intrusion. He had to know she was there. Was he trying not to wake the pups?

"Hello?" she said softly.

His tail gave a twitch and a thump, and one eye opened. "How polite. If you prefer, we can pretend you didn't see me."

Lilya knelt and reached out to tug Lore's ear. "Why?"

As the puppies roused and wriggled excitedly, the crosser rolled onto his side, propping his head on his fist. He had wolf's ears, which were taller and narrower than Ginkgo's fox ears, and his eyes were copper. She'd never heard of another Starmark crosser.

He said, "I make people nervous."

"Not me." Lilya hauled Lyre into her lap and giggled at the face-washing that earned her. "Crossers are almost my whole family. May I know your name?"

"Rude of me. Most people run before we get to a proper greeting." He offered his hands, which had smooth, callused skin on the palms but thick fur on their backs, his wrists, and all the way up his arms, disappearing under the sleeves of a loose T-shirt with **HUSH-HUSH** printed across the chest. "My name is Moon-kin Ambervelte. I'm here to visit my sisters, more or less."

"Ambervelte is a wolf pack."

"And I'm a wolf. My pack has close ties to Wardenclave. I'm Radiance's big brother."

Suddenly, Lilya realized why he'd looked familiar. "You look like Uncle Laud!"

"Understandable, since Laud is my nephew. One of Radiance's boys. Which means you must be Ever's friend. The beacon." He hesitated, nose twitching, ears cocking. "Only I can't tell. Why can't I tell?"

"Wards and things." Lilya proudly pointed out, "Papka and Uncle Argent are the best."

He reached out, then pulled back his hand.

She made it easier on him by crawling closer. "Do you want to sniffen me?"

Moon grinned sheepishly. "You don't mind?"

"No. I'm used to it. Stately House has close ties to the Elderbough pack, and wolves spend a lot of time sorting out scents." She wasn't little anymore, but wolves were big and strong. Plenty of lap space. "Kyrie and I usually end up sitting on Roo-nii's lap. He's Naroo-soh."

Without a fuss, he gathered her close. "Friends call me Moon. Why are these pups referring to you as Angel?"

So she told him about Radiance's prank.

And he told her other stories of mischief from Radiance's childhood. "My father entrusted her to me even though I was little more than a pup myself."

Lilya caught on. "You're like Quen for Ever."

"And Laud for Quen." Moon's tail swayed contentedly. "I am both Radiance's brother and foster parent. And long, long ago, I was Glint's first friend."

She recalled her errand then. "I came to talk to Glint."

"He's meeting with someone. The first of many dignitaries who'll be arriving for the Dichotomy Day ceremonies. I was able to escort him part of the way." Moon asked, "Want me to summon him?"

Before Lilya could protest, Moon whistled a piercing note.

An instant later, Glint hastened into the room, concern fading into a warm smile. "Angel," he said, sounding relieved. He sank to his knee. "You came back?"

Did he think she wouldn't?

She was still trying to figure out how to reassure him when Glint's guest strolled into view ... and struck a thoughtful pose.

Lilya guessed they did look a little strange. With Moon for her throne and Glint on one knee before them, like she was some kind of queen.

But Lapis had always been willing to play along, no matter how silly the rules of the games she and Kyrie made up. So he swept across the room and settled gracefully beside Glint, offering a bejeweled hand with all the grandeur of a fairy tale prince.

Sapphire eyes sparkling, he drawled, "Hello, sealed girl."

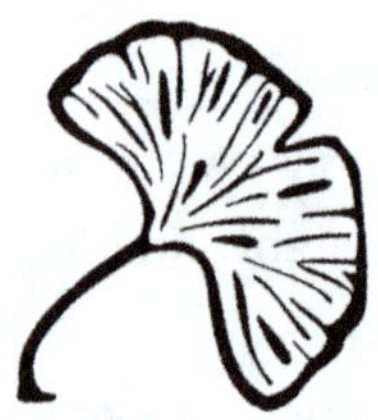

47

LIKENESS

Reveille escorted Kyrie through dense forest, skirting two mountains before slowing to stroll into a clearing ringed by camouflaged tents. Battlers and Kith alike noted their arrival, and Kyrie eased closer to Reveille, hiding in his shadow.

Lifting his arm to shoot a quizzical glance, Reveille asked, "Nervous?"

Kyrie chose a different word. "Wary."

"No use hiding behind me."

"Perhaps." Improbable as it sounded, even passing a few paces from their seats around three cookfires, most of the battlers wouldn't notice him. It was a useful trick. One his father had strongly suggested he keep quiet.

There were limits, of course. And proof of them stepped out of a netting-draped canopy.

It had been years since Torloo left Japan, but he hadn't

changed. In fact, he looked younger than Kyrie remembered, but that was probably because he was getting taller while Torloo was not. The gap in their ages was closing. Kyrie was quickly catching up, and that was incredibly comforting. He and his friend would go through their adolescence together.

"Kyrie?" Torloo's nose was working almost as hard as his tail. "I *know* you are here."

Wolves weren't much for subtlety. Reluctantly, Kyrie stepped into plain sight. "Here."

Even though Kyrie had seen Torloo the night Sinder was injured, Torloo hadn't seen him. Because Kyrie hadn't wanted to be seen or stopped. When he was littler, it had confused him that, despite the Elderbough trackers' impressive reputation, they were so easy to elude. He didn't like to mention it. Back then, he hadn't wanted to hurt their feelings. Now, it was just another trick he knew better than to mention.

Torloo darted forward so fast, Kyrie barely had time to open his arms before he was scooped into a spinning hug.

Reveille stood watching them with arms folded. "I take it you're acquainted?"

"We are *friends*," corrected Torloo.

All around the camp, reavers looked on with openly curious stares.

"When did he ...?"

"Isn't that ...?"

"Notice his eyes?"

"Didn't the briefing say ...?"

And over and over, two words cycled—*dragon* and *rogue*. Before Kyrie could ask what the battlers meant, Torloo held up a hand, signaling for silence, just as Timur and Mikoto arrived on Fend. Sinder stalked into the clearing, commanding attention.

Timur dismounted and immediately herded Kyrie and Torloo toward the canopy. "Sinder will talk to you, explain his plan for the morning," he told Torloo. "I'll fill in the rookies while they finish their breakfasts. Yes?"

"Yes. Thank you," said Torloo, who looped an arm around Kyrie and ushered him the rest of the way out of the limelight.

A ward shimmered faintly as they ducked past netting. Kyrie resisted the urge to inspect it closely, but he could tell it was Timur's handiwork. And that its primary function was dampening sound.

Although there were padded benches off to the sides, the canopy's main furnishing was a central table. Maps and lists covered its surface, their corners weighed down by an interesting jumble of stones—some rough, some smooth, some crystal.

Kyrie scanned the maps idly until he recognized the lake where they'd bathed and swapped stories. Orienting himself on that landmark, he quickly made sense of the rest and frowned. There was more to the Denholm range than he'd realized.

"Brother told me you would be at camp." Torloo placed a finger on the map, indicating Wardenclave's song circle. "My responsibilities kept me from seeking you out."

"Nobody told me." Kyrie shyly admitted, "I would have come sooner."

Torloo glanced over his shoulder and lowered his voice. "And I would have asked Timur to speak on my behalf."

Kyrie couldn't contain a pleased trill. It was good to have friends.

Touching another map, Kyrie skimmed a neighboring list. "You are training battlers?"

"Yes. Brother chose these battlers for their potential as trackers."

"And you are their teacher?"

"They are learning basic skills." Torloo began to gather up loose pages. "I will send them to my brothers before long."

Kyrie took a step back and courteously averted his eyes. Torloo hadn't said anything, but his body language made it obvious—at least to Kyrie—that there were secrets strewn across the table. He only felt a little guilty at mentally reviewing the information he'd already acquired.

Poison.

Sway.

Camouflage.

Ambush.

Torloo appeared to be teaching these battlers about tracking dragons. And Sinder was obviously helping them, which is why he'd been injured. But ... *was* it only tracking? The equipment lists included a terrifying spectrum of offensive sigilcraft, hypodermic darts, and crystal tagging.

If these were battler games, they were extremely dangerous ones.

Why would the Elderboughs be hunting dragons?

Timur batted his way past the netting and offered a gruff greeting. Fend shadowed his steps and disappeared under the table.

Torloo took a receptive posture and asked, "Is there more to this than the reunion of friends?"

"Yes." Kyrie summed up his desire to be assessed, then asked, "Where is Reveille?"

"Waiting outside," said Timur. "He doesn't need to know everything in order to keep you safe. I can't tell you everything, either, but no one can question my right to talk about myself."

Kyrie stood a little straighter and positioned his hands to promise secrecy.

Timur dropped to one knee before him, putting them more on a level. "To be clear, your Dad knows about me, as do Mum and Papka. But I don't think Ginkgo has all the particulars. Just what he's gleaned from watching me with Sinder. And neither do any of my siblings except Annika."

Annika was the sister right above Lilya. Like Timur, she held a battler's classification and had gone away to study with Aunt Sansa's people. That had to be part of the secret.

"My battler training upholds a longstanding family tradition. I specialize in dragons."

Kyrie didn't even try to hide his astonishment. "Like me?"

"Too right." Timur caressed Kyrie's hair. "Having you in my family helped me choose my courses."

It had never occurred to Kyrie that he could have brought his questions to someone besides Lapis. Like a dragon specialist. "You know things about me?"

"Not as much as Sinder, but more than most." Timur's expression gentled. "Sorry to keep something so important from you."

"I was little." Kyrie's heart thumped in anticipation of future conversations. "I have grown."

"As has my trust."

Which may have been the highest compliment Timur could have paid.

"Right. So. Torloo, Sinder, and I are working together. The battlers who just chased Sinder into the forest are learning tactics for tracking and restraining dragons."

Sinder strolled in as if that had been his cue. "Oh, don't look so surprised. All I did was circle back. Everything settled?"

Timur stood. "I was just getting around to your minigame."

With a nod to Torloo, Sinder said, "Thank you for your indulgence, leader. I'm confident that the challenge I've issued to Kyrie won't interfere with the rookies' efforts."

"A challenge?" prompted Torloo.

"His affinities interest me. I want to find out if they have practical applications. Kyrie will give chase. I'll evade. Torloo will bear witness. Reveille will keep watch."

Torloo's tail puffed and settled a few times. "Is it wise for Kyrie's test and the battlers' mission to run concurrently?"

"Why not?"

"The battlers might mistake Kyrie for prey."

Sinder smirked. "They'll never see him."

"And the traps?"

"In the unlikely event of a misstep, the traps aren't lethal, and you and Reveille will be right there. Assuming you can keep up."

Torloo looked honestly baffled. "You know my speed."

"Oh, you're faster," Sinder drawled. "But you're definitely going to run into trouble."

Kyrie immediately understood. Games like this were fun. And necessary.

"What kind of trouble?" Torloo patiently asked, though his tail was puffed double.

Sinder's smile widened. "Like now, for instance. Where is your friend?"

From under the table, where he now sat with Fend, Kyrie watched Torloo turn a circle.

"Never discount a dragon," said Sinder. "Even a young one. We're good at these games."

Kyrie liked being included, liked being Sinder's brother.

But Torloo's agitation grew, to the point that he tucked his tail. "I am forewarned."

Then something else, too soft to hear. But the winds were willing, and they carried the young wolf's troubled words to Kyrie—*he is like him.*

48

BLESSING

Lilya had always considered Lapis part of her family. His face had been bending into view since her cradle days, because he doted on Kyrie. But Lapis was too kind to part her from the brother she adored. He had two arms, and so he would carry them both away. Some of her earliest memories involved midnight blue hair, trilling lullabies, and reaching for sparkling baubles that seemed to be singing.

Lapis came to Stately House more than any of the other members of the Amaranthine Council, and she was sure that in his heart, their home was his home.

"Who banished your sparkle?" Lapis asked in scandalized tones. "Surely, it is a crime against the Maker to hide such brilliance under a bushel basket."

Lilya lifted her wrists, displaying the crystals that made up her wards.

"Lovely, well-behaved remnants, to be sure." The dragon pointed at her belly with one manicured claw, then twirled it. "Your back?"

"Yes, on my back." It was no use pretending nothing was there. More softly, she said, "Uncle Lapis, it's *supposed* to be a secret."

He sniffed. "Not from me."

She glanced up at Moon, whose tail had begun a cheery thump against the floor.

Lapis gracefully waved away her concern. "*He* is a secret, as well. We are *all* in excellent company."

"Who are we to question Argent's precautions?" asked Glint.

"I can and I do!" Lapis beckoned to Lilya with both hands. "Show me."

"Manners," groused Glint. "Surely you can see that it would be inappropriate."

"We are family. Practically." Lapis appealed to Lilya. "I suppose you have grown somewhat since I last assisted with your baths. Where *is* Kyrie, incidentally? He will vouch for me."

Lilya smiled. "I'll vouch for you, too."

"There, see?" Lapis applied himself to Moon. "Why would Glint see overtures where there are none?"

With a short laugh, Moon suggested, "Because he is a father?"

Lapis widened his eyes and tutted. "Lilya is like a daughter to me! Or a niece, at the very least. *Tell* them, Lilya."

She thought perhaps it was time to change the subject. "Uncle Lapis, did you know I found a wind dragon."

He blinked.

He blinked again.

"Surely, you jest?" he murmured. "A wind dragon? Here?"

"I named him Rifflet." She claimed one of his hands in both her own. "He has the sweetest little voice."

Lapis succumbed to a flurry of blinks.

Meanwhile, Glint leaned through the door and called, "Radiance? Would you be so good as to … arbitrate?"

She waltzed in, shook her head at them, clapped her hands, and took charge. "We don't have time for this! Snow finally agreed to this outing, and I won't see it delayed. Lord Mossberne, you are more than welcome to join us. Lilya, we're going somewhere safe for your wee ribbon monster, so fetch him along. For Lapis' sake."

The dragon looked intrigued. "May I ask the nature of this errand?"

Moon was close enough to tap Lapis' shoulder. "I'm here for the first time in a good while, and I've coaxed my sister to share my path to her bondmate's monument. I will say the words she cannot."

Lapis grew solemn. "Surely, I would be intruding."

But they coaxed, and he smiled and offered to sing a song of remembrance. Which was welcomed with such fluster, Lilya got the impression that Lapis would be doing something rare.

When he trailed after her to fetch Rifflet, she quietly asked, "Is the song special, or is the song special because you're singing it?"

"A little of both." Most of his attention was now on the soaring tree overhead. "Dragons collect songs and stories, but instead of committing them to paper, we commit them to memory. And to melody."

"You sing for us all the time."

Lapis gave a demure trill. "It is my pleasure to lavish upon Stately House what the wider world rarely hears."

Lilya stopped on one of the wide stairs. "Are you secretly

majestic, or something?"

"I am *publicly* majestic. I am secretly myself and happiest with people who take me entirely for granted."

She plucked at his sleeve. "I'll let you check my seal, but only if Ginkgo's there."

"I look forward to his opinion on the matter."

Lilya jumped down one step but lingered there. "Do you like seals?"

"In the same way I like crossword puzzles and translating ancient poetry. But not nearly as much as I like storytelling in the naproom or taking part in amateur theatricals."

That's what he called any game of make believe. Lilya knew Lapis was supposed to be a world-renowned scholar, but whenever he was at Stately House, it didn't show.

Thinking of Uncle Waaseyaa, Lilya asked, "Why don't you adopt a crosser?"

"Ah." He smiled faintly. "I could. I might. But then I would have to *choose*, and I would really rather belong to all of you."

"Truly?"

"Mostly." Lapis fiddled with the rings on his fingers. "I will acknowledge that adoption would be the most sensible course for someone like me."

Lilya thought she understood. "You don't want to be sensible?"

"No." He laughed and sighed and shook his head.

"What is the secret wish of your heart?" Lilya took a receptive posture. "You don't have to say. But I've found it helps to know that. About yourself."

Lapis smiled warmly. "Those who know me well know that I do not wish to remain a bachelor forever."

"You want a harem? Brides from east and west, north and south?"

"One bride would suffice. If she can be found."

"That would be good," Lilya agreed. "Not me, though."

He warbled his surprise. "Certainly not! I will probably always see you as a daughter."

Lilya challenged, "Even when I look older than you?"

"How forward thinking. A sister, perhaps?"

She nodded approvingly. "I'd like having both you and Kyrie for brothers."

Lapis inclined his head, but his smile was quizzical. "What put such an idea in your head?"

Before she could tell him about Glint's ridiculous list and her decisive countermeasure, something else occurred to her. "I need to know something, please. It's important."

"By all means." Lapis sat upon his step, folded his hands, and waited.

Not for the first time, it occurred to Lilya that a dragon's full attention was dazzling, even if you were mostly used to it. She firmed her posture and began. "Tenma Subaru is your apprentice."

"He is." Lapis inquired, "Did you meet him here?"

"Yes."

"I will seek him out in due course."

Lilya asked, "Do mentors have to give their blessing when it's time for them to marry?"

He pouted thoughtfully. "The boy is dear to me, and I wish to see him happily settled. No easy task, given his temperament. He longs for deep connections, and he deserves to be cherished. Yet he is tossed about by the plans of others. It is not that his trust is misplaced, but … he underestimates himself. As his mentor, I would certainly step in if I thought he was making an unwise decision. Or put a word in Harmonious' ear. He has more in the way of experience where females are … ah." Lapis stopped himself and waved a hand. "I apologize for rambling on. Did you have a question for me, Lilya child?"

"Yes. Will you give me your blessing?"

"For …?"

"Tenma-san. I chose him." Pointing back the way they came, she added, "I was going to ask Glint to write my offer."

Lapis quietly asked, "Is that so?"

"Yes." Feeling suddenly uncertain, she mumbled, "If Tenma-san doesn't like it, he can always shred it and burn it."

"I am not discounting you. Give me a moment to consider." But even as he said it, Lapis gently lifted her hands, as if to kiss her knuckles. "This *is* unexpected."

She nodded and silently studied the dragon's manicure. Today, his claws looked as if they'd been carved from his namesake stone, with the tips lightly dipped in gold.

"Lilya." He waited for her to meet his gaze. "I have no firsthand experience with bonding and matrimony, but I am no stranger to contracts and the diplomacy required to appease all sides in the most complex of arrangements. And … I am no stranger to you. Would you allow me to act as your go-between?"

Oh. That was smart. *Really* smart.

Flinging her arms around him, she whispered, "I'm so glad you're here."

"Is that *yes*?" he asked in teasing tones. "I should not have to tell you that having a dragon to speak for you is both rare *and* majestic."

Lilya nodded. "Please, speak for me."

"I will win the whole world to your side."

He was probably forgetting about Mum. But there was time, so she smiled and said, "One groom would suffice."

49

EVERY TOOL

Kyrie liked games, and he was eager to play in one that could test his limits. Even so, he couldn't see how this game was fair. "But, Sinder, I know your scent. Very well."

"Do you think trackers go into a hunt nose-blind?" He indicated Torloo. "Kith and Kindred alike have learned my scent."

"Spikenard is distinctive," he protested.

Sinder rolled his eyes. "Rely on that, and you'll be chasing decoys for days."

Kyrie appreciated the warning. But did he truly understand? "You are covered in sigils."

"*Knowing* where I am and *getting* to where I am are winds apart," countered Sinder. "And before you try to tell me that the winds are in your favor, remember this. Every hunter uses every tool at their disposal to achieve their goal. Do you remember what yours is?"

"Find you?"

"You'll find me over and over," Sinder said. "Anyone can find me. Briefly."

"Catch you?"

Sinder arched a brow. "Define *catch*. Because catching me unawares isn't the same as keeping me."

Kyrie backed up and used the language he'd heard earlier. "Track and restrain."

"Let's find out if you can," urged Sinder. "And don't look so down. I want to test your skills, but it's really just a game. Maybe you'll have fun."

"I will not hurt you," Kyrie promised.

"I won't give you the chance." Sinder's expression softened, and he gently ordered, "Close your eyes and count to three."

The instant Kyrie's eyes were closed, he knew Sinder was away. Even so, he dutifully spoke to the sudden emptiness at his side. "One ... two ... three."

Kyrie's pursuit began at a stroll. Everything had happened in such short order, he needed time to think.

His unintended snooping among the maps had given him sufficient grasp of the terrain. Sinder's greater familiarity with these treed slopes and rocky outcroppings would definitely give him an advantage, but Kyrie wasn't without resources. *Use every tool.* That's what Sinder had said. So Kyrie pondered his kit.

Surprise was a tool.

Maybe he was wrong about the spikenard and sigils giving him an unfair advantage. Sinder's swift dismissal made Kyrie feel a little less guilty for failing to mention that Sinder still carried Timur's crystal. The one that anchored the healing sigilcraft. He'd swallowed it.

What else did he have to work with?

Surprise was a tool. So was patience. And he wasn't ready to dismiss scent. Not when the winds were so willing to carry them.

Sigilcraft was one area in which Kyrie excelled, and it seemed unlikely that Sinder knew the extent of Kyrie's skills. Especially since he rarely displayed all he could do.

"Kyrie?" murmured Torloo.

He turned to face his friend. A true tracker. The one with experience in leading the hunt. Kyrie mentally added another item to his list. *Teamwork* was a tool.

With a small shake of his head, Kyrie said, "I am merely organizing my thoughts."

Reveille dropped into a crouch and set his hands into a position that communicated patient expectation. Torloo also took a passive position. "Where you go, we will follow."

"What if you lose sight of me?"

Torloo tipped his head to one side. "That would be interesting. Do not let us distract you from the trail at your feet. Even if we lose your trail, we can pick it up again."

"Or his," said Reveille in a calm undertone. "If we cannot find you, we will focus on your prey."

Kyrie accepted that with a nod.

He took a moment to confirm the hand signals he'd learned from Annika. And by mutual assent, they put away their words. Because silence was also a tool.

Taking a deep breath, Kyrie opened himself up to the winds. Wider than he ever had before. The green crystal in his armband tuned itself to his desire, amplifying it. Breezes quickly gathered. Soft warbles lured them into contact. Soft words coaxed them into collusion.

With a parting breath that lifted his hair, his invisible allies whirled away. Almost immediately they flowed back, each bringing little offerings, each hoping to please him.

They told him of barriers within barriers. They carried the scents of spikenard and sweat. They whispered of warriors and wolves, his competition in the race to find Sinder. And one very clever wind—she was a south wind, he knew—brought to his attention a faint chorus of crystals.

Tiny, yet true.

Kyrie listened closely, trilled encouragingly. And their answer was symphonic.

Slowly opening his eyes, he met Torloo's puzzled gaze and Reveille's unchanged attention. And smiled. "I need to run."

"Which way?" murmured Torloo.

Kyrie thought his friend already knew the answer. He pointed confidently in the opposite direction, where Sinder's course through the trees was setting off whispery chimes.

Torloo offered an approving nod. "How did you know?"

Would they believe him? Few ever did. But he told the truth. "Every tree in this forest has a voice."

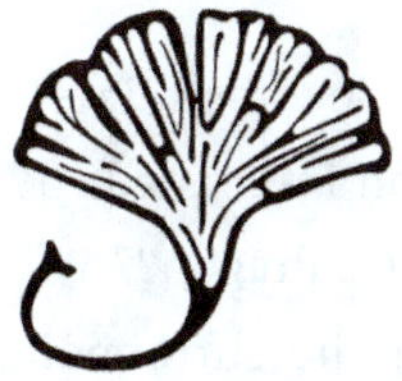

Sinder stood at attention on a rocky outcropping, listening to the sounds of a waking forest, watching for movement amidst the trees. The dawn patrol was still conducting careful sweeps on the opposite slope, far enough away to allow Sinder to focus on Kyrie.

Evading wolves had become a fairly routine challenge, but the prospect of dragon pursuit had him keyed up. He needed to take care, needed to focus.

Something that would have been so much easier if not for Timur and Mikoto having a murmured conversation at the foot of his vantage point. "Do you mind?" he grumbled.

Timur shook his head. "He's not coming."

"He *is*," argued Sinder. "That's rather the point of this exercise."

"Kyrie's father is a fox. Do you really think he'll come at you, full charge, yodeling a battle cry?"

"I used to do that," confessed Mikoto.

Timur chuckled. "Me, too."

"I suppose you think you were cute?" Sinder could picture it, though. Little battlers could be adorably idiotic. Easy pickings.

"I've improved somewhat." Timur's grin was probably meant to be modest.

Mikoto, who'd been sketching a map into the dirt with a stick, asked, "Could *you* catch Sinder?"

"I *have* caught him." Timur eyed Sinder speculatively. "I'd like to try again."

"What do you use for restraints?" Mikoto's posture was respectful, his expression interested. "If the goal is to catch and keep, how do you confine a dragon?"

With a final scan of the surroundings, Sinder dropped into a crouch beside Mikoto. "Primer time. It's not as if you need enchanted chains or anything. Rope works if it's heavy enough. Or better yet, woven cords reinforced by an ambuscade. Way back when, they'd work crystals into the weave."

"I am not familiar with such equipment."

"Specialty stuff." Ever since the Junzi had come to light, Sinder had developed a morbid fascination for the accoutrement of dragon slayers. The fabled Four Storms were one-of-a-kind, but there were records of plenty of more humdrum ways to ensnare dragonkind.

"They'd encase wardstones in rope. Which was crazy. Not only did it cost a fortune to synchronize enough crystals to properly lasso a winged dragon, but the resulting rope would be incredibly heavy."

"Weighted ropes?" mused Mikoto.

"Impractical in the extreme. Understandably obsolete." Sinder glanced at Timur, who was quietly studying his own hands. "Even if there were any of these ropes still lying about, they'd be moldering. Historical significance falls by the wayside when a financially-strapped family can unravel them in order to sell off the wardstones."

Timur lifted his gaze ... and smirked.

Sinder's confidence wavered. "Wielding them would require both physical strength and a ward's finesse."

Both of which Timur had in abundance. Dunce and double dunce.

"Surely not," Sinder muttered, all accusing.

"They're really more like whips." Timur was enjoying this way too much. "And there are still a few artisans who carry on the crafting of traditional weapons. Innovating on them, as well."

Mikoto glanced between them. "You have seen this weapon?"

"Most of the length is about this thick." Timur held out his thumb. "Leather grip. Weighted tip. And heavy as a bag of rocks."

Sinder muttered an oath. "You keep one lying around?"

"Hardly." Timur scratched behind his ear. "Battlers take better care of their weapons."

Mikoto's fascination doubled. "You *know* this weapon."

"I have the strength and a ward's aptitude." Timur lifted muscular arms and described a flowing circle over his head. "Mum started me in on ropework when I was still just a kid. Been focusing on those kinds of weapons ever since—whips, flails, chains, nets. Fend and I started practicing with the real thing this past winter."

All eyes turned to the feline, who greeted their interest with a curled lip.

Sinder wasn't used to being uninformed. "Well that's ... certainly something that could have been mentioned sooner."

"Like you said, they're specialty weapons. None of the battlers in this allotment were chosen for that kind of training."

Mikoto sighed. "I would like to try."

"Any foundation for this type of weapon?" Timur was clearly asking to be polite.

"Yes. My favorite is a chain scythe."

Timur gave him a hard look and a harder pinch. They were soon grappling on the ground like a couple of children. Finally pinning him, Timur asked, "You ride, yes? Ever done mounted maneuvers?"

"I am proficient. My partner is Merl Alpenglow."

"We are going to spar. Soon." Timur let the younger man up and slanted a look at Sinder. "And then we'll team up against our dragon friend here."

Sinder stated the obvious. "You have all the markings of a top recruit."

"That is … nice to hear."

Timur grimaced. "Don't suppose Wardenclave would let us borrow you?"

Mikoto simply shook his head.

"Right. Still." Timur clapped Mikoto's shoulder. "Over the summer, we can make good and sure that Wardenclave's headman is fully equipped to defend his home."

Sinder detected a subtle shift in the wind and straightened. "I think he's coming."

"Before things get dicey, I'll do you a favor." Timur stood and dusted off the seat of his breeches. Drawing something on the palm of his hand, he showed it to Sinder. "May I?"

It was a sigil. "A barrier?"

"You're as good as marked. My fault entirely." Timur pointed.

Sinder groaned and lifted his shirt. "Kyrie tried to warn me. The kid doesn't miss a trick."

"Pardon my touch."

He turned his face away and closed his eyes, signaling submission. Which was a little embarrassing, come to think of it. But it's how he would have presented himself to any of his older brothers in the heights.

Timur murmured, "Thank you for your trust."

It was a touching moment—literally—but any thought of brotherly bonding went out the window when jaws closed around Sinder's calf.

"Fend?" gasped Mikoto.

"Fend!" exclaimed Timur.

Sinder swore. Damned cat didn't like him much.

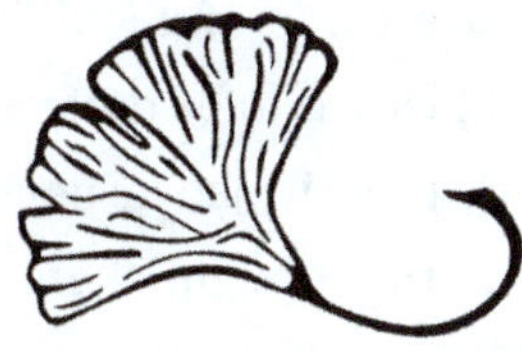

The second time Kyrie paused to wait for them, Torloo scolded. "Do not divide your efforts. Give this prey your full attention."

He found this difficult to accept. Perhaps it was Mother's influence. He did not like to exclude anyone. "If you are certain?"

"Go." Torloo's tail had developed a twitch. "In this game, we can *both* test our limits."

A balance he could embrace.

Kyrie did not look back again.

Neither did he go straight forward. For although he knew where Sinder could be found, the trees held their peace, which meant his prey was holding his position. Undoubtedly alert. So Kyrie chose a less obvious approach. Low and swift, he darted his way toward the reavers who were also on the hunt. Circling behind them, he used them as a barrier, then began teasing sigils out of his imagination.

Not the kind Michael set for lessons. Nor the sigils he'd read about in books. Kyrie needed something smaller, swifter, subtler.

Patiently, he fiddled with nuances, rejecting several attempts before he was satisfied. Then he made a dozen. And a dozen more. Anchoring them to his own soul, he sent them whispering away to mark his prey.

Three reavers walked past his sheltering shrub, close enough to brush against its leaves, but they didn't notice. He eased into the open, moved to the nearest tree, and found the crystal embedded in its bark. A blue. And pleased to be noticed.

He hummed it a little tune, which its neighbors picked up. Kyrie listened to their songs, then taught them one of his own. They wanted to be useful. He knew just what to ask for.

But sudden inspiration struck him dumb.

While the crystals around him waited, he turned the new idea over and over, considering it from every possible angle. It was simple. And beautiful. But also ... terrible.

And tempting.

Wasn't the point of this test to show Sinder what he could do?

But a summer breeze interrupted him, carrying the faint strain of music. Someone was singing again, high overhead. A compelling voice, yet elusive. As if the song wasn't meant for everyone to hear. It reminded him of the singer he'd been seeking the first time he climbed into Zisa's branches.

Were they nearby?

Heedless of the battlers and their search formations, Kyrie ran. More winds joined the first, carrying clearer snippets, guiding his way. He pushed the limits of his speed, afraid that the fleeting music would stop before he found its source.

The tree was large, but ordinary, and easy enough to climb. He clambered upward, pushing past summer leaves, and broke swaying into the muted light of an overcast morning. The sun was shrouded, yet shomething was shining. Or rather … someone.

"Hello?" he whispered, hardly believing his eyes.

Someone was resting amidst the leaves a little ways away, swaying with them. He looked like a man, but he couldn't have been, sitting with so light a touch, he didn't bend a single twig.

The face that turned his way was almost too bright to look at, like light reflected on the surface of the sea. It brought to mind the stories of angels, whose countenances were said to have flashed like lightning.

"H-hello?" he repeated, his voice trembling. "Are you the one who was singing?"

He inclined his head, and his hands framed a plea for peace. Without a word, he stood—or seemed to—and drifted nearer.

Kyrie clung to his branch, which was too thin to be steady.

The person offered his hands, but touching palms would mean letting go. One hand would have to do. Kyrie reached, and the shining person smiled. His hand was warm, and his grip offered a welcome support.

Inside Kyrie's mind, a voice gently inquired, *"Does my voice reach you now?"*

He nodded, tongue-tied.

"It would be too loud if I spoke. My voice is meant for the skies."

That was intriguing. All of this was. "Are you an angel?"

Bending closer, he smiled as if he'd been complimented. *"No, Kyrie. Not an angel. I am a star."*

50

SACRED PLACES

Lilya stared down at a plain circle of white stone, trying to understand the inscription.

PATH
FIRST OF DOGS
we walked together

"First of Dogs?" she asked. "But isn't that you?"

Glint began, "He was my ...." Faltering, he cleared his throat and started again. "Path is ... *was* .... I am not sure how to ...?"

Radiance, who stood beside Snow, said, "Path was the first Starmark Kith."

Lilya had noticed that members of the dog clans were indistinguishable from wolves when in truest form. However, Kith of the wolf clans always looked like wolves, while the dog clans seemed to represent all kinds of dog breeds.

"Who ...?" But Lilya stopped. Because it wasn't hard to guess.

This was one of those secrets that adults didn't seem to think children understood. But Ever was terrible at keeping secrets.

Looking to Moon, whose arm was draped around Snow's neck, she revisited an earlier insight. "You are like Laud to Quen. Like Quen to Ever." Beloved foster parent.

"That is the way of things," he agreed, sharing a smile with Radiance.

Stepping closer so Glint would have to look her in the eye, she asked, "Ever's Da loves *all* his sons. Was Path your Rise?"

Glint's mouth trembled, and he sank to his knees and pulled her into his arms. "So you know about such things?"

"Rise is Ever's big brother. We all love him." She wanted to tell him not to be sad, but that would be like telling him to stop caring about a member of his family. "I'm not supposed to know about Kith-sire. But I've overheard some things. And Ever explained some other things."

"Path was both my son and my companion. A packmate and a pactmate. He shared every part of my life, and I miss him more than I can express."

"Let me," said Moon. "I will speak for all here."

"Please, friend," begged Glint.

"And then I will sing," murmured Lapis, who stood to one side, cradling Rifflet close.

"You're a dear," pronounced Radiance, who was smiling even though her cheeks were wet with tears.

From within the circle of Glint's arms, Lilya watched Moon

step to one side and transform into a large white wolf. He nuzzled Snow, licked her forehead, then settled back on his haunches, lifted his muzzle to the sky, and howled.

Ginkgo was trying not to gawk at his surroundings while Hannick Alpenglow looked between him and Salali. The horse clansman's manner was patient and ponderous. As if he hadn't decided how to react to the sudden arrival of guests.

"Salali," he sighed. "What have you done?"

The squirrel beamed unhelpfully.

In an effort to break the ice, Ginkgo gave his ears a little wiggle, but Hannick's mellow gaze didn't stray. Which was kind of impressive.

He flicked them again, just to be coy.

"Burr in your ear?" Hannick inquired mildly. "I can gather a light and forceps."

"Bid for attention," Ginkgo admitted.

"You have mine."

He let his ears droop and adopted a more respectful posture. "I usually impress people."

"I usually do not." Hannick faced Salali and immediately looked fondly beleaguered. "Salali, why is this gentleman here?"

"My new apprentice would be more comfortable with a neutral party looking after his interests. Be his advocate."

"But why bring him *here*?"

Ginkgo stole another glance at their surroundings. His gardener's heart was going pitty-pat. He wanted to explore everything from the flower borders to the herb beds. Not to mention several varieties of trees that had to be both ancient and affectionate.

"He has the ear of Argent Mettlebright," Salali was saying.

Ginkgo fluttered his anew. "Both ears, actually. Family resemblance."

Salali went on. "And his enclave will be receiving a Scattering in the months ahead."

"*And* ...?" demanded the stallion.

Ginkgo's ears pricked. They were getting down to it, now. Real reasons.

With a stubborn posture, Salali said, "Linlu's lyrics mention a person between."

Unimpressed, the stallion pointed out, "*Every* reaver is a Betweener."

"A reaver stands between two cultures. A crosser brings them together."

Hannick gazed off into the sky, then nodded. "I can appreciate that kind of balance. And ... he *is* the stuff of songs."

"And you're too polite to enjoy such novelties?" Salali gave Ginkgo a little push forward.

Ginkgo braced himself for the usual formalities, but the stallion kept it simple. "I'm Hannick. A healer."

Finally, *finally*, his gaze drifted to the top of Ginkgo's head.

This was familiar territory. "Am I your first crosser?"

"Strictly speaking." Fingers twitched, and Hannick gave in to the inevitable. "May I make a brief examination?"

Ginkgo grinned. "I was hoping you'd ask."

The stallion's expression lapsed into gentle wonderment as he carefully tugged and scratched Ginkgo's ear. He eased closer and angled his head, making a display of his trust while they chatted about the mares at Stately House, some of whom were Alpenglows.

"Since I am sure it was Salali's true purpose, allow me to introduce you to some friends."

Ginkgo suspected his own delight was showing as Hannick took him around what amounted to a small village populated by tree-kin. Salali lagged behind while his apprentice was kissed and petted by tree twins. Ginkgo welcomed their curiosity and unloaded plenty of his own, quizzing their human counterparts on the contents of their gardens. Enough healers were hanging about to give the whole place the ambiance of a hush-hush hospice, with a secondary business being the preservation and packaging of medicinal herbs, teas, and pollen.

By the time he'd chatted with everyone, Ginkgo's pockets were bulging with seed packets.

"You would do well here," remarked Hannick.

Ginkgo shrugged that off. "I like people. Especially kids."

Salali casually interjected, "We could probably push for ours to go to him."

"Is that so?" Hannick led the way to a small building with colored glass set into its windows. Rapping on a door left open to catch the flower-scented breezes, he said, "I apologize for interrupting your lesson, Mare Anella, but I bring a visiting professor. He is a leading expert on crossers."

Eighteen children stared at Ginkgo with widening eyes. Half of them were human. The others looked to be Alpenglow colts and fillies.

Hannick said, "Ginkgo is our guest because his enclave will receive a Scattering."

"How many?" asked a teenage girl with a toddler propped on one hip.

Salali said, "If he takes a liking to you, he'll have no choice but to take the lot of you."

"We can stay together?" asked a surly boy of nine or ten who'd been clinging to a shyer friend's hand ever since Ginkgo stepped inside. "All of us?"

"What about us?" whispered a filly cradling a sleeping baby.

Nothing like being put on the spot. Ginkgo thought he'd sized up the situation, but he wanted to be clear. "Are you all tree-kin?"

The human children looked to Hannick and the mares first, but slowly, they each brought out necklaces. Some displayed slim capsules. Others looked more like lockets. Dad had told him about this. Kids born with a golden seed in their hand. Just like in the stories.

"And ... since this garden's jam-packed, you have to go someplace else to plant your seeds and start a new grove." Ginkgo's heart went out to them. "Is going all together an option?"

Hannick said, "If an existing grove needs a specific variety, one or two might be sent. But your enclave is starting anew."

"So it's not crazy to hope?"

The teenage girl, the one who looked to be oldest, asked, "Is there room?"

"Plenty." Ginkgo wanted to help them. "Why don't you write up some letters of introduction for my Dad. Tell him why you want to stay together."

The filly on baby-cuddling duty dared to repeat, "What about us?"

"Guess that's up to your Stallion. We have a small herd—including a few distant relatives—at Stately House. Could be like boarding school. Could be apprenticing. Maybe?"

"Perhaps," said Hannick.

Looking to Mare Anella, Ginkgo suggested, "Address the letters to Lord Argent Mettlebright of Stately House."

That stirred more than a few whispers.

"And maybe get started on language lessons. Any chance someone around here can teach Japanese?"

This time the response was clearer. Over and over, they repeated one name—*Sora. Sora. Lady Sora.*

Salali jostled him with an elbow and rolled his eyes. "Mikoto's mother came to us from Japan. Seems to me, you and yours might be interested."

"Oh, yeah?" Ginkgo's stomach did a little anticipatory flip. "Why's that?"

"Could be a distant relation." Salali quietly added, "Before taking the Reaver name, Sora was a Hajime."

Kyrie searched the star's face, struggling against the urge to hide his own. He rivaled the dawn, and his gaze seemed to slide right into the secret places of Kyrie's heart ... as easily as his voice slipped into Kyrie's mind.

"Are you certain you are not an angel?" he asked.

The shining person smiled. *"I am sure that I am not carrying a message."*

Oh, tricky. The literal meaning of angel was "messenger." Was he hiding a truth or revealing one? Perhaps angels were members of the sky clans with deliveries to make. Starry heralds.

Kyrie refined his question. "Are you an Impression?"

"That is how my people are understood." The hand that partially supported Kyrie tugged. *"Come, Kyrie. You must set your seal upon me, or I will overwhelm you."*

"Seal?" He swayed with the treetop, nearly colliding with the star.

"A sigil." The star caught him close, and they were flying. *"A ward. Lest you become drunk upon my light."*

Did stars have sway? Concentrating on his sigilcraft was more difficult than usual, so maybe it was true. Kyrie managed the lines of a basic seal and nudged it into place over the star's heart. There was an immediate shift. Almost like a good sneeze after breathing in too much pollen.

"Are you the one I heard singing before?"

"Just now? Yes."

"No. When we first arrived. Almost two weeks ago."

The star arranged himself as before, sitting amidst fluttering leaves, only this time with Kyrie across his lap. *"I am newly arrived. You probably heard Wardenclave's star."*

"Whose star are you?"

"That is a secret." The star was easier to look at now. Maybe the

sigil had helped with that. He said, *"I will give you another secret in its place. Did you know that reavers are descended from us?"*

Kyrie needed a moment to grapple with that. "Descended from stars?"

"From stars and mountains and moonbeams. Occasionally even winds. But mostly from trees."

Mother would be interested. Lapis, too, if he didn't already know. "Reavers have imps in their ancestry? Are you the parent of a reaver?"

"Not I." His smile was wistful. *"I have no desire to leave the sky."*

Kyrie nodded and nodded again. He would fly forever, given half a chance. Surely it was his dragon side that yearned for the sky. "Why are you here?"

"To shine. To sing. To greet. To guide." His gaze sharpened. *"To confront."*

"Me?"

He inclined his head. *"What have you realized?"*

Even though the question was vague, Kyrie instantly knew what he meant, and shame burned across his face. "I realized … that *tool* is just another word for *weapon*. And that I have many and more than most realize."

"And what might you do with such weapons?"

"I could find Sinder." It felt like a boast. "I did find him."

"What else?"

"I could reach him."

"And …?"

"I could catch and hold him." That would mean winning this game of theirs.

The star waited, knowing there was more.

"I could ... I could hurt him." Kyrie's voice broke on his final confession. "And I think if I wanted, I could kill him."

51
SHOW ME

Argent had warned Timur more than once that he was too quick to trust. As if optimism were a dreadful trait. Timur *liked* people, and he definitely looked for the best in them. True, it had brought him to grief more often than he liked to admit. But he couldn't help believing that things would work out. That his hopes would find a safe harbor. That he'd reach the kind of balance the herds held in high esteem.

Sinder had the potential to be that kind of friend. Timur couldn't deny his growing attachment. The dragon needed him, but that reliance might be nothing more than desperation. Even so, Timur would support him.

Once again, he probably cared more than he should.

Why was it so hard to find someone who cared back?

Fend's tail smacked Timur's thigh, and he spared his Kith partner a glance. The cat's annoyance confused Timur. Sure, Fend wasn't as much of a people person as Timur, but he'd never acted out against anyone before.

He offered his fingertips.

With a sinuous slide, Fend draped himself over Timur's lap, demanding a larger share of his attention.

Burying both hands into plush fur, he quietly protested, "It's my job to watch out for him."

Mikoto quietly asked, "What does he have against Sinder?"

"Haven't the foggiest." Timur glanced toward Sinder's latest vantage, low in the branches of a hulking oak.

"Is he a black panther?"

Timur didn't mind chatting, but he pulled a quick sigil out of the air to muffle their voices. "Basically. Fend favors his mother, who is from a jaguar clan. But cats of their coloring are often referred to as black panthers."

"How long have you been together?"

"We've been partnered for a little over a year, but he was born at Stately House. My home. I got to cuddle Fend as a newborn cub. But in cat years, he's probably older than me now."

Mikoto nodded. "That is how it is with Kith."

They lapsed into a comfortable silence.

Like they'd been friends for years.

As a battler, Timur could only approve of Mikoto. Although young, he exuded competence and reliability. Earlier, they'd spent the better part of an hour comparing arsenals, each impressing the other. A battler of Mikoto's caliber was wasted on Wardenclave. He was a front lines kind of guy.

Mikoto sat shoulder-to-shoulder with him, facing the opposite direction. Routine for battlers, since it gave them vision on all sides.

For a while, Timur pondered how far they could've gone in the annual tournaments as a two-man team. Totally unrealistic, given their responsibilities. New headman. New dad. But it was fun to ponder training menus and battle strategies.

A large owl passed overhead. A rookie's Kith. It gave no sign of having noticed Sinder, but that didn't mean it hadn't.

Sinder slipped away without a sound.

Mounting Fend, Timur and Mikoto followed.

When Sinder next stopped, Timur made sure he drank some tea before falling back to a reasonable distance. To Fend, he said, "It happened again. I was standing right there, or I might not have noticed."

Mikoto silently signaled a request for information.

Timur took more care with his sigils this time. "It's Kyrie."

"Is he coming?"

"I don't think so. Sinder would be reacting differently if Kyrie had begun his approach." Timur searched for some sign that the dragon realized what was happening. "I'm going to have to get that boy to show me how it's done."

Mikoto shook his head.

Timur lowered his voice. "Kyrie's marked him."

"With what?"

"Small sigils." His curled fingers described a circle no bigger than a coin. "They started arriving just before sunup. I have no idea how he's delivering them. Unless he marked Sinder before they parted. Or keyed off that crystal I warded. But … I don't think so."

"How far can a sigil travel?"

"Depends on the anchor. Etch a sigil into stone, and it'll go as far as you can fling it. But these are airborne." Timur squinted at Sinder. "I wonder why he hasn't noticed? I mean, he's a dragon."

Fend's big paw gently biffed him across the cheek. Then planted that paw on Timur's ankle. Where a small sigil gleamed faintly on his pants cuff.

"Oh. Well spotted," Timur muttered sheepishly. "Kyrie got me, too. I wonder why I hadn't noticed. I mean, I'm a ward."

Mikoto rubbed at his face, trying to hide his smile.

Shaking his head, Timur scanned the forest. With a scowl, he gruffly lapsed into the accent of his mother and his uncle. "A dragon who thinks like a fox. Is a dangerous combination, yes?"

As a rule, Amaranthine were patient. But Sinder had always been a bit of a rule-bender, if not an outright breaker. "Joining the dawn patrol implies attacking at dawn," he muttered. Yet the sun was nearing mid-high.

"Show me what you can do implies showing up at all." Sinder's gaze flashed across scenery. Granted, a dragon's camouflage was universally effective, but he'd expected Kyrie to leap out of a shrub or cast a barrier or ... *something*.

All he attracted were rookies, and their heart wasn't in the hunt. They were being too cautious. Not because they were afraid of dragons, but because the blessed idiots were afraid to hurt him.

Should the mission be scrapped?

He'd talk it through with Torloo.

Michaelson might have ideas, too.

Sinder checked on his support crew. Timur and Mikoto were conferring under the cover of a barrier, but Fend was staring. And it wasn't a nice stare. If anything, the big feline looked eager. Hungry? No it was more like ... anticipation.

Oh, shit.

He dove, narrowly evading a pretty bit of sigilcraft. Something like a net that promised restriction. How had the kid gotten close enough to drop it? Sinder took to his heels, only to be brought up short by a three-man cell. Dunce and double dunce. He was willing to bet the battlers didn't even know they'd been warded.

Swearing at all Four Storms, Sinder forced himself to hold position. Where?

It was no use running if you ran straight into your pursuer's arms. Where?

A breeze brushed his face. Another slid through his hair.

Definitely time to go.

Sinder ran.

Ginkgo was used to keeping track of children. It was part and parcel of life at Stately House. Wards for out-of-bounds spots. Special necklaces with etched sigilcraft. Added to those were his own eyes, ears, nose, and gut. All making sure Ginkgo was where he needed to be whenever he was needed.

Michael's and Sansa's kids were a special case. As was Kyrie.

All of them had been bound to him by sigils, pretty much since birth. That had been Dad's idea and Michael's doing. Making Ginkgo their bodyguard. Giving him every excuse to become more. Reminding him over and again that he was family.

For this trip, Michael went above and beyond with tuned crystals. Stones in Lilya's necklace, Gregor's bracelets, and Kyrie's armband had been tuned to those Ginkgo wore wolf-style, on a knotted cord around his neck.

They gave him a general direction, resonated with strong emotions, and tipped him off whenever Kyrie was working a bit of sigilcraft. So he usually knew if they were at lessons with Michael. Or mixed up in mischief.

Most of the time, he tuned them out.

This wasn't one of those times.

Ears flattened, teeth gritting, he muttered a hasty excuse and was over the wall in a bound. Salali was half a heartbeat behind.

"Any chance this is some kind of ... early warning system?" Ginkgo demanded.

"None." The squirrel blandly added, "At least, not one of mine."

"Coulda fooled me. What the hell's wrong with your trees?"

"*Somebody* is using them."

Ginkgo spared him a glance. "My brother."

With a faint smirk, Salali remarked, "The sons of Stately House do not disappoint."

"You're not bothered?"

Catching his arm, the squirrel forced him to slow. "Why are *you* bothered?"

"My brother might be in trouble!"

Salali pulled up short, and Gent wheeled tightly, coming to a rest atop the squirrel's hat. "Sinder is testing him. At your request."

"But this ...!" Ginkgo indicated the woods. "You gotta admit this is unusual."

"That, my dear apprentice, is an understatement." Salali cocked his ear and smiled. "I know full well what a mismatched jumble of shards your brother found. Barely worth a second look. But he's not only coaxed them into song, he's tuned them to each other."

"So my brother's a crystal adept. Not exactly news." Ginkgo swiveled his ears, trying to catch the music Salali was hearing. "Unfortunately, I'm not."

"Kyrie isn't any old ward."

"You're weighing in on his assessment?"

Salali peered at him from under a drooping brim. "I could. If anyone bothered to ask."

"I'm asking."

"Your brother's improvisation amounts to a trap." The squirrel gestured broadly. "He's weaponized an entire forest, and your dragon friend cannot escape."

"That's ... impressive."

"That's an ambuscade for you."

Ginkgo was catching something faint, and he didn't think it was crystal resonance. But Salali's remark distracted him. "Ambuscade. Is that a subclass?"

"Obsolete ward class," said Salali with a wry twist of a smile.

"Not the sort of thing you'd find on an academy syllabus. We had one of our own, back at Wardenclave's founding. Hemet was a good man."

"You're going to have to tell me. I'm way out of this loop."

"Hemet could use crystals as a focus. The destructive force of his soul scattered Wardenclave's attackers. And in a few memorable instances, he ended them."

Ginkgo's ears snapped forward. "What?"

"Reavers of the ambuscade classification are killers."

"My brother's not a killer!"

"I am talking about skill sets, not wholesale slaughter." Salali tapped Ginkgo's nose. "Hemet was a good man. Kyrie is a good boy."

Calming enough to think, Ginkgo caught another fragment of a melody. "What am I hearing?" he asked. "Is that someone ... singing?"

Salali pushed back his hat, unseating Gent. "You have good ears. This sort of thing happens in high places."

"Where's it coming from?" It wasn't easy to see past the overlapping sigils of Wardenclave's barriers.

"High above the blue. *Much* harder to see them, this time of day." Salali's smile was a jaunty thing. "Around these parts, the stars like to sing."

Just then, a pale blur streaked past. "What was *that*?"

"A wolf."

Ginkgo wasn't sure he liked that the wolf was heading straight Kyrie's way. "Should I be worried?"

Salali huffed and started running again. "You have a more suspicious nature than you let on."

"Let's call it a protective streak."

"First off, when the stars sing of peace, there's nothing to fear."

Ginkgo was ready to pile skeptical and cynical on top of his suspicious nature. "Like to see for myself, thank you very much."

Salali grinned at him. "Second, the wolf wouldn't be inside my barriers if he wasn't a friend."

They picked up the pace and soon burst into a clearing. The wolf—who had all the markings of a crosser—was already there, standing at the center, tail low and twitchy, arms open wide.

Ginkgo skidded to a halt at the same moment Sinder streaked out of cover and collided with the wolf, whose tail lifted into a relieved sway.

"Moon! What are you doing here?" exclaimed Sinder. "Scratch that. Don't care. You're *here*!"

"Take a deep breath," growled the wolf. "Why are you afraid?"

"The kid's terrifying. Got me good." Hiding his face against the wolf's chest, he mumbled, "Shit, that was freaky."

Timur and Mikoto, astride Fend, crashed into the clearing, all three looking harried. A handful of other battlers found their way into the open. Shouldering their weapons, they adopted receptive postures. All eyes were focused on the newcomer. Staring.

"Moon?" whispered Ginkgo.

"Moon-kin Ambervelte," Salali supplied. "Radiance's brother. He's Kith-kin."

"He and Sinder seem close."

"Fancy that."

Meanwhile, Sinder babbled on. "He's perfect. You need to get a message to Boon. The rogue's handed us our chance."

Ginkgo swore.

"His own kids could be the key."

Moon gently covered the lower half of Sinder's face, hushing him. But it was too late to call back his words.

Ginkgo stifled a groan when his little brother slipped out of the shadow of a tree. He probably should have called out, but Kyrie's cool dignity silenced the entire gathering.

"I would like to know, please." Red eyes swept every face, and his words held the faintest lilt of power. "Who is the rogue?"

52

FAMILY AND FAMILIAR FACES

Mikoto wasn't sure what was going on, so he lined up with a few of the other battlers, lowered his eyes and took a receptive posture. Awaiting orders. Presumably from Timur.

Only that's not how it worked out.

"Come away, Kyrie." Timur's voice was thick with emotion.

The boy submitted without a word, lifting his arms. Timur gathered him up, speaking to him in an undertone while setting him on Fend's back. They fled the clearing together.

Reveille arrived with a young wolf, both breathless and agitated. They singled out Salali and hurried to confer with him. When Moon bundled Sinder away, Mikoto resigned himself to a long walk home.

But then Ginkgo was right in front of him, up on tiptoe, brimming with urgency. "Mikoto. I know you have your own stuff going on, but can I borrow you?"

"What do you need?"

"Long story." He glanced around, shook his head, and muttered, "Guess I'm your ride."

Before Mikoto could frame a diplomatic protest, Reveille hurried over. "Allow me?"

"You sure?" Ginkgo checked.

"I insist." So saying, Reveille transformed, lowering himself to his belly.

Mikoto murmured his thanks and swung up behind the half-fox.

Once Reveille settled into an easy lope, Ginkgo leaned back into Mikoto's chest and asked, "How much do you know about the rogue?"

"Almost nothing." Mikoto said, "I am sure my father kept apprised of the situation, but there has been little time to ...."

"Of course," interrupted Ginkgo. He twisted enough to place his hand over Mikoto's heart. "I'm an idiot for forgetting. Sorry."

He shook his head. "All I really know is that Wardenclave is safe."

"Okay. Short version." Ginkgo's ears flattened to either side. "Uncooperative dragons are almost impossible to track, catch, and keep. The rogue is a murderer and a rapist, and Kyrie just found out that monster's his sire."

Mikoto slowly inclined his head. "Understood."

Ginkgo faced forward and slumped into him. "Not the nicest of lineages."

He grunted.

"Which is where *you* come in."

"What can I do?"

"I found out today that your mother's a Hajime." Ginkgo dredged up a wan smile. "So was Kyrie's birth mother. So was mine, for that matter."

"Are we related?"

"Probably distantly. But I'm hoping Kyrie will take comfort in the connection."

"Better me than the rogue?"

"That's the idea." Ginkgo quietly asked, "Do you mind?"

Mikoto shook his head. "I am more than happy to claim you both."

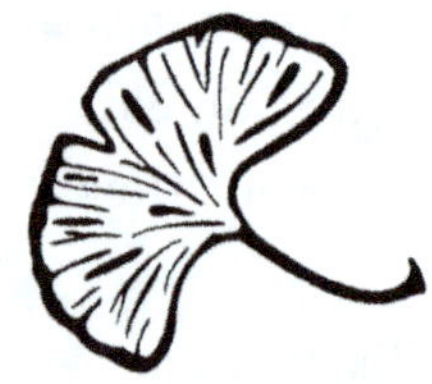

Kyrie didn't trust himself to speak, so he retreated into silence. Evading Waaseyaa's gaze, he escaped into the guest room, hiding under the coverlet. He downed Timur's tea without complaint, and he turned his face to the wall.

By some miracle, Timur let him be, and the door clicked shut behind him.

If only it could last. Kyrie didn't want anyone. Except perhaps Ever. Ever would cry for him and hold him and promise him that everything would be all right.

"Merciful dragon?" came a tentative voice.

Kyrie reluctantly turned to face Zisa.

With a soft noise of distress, the tree joined him on the bed. Swiping with his thumbs, Zisa chased the tears that Kyrie couldn't hold back any longer. He sobbed, and the tree gathered him up, cradling and rocking and crooning. And even though Kyrie had been so sure a moment ago that he wanted solitude, he clung gratefully to Zisa.

"I want Dad," he admitted brokenly. "I want my dad."

Zisa went still and turned his head. "Someone new is coming."

Kyrie's heart leapt, even though it couldn't possibly be his father. He dared to ask, "A fox?"

"No." With a kiss to soften the blow, Zisa whispered, "Do you want me to help you hide?"

"Please?"

An instant later, Kyrie was outdoors, surrounded by rustling leaves. "That is a good trick."

Zisa smiled. "I know."

They were in some kind of shallow nest, high enough in Zisa's branches that they were swaying slightly. Breezes found him, their caresses filled with gentle questions, and his nose cleared enough that he could smell the flowers hidden among the leaves.

From far below, a sharp exclamation carried.

Soothing tones had to be Waaseyaa.

And then the winds brought words. Waaseyaa said, "If you wish to climb, here are rungs."

"If I must. Will your twin mind?"

Kyrie sat up a little straighter, startled to hear such a familiar voice in this place.

"Allow me," countered another person. "I have a message to deliver, and I will invite Kyrie to join you inside."

His heart took to thudding.

"Should we run?" asked Zisa. "I have many hiding places."

Kyrie swallowed hard and shook his head. "It will be okay."

"Pardon me," called a rising voice. "May I have a word, please?"

"We are here," Kyrie replied, his voice crackling.

Gently lifting aside leaves, Hisoka Twineshaft joined them on the branch.

53

NEWS FROM HOME

Ginkgo drew up short on the threshold. "Lapis? I didn't know you'd be here."

"I did not know myself." Draped decorously upon a kitchen chair with Mikoto's dog cradled to his chest and Rifflet coiled at his throat, Lapis lifted a teacup in salute. "Who is your friend? And why has Kyrie marked him?"

Mikoto glanced down at himself. "Me, too?"

Lapis beckoned languidly. "Elbow. Achilles tendon. And a cheeky brand upon your ... back pocket."

"*Me, too.* As in other sigils?" Ginkgo took Mikoto's arm and squinted at the tiny tracer. "Who else am I going to have to frisk?"

"Timur and Fend. And Sinder, of course."

The sigils dispelled at a touch, which was almost a shame. They were as cute as they were diabolical. "Lapis, were you sent to check on Sinder?" Ginkgo could see Juuyu demanding it.

"No, no. That privilege belongs to Moon."

"Tenma, then?"

Lapis arched his brows. "I am *greatly* looking forward to seeing my apprentice again. But ... no."

Reeling a hand to hurry him along, Ginkgo wearily demanded, "What brings you to the heart of Wardenclave, O, illustrious one?"

"I am here in Argent's place."

Ginkgo's stomach plunged. "What happened to Dad? Is he all right? Did he take off somewhere? Is Mom alone?"

Lapis set aside his tea and raised a quelling finger. "Argent is dealing with a delicate task for Hisoka's sake. I am here in his place to attend Mikoto Reaver's induction as the new headman of Wardenclave."

Ginkgo wasn't satisfied. Not when *delicate tasks* could easily be dangerous ones. "Where. Is. Dad?"

"California."

Okay, that was unexpected. "Why?"

Flicking a glance at Mikoto, Lapis sighed but answered. "The fourth of the Junzi was finally located in a private collection. Argent is personally overseeing its transfer to a more secure location. Once he is satisfied, he will undoubtedly drop by."

"Oh. That's all right, then."

"Promising, even."

Ginkgo rubbed at his face. "Glad you're here. Seriously. Rough morning. Little bro just *found out*."

Lapis' low warble conveyed concern.

"I thought Timur was bringing him here." Ginkgo had been so sure Kyrie was here. But he'd probably passed right under him.

"He's with Zisa?"

"Taken aloft. Or so we were told." With a confident wave toward the ceiling, Lapis added, "Hisoka will fetch him down."

"Hisoka-sensei's here?" Pointless question. Dragging out a chair, Ginkgo slumped into it. "Where's Waaseyaa. And everyone else, for that matter."

"Next door, I believe. There was some excitement. I was invited—rather pointedly—to make myself at home here." Lapis smiled serenely. "Now, before I broach any *other* potentially sensitive topics ... who is your friend?"

Mikoto stepped forward and offered both a bow and his palms. "Lord Mossberne, welcome to Wardenclave. It will be an honor to have you in attendance at my induction."

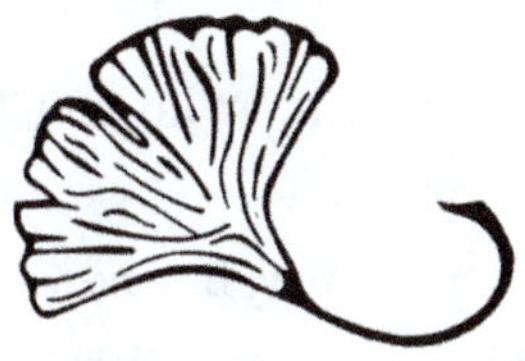

Kyrie wasn't sure how to react to Hisoka Twineshaft's arrival. Sensei visited Stately House fairly often, but he spent most of his time in meetings with other members of the Amaranthine Council. What leisure hours he stole were passed in the company of Michael, Deece, or Jacques. Not with the children. So while Sensei's was a familiar face, Kyrie was used to seeing him from a distance.

"Hello, Zisa." Hisoka stooped to look him in the eye. "I apologize for not offering my greeting sooner."

Given Hisoka-sensei's history of standoffishness, the form that greeting took surprised Kyrie.

Zisa, too. The tree touched his lips and gasped, "He kissed me!"

"He did," agreed Kyrie.

"It is so backward." Zisa's delight edged his tone with laughter. "Usually, I have to begin."

Hisoka took a seat on the branch, feet swinging free, one elbow propped on the nest's edge. With traces of a smile, he quietly revealed, "I was raised in one of the eldermost groves."

"Do you like trees?" Zisa asked hopefully.

"More than I let on," Hisoka said in a conspiratorial tone. Then the spokesperson for the cat clans said, "Hello, Kyrie."

He lowered his gaze, suddenly self-conscious about his tearstained face.

"A friend told me you were sad," said Hisoka. "I came as quickly as I could."

Kyrie's curiosity was caught. "Who told?"

"His name is Celestoria Novi, and we are old, old friends." His hands formed a plea for secrecy, but he went on without waiting for a response. "Childhood friends. Perhaps a little like you and Miss Lilya, since we are rarely far from one another."

"The star?"

Hisoka inclined his head.

This was new information. And interesting enough to loosen Kyrie's tongue. "Does anyone know?"

A small headshake. "Not even your father."

"Is your star the reason you know so much?"

"Novi is certainly part of it." Hisoka ran a hand over the top of his head. "However, I cannot deny that I have always been … inquisitive."

Kyrie was impressed. And confused. "Why tell me?"

"Is it truly *telling* if the secret has already stepped out of hiding?" Gentling his tone, he added, "Argent intended to reveal your secret at midwinter."

Ginkgo had said as much. That Kyrie was old enough to know. That Dad had wanted the responsibility. "Then why are *you* here?" Instead of Dad. Instead of Mom. Instead of Ginkgo.

"Because it was needful." Hisoka delighted Zisa by taking the tree's hand. "I am always where I need to be."

Not exactly what he'd been asking, but also very interesting. How was that even possible? Finally, Kyrie said, "That must be nice."

"Not always." Hisoka confessed, "Sometimes there are places I would prefer to go, even though doing so might not be for the best."

"So you did not want to be here?" Kyrie kept back the rest of his thought. *With me.*

Flared eyebrows shot up. "Not so. I am glad to be here. And I know that because I *am* here, this is the most important place I can be right now. Perhaps it would be better to say that there are times when I wish I could be in more than one place at once."

Increasingly intrigued, Kyrie asked, "You needed to talk to me?"

"Certainly. But not solely. I am rarely in one place for one reason. For instance, we are here—at least in part—because the stars have gathered to sing."

Perhaps hearing stars was a little bit like hearing the wind. Kyrie whispered to Zisa, "I do not hear anything. Do you?"

"Tonight," said the tree. "There will be a chorus tonight."

"Why?"

"Because Glint Starmark is much-loved." Zisa stroked Kyrie's hair. "Because a promise is kept. Because a son is given."

A son? Before Kyrie could ask for particulars, Hisoka-sensei interrupted.

"Kyrie, I made a promise to Ever Starmark. He would not let me leave Keishi until I swore a solemn oath to find you."

"Oh. Is *that* why you are here?"

"Did I not mention I have *many* reasons for being where I am? I am sure I did."

Kyrie missed Ever. So much. "He is my best friend."

"Something he made abundantly clear." From an unassuming pouch at his waist, Hisoka withdrew a phone. Tapping lightly upon its screen, he passed it to Kyrie. It was already making the soft tones of an attempted connection. The name of the call's intended recipient made Kyrie's heart leap into his throat—Laud Starmark.

Laud lived with Ever and Quen at Kikusawa Shrine in Keishi. But it wasn't Uncle Laud who answered the call.

"Kyrie? Is it you, Kyrie?"

"I am here."

"Sensei's good! And fast! I knew he'd do his best. Is Lilya there, too?"

"She is … nearby." Kyrie could tell she was below, but he wasn't sure which of the buildings she was in. Looking into the tree's sparkling eyes, he said, "I am with Zisa."

Leaning closer, the tree cooed, "Hello."

"I know that name from Da. Hi! Umm … so you'll both have to tell Lilya later, but I gotta tell you now! I'm an uncle!"

"Is that so?" Hugging the phone to his ear, Kyrie closed his eyes, greedy for every inflection of Ever's voice.

"For almost whole day now! Nobody knows. Da will call for a press conference in the morning. Everybody's been waiting and wondering and guessing."

"You most of all."

"Yes!"

There was sound of movement and a low murmur. Kyrie immediately recognized the muffled voice as Eloquence's. Ever said, *"Hang on. Here's Brother."*

"Congratulations, Quen," Kyrie said shyly.

"Many thanks, Kyrie. I'm still reeling from the events of the day." He sounded like he was smiling all the way from the depths of his soul. *"Your call is a welcome surprise, but I'm amazed that Hisoka-sensei reached you so quickly. He must have foregone all the usual means of transportation."*

Kyrie glanced at the cat, who offered a small shrug. "How is Kimiko?" he asked.

"Her happiness doubles mine. She is getting some well-deserved rest while we take turns holding the baby. Ever is prying her from Laud now."

"A girl?"

"Did Ever not say?" With a soft chuckle, Quen said, *"We named her Blessing."*

"I like it."

"Thank you, Kyrie. And behold, the triumphant uncle returns. I will give you back to Ever."

There was a soft shuffle, and Ever was there, sounding smug. *"I brought her. Wish you could see."*

"Does she look like you?"

"Yes! Starmark colors. We're kin for sure."

"Does she have your ears?"

"And my tail!" In a very different tone, Ever coaxed, *"Say hello, now. You can do it. Say hi to Uncle Kyrie."*

On the other end of the connection, a soft snuffling could be heard. Then a tiny whine.

Zisa hugged Kyrie and whispered, "A baby!"

Ever's giggle was pure joy, and he explained, *"She's trying to eat the phone, and it's no good. You say something, Uncle Kyrie."*

"Hello, pretty pup. Save some room in your affections for me and Lilya. We will come and see you as soon as we can."

"She will love you," promised Ever. *"Hey, Kyrie? Da is going to be there—where you are—next week. For Dichotomy Day. There's a ... a thingie."*

"Induction ceremony?" guessed Kyrie.

"Yes! And Da offered to bring me along. You know, if there's room for me. With you guys. Maybe?"

"You do not want to stay with Blessing?"

"I have almost a whole week to make sure she knows my voice and my scent. She won't forget me." More quietly, less confidently, Ever asked, *"What do you think?"*

"That would be ...." Kyrie's lips trembled, and his voice wobbled. "Please, come, Ever. I want you."

"I'll be there," Ever promised. *"You can count on me!"*

Kyrie whispered his thanks and then his goodbyes. Hisoka-sensei eased the phone from his grasp. Next, the cat eased Kyrie from Zisa's arms. It was less awkward than Kyrie had expected, clinging to someone who was suddenly more than a familiar face.

Friend of Stars.

Lover of Trees.

Teller of Secrets.

Maker of Miracles.

"You flew to me?" Kyrie whispered against Hisoka's shoulder.

"Like a shooting star."

"Thank you."

"You are most welcome."

Hisoka moved into the nest with Zisa, who did his share of patting and petting while Kyrie gave in to another wave of tears. He couldn't remember ever being so mixed up before. Maybe he was a little like Eloquence—still reeling from the events of the day.

Once he'd calmed, Hisoka-sensei said, "Your parents have earned my admiration over and again. They have always been willing to carry through with their responsibility to you, but I will ask you to allow me to ease their burden. I can spare them this conversation. Ask me anything, Kyrie. Ask me everything."

"Do you know who my Amaranthine parent is?"

"Mostly by reputation. Your biological father is a dragon commonly referred to as 'the rogue.' We are trying to put a stop to his crimes. However, we have been unable to discover his name. He was not hatched in the harems, so his origin is as much a mystery as his current location."

Zisa tittered.

Hisoka glanced at the tree and averted his eyes.

Kyrie asked, "What?"

"He said something silly," said Zisa. "There is no mystery. Not for a friend of stars. Not for someone raised in an eldermost grove."

"We cannot find a record of the rogue in any of the dragon clan lineages. They have been thoroughly vindicated." Hisoka-sensei rubbed a hand over the top of his head and sighed. "But all that means is that the rogue was not born in the usual way. He may have impish ancestry."

"Or ...?" prompted Zisa, all smiles despite the gravity of the situation.

"*Or*," Hisoka dutifully echoed. "His parent may have consumed a golden seed."

54

SOME EXCITEMENT NEXT DOOR

Ginkgo needed *something* to do, and his options were few. On any other day, he'd escape into the garden or drag a bunch of the boys down to the beach. Being cooped up inside was giving him a bad case of the fidgets. He had no idea how Waaseyaa was content to stay in one place for so many centuries.

With little else to busy his hands, Ginkgo announced, "I'll just … put on the kettle."

Kitchen puttering was better than nothing. The room was spotless, so he couldn't really pitch in. Instead, he rummaged through tea cannisters and found some snacks.

He was sneaking tidbits to Noble when Reveille walked in.

"Tea?" he offered. "Or if you're hungry …?"

Reveille put up a hand. "You need to come with me."

Ginkgo tensed. Again. "Something happen?"

"You could say that. Transcendence is asking for you." With a cocked brow that was so like Harmonious, he added, "My aunt? Snow."

Now that he knew the lady wasn't Kith, Ginkgo was feeling a little awkward. "Why me?"

"Who can know the mind of a female?" Reveille gestured to the door with both hands. "But orders are orders. She wants you at her side. Now."

"Her time?" asked Mikoto from his seat across from Lapis.

"Finally," confirmed Reveille.

Ginkgo could feel the color draining from his face. "I don't know the first or last thing about whelping pups!"

Reveille raised both hands and took a soothing tone. "You and me both, but I'm not asking you to play midwife. The pup was born a little after mid-high. It's probably the *only* reason she let me chase Kyrie through the forest instead of doing it herself."

"She needs a nanny?"

"You're standing in for Path." Reveille kept edging toward the door, clearly eager to fulfill his aunt's wishes. "You'll speak for him. Present the pup to our Da and announce his name."

"But I never met Path." Ginkgo tucked a bewildered tail. "I'm not even a dog."

"Auntie has always been ... contrary. And slow to trust." Lowering his voice, Reveille added, "And short on patience. So hurry it up."

Mikoto rose and asked, "May I attend?"

"Of course, headman. She liked you even before your promotion."

With a small smile, Mikoto admitted, "It can be difficult to tell."

Ginkgo shot a questioning look at Lapis.

The dragon indicated Noble and Rifflet. "I have all the company I need until such time as Hisoka returns with Kyrie. Hurry along. It does not do to keep a lady waiting."

"Coming, coming!" sang out Reveille, who practically carried Ginkgo to the low building.

Several important personages milled outside. He recognized Hannick and Salali, and he could only assume the rabbit was head of the Duntuffet clan. But Reveille bustled him straight inside, where an abundance of fresh straw *almost* covered the scents he associated with birthings.

His escort gave him a bump in Snow's direction, so Ginkgo hurried past anyone else in the periphery and said, "I'm here. I'm also a little confused but mostly honored. You sure about this?"

Transcendence—he really needed to remember her rightful name—angled her head toward the pup nuzzling at her belly.

Ginkgo melted. "Now *that's* what I call cute. Okay if I say hey?"

Without really waiting for an answer, he hunkered down next to the pup, leaning into Snow, surrounding himself with the homey scents of motherhood and milk.

"You're a Starmark for sure." The puff of puppy down was red, and Ginkgo had little doubt it would grow out into the silky curls that made combing Rise so much fun. "You know, I've never been this close to a newborn pup. Cubs for days, but you're my first baby dog."

The little guy stopped nursing and thrust his nose in Ginkgo's general direction.

"Clumsy little wobbler." He gathered the pup onto his lap and urged, "Get a whiff, why don't you?"

The pup's ears had a decided droop, and he thought the tail

would have a respectable sweep. "Odds are on copper, but maybe you'll please your grandsire with a show of silver."

His little voice piped, and he lipped Ginkgo's chin.

"Now you listen to me," he gruffly ordered. "Your mother is a growly nipper, but she knows what's what. That's why I'm here. *Nobody* loves little ones more than me, and I have some stiff competition."

Transcendence did nip his ear then.

Which brought his attention up. "Oh. Hey, Resplendence."

"Auntie had me write down the words you need to say." The guard he'd met at the front gate radiated happiness. "They are Path's message to Da."

Unfolding the page, he read the pronouncement through a few times. "Got it."

It was incredibly sad that this pup's father wasn't here to help welcome him. He was missing out. And Snow was undoubtedly missing him. Ginkgo lifted his hand and said, "You did good, mama."

She bypassed his hand to nip his ear again.

"Watch it, little mister," he grumbled to the pup. "She'll be after yours next. But don't let it worry you too much. I'm pretty sure it means nice things."

A throat cleared, and people filed inside. All five founders. Resplendence and Reveille, who Ginkgo guessed were Glint and Radiance's youngest children. Waaseyaa entered, as did Wardenclave's headman. Ginkgo offered a little wave to Mikoto, whose mystification softened into a smile.

Salali sidled over and helped Ginkgo to his feet. No easy task, given the pup's heft. Before retreating, the squirrel tucked a crystal into his pocket and whispered, "If motherhood interests you, I can pull a few strings, bend a few branches."

Ginkgo rolled his eyes, but he had the uncomfortable suspicion that his mentor was only half-teasing.

And suddenly, it was time. There was no way Ginkgo was going to mess this up. Not when it meant so much to Snow. And to this pup. And to Glint, whose cheeks were already wet.

Taking a deep breath, Ginkgo said, "I speak for Path Starmark."

Glint shuffled forward. "I am listening. I will hear."

"We shared a den. We shared a pack. We shared a promise."

"I remember." Glint quietly added, "I will always remember."

Ginkgo blinked hard and continued. "I did not forget our pact. A son for a son."

"Your promise is fulfilled. And he is beautiful."

"May he be a tribute to the Starmark clan, and may he be a comfort in my absence." Ginkgo couldn't quite keep the tremor out of his voice now. This was breaking his heart.

Glint wasn't trusting his voice at all. He simply nodded.

Ginkgo glanced at Snow, who inclined her head. So he smiled shakily and said, "Father?"

"I *am* Path's father."

"A son for a son," Ginkgo repeated. "Here is my promise kept. His name is Pact."

55

LEVELS OF STUPIDITY

Lilya couldn't help feeling that something was happening. Like Stately House on the eve of the Frost Festival, or when Uncle Jackie returned from a trip with Uncle Argent and began doling out souvenirs for each of them. The air seemed to be humming with anticipation. Or maybe she really was hearing humming.

Gregor propped on her hip, she hurried after Timur, scanning the sky for any sign of singers. "Maybe it's the wind," she said to Gregor.

He lay his head on her shoulder and said, "Pah-kah."

"Yes, your papka needs us."

Inside Zisa's little house, which was now swathed in creamy yellows and golds, she found her big brother already slouched in a chair that had been dragged to the corner and Sinder huddled on the larger of two beds.

Timur beckoned for her to pass him Gregor. "Thank you, Lilya. Take care of Sinder for me."

"Wouldn't it be better if *I* held Gregor so *you* can ...?"

"No." Timur's tone was tightly controlled. "I will stay right here, and I will hold Gregor, and you will take care of Sinder."

"Why?"

"Because I am angry."

Lilya had never seen Timur angry, but she'd seen Mum angry. Once. Things could get scary without someone—in Mum's case, Papka—to calm everyone down. "Where's Fend?" she asked.

"I shut him out."

"Why?"

Timur's jaw tightened. "He's even angrier."

"Right, then." It was clearly up to her. "Tell me what to do."

"Remove his bandages. Clean him up. Reapply ointment." With his gaze firmly fixed on Gregor's face, he gruffly added, "Better check his leg, too. Fend bit him."

Lilya studied Sinder, who looked increasingly wilted. "What did you *do*?"

"I messed up."

"Anyone can make a mistake." Lilya located the medical kit and pointed to the foot of the bed. Sinder scooted to the edge and sat with eyes downcast.

"Mistake?" Timur's accent thickened. "This was a debacle."

"You know the rules." Lilya patiently quoted, "You can't point to consequences without weighing them against intentions."

"He made a grievous error."

"Unintentionally?"

"Carelessly."

Lilya propped her hand on her hip. "That falls under simple stupidity, and you know it."

Sinder blurted, "What are you two on about?"

"Uncle Argent says there are levels of stupidity, but those who climb them sometimes achieve genius." She gestured for him to remove his tunic. "There are also depths of stupidity, and those mired in them rarely get by without help."

"That's probably why I need a partner," Sinder muttered.

Lilya placed a hushing finger over his lips. "That was a secret, yes?"

Sinder winced. "I'm sorry."

"Saying *sorry* is a good start." Lilya eased gauze away from an injury that was healing nicely. "What did you do?"

"Confess," ordered Timur. "Tell my sister the tale of your thoughtlessness. You can spare Kyrie that much, yes?"

Lilya gave her brother a hard look and went into the bathroom to fill a basin with hot water. She sometimes helped the mares and Mum with this kind of thing. Everybody at Stately House learned the basics of the healing arts. She wasn't completely hopeless, so long as she was following orders, but she didn't like seeing people in pain.

Right now, both Timur and Sinder were in pain. And she wanted to help.

She quietly cleaned Sinder up. He endured it while stealing glances at Timur.

"You are depleted," Lilya said. And to Timur, "He needs tending."

"I am in no fit state," her brother said firmly. "Is Mikoto still around? Or Tenma. He'd be best."

Lilya was tempted to ask his opinion of Tenma. But she wasn't about to bring up her impending contract while Timur was angry. Instead, she busied herself with ointment and gauze. "Sinder, what does Kyrie have to do with what happened?"

He met her gaze. "I blabbed a secret, and he overheard. It was about his biological father."

"Why would that be bad?" She risked a look at Timur, whose expression was unreadable.

Sinder sighed. "How much should I say?"

"*Now* you weigh your words?" asked Timur.

"She's just a kid." When Timur offered no guidance, Sinder looked ready to be sick. "We've been training battlers to hunt dragons. Because there's this one dragon. He's a very bad person."

Lilya helped Sinder into a clean shirt. "Kyrie's actual dad is some kind of criminal?"

"The worst kind." The dragon whispered, "Terrible and terrifying."

She rested her hands on his shoulders and firmly said, "That's not your fault."

"But I told ...!"

"The truth." Lilya knew Kyrie better than she knew herself. "He would always rather know the truth. Secrets bother him almost as much as lies."

Sinder looked like he really wanted to believe her. But didn't trust her. Or himself.

Suddenly, she knew what to do. "Timur, go get water for tea?"

Her big brother grunted and hauled himself out of his chair, carrying Gregor out.

To Sinder, Lilya said, "Don't tell."

His brows shot up when she pushed her knuckle between his lips and past his teeth. "Li'ya?" he mumbled around her finger.

"Hush. There are so many wards, I can't hurt you. It's safe. Papka made sure."

A muffled warble. He was uneasy.

"Tending will do you good." She pressed firmly. "This is the only way past the seal, so bear with it. And don't worry about Timur. He never stays grumpy for long. He'll still be your friend."

Sinder slowly bowed his head, letting it come to rest on her shoulder. Lilya felt him give in to trust. That's when the first hot drops splashed, and she knew he was crying.

"Don't be afraid." She petted his hair. "You have good friends."

They pulled away from each other when Timur returned. He'd turned Gregor over to someone else, and he carried a tea tray. "I made it extra strong," he said grimly.

Swiping at wet lashes, Sinder adopted a meek posture. "Thank you."

Timur's anger fled, and he sank to his knees beside the bed. First checking Lilya's work with the bandages, he relented completely. "Lilya's right. It's not your fault that Kyrie's father is a monster."

"I'm sorry."

"You will apologize to Kyrie, yes?" Timur ordered.

"I will."

"Go on, then. Get back to it."

Sinder stilled, and Lilya blushed.

Timur blandly said, "You think I can't tell when a beacon is bestowing a blessing? It's fine. She needs the practice, and you need the heartening. But first ... tea."

Choking down his dose, Sinder allowed them to chivvy him into a more comfortable position, sitting against the headboard, propped on pillows. Lilya sat with him, tucked against his side, going through the motions, even though Papka's and Uncle Argent's sigils regulated everything.

After a scant half hour, Sinder removed her finger and kissed the knuckle. "Better stop there. Staying close is enough."

She knew from Papka that some Amaranthine withheld themselves from direct tending. A pleasant atmosphere was enough to lift their spirits. Cossets were especially good at that sort of thing. So was Aunt Tsumiko, according to Kyrie. Except that Uncle Argent was forever shuttering his beacon, keeping her all to himself.

"Don't go falling in love with me."

"Same to you." She was relaxed. Eyes closed. Calm.

A few beats later, Sinder tentatively said, *"I'm much better at getting people to hate me."*

That was probably an exaggeration. "Like who?"

"The battlers, since I make their training a misery. Your brother, since I hurt someone precious to him. And don't even get me started about Fend. Was that cat always a menace?"

Lilya giggled. "You're rivals."

"Excuse me?"

"You've been sleeping with him, yes?"

"Who can sleep? Timur snores worse than a seal with a stuffy nose."

Sinder was sounding more like himself, which was a relief. She pointed out, "But that's *his* usual spot."

"He's jealous?"

"And territorial. And temperamental."

"Lilya?" called Timur, an odd note in his voice.

She opened her eyes, arched her brows. "What?"

Timur's brow furrowed.

"Maybe he's jealous?" suggested Sinder.

"Of what?"

"Good point. But he definitely thinks I'm up to mischief."

"You can't *do* mischief. You talk too much to get away with anything."

"I could give you a list of all the people who agree with your assessment. But here's the thing, Lilya. While I'm probably always talking, it's not always out loud."

She turned enough to study his face.

Sinder's lips quirked. *"Took you long enough."*

He hadn't opened his mouth, yet his voice carried just fine. "Why can I hear you?"

"I think we've accidentally narrowed down your classification. Congratulations, Miss Lilya. You're a fellow."

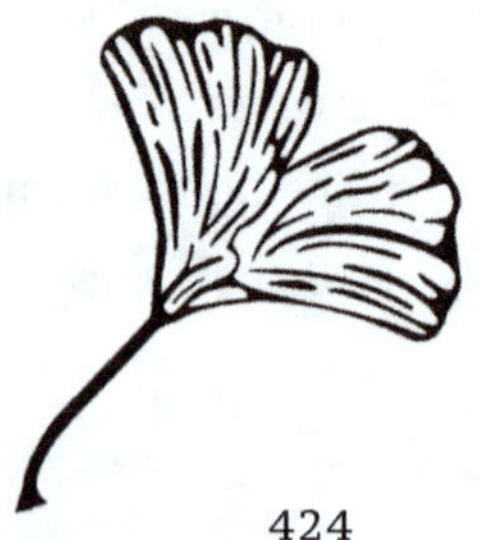

56

GAIN THE SKY

Sinder spent the next few days effectively confined to quarters. It was no use trying to argue that there was a mission at stake. Not with Hisoka Twineshaft backing Timur. So Sinder was forced to endure a full course of remedial teas and handholding.

Sure, they *said* they needed time to revamp their strategies, but the suspension still felt like punishment. Sure, the rookies would've taken a break anyhow, what with the long holiday for Dichotomy Day, but did they have to ban Sinder from the woods?

He was restless.

He wanted to run.

Lilya came as often as her courses allowed. Kyrie came even more, since he slept less. Moon was scarce. Family stuff, no doubt. Hisoka's visits came at odd intervals—brief, intense, and all business. Everyone had other places to be, other things to be doing. They were moving forward, getting on, busy elsewhere. Only Timur ever lingered. Usually to reinforce the whole bed rest thing by snoring in Sinder's ear.

He needed air.

He wanted a look at the sky.

Easing out of his healer's clutches, Sinder stole barefoot across an extravagance in tapestries Timur had strewn across the floor. The man had transformed Zisa's home into a sanctuary fit for any dragon, and Sinder appreciated the pampering. But not tonight.

He wanted something else.

He needed something more.

Dawn was still an hour or two off, and the humans were all abed. He tiptoed through the hush, half expecting Zisa to swoop in for a surprise snuggle. But the hush held.

Dew beneath his feet. Breezes tugging at his unbound hair. Stars adding luster to a moonless sky. He wished he could touch them. He *thought* he could hear them.

Snatches of a song caught and held him, winding him up inside.

"Hey, Damsel." Ginkgo tossed him a wave from where he was lounging among Zisa's roots. "Nice, huh?"

Sinder drifted over, hugging himself against the chill, even though he was too warm.

"Strangest music I ever heard. Or almost heard. Reminds me of a meteor shower." He drew a line in the air with one finger. "There and gone in a wink, but a nice surprise. It was clearer the other night. Probably because there were so many of them. All the fragments became a line, and the melody was sorta … otherworldly."

He hadn't heard their chorus. Not this time. Which only meant it hadn't been for him. But Novi was close, and he was in a tuneful mood. Definitely a portent.

"Something wrong?" asked Ginkgo.

"Not sure." Sinder pivoted and strode away.

"Where are you headed?"

"Into the open. Out from under these branches." He kept right on walking. "I want to see that star. I want to run."

Footfalls. Ginkgo caught up and matched his pace. "I usually run with wolves, but I like a change of pace. Mind the company?"

He was rattled.

He was desperate.

Sinder was barely holding it together, which made it easier to admit the truth. "I don't want to be alone."

Ginkgo's ears dipped and flicked, but his manner was as casual as usual. "Not a problem."

So Sinder ran, could *only* run.

Headlong, as if there were a pack at his heels.

But he couldn't outrun the haunting melody that seemed to howl and shriek against his bones. Ignoring the slap and sting of needle and thorn, Sinder plowed on. He needed to silence this wailing need, but where was relief?

He wanted Juuyu.

He needed help.

"Damsel? You blundering idiot! Sinder!" Ginkgo swung into his path, lifted him off his feet, and bullied him into a broad tree trunk, caging him there. "What's come over you?"

Sinder could only swallow thickly and shake his head.

"What's going on. Talk to me," he ordered sternly.

"Feels strange." Sounded strange, too. He could barely hear his own voice, what with the ringing in his ears. He rolled his shoulders and winced at the bite of bark against his back.

And Ginkgo's whole expression cleared. "Hey, okay," he said gently. "I get it."

He did? Sinder tugged at his shirt, desperate for answers. "What is it?"

"Hang on a sec." Ginkgo half-turned and raised his voice. "Who goes there?"

Kyrie slipped out of the shadows. "Here I am."

"What's up, little bro?"

"The winds woke me." He frowned slightly. "And the stars. What are you doing to Sinder?"

"Helping him. I hope."

Sinder warbled miserably, and Kyrie answered with a gentle trill.

Ginkgo asked, "Which form is best for wings? Because there's not much room here." And when Sinder didn't answer, he pressed, "That's what this is, isn't it?"

Was it?

"You've been tended by a beacon for how many days? And Timur and Tenma before that. And Waaseyaa's influence is probably in the mix." Ginkgo gave him a little shake. "This is the change every dragon awaits ... works toward ... right? This is *good*."

It didn't feel good.

But Sinder couldn't deny that yes, that's what must be happening. And he had no idea if he was supposed to do this in truest form or speaking form. Stories spoke of both. Did either have an advantage.

"I ... I want Michaelson."

Ginkgo nodded, turned to Kyrie, and lifted his chin toward the village. "Fetch Timur quick."

"I will hurry."

Sinder barely registered his absence. Drawing himself up, he tried to remember his lore. Information was his thing. He should know this stuff, probably did. But being in the middle of his attainment left him incoherent.

Slowly releasing his hold, Ginkgo took Sinder's hand and tugged. Moving forward was better than staying still. Sinder locked his fingers with the half-fox's and was glad he wasn't alone.

The lake. He hadn't realized they were close to it. Stars glittered on a surface that was glassy-smooth. Only then did Sinder realize how still the night had grown. Not a single breath of wind. Had they all followed Kyrie when he left?

"I don't know what I'm supposed to do."

Ginkgo nodded. "When I came into my inheritance, I needed Dad's help. But it's probably different for crossers. I ended up needing both him and Tsumiko. They struck the right balance between my human part and my fox part. But Dad's the one I wanted most. Say, should we have sent for Lapis?"

Sinder shook his head. He wanted Timur. Trusted him.

Rolling his shoulders, Sinder asked, "What was this inheritance?"

"My tail. I wasn't born with one." He gave it a lighthearted swish.

"What happened?"

"My bones were on fire, and I could hardly sit still. I was pretty damned scared, and I couldn't figure out how to display for Dad. But he guided me."

Sinder asked, "How?"

"You ... *probably* don't want to know." Ginkgo's ears angled toward the tree line. "They're coming."

Timur charged out of the shadows, Kyrie riding on his back. Winded and worried, he rushed forward, stopped short, then bowed low. "Thank you for inviting me to attend your Ascension."

Sinder was speechless.

"Where's Fend?" Ginkgo asked.

"Unable to attend," Timur said shortly. "Probably for the best. I apologize for any discomfort you've had to endure because of my delay. I'm here, Sinder. Right here."

Admitting it to a Spomenka was hard. "I don't know what to do."

"Ah, Zolottse. Nothing to it, really." Timur's confidence had a calming effect. "This dawn will see you soaring."

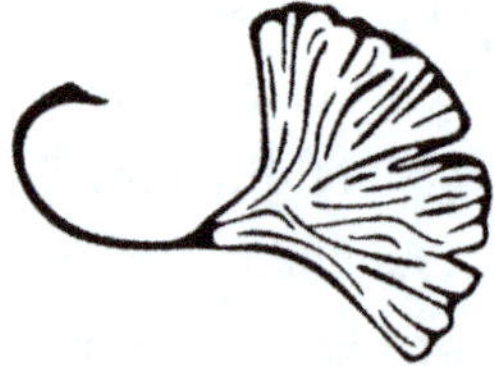

While Timur arranged things, Sinder balled and relaxed his fists over and over. The man's shoulder bag clinked with an abundance of flasks. Had he brought medicine? Bandages? Would breaching wings leave him bloodied? Why wasn't this in the lore? Then again, would anyone seek the sky if they knew the cost?

A smaller hand slipped into his. Kyrie. "Does it hurt?"

"Not exactly. It's not comfortable." Sinder was beginning to feel betrayed by his own body. "I didn't know it would be like this."

Kyrie pressed closer. "We are here."

"We are four," said Timur, who was working on starting a fire. "That's auspicious."

"Are there other favorable conditions?" asked Kyrie.

"Plenty." Flashing a smile at the boy, Timur asked, "Don't suppose you could summon an east wind for him?"

"I will ask."

Sinder eyed him skeptically. But a breeze rose from the direction of the lightening horizon, cooling his flushed face. Carrying with it a whisper of Novi's song.

"Does he need to shift forms?" asked Ginkgo.

"Wings will manifest in either form, but in recent centuries, it's become popular to remain in speaking form." Timur's voice was pitched to soothe. "It makes it easier to maintain a partial transformation later."

"Wings in speaking form?" checked Kyrie.

"Like a wolf and his tail," said Ginkgo. "Or a stag and his antlers."

"That's the idea. Sinder, may I have access to your blaze?" Timur seemed to tower over him.

No sense holding back now. He shrugged out of his tunic, presenting his bared shoulder.

Pushing aside Sinder's hair with one finger, Timur asked, "Can we tie this out of the way?"

"Let me," said Ginkgo. "I'm a pro at braids. In high demand by all the kids."

Sinder frowned. His injuries had healed enough, he could have managed on his own. But Ginkgo was already smoothing and sectioning. Was everything spinning out of his control?

"Calm down, Damsel," ordered Ginkgo.

"How can I?" He peered over his shoulder into pale eyes. "I still don't know what to do."

Timur was fiddling fireside, and the scent of warming oil filled the air. But he returned to Sinder, hands framing his face. "Truly, there is nothing to fear. All you had to do has been done. Your strength is gathered, and your wings await."

Sinder's agitation doubled. "How am I supposed to …?"

He didn't even have words for the hurdle before him.

"Take from me." Timur flashed that ridiculously winsome smile of his. "My turn to tend you, Zolottse."

"That's all?"

"Simple as that." And without hesitation, the dragon slayer offered his soul as a refuge, so that one dragon could gain the sky.

A starry soul, more potent than pollen. Heady and homey and his for the taking.

Sinder lost track of everything but Timur, who stole the ache from his bones and flooded him with certainty. All would be well. Nothing to it, really.

Kyrie's trill called him back. He fluted in harmony with Novi's swelling song.

Ginkgo's voice was there, too. Right beside him. "Rise from here, Damsel," he urged, stroking firmly at his back.

"Whenever you're ready," said Timur, who held him snug and steady, one large hand covering his blaze.

Then the sun crested, and Kyrie gasped. Sinder writhed.

"That's the stuff," praised Ginkgo. "Spread your wings for us, Sinder."

"Please?" Kyrie added in an awed whisper.

He trembled with the effort, but he managed.

Timur spoke the traditional rites in Old Amaranthine first, then boomed a joyous, "Well done!"

57

WOO THE WIND

Mikoto sought out Merl.

When had they last spent any time together? Too long. True, Merl was essentially running the camp this summer. And everyone was extra busy with the upcoming induction ceremony. But Mikoto was suddenly certain that he needed his brother. His best friend.

"Hear me out?" he begged.

Merl ushered him into the garden behind his house, unlocked the small shed that served as their shared armory, and readied himself to spar. Because this was how they did things. Mikoto always needed a while to figure out how to say what was on his mind.

They bashed around for a bit, changed weapons, and clashed some more.

After another exchange, Merl silently passed him a trowel,

and they weeded most of the herb garden before Mikoto began to talk. There was so much. He knew he was forgetting details, but he managed the basics. And Merl listened closely, often pausing in his work to watch Mikoto's face. The colt was amazed by it all. Every word.

So was Mikoto, come to think of it.

"Your connection to her must be strong if Tenma mistook you for one of us," said Merl.

Mikoto grunted his agreement.

"So?"

He looked up.

"Have you made your choice?"

"I have." He studied his hands. "Will it cause problems?"

Merl whole expression warmed. "Fewer than you seem to realize. But if problems arise, you can count on Wardenclave's support."

Mikoto nodded.

"Have you told Yulin?"

"No."

"He will be the most help, so go to him next." Merl rose smoothly. "But first ... wait here, please."

The colt disappeared inside, returning a minute later with a little bell, which he suspended from a branch of the plum tree in the corner of the yard. It chimed once, then settled into silence.

"But first," Merl resumed. "Talk to her."

"How?"

"Even if you cannot hear her, she can hear you. Tell her what you know, what you want. Give her as many reasons as you can to find her way to your side."

Mikoto glanced around. "Can we be sure she is listening?"

Merl pointed to the bell.

It chimed.

"Maker bless," murmured the colt, who went all soft-eyed. "Take your time. I will be inside."

The cottage door closed.

Mikoto picked himself up out of the dirt, brushing absently at his breeches. "Is it you?" he asked uncertainly.

A breeze ruffled his hair, then nudged the bell.

"I did not know," he began awkwardly. "And now I do."

He waited, but of course she didn't have anything to say. Or at the very least, no way to say it.

Clearing his throat, Mikoto got on with it. "You need to know that my feelings have not changed."

The air went still, and it was hard to breathe. This was so embarrassing.

"All the things I loved about Lupe ... were you." He could feel the flush creeping, but she needed to hear it all. "More than anything, I wanted her to see me. Was it that way for you, too?"

The bell pealed several times.

He nodded.

"I do not know if this is enough, but ...." Mikoto took a steadying breath. "Tzefira?"

Wind brushed his face. She was listening.

"Tzefira," he said more confidently. "I want to see you."

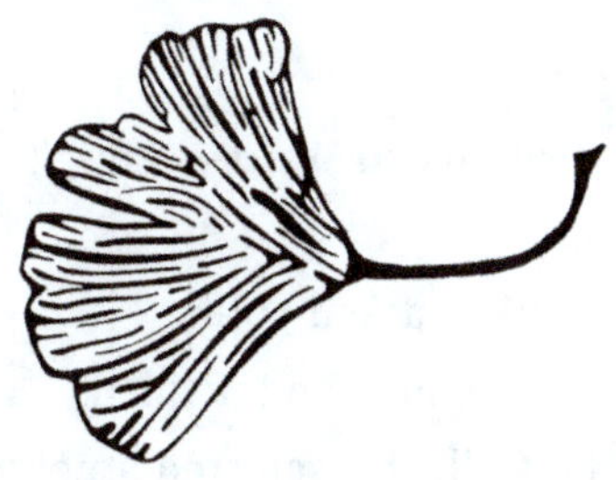

Mikoto wasn't used to being in charge. "Would you please arrange a ... a gathering?"

"Very well." Yulin set aside a stack of folders and clasped his hands. "May I know the particulars?"

He really didn't want to go through the whole long story again, so he skimped. "I am going to woo the wind to my side. If it works—*when* it does—I am fairly certain I will be engaged. Or would it be considered a betrothal? I do not know the etiquette."

Yulin gaped.

Mikoto settled for an apologetic posture.

"Precious noble," Yulin said faintly. "How long has she been courting you?"

"The accident by the river. Since then. Maybe even before."

Folding his hands over his heart, Yulin asked, "That long?"

"Sinder thinks I am wind-kissed."

The moth stepped forward and touched Mikoto's cheek. "And you wish to kiss her back?"

It was his turn to flounder for words.

Yulin inclined his head. "When you do, it will bind you irrevocably. You are right. There should be witnesses. Who did you have in mind?"

Mikoto had expected more resistance. "You do not disapprove?"

"Why would I?"

"I have a responsibility to Wardenclave. To serve as headman. To have a son."

"Does she know this?" asked Yulin.

Mikoto supposed she must and nodded.

"Then all will be well." He selected a notepad and stood with pen poised. "Dear me, there is so much to do! But the task is hardly insurmountable. Everyone will already be here for your induction."

"Oh, I was thinking a smaller group. Something more … private."

Yulin was already jotting. "For the Descent, surely. An intimate gathering for an intimate moment. I was referring to the solstice. What better time?"

Dignitaries were already arriving from all over the world, along with news crews, journalists, and Amaranthine enthusiasts. Every hotel, tavern, and bed and breakfast in Denholm was booked solid.

Mikoto watched Yulin scribble for a full minute before daring to ask, "Do you mean Dichotomy Day?"

"Noble heart," Yulin said kindly. "I mean your wedding day."

58

INTIMATE GATHERINGS

Part of Kyrie was jittery with anticipation for tomorrow, when Harmonious Starmark would arrive, Ever in tow. But today had an excitement all its own. Before leaving Waaseyaa's door, he checked to see if Lilya also had her invitation.

"Ready?" She lifted the small envelope where her name was written with an extravagance of loops and flourishes.

He reached up to touch her hair, which Zisa had braided into a crown and flourished with his own flowers. Lilya adjusted the fold of Kyrie's sash, which bore both the Mettlebright and Stately House crests. They'd dressed in their very best, since today was extra special.

With the help of Lapis and Sinder, Mikoto would woo the wind to his side.

The invitations, which were hand-lettered works of art, called this transformation a "descent." Which matched every story Kyrie knew of the various sky clans. Moon maidens, stars, and storms were difficult to capture, for once they touched the ground, they could never return to their former home in the skies.

"Ready," he agreed.

A few others were already gathering. This is where everything would happen, since Waaseyaa and Zisa couldn't have attended otherwise. Ginkgo was already there, speaking in Japanese to a woman in a luxurious kimono. Timur and Salali were fussing with a lovely set of wardstones. Lapis had somehow ended up with Gregor, and each seemed entirely pleased in the other's company.

Lilya made a happy noise and ran to speak to the Dimityblest at Mikoto's side. "Did *you* write these?" she asked, proffering the invitation.

"I did." He smiled gently and covered her hands. "Keep it as a memento of the day."

"I'll treasure it always." And turning to Mikoto, Lilya said, "It's like a fairy tale."

Kyrie hung back. It was nice that she'd made friends. She might not even realize that, in her own way, she'd begun to feel at home here. Already their paths were beginning to diverge.

Turning aside, Kyrie slipped his hand into Sinder's. "Is this a wedding?" he whispered.

"Hope so." His smile was wry. "Do I look as awkward as I feel?"

Kyrie studied his attire, which was certainly more lavish than the stuff Sinder usually wore. "Lapis usually dresses in a similar style."

"There's a good reason for that." Fiddling self-consciously with gauzy layers of sheer fabric, he muttered, "He loaned me this get-up. I managed to talk him out of most of the jewelry."

"You look very pretty." Touching the necklace Lapis had loaned him, Kyrie added, "I feel special."

Sinder grudgingly admitted, "It's not so bad. Once in a while. To pretty up a bit."

Wardenclave's founders arrived together, and Radiance swept to Lilya's side. She and Glint were clearly taken with her. So much so, Kyrie couldn't help wondering if Ever would be jealous. Which reminded him of something.

"Will it cause a problem that Mikoto's children will be crossers?"

"They won't be."

Kyrie hesitated. "They are not compatible?"

"No, no. If the stories are to be believed, they'll have no trouble. Untouched by the Waning, and so forth. However, I have it on good authority that an imp's contribution to a mixed mating is … unmixed."

"Could you clarify?" asked Kyrie. "If it is not a secret."

"Nah, not this. It's lore." Still, Sinder kept his voice low. "If a moon maiden accepts a wolf as her bondmate, she'll give him strong cubs. If a wind joins with a dragon, all their young will be exceptionally beautiful dragons. If a tree gives its fruit to a phoenix, the resulting child will be a phoenix."

"So Mikoto's children will be human, even though their mother is a wind imp."

"Not just human. They'll be *reavers*, and they'll probably rival Waaseyaa's lot for power once they're ranked." Sinder's gaze settled on Wardenclave's headman. "Couldn't have happened to a nicer kid."

Just then, Ginkgo signaled for Kyrie, so he excused himself.

His big brother was still with the Japanese woman, and Glint had joined them. They'd switched to English, probably for the dog clansman's benefit.

"I was going to tell you, and then I didn't." Ginkgo's ears went all cockeyed with embarrassment. "This is Mikoto's mother. She's from Japan, and her maiden name is Hajime. Sora-san, this is Kyrie Hajime-Mettlebright. Like I was saying, I also have Hajime ancestry, so in a way, we're kin."

Kyrie looked up into the woman's face, searching for any resemblance to Mom. There were commonalities, things typical to the Japanese people, but that was all. He offered his hands in greeting.

"My pedigree is a matter of record." Sora looked thoughtfully at Glint. "If anyone can trace our connection, it would be you, Lord Starmark."

"Odd thing, that." Ever's grandsire casually offered a hand to Kyrie. "Your father personally searched our records. Quite thoroughly. He was researching Tsumiko's heritage. Even unregistered reavers can usually be placed on a chart if we cross-reference family registries."

Ginkgo's ears pricked. "He never mentioned that to me. What did he find?"

With a low chuckle, Glint said, "He never mentioned that, either. Although I got the distinct impression he was … annoyed."

Kyrie had been so focused on the dragon half of his heritage, it had never occurred to him that being a Hajime might be special in its own way.

Yulin encouraged Mikoto to limit his guest list to the bare minimum. His mother and his best friend. His five mentors. He'd wanted Waaseyaa and Zisa in attendance, so they were hosting. They needed Lapis and Sinder, who'd outlined a plan that required Timur's support.

He'd promised a place to Kyrie, and it was only natural to include Lilya. And Ginkgo for that matter. Lupe had also been invited, but she'd politely declined. Maybe that was for the best. Mikoto could only assume that she was being considerate of Tzefira's feelings.

"Cold feet?"

Mikoto hadn't specifically invited Radiance, but neither would he dream of excluding her. Lady Starmark found a warm welcome wherever she went. He considered her teasing question and answered seriously. "I have no doubts."

"Good boy." She bumped shoulders with him. "Did you know that your parents didn't meet until the day they exchanged vows?"

He shook his head.

"It was the same for Glint. He was adorably flustered when I ambushed him. But like you, he squared his shoulders and faced me." Radiance dimpled. "I'm happy for both of you."

Mikoto slipped into a grateful posture, but he wasn't sure what to say. Wasn't it too early to celebrate? They weren't even sure this would work. Then again, if it didn't, they'd keep trying until something did.

"She has only been here for summers." He liked knowing Radiance would support their choice. "She will finally see our village in autumn and winter and spring."

"May all the seasons ahead be joyous."

He wanted that, too.

"Mikoto," called Timur. "We're ready for you."

He hurried into a circle set with wardstones. Most were pale blue, but at the center Timur placed a single red crystal.

Timur grabbed him by the shoulders and backed him out of the ring. "You'll be on *this* side of the barrier. Otherwise, our dragons may inadvertently woo *you* to their side, and that would leave your lady lonely."

"Understood."

"I'll monitor things from inside. Ginkgo and Kyrie will keep watch out here. Lapis and Sinder will be piling on the charm, and nobody here would be able to resist."

"Because they will be singing a love song?"

"A traditional ballad with admittedly amorous subtext." Timur indicated the crystals. "I'm pretty sure one of the reasons Lapis insisted on the barrier is because it's a clan secret."

"If they're inside a barrier, how will Tzefira be able to hear them?"

Timur blinked, then chuckled. Gesturing with both hands, he explained, "It'll be switched. You and your guests are on lockdown. Lapis and Sinder will be singing to the open sky."

"What if they attract more than they intend?"

"Won't matter," assured Timur. "Even if the stars themselves are lured in by their song, they don't have Tzefira's reason to stay."

"And the song will help her know what to do?"

"That's what they tell me." Timur lowered his voice and took a more serious tone. "It's a very old, very long ballad that teaches by example. A dragon friend slipped me the transcript once. It's called 'The Temptation of Lord Beckonthrall.'"

Mikoto started out nodding, then shook his head. "What good will it do to hear about him? I cannot duplicate his methods."

"You've got it switched again, my good man." Timur's eyes sparkled. "According to tradition, Persiflage Beckonthrall was the one who succumbed to temptation. And the song was composed by the four winds who wooed him."

That wasn't in the song Sinder had shared. Mikoto was almost afraid to ask. "How did they do that?"

Timur's smile had a hint of smirk to it. "I think you're about to find out."

Because of the barrier, Kyrie couldn't hear Sinder and Lapis, so he gave the blue wardstones a bit of encouragement—they were doing their job well—and slipped away. Certain the song would rise, he found the rungs set into Zisa's trunk and clambered upward.

Only when he'd reached the lowermost branches did Kyrie realize that someone else had the same idea. Salali rolled his eyes, signaled for silence, and continued his own nimble ascent.

A voice filtered down. Zisa's.

"You know he is in earnest. He is serious about *everything*."

A pause.

"Has he neglected something? I thought not. Well, then ... what more is there?"

A longer pause.

"Does that matter? I never gave it a thought. I simply happened."

Salali revealed himself, strolling along the limb. "Who have you coaxed into my nest, Zisa?"

The tree looked relieved to see them. "Come, Salali. Come, Kyrie. What should I do?"

Squatting before the nest, Salali asked, "What's needed?"

"Tzefira is not sure how to appear."

"Isn't that what the song's for?" reasoned the squirrel.

Kyrie climbed one branch higher and stepped lightly along its length, intent on catching the dragons' song. To his delight, once he was far enough away from the trunk, he met Timur's barrier. However, before Kyrie could coax it to give him a tiny hole to listen at, Salali's words snagged his attention.

"... was always easier for Amaranthine because the forefathers and foremothers were once human themselves. But for Impressions, who are the embodiment of the natural world ... well, it's trickier. The first to manage it were either commanded by heaven or inspired by love."

Eager for more details, Kyrie stole back and perched directly over the nest. "Are they in love?"

Salali huffed. "I'm hardly an expert, and that boy simply isn't the sort to spout poetry or sing ballads. But once he commits himself ... I mean ... isn't loyalty a kind of love?"

Zisa waved his hands. "All of that may be important, but this is not a matter of means. Rather, Tzefira must decide how to appear."

"We are talking in circles, friend."

Kyrie, who had many sisters, said, "Radiance has a robe waiting."

Salali blinked, then hauled his hat low over his face. "Maker have mercy. She wants to be pretty."

"She certainly does." Kyrie understood all too well. "I would want to be found beautiful in the eyes of my beloved."

Zisa nodded.

Salali sighed. "Impressions in speaking form often resemble their true form; however, they can also borrow their appearance from someone they admire. Their mentor. Their friend. Their kin. Their love."

Kyrie stowed these new details before asking, "Why do you know so much about Impressions? Most people think they are myths."

"Some of it's age. There are those who remember what the world was like before the imps completely faded. And wrote the stories that passed into legend."

"Are you a forefather?" guessed Kyrie.

"I hardly qualify. Never been a father." Salali went on. "Some of it's this place. We've been preserving reaver lines and tree-kin from the beginning. But a few of us have been quietly preserving ties with imps. For instance, Starmark Kith have always had ears to hear the songs of stars."

Kyrie believed that. After all, he'd always had ears to hear the whispers of winds.

"But the main reason we have so many connections with impressions would be Linlu Dimityblest. His knack brought them flocking. We always had a star or two hanging about, keeping Jori company."

"He is Wardenclave's star," supplied Zisa. "And there is that rainbow who visits most summers."

Salali nodded. "We're on the course of a comet, as well, but I think his last pass was before Tzefira's time."

"No other winds?" asked Kyrie.

"They're not usually the sort to linger." With a sidelong look that was probably meant for Tzefira, he added, "Mikoto has always lived for summer's arrival. Now, we know why."

"Linlu would have known sooner," Zisa said sadly.

Kyrie studied their faces. "Is he away?"

"Well, he's certainly not here." Salali grimaced. "He's missing. Went away with some secret purpose and never returned."

"He would if he could," murmured Zisa.

"We should set aside those cares for another day. Mikoto is waiting for his bride's appearing."

Kyrie exhaled on a slow warble. "I have never seen a wind, so I do not know if they resemble one another."

"Oh!" exclaimed Zisa. "Oh, I know! I am comely, and Mikoto loves me. Tzefira, let me be a brother to you, and I can stand beside you when you claim your husband. Wouldn't that be nice?"

The wind twirled, scattering leaves and flower petals, before spinning away.

Salali, one hand clamped firmly over his hat, whispered, "That worked?"

Zisa tittered and vanished.

"Hurry!" gasped Kyrie.

Sighing mightily, Salali scooped him up and dropped.

Mikoto knew how to hold a position. To stand at his post, alert for any change, poised to respond to any situation. This was a little different, perhaps, but it felt the same. Requiring patience. Requiring courage. Mikoto wasn't awaiting further orders or anything resembling an attack. Still, he would have felt a little better if he were armed.

Sinder and Lapis were singing, but the barrier was funneling their song away. It was supposed to call to Tzefira, but Mikoto couldn't help but think that *he* was the one who should be doing the calling.

Mikoto lifted his chin and declared, "I am here, Tzefira. I am waiting."

Something changed.

Timur signaled, and the dragons traded a look. They ended their duet with a prolonged flourish, and when the barrier collapsed, the final note was somehow still ringing. An echo? An overtone? Or perhaps a star. Radiance swore they sang for those who needed to hear them.

Lapis stepped back, and Sinder hurried to Timur's side, making room.

Diffuse light began to coalesce, and Radiance readied a kimono. It was an heirloom from his mother's collection. Again, something changed, and chimes sounded—tiny and tinkling. Radiance was fussing with folds and knots, which meant there was someone wearing all that silk. Mikoto desperately wanted to look, but he didn't want to see too much.

Lowering his gaze, he went back to what he knew. Holding a position.

"Lovely," declared Radiance, which meant it was safe.

"We are," agreed Zisa. "I helped."

That was so like him, heedless of ceremony, quick to greet a newcomer.

He and Radiance stepped aside, parting like a curtain to reveal a young woman. She was the same height as Zisa, though with a much more curvaceous aspect. Her feet were fair against the springing mosses, and when she stepped toward him, bells jingled anew.

There they were. Golden bells gleamed softly against light brown hair, so like Zisa's. The similarities could not be a coincidence. Mikoto probably should have put more thought into his first words, but he blurted, "She looks like you."

"We made a pact," Zisa announced proudly.

Waaseyaa hurried forward. "Brother, what have you done?"

"I have become her brother!" The tree caught his twin's hand. "That way, she has more than nothing and the best of everything. Us as a family. And Mikoto for a groom."

Mikoto marveled at Zisa's foresight. "You are always so generous," he said. "Thank you, Zisa."

Slipping from his brother's arms, Zisa twined around Mikoto. "I have a sister!"

"She will rely on you greatly."

"And visit often." With a blissful smile, Zisa said, "You may call me Brother."

Laughter broke out, and everyone had relaxed into indulgent smiles.

Zisa turned him loose and whispered, "Go."

Mikoto stepped forward and looked into green-gold eyes and liked the familiarity. This might be their first proper meeting, but she wasn't a stranger. Not really.

"Hello, Tzefira."

She tipped her head, and bells tinkled. Yet she didn't speak.

Suddenly, Kyrie hurried over, catching Mikoto's sleeve. But his gaze was fixed on Tzefira's face. "Are you like a star? Do you also have a voice intended for the skies?"

Tzefira tapped the boy's nose, then sought Mikoto's gaze, touching a finger to her lips.

His brows shot up before he could school his expression, which *may* have been rude.

She winked solemnly. At least there were no hard feelings.

Kyrie tugged at Mikoto and explained, "You will need to be touching if you want to hear her voice."

Startled by this development, Mikoto offered his palms in the usual way.

When their fingertips met, he thought he caught a whisper, but it was too faint. So he clasped her hands securely, and furrowed his brows in concentration.

All that came through was a laugh. But it meant there *was* a connection. And she sounded happy.

Mikoto's own happiness spilled over, more inwardly than outwardly, and Tzefira swayed into him. Reaching up with both hands, she pulled him into a kiss.

"Mikoto." Her voice was light and teasing as the breezes that had always tugged for attention. *"Does my voice reach you now?"*

He managed a small grunt.

She laughed again, then repeated his name in reverent tones.

Would pulling away be like refusing to listen? He didn't want to be rude. There were probably lots of things they should talk about, but words were quickly fading in importance. She was all soft curves and familiar scents. There was silk and the sound of bells, and the swirl of her tongue against his.

Mikoto hadn't meant to tend her, not specifically.

He was willing enough. Maybe even eager, because she wasn't like anyone else he'd ever touched. The Amaranthine were deep and dense, a darkness that craved his light. But she was luminous, with a sparkle that slipped in and suffused his mind.

"More," she sighed into his thoughts. *"Oh, lovely one … more."*

A throat cleared, and hands closed around Mikoto's shoulders. "That will do for now, my boy." Glint's smile was sympathetic. "I take it she is willing to have you?"

Radiance, who had Tzefira by the shoulders, sported a decidedly rakish grin. "And have him you shall, you brave and beautiful breeze. But there's your bridal attire to arrange, and your lovely boy has dignitaries to greet and a wedding announcement to make."

Jostling him slightly, Glint asked, "What did she say?"

As if their kiss had been nothing more than a conversation. Mikoto wasn't sure he wanted to attempt an explanation, so he chose the simplest answer. "Yes …?"

"You sound uncertain," Radiance said lightly. "Did you need more time to … talk?"

Mikoto blushed, but Tzefira's gaze was as steady as her hand over his heart.

"You are willing?"

He covered her hand. "I am willing."

With an impish smile, she ordered, *"Bend."*

"Like this?" he mumbled, bowing at the waist.

Her hand slipped into his hair, and her lips pressed his forehead. *"Lovely one, you are mine."*

"Oh, that's done it." Radiance actually giggled. "I wonder if it will show up on camera?"

Glint turned Mikoto's face, studied his forehead, and huffed.

Someone—Mikoto was fairly certain it was Ginkgo—gave a piercing whistle and started off a round of applause. There was much stomping of feet, and everyone wanted to ogle him and meet Tzefira. Amaranthine introductions being what they were, Radiance slid into the role of mistress of ceremonies.

Mikoto watched from the sidelines, relieved that his friends and family did all the talking. Tzefira didn't seem inclined to kiss anyone else.

"Brings back memories," murmured Glint.

"Do we need a contract?" checked Mikoto.

Signaling to someone, Glint gruffly said, "Nothing like that. The contract between you two has been made, accepted, and sealed. You are hers. She is yours. May your household flourish."

Yulin came alongside and touched Mikoto's elbow. "Rather than a contract, you shall have a chronicle. I hope I can do justice to the day."

Mikoto mumbled something grateful, though he lost track of the sentence midway through. The Five had come to surround him—Starmark, Fullstash, Duntuffet, Alpenglow, and Dimityblest. On every side, they gazed at him with universal satisfaction.

"Is it really that strange?" he managed.

"We need a mirror," remarked Hannick.

Salali snapped his fingers. "Ginkgo. Your phone?"

The half-fox bounded over and produced the device. Snapping a picture, he studied his phone's screen, and eyed it critically before handing it off. "It's prettier in person."

In the photograph, Mikoto's eyes were as wide as a first-time camper's fresh off the bus. And in the center of his forehead was a mark. Not quite a sigil. It seemed to be more decorative.

"The colors keep shifting and changing," said Ginkgo. "Betcha Tenma calls it *prismatic*."

"Is it a blaze?"

Glint took his arm and cleared his throat. "Radiance would call it a miracle."

Mikoto smiled at that. It was her pat answer whenever anyone asked her about the star that marked her forehead.

"My boy, do you understand what this means?"

"He doesn't," said Salali. "Who wants to tell him?"

"Choose me!" Zisa wiggled into their midst and flung his arms around Mikoto's shoulders. Just like always. "I am his brother-in-law, so it should be me."

All five yielded with smiles.

"What do you wish to tell me, Brother?"

For once Zisa didn't fritter around the edges. "Waaseyaa has my blessing. You have Tzefira's. Which is different, but the same. Are you glad? Glint is."

Mikoto scanned the group. Hannick was thumping Glint's shoulder. Bram Duntuffet and Salali were laughing against each other's shoulders, as if to hold each other up. What was so funny?

Waaseyaa eased to Mikoto's side, slipping his arms around his waist and hugging him with more emotion than he usually showed.

"Uncle?"

"I live on because I have the benefit of a tree's blessing." Waaseyaa laughed in a way that made him seem much younger. "Mikoto, brother of my brother, you have a wind's blessing. It means you will *live*."

Then Glint was grappling all three of them in a spine-bending hug and doing a poor job of hiding his sniffles.

Yulin lent his support, one hand firm at Mikoto's back. "As you are aware, noble heart, Glint has never liked letting go. And you have spared him the necessity."

Mikoto could only be boggled, so he settled for a nod. And hoped they'd let him return to Tzefira soon.

"Well, boys! Guess we'll have to train him up right, since he's the only one we'll ever need." Salali tipped his hat. "Mikoto Reaver, Eternal Headman."

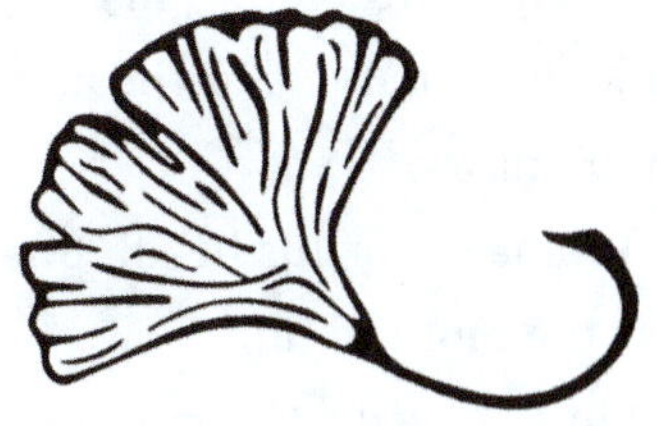

59
UNIONS AND REUNIONS

Tenma prodded at his ice cream, lost in thought.

"She'll be here any second." Ginkgo waved a spoon loaded with mint chocolate chip ice cream. "What's got you so morose?"

"I am twenty-six years old."

"So?"

"I am twenty-six years old, and this is my first date." Gesturing between them with his own spoon, Tenma said, "A chaperoned date with an eleven-year-old girl."

Ginkgo snickered. "I'm going to hire us a Dimityblest chronicler while we're here. And those very words will begin the history of your dynasty."

Tenma shook his head. "She wants to add to Michael's dynasty. Give the moth to him."

Lilya arrived a few minutes later, arm linked through Kyrie's.

The brothers Mettlebright went to get more ice cream, blatantly giving Tenma a few minutes to speak with Lilya.

"Are you very sure about this?" he ventured.

The girl fixed him with a look that reminded him very much of Isla. "Yes."

"Wanting something similar doesn't necessarily mean we'll find it in each other."

"Not similar," she countered. "*Same.*"

"And there's the difference in our ages." He'd promised to address every possible hindrance. Surely, it was his responsibility.

Lilya said, "I'll grow."

He let his head hang. "But your parents might not like it."

"Why not?"

"It's … hard to explain."

Stretching across the table to touch his hand, she asked, "Will Papka and Mum have *good* reasons? Because I think everything will work out."

Ginkgo returned tail swaying, and Kyrie followed, carrying dishes for himself and for Lilya.

Ignoring them, Lilya pressed, "Don't you?"

Tenma would be honest. "I would love to call Stately House home, but it's hard to picture you as my wife, Lilya-chan. You're so young. It's too soon."

Ginkgo nodded approvingly. "That's a proper attitude. Plenty of time for that later."

"I like having things settled," said Lilya. "Nobody will worry about my future because you'll be waiting."

"What if you change your mind?"

She stared at him again. There wasn't any hostility there, but her next words were a blunt force. "Do you take promises that lightly?"

"No!" he gasped. "But …."

Tenma found that he couldn't voice any further protests. He'd only wanted to give her a chance to reconsider, but anything more would be an insult, both to her and to the wish they shared.

"I will not shy away from this choice if it's allowed to me." Tenma sat straighter and placed his hands on the table. "You have my promise now, before others call for vows. I accept, Lilya-chan."

With a straightforwardness he was growing to appreciate, she said, "Right. We're set, then."

And conversation moved on to the impending arrival of Harmonious Starmark.

However, when the time came for Ginkgo and Kyrie to clear away evidence of their midnight raid on the kitchen, Lilya tapped Tenma's arm and said, "I did think of one thing. I'm not sure if it will be a problem."

"Yes?"

"Looking him up and down, she eased closer to whisper, "I'll grow."

Tenma could only agree.

Lilya bluntly announced, "I'll probably be taller than you."

Once again, Tenma could only agree. He was still laughing when Ginkgo and Kyrie returned.

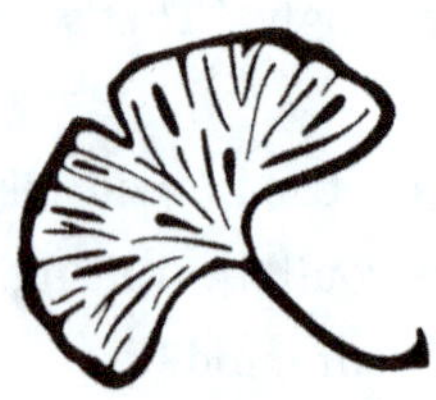

Ginkgo wasn't sure he'd ever had more fun than keeping Dad posted with texted asides about Lilya's impending betrothal. True, he loved the gossip. But some of the elation was knowing that Dad was safe enough to be snide.

Ribbons for days

Do not dismiss them lightly
He pioneered embroidered sigilcraft

Gonna start adding them
to my work shirts?

So you had not noticed?
NOW who is amused?

"Apologies for denying you rest." At four in the morning on Dichotomy Day, Glint greeted them at his back door in formal attire. Flapping a hand Yulin's way, he explained, "Every minute of my day has been scheduled."

"Thank you for making time," said Lapis.

Lilya said, "More importantly, look who's here!"

Our girl is putting Ever
ahead of marriage

I see no issue with her priorities
Or have you forgotten
that she is a child?

How can I forget?
Tenma languishes a *little* less
over the age difference

It might be amusing to mention the years between Tsumiko and me

Are you trying to encourage him?

Let us say that I am willing to indulge Lilya

Nice out

Have you progressed past sniffening?

Almost

Dogs

Ginkgo surveyed a receiving room that would probably see dozens of couples over the course of the summer. Banners emblazoned with the Starmark crest decorated the walls, and the drapings on the table also shimmered with copper.

The central table was a large square, with seats on either end for those scheduled to sign contracts. Glint presided between them, presumably to bear witness to the vows and to add his seal to the attendant paperwork.

Yulin and a small group of moths fluttered about narrow tables along the room's edges, straightening already-tidy piles of paperwork.

On the groom's side of the table, Tenma sat between Harmonious and Lapis.

"An honorary Starmark, you say?" asked Glint, peering at Tenma with new appreciation. "But Lord Mossberne, are you not Lilya's go-between?"

Lapis tucked his arm through Tenma's. "This boy is my apprentice. And Miss Lilya has enough support."

On the opposite side of the table, Lilya hugged Kyrie and Ever to her sides.

Snapping a couple of pictures, Ginkgo sent them together.

> **There is a certain symmetry**
> **Each with a dog and a dragon**

I don't dare point it out
But doesn't it mean they're
kind of perfect for each other?

> **Show me Tenma**
> **Again**

Ginkgo zoomed in and snapped another picture. A good one, since it showed Isla hovering at his shoulder, talking his ear off. She'd arrived with Harmonious, and she was taking her duties seriously. Not as Tenma's go-between this time, but representing her parents' keen interest in these arrangements.

He blushes like a maiden

> **Is she his choice?**

More like WE are

> **A practical alliance**

For now, but probably not for always
Tenma reminds me a little of Mom
He wants a family, a home

> **He shall have them**

At a wave of Glint's hand, Scribe Dimityblest placed a handwritten contract before Tenma. Lilya's offer for him, now in its third revision after Lapis and Isla had spent most of yesterday on the phone, quibbling over details.

Tenma's only condition hadn't changed—mutual exclusivity.

For the rest, he bowed to the wishes of Lilya and her family.

"Under normal circumstances, I would not have imagined, let alone arranged this union," said Glint, who seemed oblivious to the intense looks he was receiving. "But the young lady is most insistent, and her parents are adamant in their support of their daughter's right to choose her own happiness."

"That would be *you*," murmured Harmonious, his eyes shining with pride.

Glint went on. "Tenma Subaru, your existence is unique, and your future wife is counted among the stars. May your joy in one another create a new constellation on the horizon. Will you take a new name for the house you establish?"

Behind him, Isla gasped.

This was probably a huge honor.

"Do I have to declare that now?" asked Tenma.

"No."

"Then I would prefer to wait. I'll want L-lilya's opinion on the matter." He was such a schoolboy. Dropping the honorific didn't have to be a big deal. The others probably didn't even notice.

Ah, but there. Kyrie both noticed and knew. His small nod accepted the intimacy.

Lapis pressed a pen into his hand. Harmonious indicated the place for his signature.

With the faint scratch of a nib across parchment, Tenma chose his own happiness, sure that it would be shared. "Right," he murmured to himself. "We're set then."

60

MY HALF

Timur dragged into Zisa's cottage and stood mute in the hush, caressing Gregor's silken curls. He was tired of smiling, tired of feasting. Worn out by toasts and dancing and laughter.

Everyone had presented themselves well.

Mikoto's nobility throughout back-to-back ceremonies— induction and wedding.

Hisoka's Dichotomy Day address, with Isla standing just behind, looking so sophisticated.

Harmonious Starmark's booming re-announcement of the birth of his first crosser grandchild.

Timur had soldiered through, stiff upper lip intact, but he'd found his limit. "Here, now." His voice crackled. "Is Papka's little battler ready for a bath?"

Propping Gregor against Fend's flank, he went to fill the tub.

For the first time in days, he ignored the collection of herbs and scents he'd have used to appeal to Sinder. The dragon would be back to work, same as everyone else, once the Dichotomy Day celebrations came to a close at the end of the week. They wouldn't go to waste, but they weren't needed now.

Plain water.

Plain soap.

Plain facts.

It was a terrible thing, taking after both parents. Like Papka, Timur easily formed attachments. But like Mum, he guarded them jealously. So he took it too personally when people moved on.

When a glowering phoenix in a fine suit had descended on Wardenclave like a thundercloud, Sinder hadn't even looked back in his hurry to reach him. Knowing he and Juuyu were partners made Sinder's vanishing act understandable. Still hurt, though.

Timur should probably be grateful for the reality check. He wasn't going to find what was missing in a summer friend. Everyone here had lives to go back to. Even him. And he shouldn't be whinging about what he lacked. Not when he'd struggled through so much in order to gain a son.

Shedding feast day finery, they dawdled through bathtime. Whimsical sigilcraft, cradle songs, and enough exuberant splashing to earn a few hisses from Fend.

Gradually, Timur calmed enough to smile for Gregor. "What is good is hard. But is still good, yes?"

Timur was suddenly awake and seriously confused. The room was dark, and someone was sifting fingers through his hair. He could feel the gentle scrape of claws. "Ginkgo?"

"No."

Whoever it was licked a long stripe up his cheek.

He didn't know who it was. Didn't smell like Zisa. Didn't smell like a stranger. Who even had access to Waaseyaa's and Zisa's haven?

"You aren't usually this indecisive when attacked."

"Not sure this is an attack."

"Full points. It's not."

Crisp enunciation and a cultured accent. A flatness that suggested a dry sense of humor. But with a slight lift that was almost ... flirtatious.

Timur flipped his assailant, pinning his arms.

"Mind the baby," said the stranger, clearly unconcerned by the arm across his throat.

"Who ...?"

"Missed an appendage," interrupted his captive. Something boffed Timur across the face. "Light a couple of crystals. I'm curious to see what else I have to work with."

Now he was giving orders? Timur growled, "Who put you in charge?"

"I may not have your bulk, but you don't have my strength."

For one disorienting moment, Timur lost contact with the bed. Flipped, dropped, and pressed into the mattress, all he could think to say was, "Mind the baby."

"I always do." His captor's voice was at his ear then. "And I've *always* been in charge. Now, light a couple of crystals."

Timur hesitated. Because a strange possibility had finally occurred to him.

"You can finally hear my voice. *At least* have the good grace to listen."

"Crystals are on the bedside table."

A long stretch. Warm fingers. Cool stones.

Timur lofted one and then another and stared blankly at an Amaranthine who looked more or less his own age. Brown skin, dark brows, thick lashes, and vividly orange eyes with slit pupils.

He left off studying his claws to fix Timur with a decidedly smug gaze. "Opposable thumbs. I'm thinking they'll be a game changer."

"F-fend?"

"I'll permit your perusal, so long as you keep what we find in the strictest confidence."

Which was definitely another order.

Timur sat up and helped his Kith partner explore his speaking form. The feline arched his back, wriggled his hips, rubbed his hands together, and flex and retracted the claws in his feet, which were more like elongated paws. Everything must have proven satisfactory because he began to purr.

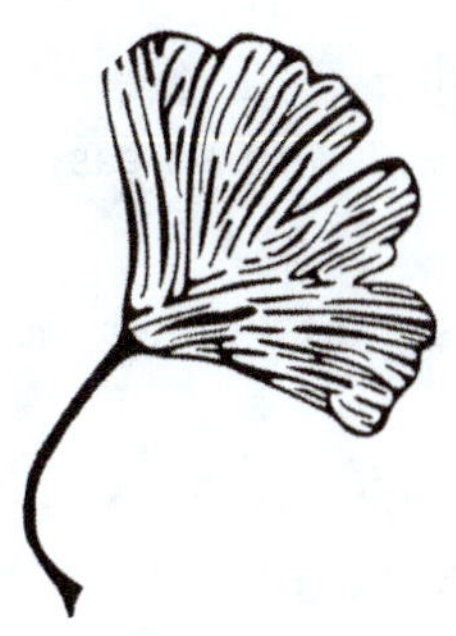

"Fend?"

"Hmm?" He sprawled limply over Timur's chest, now clad in boxers and luxuriating in the petting of the velvety panther ears atop his head.

"How long have you been Kith-kin?"

"Probably since conception. All in the genes."

Timur chuckled. "Fine. How long have you *known*?"

Fend's tail, which was exceptionally long and dexterous, flicked Timur's nose. "About two minutes longer than you."

"Why, though? Why the sudden change?"

"You were crying in your sleep."

Timur scratched through Fend's short hair, which had the same dense silkiness as his fur. "That's all?"

Fend lifted his face to glare. "What's so wonderful about dragons, anyhow? Flighty as the winds they follow."

Unable to resist teasing, Timur asked, "And felines are famed for their constancy?"

"Stop pining after someone else's partner." Baring his fangs, Fend said, "You are *mine*."

How long had he waited?

To be deeply attached.

To be jealously held.

"Yours," Timur agreed with an easy smile. "We make a good team, yes?"

"Not good enough. I want another pact," Fend demanded.

"Yes."

"Yes?" The feline sniffed. "You haven't even heard my terms."

Timur shrugged. "Still yes."

"Reckless as ever." Fend bent to rub their cheeks together, his purr gaining decibels. "Trust me, *ma moitié*. Together, we will be unstoppable."

never more than
FORTHRIGHT

a teller of tales who began as a fandom ficcer. (Which basically means that no one in RL knows about her anime habit, her manga collection, or her penchant for serial storytelling.) Kinda sorta almost famous for gently-paced, WAFFy adventures that might inadvertently overturn your OTP, forthy will forever adore drabble challenges, surprise fanart, and twinkles (which are rumored to keep well in jars). As always... be nice, play fair, have fun! ::twinkle::

FORTHWRITES.COM

Abundant thanks to all who lend their support by reading, rating, and reviewing my stories, wherever they may be found. ::twinkle::

ALSO BY FORTHRIGHT

AMARANTHINE SAGA

Tsumiko and the Enslaved Fox
Kimiko and the Accidental Proposal
Tamiko and the Two Janitors
Mikoto and the Reaver Village
Fumiko and the Finicky Nestmate

SONGS OF THE AMARANTHINE

Marked by Stars
Followed by Thunder
Dragged through Hedgerows
Governed by Whimsy
Hemmed in Silver

AMARANTHINE INTERLUDES

Lord Mettlebright's Man

PATREON EXCLUSIVES

Bard & Barbarian

When I reach 400 patrons, I'll begin publishing a new subscription-based storyline on Patreon. Loosely based on the old Amaranthine tale, "The Wolf and the Moon Maiden," this serial will involve three sisters, twelve pledges, and the long-awaited stirring of a sleeping landmark.
Kimiko and the Cycle of Moons
Become a patron at https://www.patreon.com/forthrightly

She could make a mess of everything. Especially him.

The Junzi—also known as the Four Gentlemen—are a set of ancient weapons fashioned from remnants. Dragons refer to them as the Four Storms, and Hisoka Twineshaft believes they will make a difference in the hunt for the rogue. But someone else is interested in gathering up these crystal masterpieces. The so-called Gentleman Bandit is responsible for two thefts already, and Hisoka is concerned for the Bamboo Stave. So he deploys an elite taskforce to guard the treasure. And to catch a thief.

Juuyu Farroost and his teammates regroup at a safehouse tucked under the boughs of one of the oldest—and most heavily fortified—orphan trees in the Americas. Fumiko and her tree twin have enough rooms for all of them. If they can shift enough of the woman's clutter to set up their equipment. Juuyu's expertise is essential to the success of their mission, but he can barely focus thanks to Fumiko, her messes, and Akira, who apparently owes Boon a favor.

Fairies in the garden. Frost on the pumpkins. Farmhands at the dance.

Wyn Outler doesn't talk about where he came from (or how long ago). All part of the vows he took when he and his best friend turned their backs on the In-between. Decades later, when a letter arrives from an orphan boy who thinks he's found his uncle, Wyn faces the monumental task of welcoming two children into a household rife with secrets.

Alfie is quite sure Merritt House is magical. Uncle Wyn's quirky rules only add to the farm's mystique. He'd do anything to stay. Even if it means pretending not to notice that the chickens are enormous, the cows are a little too clever, and the cook has a tail. However, his baby sister Hazel, who is forever bending the rules, grows up with some peculiarly romantic notions. First love will make things awkward for everyone, especially the three farmhands who live in Cozy Cottage.